The Agony of After

Scott Hale

This is a work of fiction. Names, characters, places, and incidents either are the product of the author's imagination or are used fictitiously, and any relevance to any person, living or dead, business establishments, events, or locales are entirely coincidental.

THE AGONY OF AFTER

All rights reserved.

BOOKS BY SCOTT HALE

The Bones of the Earth series

The Bones of the Earth (Book 1)

The Three Heretics (Book 2)

The Blood of Before (Book .1)

The Cults of the Worm (Book 3)

The Agony of After (Book .2)

The Eight Apostates (Book 4)

Novels

In Sheep's Skin

The Body Is a Cruel Mistress (Coming Soon)

THIS BOOK CONTAINS SCENES OF
EXPLICIT VIOLENCE AND GORE

CONTENTS

WHERE THE DEAD GO TO DIE

Despite being at the center of everything, Brooksville Manor couldn't have been less of this world. Six miles from the highway and five streets from the main road, the low-income housing complex was three sprawling stories of old brick and busted blinds at the bottom of a steep hill that overlooked the river. The Manor's grounds were an ocean of cracked cement that glistened with shattered glass when the sun hit it just right. The yellow swing-set, green picnic benches, and brown dumpsters were the only true sources of color in the otherwise monotone realm. Everything else, be it from the few cars in the lot, to those fleeting shapes of the souls that lived here, was covered in a grayish wash, like the dirt or dust thrown after some great machine's take-off. According to those who lived or had lived at the Manor, things had always been this way, which meant both forever and for as long as they could remember. The same could be said for the appearance of the housing complex, which hadn't seen a hammer, nail, or a fresh coat of paint since its construction in 1950. Brooksville Manor was a place out of time, existing and not-existing. Those who had escaped its gravity never drifted far from its orbit, and those that lived there were seldom seen in the surrounding community. It was a place known solely by its history, for those who might've realized its future were never heard from again.

Dario knew these things because everyone knew these things. It was the worst kept secret in Brooksville, and yet, somehow, it was secret all the same. Leaning forward over his car's steering wheel, he watched from the farthest end of the parking lot as two kids hauled ass after a dog that looked like a shag carpet with legs. They didn't get but a few feet before the heat hit them hard and laid them out against the Manor's façade. They held up there, sweating into their hands and the sleeves of their shirts. Dario checked the clock—4:25 PM—and when he returned his attention to the kids, they were gone—long shadows where once their melting bodies had been.

Dario fell back in his seat. His hand hit the windshield wipers. They screeched across the sun-scorched glass and gave him a minor heart attack. Flicking them off, he pinched the bridge of his nose and hated himself and the anxiety bubbling in his gut. He'd bounced around most of his early life between places like Brooksville Manor. They all had their stories, and they were all some parts bad and some parts good. Villains and victims. The vindictive and the vindicated. Single mothers. Loving fathers. Alcoholics and Sunday regulars. No, it wasn't the people here or anywhere else that made him nervous. It was the building itself. In some ways, it was more alive than the few individuals he'd seen roaming around it. Maybe it was the urban legends. Maybe it wasn't. But he wasn't here for that, and here he had to be, for an unknown duration, until the person he'd come to see was better, went missing, or just fired him altogether. Even in the bleakest bowers, it couldn't be about him.

Because he was a social worker—a mental health therapist, more specifically—and he wouldn't be any good to anyone if, during sessions, all he thought about was himself. Early into his career, he'd thought the possibility unlikely. But after having spent some time in the field, he came across many professionals just as lost as those they were trying to help. Misery loves company, if only to get a chance to break out its tools and peel back the flaps of those worse off, to see itself reflected in the glistening folds and find its answer in the agony of others. Dario didn't want to be like those other social workers, who brought their work home with them every night and let it fester in all the cracks they refused to patch. For eight hours a day, he just wanted to do right by those who'd been wronged for so long it'd become routine.

He was cynical, and naïve, and not very popular.

Dario checked the clock again—4:28 PM—and turned off his car. At 4:35 PM, he had an appointment with Oblita Vesper—a sixty-five-year-old Caucasian female with a name that sounded like something his daughter might make up. She had been referred to his office a year ago, but she never followed-up beyond the initial phone call. Last week, Oblita contacted the office stating that she needed help with her depression and feelings of guilt, and that although she wasn't suicidal or self-harming, she wasn't doing well. Oblita Vesper lived alone on the third floor of Brooksville Manor. She was Dario's last client for the day.

Grabbing his bag, he got out of the car, locked the door, and then locked it again. Without his air conditioner shield, the heat had its way with him. It moved like clammy hands over his body and filled his lungs with sickly breaths. Quickly acclimating to hell's climate, it was the smell that blindsided him next. Though the river was hidden behind the Manor at the bottom of the hill's sheer drop, its presence was undeniable. The air was musty, humid, with hints of chemicals and bitter notes of dead insects. It smelled like a shed might smell in the fall, when all the creeping things inside decided to die before letting winter get ahold of them. To Dario, it was a precise odor he could never place. A certainty he was never certain of.

Brooksville Manor was the shed its community leaders had forgotten. The naïve man inside him told him it was because of funds. The cynical man inside told him it was on purpose. He was biased, being of the gutter himself, but the lower-class were the creeping things everyone else could do without. It was so cliché it was stupid, but it was true, wasn't it? Squandered potential. Hard men, women, and children made harder, stronger by their hardships. Weak men, women, and children given over to shadows and erosion. Good and bad. That's what made the shed stay sealed shut. Everyone wanted one or the other—good or bad—otherwise, for most, it wasn't worth looking up from the cell phones for.

Starting to feel something like a hateful martyr, Dario furrowed his brow and crossed the parking lot. The closer he drew to the Manor, the more tangible its atmosphere became. He could hear TVs blaring at full volume from the first and second floor, and pockets of Hip Hop thudding like a chain of throbbing nerves all across the building. Laughter, too, and voices he couldn't place.

He stepped up to the sidewalk and headed to the front door, which stood underneath a skybridge that connected the second and third floors of the divided buildings. There were people up there, behind the glass, but they weren't paying him any attention. Sometimes, Dario felt like a person of interest as a social worker, or even an uninvited guest. But most of the time, most people didn't really give a shit.

The front door was a heavy metal barricade that had seen its fair share of beatings. Dario went for the handle and then noticed the keypad and intercom on the wall. He hated these things. They barely worked. Most of the time he would just slip into the buildings as someone was leaving. But no one was leaving Brooksville Manor today, because no one ever did.

He opened his bag, peeked inside Oblita's folder, and found her phone number. Sweat stinging the corner of his eyes, he squinted it out, punched in the digits on the keypad, and then pressed pound.

While the system dialed her number, he glanced inside the building through the horizontal glass that was framed within one side of the door. Blue patterned carpet covered the floor. Seething fluorescent lights lined the ceiling. He noticed a door opening at the farthest end of the hall. Instinctively, his hand went up—he wasn't about to be standing out here for fifteen minutes on a day like today—but before he could knock, the intercom buzzed and the door was unlocked.

Oblita Vesper had let him in without even asking who it was or why they were there, calling her number. He made a mental note of this, for the progress note to come, and let himself in.

The long hallway didn't offer much in terms of what he could expect from the Manor. To his left, there was a bank of mailboxes too stuffed with letters and catalogues to be locked. To his right, there was a sign that read "Office" and underneath it, a puddle of tobacco chew from some undoubtedly disgruntled tenant. And up ahead, past several apartments, was the door Dario had seen opening through the glass. Beside it, a large man stood in baggy sweat pants and a pristine white tank-top.

He gave Dario a nod and said, "Hot enough out there yet, brother?"

"Too hot." He pointed to the doorway beside the large man. "Stairs?"

The large man's eyes went wide for a split-second. "Who you here to see?"

Dario gave him a shrug that told him he couldn't really say and said, "Just need to get up to the third floor."

"These go down to the basement," the large man said, pointing with his thumb at the door beside him.

Dario nodded and started down the hall. He passed the Office, whose door was shut and whose lights were out, and gave the large man a small smile. Some of the apartment doors past the Office were decorated. A few with fist marks, others with stains. The apartment nearest the large man, who wasn't budging, was covered in pages that had been torn from the Bible. A portrait of a black Jesus drawn in crayon crowned the display. It wasn't half-bad, except for the fact that the artist had drawn what looked like maggots onto Jesus' open palm. The other hand was a fist, and red faces, like blood drops, were dripping out of it.

"Kind of freaky," the large man whispered, wrinkling his nose. "What do you think?"

Dario went sideways to slide past the man, to get around the corner.

The large man touched his gut, sucked it in, and said, "Sorry."

Dario kept smiling. Around the corner was another set of doors that split the hallway in two. He wondered if the whole building had been built like this, in segments, so that portions of it could be closed off from the others.

There was that smell again, that river smell; this time laced with incense. It was coming from behind, out from under the door the large man said led to the basement. The scent reminded Dario of church. He breathed it, and it took him back, ten years ago, to a Sunday with his grandmother, in the pews, on their knees, the smells of her kitchen drifting around her, promising his seventeen-year-old-self a meal she'd worked too long on, and one he'd take for granted. It had been, as his mother put it, their last supper.

"Hey, bro, how long you staying?"

Dario shook the memory and turned. "Not really sure."

The large man kept holding onto his gut. "It's easy to get turned around in here is all. And people get a little... strange at night. Listen, if anyone gets in your ass about anything, tell them to take it up with Jam."

Jam held out his fist.

Dario channeled is inner bro and gave it a hearty bump. "Appreciate it, Jam."

Jam's gut rumbled. He cringed.

"Third floor past these doors?" Dario asked.

Jam belched up a cloud of onions. "Yes, sir. Stairs go down to the basement in that well, too."

There he was warning him about the basement again. And there it was again, the anxiety in his stomach, boiling over like a chemistry experiment gone wrong. He didn't want to ask, but the social worker (and survivor) in him deemed it pertinent. "What's wrong with the basement?"

Jam traced the outline of a Fu Manchu on his face, said, "Nothing," and walked away and out of the building.

Dario went through the second set of doors. There were more apartments on the other side, and a kid. It wasn't one of the boys he'd seen earlier. This one was sprawled out across the bottom step of the stairs he needed to climb. He had to be about ten going on twenty. With designer jeans, a haircut so high and tight his forehead might snap, the latest smartphone in his tiny grip, and a cigarette behind his ear, the kid looked so cool and hard he could have sunk the Titanic.

"Sorry," Dario said, stopping a few feet away, "have to get up there."

"You going to see Oblita?" the kid asked, pocketing the smartphone. "Basement's not open until six." He wiggled his feet excitedly. "Got a light?"

Dario shook his head and said, "Just need to get to the third floor."

Taken aback, the kid pulled his legs in. "You play video games?"

"Yeah, when I have time."

"MichaelIndomitable. Look me up."

Dario grinned.

"What's your tag?"

"MichaelIndomitable1."

Michael snorted. "Shut up. For real, though, if you're here to see Oblita… don't."

Dario, trying to hide his concern, said, "Why's that?"

He didn't answer.

Dario's bag was starting to feel heavy at his side. Suddenly, the little information he had on Oblita Vesper became crucial clues to a potentially problematic puzzle. Initially, she had been referred to the office by her primary care physician, Isabella Ødegaard, for social anxiety, which may or may not have been the manifestation of an undiagnosed body dysmorphic disorder. From reading the documentation, it wasn't entirely clear to Dario how Isabella Ødegaard came to that conclusion, as that visit had not only been Oblita's first, but also her last. And in an off-the-cuff comment reportedly made by Oblita during her appointment, that had been the first time Ms. Vesper had ever visited a doctor in her entire life.

"Have a good day," Dario said, going up the steps. It was his go-to phrase for strangers that carried on conversations like they were the plague.

Michael called after him, "Hey, how long are you going to be here?"

Dario looked down from the sticky second-floor landing, where the falling light shone through the eight opaque, square glass windows. "Awhile," he said with a smile, but the boy was already gone.

At the door that led into the third floor, Dario stopped, checked his surroundings, and took out his phone. Oblita Vesper was either dangerous, or she had spent the better part of the week talking up an appointment with her therapist to anyone who would listen. It didn't fit the symptoms of the social anxiety she supposedly had, but that was mental health, wasn't it? A blueprint done in crayon; consistent until it wasn't. Sometimes it made him wish he had pursued a career that dealt with more tangible issues. Not the ghosts that haunted our skulls.

He texted his supervisor a reminder of where he was, what he was doing here, and when he expected to be finished. She responded almost immediately with a "Sounds good."

Dario pocketed his phone, and his stomach rumbled at the smell creeping through the third-floor door. It was the smell of cinnamon and bread, with an underlying aroma of marijuana. Compared to the odious odor lifting off the river, it might've well been the fragrance of heaven itself. The mixture reminded him of his grandmother and aunt—the two biggest potheads he'd ever met in his life.

So he breathed it in—the memory and the nostalgic pores carrying across his mind—pulled open the door, and stepped onto Oblita Vesper's level.

After everything—the stories about Brooksville Manor, and Jam and Michael's strange behavior and warnings—what Dario expected to find on the third floor in no way matched what was actually there. In fact, this part of the Manor put his own apartment complex to shame. The floor wasn't carpet, but spotless tile checkered with red and black diamonds. The walls weren't painted, but wallpapered with a seamless, spotless pattern of pink, art nouveau-styled flowers set against a soft, green field. Gone were the buzzing fluorescent tubes; in their place, small chandeliers hung—twelve in all, one for each apartment on this floor, they cast their sleepy light up and down the windowless hall. Given the state of the Manor and the neglect shown to it, Dario couldn't believe these decorations had been part of the original construction. In a place where half the community was hoping it would fall into the river, who the hell had taken the time to transform a part of it into what was, more or less, a Victorian hideaway?

Oblita Vesper seemed the obvious answer. But she was probably on a fixed income that was just enough to keep the grave away. Dario didn't know what he had stumbled into, but he kind of liked it. He liked when people went against the expectations placed upon them. It was too easy to assume, too convenient to stereotype. He liked to think people were more than what the rest of the world had decided they could be, even if they became exactly what the world decided them to be. Too often he had too many clients who had no idea who they were or what they wanted. They constantly sought out answers for problems they couldn't begin to articulate. So maybe the residents of Brooksville Manor were freakish to most, but hell, at least someone here knew what they wanted. With that alone they were doing better than most.

He was looking for apartment 312. Apartment 306, the first that he passed, had the door open. Inside, a skinny man with no legs was sitting in his wheelchair, masturbating to TV static.

"Just watching a sex tape," the man said, never taking his eyes off the television, never losing rhythm. "Oh yeah."

Dario tried not to look at the man's penis, but like passing a car accident on the highway, he did anyway. He waved the man off as he got off and continued down the hall. His naivety had come and gone, and cynicism was setting in again. His wife said he was of two minds. She didn't know how right she was.

He continued on, past 307, where someone was crying behind the closed door, and jumped. Out of 308, a little girl with tourniquet-tight braids bolted, a squirt gun in her right hand, because her left hand was missing at the wrist. Before Dario could say anything, her mother, stocky and out of breath, ambled awkwardly through the doorway. She had a squirt gun, too, and her drenched shirt told Dario she was losing this fight badly. The mother's smile was more gum than teeth, and more pain than happiness in that glowing grimace. This woman was an amputee, too. She was missing an index finger on both hands; from the way she walked, she seemed to be missing toes, too.

The little girl grinned at Dario.

Her mother mouthed an apology, checked her watch, and then, eyebrows raised, gunned down her daughter until they both made it around the bend.

When it came to conducting therapy, one's environment could be just as important, if not more so, than the mental illness they presented with. It would be hard for anyone to manage acts of aggression when they were surrounded by groups of people who taunted them on a daily basis, or bullied them on the first of every month for their government assistance. When one's apartment is ravaged by bed bugs and a complete lack of attention from the landlord, depression and guilt over one's own squalor isn't all that unimaginable. A person with schizophrenia might not prosper living with a reluctant relative with thin walls or prying company. Just as someone sexually attracted to children, possibly from their own sexual abuse, might not be able to resist the temptations before them with a school in their backyard.

Environment could be a cause, or it could be an aggravator. If Oblita Vesper was to be believed, then this was the first time in her life she had reached out to professionals for help. Dario refused to believe the fact her living in Brooksville Manor, a hive for all sorts of urban legends, and on the third floor, where the physically disabled had a run of the opulent halls, could be chalked up to pure coincidence.

Encouragement, curiosity, or a court order often led to clients coming into Dario's office. But regardless of the reason that brought them, the catalyst for doing so was almost always the same: They could no longer cope.

So what had really brought Oblita Vesper's name into their office? Her name was awfully well known and, in some ways, respected for someone who supposedly had crippling social anxiety. The body dysmorphia was starting to make more sense given her neighbors, but with that train of thought, did she find her surroundings repulsive or empowering? Or was it something else? Something in the environment? On an appointed hour? For a place frozen in time, maybe it made sense for everyone to be obsessed with it.

Speaking of time, Dario was going to be late. With an hour to complete the intake and dinner with the wife at six-thirty, he couldn't afford being locked up here all evening. Twisting his wedding ring off his finger, he took out his wallet, dropped it in its usual bulging pocket, and, fighting fatigue, reminded himself to give a shit. Social work was, if nothing else, a balancing act after all—an unstable harmony of function and feasibility, like most things in life.

Apartment 309, and again, the door was open. Dario peeked inside and found only a dimly lit living room with an air conditioner on full-blast. He could hear a toilet flushing somewhere deeper in the den, and the metallic clicks of a walker or cane on tile.

The single chandelier above apartment 310 was out. Had it always been? Dario could've sworn it hadn't been, but the heat had also robbed him of his memory of the trip here, so what did he know? Someone was home behind the scratched-up door, though. Two people, maybe. He could hear them in there, cleaving through dinner ingredients on a counter or cutting board.

Coming up to 312, Oblita Vesper's apartment, Dario paused mid-knock as the door to 311 creaked open behind him. He waited a few seconds for whoever it was to come out, or for the door to shut, but neither happened. Whoever it was, they were watching him. He could feel their burning gaze upon the back of his neck, the searing judgment that came with their sharp breaths.

Dario ignored them and knocked twice upon Oblita Vesper's door. The wood was humid to the touch, and left his knuckles glistening.

"You're man enough," apartment 311 whispered behind him.

Dario couldn't make out whether the speaker was male, female, or some combination of the two. Instead of turning around, he made two fists and waited.

Apartment 311 started playing with what must've been the chain lock and mumbled, "Thank you."

As apartment 311 shut their door, apartment 312's opened, and there, at last, she stood.

If Oblita Vesper was sixty-five, then she was an easy sixty-five going on forty. Time had been kind to her, and if this place was frozen in time, then so was she, because not only did she look younger than she claimed, but she had the quality of someone who had just climbed out of a bath. It wasn't that she was wet—it was the way her cult-style hair fell well past her hips, and the way it stayed together; the way her skin was simultaneously pale and subtly flushed. She was attractive in the way people from old, black and white photographs were attractive: bred out features made soft by the light, or emboldened by the dark; and intensely alien in how she carried herself, as if she were a subject who had stepped straight out of its portrait. She wore no jewelry, perfume, nor make-up, but she was well-kempt, and the clothes she wore—a modest blouse and blue jeans—were, except for some occasional fraying and dark stains on her cuffs, clean. He searched her for tattoos and scars. While he couldn't locate the former, the latter leapt out at him almost immediately. Oblita Vesper had two vein-like scars that ran from the corner of her mouth, down her throat, to somewhere underneath her shirt. They looked fresh.

"Hello," Dario said, cheerfully. He extended his hand: "Dario Onai, from the Brooksville Community Health Center."

Oblita Vesper smiled and took his hand. "Oblita Vesper. It seems we both have strange names, Mr. Onai."

"Dario is fine."

Still holding his hand, she said, "Italian… and African?"

"Yes." Was she rubbing his wrist with her thumb? "Father was Italian. Mother was African. She was fiercer, so we took her last name."

Finally, she let go of him. "It is a shame those things a woman still has to fight for these days—" Oblita's eyes went dim, "—but please, come in."

Dario did as he was told and went with Oblita across the threshold.

For a social worker, home visits could prove to be invaluable in the therapeutic process, as they often times gave glimpses into an unguarded realm of the client. The smell of the home and the condition it was in; the decorations and décor, if there were any at all; the evidences of excess and the phantoms of frugality; the state of the bathroom, the bedroom, and contents of the kitchen—all of it meant something, even if it didn't mean much at all. Were there pictures on the wall, and if there were, who or what was in them? Was the home a place where someone was living, or just getting by? Was it the best they could do? Or was it all they told themselves on a daily basis they deserved?

In some ways, a home was what inhabited it. What was it, then, that inhabited the apartment of Oblita Vesper? Staring at it from the entryway, Dario couldn't be sure. If the hallway had been the corridors of a museum, then the apartment of Oblita Vesper was a veritable gallery. It was a studio space that, by illusion or architectural trickery, seemed to extend beyond the confines of the Manor itself. The color palette was red and white, and a pinkish tone bordering on bloody milk. The walls were the very off-putting off-white, while the bed, tables, couch, and loveseat were deep, Valentine's Day red. The carpet was white, and so, too, were the curtains; the appliances—the refrigerator, microwave, CRT television, phonograph, and police scanner—were white as well. Everything appeared to be placed very particularly, so much so that Dario imagined there must be chalk outlines underneath each piece of furniture. There was no garbage, nor were there any dirty clothes, or hints of the insects that would enjoy nesting in either.

Other than the color of the apartment, which, morbidly, reminded Dario of the birthing videos from high school health class, there was something about the place he couldn't place. Was it a sound? Or a presence? It was definitely the walls. Something in the walls. Scratching, maybe, like birds or rats, or even squirrels stuck or trying to come through. Dario had the same thing happening in his attic. His wife liked to give him a hard time and say the only thing he should be worrying about were all the bats in his belfry. If Oblita was sixty-five going on forty, then his wife with all her old person mumbo jumbo could've easily been Oblita's opposite.

Dario smiled, rubbed his finger where his wedding band had been, and said, "Thank you so much, Ms. Vesper, for meeting with me today."

Oblita waved him off, went to the refrigerator, and half opening it, offered: "Bottle of water?"

Typically, social workers were encouraged not to accept anything from clients, but Dario nodded, anyways. Many of Brooksville's population in the lower socio-economic range were from the nearby mountains, where niceties such as offering a guest something to drink were taken as seriously as Sunday Mass. He didn't know anything about Oblita, not even after seeing her funky ass apartment, so he wasn't about to step on her toes right before their big dance.

Dario grabbed the top of the kitchen chair and asked, "May I?"

Oblita, carrying a bottle of water for him and her, nodded.

He placed his bag on the ground, his ass in the chair, and waited until she was sitting opposite him.

"This summer has been too damn hot," Oblita said, sliding him the bottle of water.

He took it and nodded. "Not a fan."

Oblita's gaze narrowed on his hands. "Divorced?"

"Oh—" he touched the pale mark on his finger from the wedding band, "—still married."

Oblita bit her lower lip. "You really a therapist? Or a gentleman caller?"

"Ah, ha, uh… no, no. It's… habit. Some of the individuals we work with have done some very violent… things. Some have… gone out of their way
to track down service providers. Just a habit."

"I take it you do not find me to be a threat?"

Dario shrugged. "I'm sure you're a force to be reckoned with when you want to be."

Oblita leaned forward, resting her head against her palm. "Mm, perhaps."

"Well, we do have a lot of paperwork to get through today—"

"Shame."

"—but mostly, I really just want to get to know you."

"Of course."

"But I'm the stranger in your house, so I feel like I should properly introduce myself."

"Sure."

"Again, my name is Dario Onai. I'm a licensed independent social worker from the Brooksville Community Health Center. I've worked there for about four years."

"Do you like your job?"

"I do. What about you?"

"I don't work."

"Used to?"

"I was a glorified gardener, if you will."

"Oh. Very cool. Do you miss it?"

"I still garden on the side, but I just couldn't stand the people I worked for. As I've gotten older, I've changed."

"You're sixty-five."

"Sadly."

"You look about half that."

Oblita Vesper twisted her mouth in a smile. "And who says therapists are useless? I feel better already. I think it's just from being around all the plants all the time."

"Your referral came from your PCP, Isabella Ødegaard. Was that her idea, or yours?"

"Hers. And then, after I thought about it, mine."

Dario nodded. With his foot, he nudged his bag closer to him.

"I have a lot going on. I have no one to really talk to."

"Family?"

"No," Oblita said, sharply. "And I feel guilty about things. I've lived in this building since it was built, you know?"

"Really?"

"Yeah. And I haven't ever really left it since."

"It sounds like you have so much on your chest these days, it's almost as if you can't breathe."

"Exactly." Oblita bit her bottom lip again. "Yes."

Dario took two pens out of his pocket. He could tell by the way she was sitting and speaking that she was ready to move forward. He leaned down, took her folder from out of his bag; and from that folder, he removed a small stack of intake paperwork and laid it out before them. He handed her a pen. Therapy was supposed to be a collaborative effort, not the therapist telling the client to live their life the way the therapist would themselves. If she wasn't doing this for her, at least, eventually, then what was the point of doing it at all?

One by one, signature after signature, they went through the process together. The consent to treatment, the notice of privacy practices, and an explanation of HIPAA (Health Information Portability and Accountability Act) and how it related to Oblita and how it protected her. They went through the billing for her insurance, and her releases of information, if she ever wanted Dario to speak to or be spoken to by anyone else in regards to her treatment (she didn't). All that remained were the physical and the mental health status exam, and whatever Dario could manage to get for the diagnostic assessment.

Well-kempt, attentive, euthymic, oriented, without any obvious delusions or paranoias—Dario checked the appropriate boxes while never breaking eye-contact with Oblita.

"I know that you said you have lived in the Manor since it was built, but have you lived in Brooksville all your life?" Dario asked.

"I have not."

Dario's head twitched. Something about her voice, the way she answered him.

"What about yourself?"

"I've bounced back and forth between the Brooksville, Bedlam, and Bitter Springs tri-county area a lot."

"Had a hard time making roots?"

Dario hummed. "You?"

"I've made roots here just fine," she said, "but a lot of moving around before then."

"You said you've lived here since the Manor was built?"

Oblita nodded.

Dario said, "I bet you've seen it go through a lot of changes," but what he really wanted to make mention of was how that was impossible; how the building was older than she was by a few years, and if she did do a lot moving around before coming here, then there was no way she had been here since the '50s. But this was their first session. Confrontation was a tool not to be used lightly.

He went on: "Do you have any siblings?"

"A brother, but he passed away some time ago."

"I'm very sorry to hear that."

"Thank you. I think of him often."

There it was again. The strange inflection in her voice, almost like an accent.

"Mother and father?" Dario asked.

"Gone as well."

He made a sympathetic noise, said, "Were you close to them?"

"My mother? Yes. I never knew my father well, but by all accounts, he was a mean man."

Dario searched Oblita's body for non-verbal cues; for those often-uncontrollable hints of the thoughts and feelings going off like overloaded lights in one's mind. He glanced at her face and the vein-like scars that started at the corner of her mouth. They looked fresh, but maybe they weren't. Or maybe they were, and there were others beneath her blouse—ones from her childhood, when her father was still around.

"Was she a gardener? Your mother?"

Oblita's eyes lit-up, got smaller. Coyly, she said, "For a time."

"Anyone else that you are or were really close with?"

"I don't know. My uncle, I suppose." Hate locked Oblita's jaw into place. "That's the bad thing about getting older, Mr. Onai. People will eventually disappoint you, and those that don't, die."

"I appreciate your honesty," Dario said.

Oblita took the bait. "Thank you."

"Do you find people disappointing?"

"Absolutely. All of them."

"How come?"

"Oh, I don't know. You'll think less of me."

"I'm your therapist. Anything you say to me is confidential. Again, I can only break that rule if you tell me you want to hurt yourself, someone else, or if you know a child is being hurt. And even then, it's a judgment call on my part.

19

"But for everything else?" Dario leaned over the kitchen table. "I'm not here to judge you. I'm just here to help you make sense of things, and to help you find the path that you want to take. At this point, I've heard just about everything."

"I wonder if you really have," Oblita said. "I'm sorry."

"Don't be. This is the first time we've met. I don't expect you to tell me everything right away. I have to earn your trust."

"I'm sure that you will."

Dario thought about redirecting the conversation back to Oblita's reported disappointment with others, but on that topic, she was guarded. He checked his watch—twenty minutes left—and decided to move onto something else. He didn't have to get her life story right here and now. That's what next week was for, and the week after that, and the week after that, and so on, and so on, until all the goals were met, or the insurance coverage ran out.

"Your apartment is amazing," Dario said.

Oblita laughed and gestured for him to drink his bottled water, which he hadn't touched.

Dario twisted off the cap, had a sip, and then, temptation taking over, guzzled almost all of it.

"It's taken a long time to get things the way I've needed them to be," Oblita said.

"Even in the hallway, it's... not what I expected. Did you have something to do with that?"

Now, Oblita was beaming.

"Are you the landlord?"

"No, of course not. Well, maybe, in a way. I take care of a lot of people here."

"I thought you said people disappoint you."

"They do, but I try to make them be better."

"How do you do that?"

A scratching sound came from the walls, and disappeared somewhere behind the ceiling's sharp, unsmoothed plaster.

"Everyone knows everyone in the Manor very well," she said. "Everyone is good for something, even if they do not realize it."

"Is there something special about the third floor, though?"

Snidely, she quipped, "Other than the fact that I live on it?"

"Other than that," Dario said, faking a laugh.

"Well, yes, actually." Oblita straightened up in her chair. Her long, dark, almost tail-like trunk of hair fell over her gaunt shoulders. "Did you run into any of my neighbors?"

Dario said he did.

"Notice anything about them?"

"The few I saw had a physical disability in some way."

"They all do."

"Do you take care of them?"

"I try to. They've given a lot."

"That sounds like a lot of work."

"More than most realize."

"Do you help them outside of the Manor?"

Oblita's brows furrowed. "No, they never leave. They do not need to."

"Food? Activities?"

"Everything they could ever need is up here, with me."

Dario pressed his pen hard against the diagnostic assessment form and started unconsciously drawing a circle. "Do you take care of the others on the floors below?"

"When they've earned it," Oblita said. "I know it is strange to hear all of this—"

"No—" he stopped drawing, "they are very fortunate to have someone so dedicated to them."

"It goes both ways," Oblita said, with a clear, British accent. "Doesn't it?"

"It does." Dario agreed just to agree. "We don't have a lot of time left, but you said you wanted to begin therapy because you feel guilty for things you've done."

"Yes."

"Things in the past? Or things you've done recently?"

"Both, I suppose."

"But it sounds as if you do a lot of good here."

"I am trying."

"This guilt… how does it make you feel?"

"Sad," Oblita said. "Angry."

Dario made a note of each affectation on the assessment and asked, "Anxiety?"

"Not anymore."

"Used to?"

"When I didn't know myself so well."

"Do you feel comfortable in your own skin?"

At this, Oblita leaned back in her chair and let out a loud laugh that might as well have been a bark. "I've become accustomed to this skin, I suppose."

"Have you lost interest in things you used to enjoy doing?"

"It's routine."

"Okay," Dario said. "Do you have as much energy as you are used to?"

"I'm sixty-five. I wake up early, and go to bed early."

"Fair enough. Have you ever been a violent confrontation with someone?"

"Yes," Oblita said.

"Bad enough to have the police called?"

"I suppose, if the police ever came out this way."

"What happened?"

Oblita shrugged.

"That's fine," Dario said. "You don't have to tell me. But do you feel safe here?"

"Oh yes." She looked at Dario as if the question was the most absurd thing she had ever heard.

"This sadness... this guilt... has it ever made you want to harm yourself?"

Oblita chewed on the question like a piece of meat. Surprisingly, most clients would answer any questions about harming themselves or one another with very little hesitation. Dario had always thought it would be the opposite when it came to those topics unprotected by confidentiality, but it wasn't. Once the doors of the mind were unlocked, all manner of things came crawling out.

"When I was younger," Oblita admitted, touching the vein-like scars beside her mouth. "Not anymore."

Dario checked the time—eight minutes—and went into wrap-up mode. "I'm really happy to hear that. But if you do ever feel that way, you can tell me."

Oblita hummed in agreement.

"Somehow, we're almost out of time."

"Already?"

"Unfortunately. But before I go, I want you to think about one or two things you would like for us to work on in therapy together."

Oblita played with her bottled water. She still hadn't opened it. She was thinking about something, the same way a child might think of a wish before blowing out their birthday candles on a cake.

Packing up the papers and folder and placing them back into the bag, Dario said, "Do you mind if I use your bathroom before I leave?"

Oblita cocked her head. Again, there was a light in her eyes. A red prick of light that could've been some refraction from the walls. At first, she looked as if she was going to say no, and Dario prepared himself to tell her not to worry about it. But instead, she scooted her chair back loudly, came to her feet, and with a very obvious British accent, said, "Ignore the mess, if you can."

"I'm sure it's fine." Dario stood and placed his bag on the chair he'd been sitting in. "Thank you. I'll be right out."

Dario went left, across the apartment, where three doors formed the ends of the small hall there. Oblita, her voice distant, told him to go to the right. And without looking back to see why she sounded so far away, he opened the door on his right.

The bathroom was the very definition of cramped. It was nice—the sink was marble, the toilet white porcelain with a red flower around the base—and like everywhere else, impeccably clean. The bathtub was white as well, but the shower curtain was pulled over it, so beyond the vague shapes he could see through the covering, there wasn't much to note there.

Dario tried to lock the door behind him, but there was no lock. He didn't really have to go, but he wanted to see Oblita Vesper's bathroom, and maybe even what was in the garbage cans. Except there weren't any garbage cans. Nor was there any toilet paper, hand soap, or towels. Unbuttoning his pants, he lifted the toilet seat and lid and started to piss. Curious, he leaned over the sink, reached for the medicine cabinet, and pulled it open. The shelves were empty, except for a few dried-up roots that appeared to have come through the drywall behind the cabinet.

He shut the cabinet, gave himself a few good shakes, buttoned his pants, and turned on the faucet. The water sputtered out brown, and then, after a few seconds, it was clear. He didn't have any soap to work with, but he figured he may as well make the effort. On another day, he might ask Oblita about her lack of supplies in the bathroom, or if she had some, why she had decided to hide them for when guests came over.

Thinking about his new client, as well as the group he had to run tomorrow (families in Bedlam whose children had gone missing), his eyes wandered over to the base of the toilet and the floral decoration he had more or less dismissed.

Because now the red flower didn't look so much like a red flower. It was dripping down the toilet in chunky streams to the floor, where the tiles were dotted with wet, faintly red splatters.

He stared at the bathtub, and at the shower curtain, and what might lay behind it. His first thought was of himself, and then of his family. He took out his cell phone in the event he needed to dial 911. Oblita Vesper was an old woman who clearly had something to hide. She spoke of guilt regularly; maybe her guilt was all over the tub. She had to have known he would find this.

Footsteps outside the door. Dario's heart let out a thunderous beat. He grabbed the side of the sink, steadied himself. It wasn't a body. This woman needed help. She was reaching out for help. This wasn't an accident. He was here, in this bathroom, for a reason.

More footsteps. Something brushed against the doorknob from outside. Dario summoned the coping skills he never used and preached to his clients as gospel. He looked at the toilet again, and the blood dripping off it. He remembered the stains on Oblita's cuffs, and how she had been acting strangely. Had she been bleeding out the whole intake?

Dario shook his head and grabbed the shower curtain. She didn't have a body her bathtub, he told himself. And telling himself this, he flung the curtain back.

Oblita Vesper had a body in her bathtub.

Dario gasped and choked on his words: "Oh fuck!"

He spun around to make sure he was still alone.

He was.

Forgetting about the phone in his hand, Dario, cringing, leaned forward.

Inside the bathtub was the body of an old man who looked to be in his eighties. He was covered in a heavy blanket from the waist down, as if Oblita had been wrapping him up the moment Dario rapped upon her door. The old man's neck was cut open, deeply; straight down to the bone, the ravaged gulch was the cause of death, and the source of the blood that coated the bottom of the tub.

Dario thought of his wife and daughter. For a moment, he saw himself in the tub. He moved the phone around in his sweaty palm, thumbed the number pad on the screen…

"Isn't that something?" Oblita said behind him.

Before Dario could react, she cracked the back of his elbow with a hammer, sending the cell phone flying into the tub of blood.

He screamed, spun around, and slammed against the bathroom wall.

"Please," Dario cried, holding his throbbing elbow, his blood-mushed skin there making his stomach sick. "Please, I can… I can help."

Oblita lowered the hammer to her side and bounced the head of it against her thigh, over and over. "I do feel guilty about killing Herbert North, but I feel worse about what I've been doing in the basement. Come, Mr. Dario Onai, let me show you. I still want to unburden my soul."

He shook his head. "I'm not… I'm not the right person. Police… a priest… if you want to confess."

"A priest?" Oblita chuckled. "No, no. If I told a priest about what I've been doing—a real priest, mind you, who worships the true God—they'd only encourage me to keep going. I'm not confessing. I just want your opinion."

She held the hammer outward and bared her teeth.

"Your professional opinion. Can you do that for me? That's why you're here, isn't it?"

Dario pressed himself harder into the wall, like a rat trying to dig away from a threat. It took a lot out of him, but he managed a nod and a pathetic, "Mm."

"Excellent use of active listening, Mr. Onai," Oblita said. She went sideways and gestured for him to pass in front of her. "Go ahead. Attack me if you'd like on your way out, but it will not do you any good. A man's hands have never been enough to stop me."

Dario swallowed the bile of hate and terror clogging up his throat. Slowly, he slid across the wall, closer and closer to Oblita. He thought about attacking her, or running, and yet neither seemed possible. She was psychotic, or, at the very least, decompensating. No amount of pain he inflicted upon her, unless it led to a coma or her death, would be enough to stop what she had in store for him.

In a flash, Oblita swung the hammer and bashed the side of his face. Screaming, he grabbed his face, where his left eye was already beginning to swell from the bludgeoning.

"God, stop!"

"You had a look in your eye like you were about to do something stupid." Oblita grabbed his hand and pulled it away from his face. She surveyed the bleeding bulge. "It's gone now."

Dario told himself to be calm, but that only made him all the more terrified. Going past Oblita into the hall, he tried to think of something to say or do to take control of the situation. He'd had classes on this sort of thing, and training, both online and in-person. He had even signed a fucking form stating that he felt qualified to de-escalate situations where a life was in danger. But he couldn't think of anything. Not a goddamn thing. All he had to work with was the sick feeling in his stomach, and the stupid things it might drive him to do or not do in the name of self-preservation.

Back at the table, Oblita Vesper practically nipping at his heels, Dario grabbed a kitchen chair, spun around, and smashed it into her face. She went down hard; a geyser of bright red, black-speckled blood spurt out of her head, across the carpet.

"Good thing you weren't next to the couch, Freud!" Oblita said, laughing.

He didn't look back. Cradling his busted arm, fighting against his failing vision, he hurried to the front door. As he reached for the knob...

The door pushed open and something his mind couldn't reconcile came through. The nearly naked thing had the frame of a drug addict—hard limbs and thin skin on a body caving in as if there was a black hole inside it. It stood on two legs, and it had two arms, but it might as well have been a reject from god's petri dish. It wore a leather apron and leather gloves, and there was a massive butcher's knife fixed to its leather belt. Wrapped around its head was the last of the creature's clothing: a cobweb-colored scarf that left only its eyes exposed. From those diamond-shaped cavities, vermillion veins poured, like calcified tears, down its face, obscuring most of its mouth.

Dario took two steps backwards before he bumped into Oblita and her hammer.

"His name is E.A.973," she whispered, her lips wet against his ear. "The Manor can be unstable during this time. He will guide us to the place."

Staring at E.A.973 robbed Dario of any courage he had left in him.

He was shivering out a monsoon of sweat. His mind was full of prayers; not his prayers, but his grandmother's prayers—those feverish exultations that left her pallid and everyone around her speechless. And then there were his wife and daughter; the shapes of them; the hate of them; the disappointment, the dinner, and the emptiness between them. Why wasn't death worse than missing tonight's date?

"I don't know what drove you to this," Dario said, as Oblita came around him and stood beside E.A.973. "But… I know it must have been… awful for you."

Oblita arched an eyebrow. "You hit me with a chair—"

He had, and all she had to show for it was a patch of skin on her face bubbling, like foam, until it didn't.

"—and now you want to reason with me?"

His eyes darted back and forth between Oblita's hammer and E.A.973's butcher knife.

"I prefer violence, Mr. Onai," she said. "It is the only truly reliable way to survive. We are all survivors at the Manor. What have you survived?"

Dario's thoughts were fragmented, held together only by the threads of fight and flight. He had told himself that he wasn't like some of the other health care providers he'd met—damaged and deranged, and desperate for vicarious validation. But something was breaking apart inside him. A dormant memory had metastasized; a traumatic tumor he'd thought he'd removed with time itself. The hammer and the pain it caused him hadn't been the trigger. No, it was the way Oblita Vesper was standing before him, lording over him; the way she might one of the creeping things that came crawling out of the shed. It was the disgust, and it was the delight, and the deadly combination the two of them created. She was going to do terrible things to him, and she knew as well as he did there was nothing he could do it about it. He was powerless. Again.

Oblita reached out, grabbed him by his bloody, likely broken elbow, and wrenched him forward. Yelping, with hot stars of pain burrowing into his bones, he went past her and her monster, through the front door, and out into the third-floor hallway.

Except it couldn't have been the third-floor hallway. Gone were the spotless tiles checkered with red and black diamonds—in their place, a long stretch of smoothed dirt, with fleshy, throbbing pustules bleeding maggot-white liquids around themselves. Gone was the wallpaper and garden of pink flowers it played host to—like a dirty magnifying glass pressed to ancient art, the designs were enlarged, unfocused abortions of color behind the fatty walls. Gone were the chandeliers that twinkled out twilight light—from where they were now hung roots, vermillion veins not unlike those in E.A.973's eyes, and in their clutches, bones.

The air was oppressive; wet, scummy, it was like the bottom of an old rock in a sewage pipe. Dario could hear water running all around, as if it were raining inside the opaque walls; or as if the Manor had finally plummeted into the river.

There was no sunlight, either, because there were no windows. The only light that lit the hallway came from the tenants holding candles in their yawning doorways. Four to Dario's left and five to his right, each tenant was different when it came to age, sex, and ethnicity. The commonality that which they could all claim was that someone or something had claimed a part of them. Each tenant was disfigured, disabled; each one was missing pieces of themselves, and they wore the badge of their amputation proudly, practically waving it at Dario to give witness to their sacrifice.

There was the mother and child he'd seen earlier with the squirt guns, and past them, the jackass who had been jerking off to TV static. And then there were the others. The gray-haired guy with gecko-like features, whose lips, as far as Dario could tell by the gouges in his enamel, had been literally ground off. The twenty-something woman with rainbow-colored weaves, whose cleavage was the gray scar tissue from where her breasts had been removed. The four-hundred-pound bowling ball of a man, whose skin was craterous and whose right arm was missing completely. The little boy with the fast-food crown and one hundred-dollar bills exploding from his pockets, whose throat had been ravaged and whose body sagged, as if bones had been removed. The elderly woman, with no eyes or feet, who leaned against a coat rack with IV bags hanging off it, alternating between puffs on her cigarette and asthma inhaler.

And then there was the person he must have heard earlier, the one who'd spoken to him as he knocked on Oblita's door—the one who he couldn't tell was male or female by their voice alone. Looking at them now, he still couldn't discern their sex. They had no arms or legs, and pouches were attached to their torso, where urine and feces passed through plastic tubing that fed in and out of their body. They had been shaved, and they looked soft, pliable; bed sores or some form of pso-riasis left them looking raw. The candle they held was wedged into their belly button. They didn't seem to mind the hot wax that coated their stomach, or the flame that was inching towards it. And why should they? For all they'd undoubtedly endured, the pain had proba-bly gone so far it might've transformed into something like pleasure. Transubstantiation of the most terrible kind; a cannibalized coping skill.

Dario's sensations were shutting down. One by one, feeling by feel-ing, thought by thought, his body orphaned him to numbness. He didn't know what he was looking at, or where he was, or what was going to happen to him. His arm was useless to him; his elbow was swollen like a balloon, and he could feel things breaking inside his flesh when he tried to move it. His eyeball felt like a marble in his skull; the skin around his face felt tight, as if it were constricting into one great mound. There was no getting away, only going along. He had been marooned here once, in the same kind of dangerous, unknown hell, and here he was again—nothing learned; everything gained, immedi-ately lost.

E.A.973 took out the butcher knife and gently pressed its blade against the back of Dario's neck. It cut into his skin, worked itself into a gap between the bones of his spinal cord. Using it like a rudder, the creature guided Dario to where it and Oblita wanted him to go.

Dario didn't dare resist; he knew all too well what would happen if he did. He walked past each tenant, and as he did, they blew out their candles and retreated into their apartments. The only person who didn't move was the one who couldn't: the sexless puddle of flesh, kept alive by some maniac's miracle, who lay in the middle of the ground, chewing on the tubing stuffed down their bulging throat.

"This floor is reserved for those who have given to the cause," Oblita said.

Dario blinked the tears out of his eyes. He had worked with many people who had been born with disabilities. He knew the capabilities, the strengths they possessed that not even the so-called "able-bodied" could compete with. This trunk of a person wasn't disabled; their body was a massacre made flesh.

"It has been here longer than the others. It has given almost every-thing, and it has been rewarded greatly."

"It?" Dario said, shaking. "That's a person."

Oblita snorted and asked the quadriplegic, "What are you?"

They struggled with the spit in their throat. "Whatever... I—" vomit dribbled down their chin, "—need... to be."

"See? With the right sacrifice, a person at the Manor can be anything they need. And what need have they for limbs they do not use? What good are legs if a person does not leave? What good are arms if a person is fed and bathed and clothed by another?"

Oblita tapped E.A.973 on the shoulder, and it urged Dario forward.

"Tongues are unnecessary, when I can speak on their behalf," she said. "There are so many parts of the human body that can be put to a better use. Those that live in the Manor are not living. This is where the dead go to die."

Dario stopped at the cavernous hole in the wall where the stairwell should have been. He turned to face Oblita, and in doing so, noticed that all the candles had gone out, and all the tenants were gone.

"These are people," he whispered. "They're not things."

"They are useless. They feed off those who have more, and give almost nothing in return. They are parasites, spreading their disease of poverty throughout their communities. If it ended with them, I would understand, but it continues on with their children, and their children's children."

"Bullshit," Dario said, regaining some of his courage. "I've known... so many. I've seen so many. You can't... say that. I was one of them."

"And yet here you are, where you've always belonged." Oblita cocked her head. "I can help them in ways your programs cannot."

"By butchering them?"

E.A.973 applied more pressure to the butcher knife. Dario could feel hot blood slipping out of the cut on his neck, down his back.

"Trimming the fat, bringing them back to their most basic needs. I get what I want. They get what they want."

Dario slipped into the darkness filling the stairwell, using the tips of his toes to prod for steps. "What do you want?"

"What you'll all want, when the time comes," Oblita said. "Now, hush, please. It's best to limit communication while crossing the Membrane. We wouldn't want to draw... unwanted attention."

The Membrane? He wanted to decipher her cryptic statement, but navigating his surroundings was more important. She was leading him somewhere, to some unspeakable act; if there was an escape along the way, he had to take it, despite how badly his biology was begging him to do otherwise. Action would solicit a reaction. All his life he had been a deer in the headlights; never killed, only clipped by the oncoming atrocity, it had worked so far. But something deep inside him, something primal, told him that wouldn't work anymore. He couldn't stand by, like he'd done when he was young, and watch the beatings, and take the leftover licks. Those three were only kids, like himself; it had gone on for too long, but...

Dario felt a sinking feeling in his groin as his feet slipped off the edge of something in the stairwell's dark. He scrambled backwards, into the slimy embrace of E.A.973's leather apron. Oblita whispered something, plucked something; in her outstretched palm, an orb burned with nightmarish green light. Immediately, the stairwell was illuminated, and like back the way they'd came, nothing here was the same. She handed the orb to Dario.

The stairwell itself had been transformed into what appeared to be a large drainpipe. There were no steps, only a single path carved into the gunk-covered stonework. Even with the limited light he held, Dario could tell that this vertical drop went far beyond the original property of the Manor. Listening closely, he could hear what sounded like water roiling in those black depths. But when he leaned farther over the ledge and his nose caught the bitter updraft, he realized it wasn't water at all, but blood. A whole river of blood, flowing beneath them.

E.A.973 jammed the butcher knife deeper into Dario's neck. A sharp stinging sensation shot into his skull, and so he made the descent.

Dario was a religious man. He believed hell came in many forms, whether it was homelessness, spousal abuse, or even war itself. But the truest form of hell? It was personal; specific and unique to every individual. That was what his mother had taught him, and that was what he believed with every ounce of his being, especially now. Because he was in hell. And this drainpipe? He recognized it. Maybe it wasn't the same as before, but he got the hint. After all these years, it was time for him to be the one who truly suffered.

There were cracks in the walls. Large enough to look through, so he did. On the other side, across what seemed like a chasm, was another vertical shaft with a path carved directly into it. Marching down this path were people, too—tenants, he assumed—holding candles, or holding one another, depending on the nature of their mutilation.

Dario's busted eye started to hurt badly. He tried to apply pressure to it with the arm Oblita had bashed and retched from the pain it caused him. His head felt fuzzy, like the TV static the wheelchair-bound man had been jerking off to. Desperate, he took the ball of green light Oblita had given him and held it to the swollen pouch of skin around his eye. It was simultaneously warm and cool to the touch, and numbing. It was good enough.

At the first door-sized hole in the drainpipe, Oblita told him to stop. E.A.973 flattened Dario against the wall with its arm to his neck, to give her enough room to get by. She slipped into the hole, the hammer raised high, and disappeared into the darkness it held.

"She…"

Confused, Dario glanced at E.A.973. The thing was trying to speak to him.

"She…" It sucked on the vermillion veins that poured out of its eyes. "Trusts."

Dario did a double-take of the doorway—she was still gone—and said, "Please, help me."

"Help… her." E.A.973 pressed harder with its arm into Dario's neck. "She… trusts."

Dario closed his one good eye. Tears, like burning pitch, melted down his face. "I don't know what the fuck…"

"Listen. See." E.A.973 pressed the butcher knife to Dario's forehead and dragged the blade down his skin.

Immediately, his eyes snapped open, and he let out a stifled scream. E.A.973 nodded and said, "See."

Dario gulped for air as the creature jammed its arm harder into his windpipe. For its bulk and brutality, there was a child-like quality to it. The thing wasn't just guarding her; it was almost as if it loved her. Was she a witch? Had she conjured it from this Membrane place? It could have been one of the tenants; its body and brain taken far beyond the limits of pain, to something almost transcendental. She said she was making the most of them. Was this the most of them?

He could hear Oblita returning, so quickly Dario asked, "What are you?"

"Better."

"Than what?"

"The last."

"Nine-seven-two?"

It nodded.

"There were nine-hundred-and—"

Oblita emerged from the doorway. She was smiling and swinging her hammer back and forth, gleefully. Her hands were covered in shit, and the festering stench of it almost knocked Dario off his feet. She'd been digging in something.

"Let's go. I don't want this to be one time She stops turning a blind eye." Oblita was consistently using her English accent now. "Come, now."

E.A.973 finally removed its arm from Dario's throat. He took a big gulp of air and massaged that knotted, choking sensation from his neck. As Oblita took one impatient step after the other towards him, Dario realized how bad of an idea it had been for him to have stopped moving. Like the man or woman who lifts a car off a loved one, his body had been so tightly-wound and adrenaline-soaked that now it was damn near useless to him. His muscles ached in ways and places he'd never experienced before.

Yet, he was moving. Drifting, really, towards the center of the drainpipe, where the blackness yawned and blood flowed. It was like he was being sucked inwards, called forth. His mind named it the Abyss, and it seemed so obvious, as if he'd known it before, and would know it again.

Oblita grumbled, spun the hammer. She drove the hammer downwards, claw first, into Dario's right shoulder. It sank into his skin, let loose the blood within. He screamed in her face. She ripped the hammer away, out of his shoulder, sending a fleshy chunk of him into the salivating dark.

"Stop. God, please, stop!" Dario shambled forward, unable to apply pressure to the wound, because his left arm, his bad arm, couldn't reach it. He dropped the orb of light into the Abyss. "Goddamn it. I can't take this anymore."

"They could," Oblita said, gesturing to no one in particular. "Come see what I have brought you here to see, and listen to what I have to say, and then this will all be over."

"I don't know what this is!" Dario screamed.

E.A.973 fixed the butcher knife to its belt.

Oblita wiped her shit-covered hands on her jeans. "The Membrane? It's somewhere in between Earth and elsewhere. The barrier was weakest here, and it has been growing weaker with every passing year. It is the perfect place for my work. I wouldn't worry about it."

"You're not going to let me go—"

The images finally hit him: Darnell, and his two over-privileged cronies, Mark and Brad, closing in on some snot-nosed kid whose name Dario couldn't even remember. He had been their first of the day.

"I have a family—"

He wondered what time it was, and if it was too late. His wife had said it was too late, already, but she didn't really believe that, did she? She wouldn't have made the call or the invitation. Another image of his wife and daughter, sitting down to have dinner with Darnell, Mark, and Brad—and Dario was the main course.

Oblita raised her hammer, as if to strike him again, and then said, "I had a family, too. It's why we do as we do." She took a deep breath. "Do as I say, or I will feed you to it, too."

Dario's tightly wound body began to unravel. Her threat hit him just as hard as her hammer would if he didn't do as she told him. He didn't know what she was referring to, but if it was anything like E.A.973, it was undoubtedly ungodly. Pain meant nothing to this woman, he realized, but the plan, her plan, was everything. If he could just get his shit together long enough to see it through, to make her happy… maybe there was still a chance.

With a battered eye, a broken elbow, and a bleeding shoulder, Dario went down the slope and entered the darkened doorway.

"Oblita Vesper isn't my real name," she whispered.

Dario stumbled, caught himself against the ribbed walls. Blinded by the blackness, he skirted the edge of this second tunnel. Occasionally, his knee would give out, as his foot dropped into a small hole, or ditch. If this was hell, he was being tested. Social work had been his penance, but apparently, it wasn't enough.

"Surprised, I'm sure. I was young. It means something along the lines of 'forgotten evening star.' Again, I was young, but it stuck with me."

Light, and sound. Dario strained himself to see father ahead, but it was still too dark. Preoccupied, he slipped, crashed down to the ground; cracked his chin against something somewhere along the way. His teeth clenched together, catching a bit of his tongue. They sank into the muscle, and like a vampire, drew blood. He gagged, drooled, and got back up.

"My real name is Ruth Ashcroft."

She shoved Dario, and he went spilling into the next, dimly-lit room.

"In time, it will be the only Ashcroft name history will bother to remember."

Dario scrabbled forward, eye still adjusting to this new place, and slammed into a washer and dryer. He glanced up, gasped. Four faces a few feet above glared down on him—their glazed looks seeing him, and seeing him for what he was supposed to be. Backing away, he spun in semi-circles, getting a measure of the place and those that filled it.

He was in a basement, that much was clear to him. Ugly and grey, it had all the staples a basement in this kind of building would have. Washers and dryers with worn down slots from the weekly quarter deluge; exposed piping that snaked across the wall, leaking their clouded, yellow venom in pools and stains; an uneven floor, broken up by rusted drains and the cracks that crossed it—the Manor's splintered timelines.

But that was all that made it a basement. What was different was what mattered the most. It was the way he couldn't see the ceiling, the way the walls caved in as they ran upwards, as if coming to a point in that impenetrable blackness of that distant pinnacle. And it was from these walls the tenants of Brooksville Manor looked in on the basement. They were standing at balconies that let out to the basement from their own apartments. To Dario, the entire effect gave the impression of an operating theater, and yet, he wasn't the piece of meat on the slab to which their attentions were tethered. It was something else. Something behind him.

Dario turned around. There was E.A.973, stroking the vermillion veins growing out of his eye sockets. And there was Oblita... no, Ruth Ashcroft, smiling and nodding and pleased with herself. Past her was a gurney with restraints hanging off it. And farther back still, framed in orbs of nightmarish green light, the wall gave way to a scaled orifice inside which something white stirred.

Ruth asked him, "Can you guess what my favorite thing about humans is?"

Dario didn't respond. The orifice trembled with life. The white thing creeping inside it moved towards the exit of that weeping portal.

"How easy it is to make them believe something is a god."

"That's... not... god," Dario said, backing away, towards Ruth and E.A.973.

"No, it is not," Ruth whispered, as if she didn't want the tenants above to hear. "But when it is grown, it shall do godly things."

Doors slammed open behind Dario. He turned around and in came Jam, the man he'd seen coming up from the basement earlier, with someone slung over his shoulder. His pristine, white tank top had a single stripe of a blood and vomit sludge mixture running down the front of it. The person over his shoulder was flailing, screaming high, pathetic, pre-pubescent pleas for help.

E.A.973 grabbed Dario by the back of his shirt, but he had no intention of intervening. He wanted to. He told himself he should. But then there they were again—Darnell, Mark, and Brad—taking center stage for the longest-running play his mind had ever known. They had another kid this time, a little boy, and his blood was on all their knuckles. Dario did nothing then.

And he did nothing now, not even as Jam walked past him, and he saw who was slung over the man's shoulders.

Michael. It was Michael, the ten-year-old from the stairs who looked older than he was, and who asked if Dario liked to play video games. MichaelIndomitable. The kid who was so cold and hard he could have sunk the Titanic. Now he was bawling his eyes out, kicking his legs up and down, bashing Jam's chest to no avail.

"Help! Help! Help!" He outstretched his hands and clawed at the air, for Dario. "Help me!"

Dario jerked away from E.A.973's grasp. He made it two steps before the creature had a fistful of his hair. It yanked him backwards, kicked his legs out from under him, so that his knees slammed into the cement ground.

"They're going to kill me!" Michael cried. "They're going to—"

Jam spun Michael's body around and threw him onto the gurney. The boy exploded upwards, trying to get free, but with the restraints, Jam was faster. Arm by arm, foot by foot, the man, silent but for his heavy breathing, tied Michael down. He had done it so quickly, so effortlessly, that this couldn't have been the first time.

Michael heaved and twisted on the gurney. The brake-lock wheels that kept it in place kept coming off the ground, but never enough to tip it over.

"Momma!" he cried to the tenants watching the scene from above. "Momma, please! Momma!"

Jam walked up to E.A.973, not acknowledging Dario at all.

"What the fuck are you doing? He's a kid!" Dario tried to throw himself at Jam, but E.A.973 had grabbed a fresh batch of hair. To Ruth, he yelled, "Don't do this!"

Jam cupped his hands together and held them outwards.

E.A.973 removed the butcher knife from its belt, made a symbol in the air with it, as if blessing the man, and then placed the weapon across Jam's palms.

"Momma. Momma. Momma." Michael went on, his voice hoarse, his mouth full of spit.

Above, the tenants shuffled and whispered amongst themselves. There was clapping, too; praise.

"Your mother has five other children, Michael," Ruth said, never taking her eyes off Dario. "If you weren't a mistake, then why are you here?"

"Momma. Momma. Momma."

Jam took the butcher knife with both his hands, turned, and slowly started walking towards the gurney.

"Jesus fucking Christ!" Dario said.

He groaned as E.A.973 lifted him by his hair to his feet and then held him there, its boney arm once again pressed to his neck.

"Momma. Momma."

More clapping from the onlookers. Somewhere in the nosebleeds, the sound of a door shutting. Michael's mother, maybe, no longer able to witness what she'd wrought.

"Don't do this," Dario said.

Jam stopped at the end of the gurney and turned to Ruth Ashcroft.

"Momma. Momma."

Dario closed his eyes—there was Darnell, waiting for him; always waiting for him—and then he opened them.

"Momma."

Jam took one hand off the butcher knife and used it to grip the side of the gurney.

"Momma."

He raised the butcher knife above his head.

"Momma."

And drove it into Michael's leg.

The ten-year-old let out a blood-curdling scream.

Faster and faster, Jam hacked Michael's leg, chopping through meat and bone, until the cleaver clinked against the metal surface of the gurney.

"Mom… M—"

Blood poured off the gurney, splashed against the ground.

Dario mumbled a weak, "Stop it," but there was no stopping it now. This was ritual. This was routine.

Jam crossed in front of the gurney, to the other side of Michael. He sliced into Michael's left leg. With each cut he made, he dragged the butcher knife out of the wound, so that it caught on stray muscles and tendons. Once again, after a few seconds, the cleaver hit the top of the gurney, and so it was time for Jam to move on.

Michael had stopped speaking. Dario hoped that he was dead.

Jam went to Michael's left arm, lifted it, and started chopping through the bicep. The boy was skinny. His bones like a dead tree branch. With the final swing, his arm came away raggedly from its spewing stump. Jam dropped the severed appendage beside the boy's head, and then walked behind him, to the other side of the gurney.

"Stop," Dario said, to anyone who might be listening. "Stop."

The front of Jam was completely doused in blood. His hands were slick. He could barely hold the butcher knife. He grabbed Michael's right arm, paused for a moment, and looked at Dario.

"Don't," Dario said, feeling the faintest hope. "You don't have to—"

Jam jerked Michael's arm, bringing the boy's blood-gushing torso closer to him. In one strike, he separated his right arm from his body and dropped it on his chest.

"Momma."

Shocked, Dario's swollen eye almost opened in surprise. How the hell? How the fuck? He couldn't still be alive.

Jam went to the top of the gurney and took Michael by the hair. He reared his arm back and aimed it for the boy's glistening neck.

Dario closed his eye to escape what was to come, but the sounds found him all the same. The sudden, thick chords of nauseating noise: the wet splash of gore; the hollow echoes of blood drizzling on steel. He could hear bones being uprooted from their soil. Michael continued to beg for his momma, even though he couldn't.

This was hell. He was in hell, and Dario knew exactly what he had done to deserve this. When he was thirteen, a twenty-year-old from his building, Darnell, hung out with the two high schoolers, Mark and Brad, he dealt drugs to. One day, on Dario's way home from school, he caught Brad giving Darnell a blow job by the dumpster near the back door to the building's basement. When Dario tried to sneak away, he ran into Mark, who had a condom wrapper in one hand and a woman's purse in the other. Both of them owed Darnell money. Sex was the only payment outside of cash the drug dealer had been willing to accept.

Dario opened his eyes. Jam was finished. Michael's arms, legs, and head had been cut from his body. The blood pouring off the gurney was slowing down to a steady trickle. Jam, looking weak, looking as if he finally realized what he had done, started towards E.A.973.

After they caught Dario, Darnell, Mark, and Brad didn't lay a hand on him. Darnell knew Dario—they'd both lived in the building for as long as the other could remember—and knew how much his grandmother meant to him. Darnell called him a faggot and had Mark spit what was left of him in Dario's face. They weren't going to hurt him. They were going to give him a choice.

Jam stopped beside Dario. His eyes were cold, empty. The tenants above were beginning to disperse. The show was over. What was done was done, and with it done, Jam gave E.A.973 back its butcher knife.

Randomly, Darnell and his gang would jump Dario, be it before school, after school, or somewhere in the community on the weekends. They reminded him he was a faggot, a coward, and useless. They threatened to beat his grandmother, rape his mother. But if he chose someone else to take the beating, then they would be spared. He could've chosen himself, of course, but he never did. Instead, he chose kids at school, the ones who picked on him, the ones he hated. It seemed fair. It wasn't at all.

E.A.973 finally let go of Dario and pushed him away. Ruth Ashcroft closed in on him, her trusty hammer poised to strike, and said, "We are almost finished here."

Jam's arms dropped to his side defeatedly. E.A.973 pulled back its arm and swung the butcher knife into Jam's head, cracking open his skull. It dragged the blade out slowly, the same way Jam had done to Michael, and went at him again and again, sending pieces of flesh and bone fragments across the basement, until Jam collapsed, dead.

E.A.973 knelt down beside the corpse and started hacking it to pieces. Not just the limbs, but fingers and toes; the creature cut off every feature of Jam's pain-wracked, death-paralyzed face. And with a handful of nose, eyeballs, lips, ears, and a tongue, it threw them onto the gurney.

Darnell's punishment went on for months. Dario would choose a kid from his school, and Darnell, Mark, and Brad would stalk them. Dario would have to follow. They never raped anyone he chose, and he only chose boys, because he was afraid they would. Instead, they stole whatever belongings they had and, in the sewer tunnels that let out into the local creeks of Brooksville, beat the kids into unconsciousness. Dario saw it all from the shadows. Every awful thing he let happen to others, because he couldn't face having it happen to himself. He was helpless, and made others helpless with his helplessness.

With Jam in a pile of stinking, steaming bits, E.A.973 scooped up the remains into its arms, and what it couldn't carry, the vermillion veins curled around and held, like tentacles. In one trip, it hauled all of what had been a man to the gurney and deposited the two-hundred-pounds of gore, burying Michael beneath it, as if he wasn't even there.

Ruth Ashcroft said, "Thank you, Edmund," to E.A.973 and left Dario's side for the gurney.

By the third month of Darnell's punishment, Dario was having such bad anxiety that his mother took him to a therapist. His grades had begun to drop, as well. There were rumors at school he was somehow connected to the bullies who were beating up the kids across Brooksville. Mark and Brad had started to stare at him in ways that turned his stomach, and Darnell kept making him drink the swill at the bottom of his beer bottles. It tasted differently every time.

Ruth undid the brakes on the gurney, stood up, and started pushing it towards the large orifice. The wheels let out a piercing screech, despite the blood that oiled them. The closer she drew to the orifice, the more excited the white thing inside it became.

Dario often thought of killing Darnell, Mark, and Brad. One day, he stole a butcher knife from his mother's kitchen and put it in his backpack. He had convinced himself it was the right thing to do, and no one would miss people like them.

Ruth slowed the gurney to a stop inches away from the orifice. With a grunt, she lifted her end up. The pile of Michael's and Jam's remains came together in a foul avalanche of gore and slid down the gurney, off it, and into the disgusting hole in which the white thing thrived.

For once, Dario had gone out looking for Darnell, Mark, and Brad. He checked the building and all the places where Darnell was known to deal drugs. He checked the clothing stores and gas stations where Mark and Brad were often seen. But he couldn't find them, nor could he find anyone who had any idea of where they had gone.

Once the last of the limbs finished rolling off the gurney, Ruth quickly dropped it and backed away from the orifice.

All of the tenants were gone, now. It was just Dario, E.A.973, and Ruth.

"See," E.A.973 told Dario.

A day later, Dario discovered Darnell had been busted for drug dealing. Mark and Brad had ratted him out, after having been caught by the police with heroin on them.

Mark and Brad did some time, and Dario never saw them again; at least, never face-to-face. Years later, Gratify, a social media platform, suggested Dario friend them, on account of having grown up in the same neighborhood and having gone to the same school.

Dario did run into Darnell once. It had been at baseball game in Bitter Springs. He had been wearing a nice suit, and spent most of the game yelling at his girlfriend, whose name he kept mixing up with someone else's. When Dario, who had been desperately trying to avoid him the entire time, ended up running into him in the parking lot, Darnell looked at him as if he had never seen him before in his entire life.

Darnell, Mark, and Brad had never been punished for what they had done.

And Dario, who had never told anyone about his involvement in the beatings, hadn't either.

The white thing inside the orifice was larger than Dario realized. Distance had disguised its length and throbbing girth. It crawled forward, its upper half going first, its lower half following close behind. It navigated the insides of the massive orifice that checked the basement with a fierce intensity, the same way a leashed dog would drag its owner towards a cornered animal.

When it reached the edge of the orifice, the creature reared back, and Dario saw in full its grotesque glory. It was the length and width of a pick-up truck, with two brown chevrons and two black pincers as its defining facial feature. There were smaller, darker markings that ran up and down both sides of the beast; the markings and the coloration came together in a deep black patch at the thing's tail-end. At first, Dario thought it was a worm, but it wasn't a worm at all.

It was a maggot.

The Maggot jammed its face into the gory remains and began gulping down the skin and organs. When it came to liquids, the overgrown grub absorbed them directly through its piss-colored outer-layer. Like a chameleon, it took on the color of carnage, and then the blood receded into the thing's starving depths.

"What do you think?" Ruth asked.

Dario didn't respond.

E.A.973 turned away and walked off into the shadows.

"You must have a lot of questions," she persisted.

Dario didn't. He really didn't. Over the course of two hours, everything he had ever known or thought he knew about the world and the people who inhabited it had been destroyed, and then desecrated. In the back of his mind, he knew he had a date to keep, but his dates had no need to keep him now. When a social worker didn't take care of themselves, or took too much of others and their problems in, they often suffered burn-out. Dario was beyond that now. Ruth had scorched his reason, his sanity; she had incinerated his soul.

The Maggot, having finished its meal, glanced up from the orifice and into the basement. Though it could not express any emotions, Dario recognized that absent look. The creature was hungry. It wanted another meal.

But as it lurched forward to claim the fresh meat before it, the orifice faded into non-existence. Like a hologram giving out to electrical failure, the wretched window went fuzzy, out of focus. And then, as if it had never been there at all, it was gone, replaced by a bland, water-stained cement wall.

It didn't stop there. The grand, slanted ceiling had vanished as well. The operating theater closed down in a matter of seconds, and whereas before Dario couldn't see the top of the basement, he could now nearly touch it if he stood on the tips of his toes.

Glancing over his shoulder, he saw that the basement had shrunk, too, in width and length. There were more washers and dryers, and a clothesline with drying clothes hanging from it. More piping, too, and the catchy chorus of a pop song coming in from underneath the metal door that led into the place.

Dario gasped and gave everything he had to keep from fainting. The Maggot was gone. The Membrane was gone. He had seen what Ruth Ashcroft had wanted him to see, and he had heard what she had wanted him to hear. It was over.

Ruth pocketed the hammer into her jeans. She shrugged, smiled, and said with her arms outstretched, "Well, are you ready?"

The question drove tears out of Dario's eyes. "What?"

"To get started."

He closed his eye, shook his head.

"I'm ready to talk now."

He shook his head harder.

"Isn't that why you came here? To get to know me? To help me?"

Dario swallowed hard; his jaw was quivering so badly it made his teeth hurt.

"Let's give the session another go."

Dario opened his eye, and saw from the way she flirted with the head of the hammer he had no choice in the matter. "Why?" he said with a rasp.

"Why do you do what you do at all? Can't everyone change if given a chance?"

"I don't... have a choice... in this," Dario said.

"You do, and you did," Ruth said, extending her hand to him. "You chose to do nothing. Doing a little more nothing isn't going to kill you. It's the opposite you have to worry about."

Hand-in-hand, Ruth led Dario through Brooksville Manor like a mother would an overwhelmed child their first time at the mall. As it had in the basement, the Membrane had vanished, leaving no trace of its otherworldly presence or the putrescent, bio-organic material of which it was comprised. Everything was exactly as it had been a few hours ago, except it all carried a different meaning, a different tone. He was losing his mind—that much he could be certain of—but the place seemed changed, or at least, revealed. It had the atmosphere of a building locked-up for the evening; too quiet, too stagnant; where anything could lurk around any corner; and the things that had been hidden in the light gave themselves over to the trusted embrace of the dark.

Coming out of the basement, from the doorway Dario initially met Jam at, they passed the apartment with the picture of the black Jesus who held blood drop-shaped faces in one hand, and maggots in the other. Seeing it again, Dario bit his lip so hard he took a chunk out of it. The writing had been on the walls. He just hadn't yet learned the cryptic language of the cult.

He went up the stairwell as if he were going to the gallows. In his mind, he replayed his past and present crime of inaction. He couldn't remember the names or the faces of the children he'd led to Darnell's fists. And try as he might, he already felt Michael leaving him, like a sickness his body had decided it needed to be rid of. It was easier that way, to remember the remains than the thing to which they belonged. The more ambiguity, the hazier the recollections became.

He told his clients it wasn't healthy to bury the guilt, the hurt, but there he was again, as he had been before, shovel in hand and a grave before him. All the old corpses were there, just as fresh they'd been the day he threw them in. Some, like Darnell, had clawed their way out, but he was still strong enough to put them back. The problem was the memory of Michael, and the event that had been his marriage. They wouldn't budge. His mind was clinging to them. They refused to be cast like old stones into a well, to be forgotten until they were new again.

Then it came to him, from where he least it expected it.

Ruth Ashcroft, reaching the third floor, turned and asked, "What have you learned from hell?"

The immediate answer that came to mind was nothing, but that wasn't true. At the risk of sounding like a suicidal teenager, hell had been his mentor his entire life. By its hammers and fires he had been molded and shaped. For years he had convinced himself that he wasn't like a lot of the other social workers he met, but he was. For eight hours a day, he absorbed the agonies of others and used it as glue to seal the wounds in ways alcohol and pills hadn't been able to. He was still cynical, and he was still naïve, and he wasn't very popular, not with his wife or daughter or his so-called friends, because in all his helping years, the only person he was trying to do right by was himself, and he had been doing it in every wrong way.

Social work was the shell in which he hid. It had never been about the client, and because he told himself it was, it had never been about him, either. He had been spinning wheels, choking on the fumes. He usually made one grand show of things—hitting Ruth with the chair— and when it failed, as it inevitably did, he caved-in to what he figured was fate.

But not this time. Not anymore. He didn't have enough fingers on his hands to count those he'd damned. Dario had a duty to protect, a duty to warn; a duty to do something other than let Michael's tortured cries for his momma ring out through his head. The boy deserved better. They all did. And if Dario lost it all trying to get it for them, then he would lose it all.

He would trust in god now, like his grandmother had always told him to. The real god, the true god; not the Maggot that infested the Manor's bowels, or the beasts Ruth warned of in the Membrane. If he had learned anything, it was that, through hell, he could finally find heaven.

Ruth led Dario into the third-floor hallway, where, once again, the floor was tiled and the walls wallpapered, and the chandeliers were transformed back into their gentler selves. Whispers fell in on them from every direction, as the curious undoubtedly tracked them behind their apartment doors and through their peepholes. He noted surprise in their voices, as if they couldn't believe he was alive.

The chandelier that had gone out earlier flickered back on above 310. Dario wondered if Michael's mother and siblings had just moved in there, and if they were reaping the spoils of their slaughter. It made him sick to his stomach, so into his shell of social work he retreated and acknowledged with monkish indifference the decision they'd made. A colony run by a monster did make of those who lived there monsters. Through therapy, he had connected with and even cared for criminals, whether they were murderers or sex offenders. At least when it came to the tenants of Brooksville Manor, he knew it wasn't ghosts that haunted their skulls, but a demon possessing their bodies.

Ruth pushed open the door to her apartment. It was unlocked. Dario imagined it always was. The fruity rot of the old man, Herbert

North, greeted them like the help. Ruth picked up the chair that Dario had used to try and beat her brains in, and Dario went and stood beside the table and his work bag next to it.

For a moment, his mind swam in the high-tide of déjà vu. He had been here before, not long before, but to say that everything was the same would ask of Dario to be that same scared, cowardly kid he had always been and just recently shed. His eye was swollen shut; his left arm was broken; his right shoulder was a bloody emblem of idiocy; he was dehydrated badly; and there, in his mind's eye, the death of MichaelIndomitable looped, one cleaver cut at a time. It would be there forever. It shouldn't be archived. He didn't want it to be.

Dario cleared his throat, killed his thoughts, murdered his feelings, and with the cleanest of affections, said, "Hello, I'm Dario Onai from the Brooksville Community Health Center. You must be Ruth Ashcroft?"

Ruth nodded, apparently pleased that this was about to play out exactly as she wanted it to. "I am," she said, in a proud English accent. "Thank you for coming to see me. I imagine it must have been hell getting here at this hour."

He swallowed his revulsion. "Yes."

She laid the hammer on the table in between them. It was a dare, a part of her violent dance. She'd spent so long in this depraved kingdom she seemed to relish opportunities such as these, where her rule could be challenged, and those that dared challenge her could be put down with ease.

"You may have heard this before," Dario said, "but anything you tell me is confidential."

"Unless I intend on harming myself, someone else, or if I know a child is being harmed."

"Yes—" *Momma, Momma,* Michael cried out in Dario's head, "— that's correct."

Ruth twisted a long strand of hair around her finger. "Where should I begin?"

"With the thing that has been bothering you the most," Dario said—his swollen eye, broken elbow, and mauled shoulder singing in seething harmony. "Start with… where all this started."

"I was born 1878." She paused, as if waiting for his shock.

He gave her no response. After everything, she would have to do better than that.

"I was born in 1878 in a small village in England. My mother's name was Amelia Ashcroft, and my brother's name... Why aren't you writing this all down?"

Dario swallowed blood, leaned over, took out her folder from his bag, and started documenting what she'd told him.

Frustrated, she carried on. "My brother's name was Edmund Ashcroft."

Edmund Ashcroft. E.A.973. Dario's pen skipped across the page. Nine-hundred-and-seventy-three.

"He and I have different fathers. I cannot remember their names, but they were abusive, to us and my mother. She killed them, my mother. Stabbed one, kicked the other down the stairs."

"Was she arrested?"

"No, the Ashcroft family was once a powerful family, and it had many ties. Unbeknownst to my mother, the last surviving member of the Ashcroft family other than ourselves was keeping a close eye on us, keeping us the best that he could out of harm's way. His name was Amon Ashcroft, and he was my great uncle.

"He wrote to my mother one day. They had once been close, almost inseparable, when she was a little girl, but then he disappeared. She had thought he was dead. In his letter, he begged her to return to the family estate, to allow him to make right everything that had gone wrong. Reluctantly, my mother agreed, and we then set out for the countryside.

"There was something very wrong with the land near the Ashcroft estate. Villages were abandoned, and a strange pestilence was rooted there. It took the form of vermillion-colored veins."

Dario whispered, "Like those coming out of E.A.973's eyes?"

"The very same, actually. But all will be explained in due time." Ruth exhaled slowly, smiled. "There was something wrong with the Ashcroft estate as well. The pestilence hadn't spread there, but originated from that ruin. I said that the rest of the family had died out, and this is true. While my grandmother and grandfather, uncles and aunt had died due to natural causes, those that came before them perished for a more sinister cause. Sacrifice."

Dario felt himself drifting into her orbit, the same as the poor and the destitute drifted into Brooksville Manor's. He reached across the table, grabbing the bottle of water that was still there, and chugged it. She wanted him to fall under her spell. He couldn't let that happen.

"The Ashcroft family, for as long as anyone could remember, had found fame and fortune in the forging of an unholy alliance with a creature that lived far below the estate, where, like here, the barrier between our world and the Membrane was weak. The price they paid for Its services was bodies. Children of the Ashcroft line had to be sacrificed to Its insatiable hunger. And they were. The women of the family were bred like cattle, so that those who had been given a pardon from the ceremony could live, while others, such as newborns with deformities, or children with little potential, could take their places."

If Ruth Ashcroft had told him this earlier, when they had first met and she still went by Oblita Vesper, he would have immediately diagnosed her as psychotic, schizophrenic, or as having some other delusional disorder, possibly brought on by a medical condition. But he'd seen what lurked in the basement, what lurked beyond the walls of this reality, and he believed her completely. She had planned this perfectly. But why? Why did she give a shit about what he thought?

He engaged her to show that he listening: "Did Amon know?"

"Yes, that is why he called us back. The creature needed a new pawn, my mother. However, Amon had other plans. He had discovered a weapon in those years he was away, a weapon that could possibly destroy the monster. He thought my mother could get closer than It would allow him. He was a cowardly man, and my mother was the bravest woman I've ever known. When the creature's minions stole my brother and I, she went into the bowels of the house and destroyed the creature. Or at least, she believed she had.

"When my mother returned from her ordeal, Amon was changed. The vermillion veins had consumed him. He became an agent of the creature, a harbinger. Or perhaps it was only a copy of Amon created by the beast. I never knew. The house released my brother and me, and with my mother, we were infected with the vermillion pestilence.

"My mother, brother, and I were recruited into the creature's cause. We went with Amon from the estate to a neighboring village, Cairn, and there we set about spreading the pestilence, the influence, if you will, of the creature further. We did fairly well, until an investigator arrived to stop us.

"His name was Herbert North."

Dario clenched his jaw. "The old man in your bathtub?"

"The very same."

"But that was so long ago."

"Yes, it was," Ruth said, dreamily, "but we had attempted to convert him to the cause. In doing so, he was given an extended life, like me and my brother and mother, and Amon. He overcame the vermillion hunger, though, and killed my brother and my mother. We killed many people in Cairn, and I burned down the village before Amon and I slipped away. I thought the killing would make my grief go away, but it did not."

Dario lurched forward; the pen twisted up in his hand before dropping onto the table. He closed his eye. In the noisy darkness of his lids, he saw the veins and amorphous shapes, and other things his optometrist told him not to worry about, and yet he did now more than ever, because what if they hadn't always been there?

He had lost a lot of blood from where Ruth had taken a chunk out of his shoulder, and his body's reserves were running on fumes. Feeling a pressure on that same shoulder, he opened his eye to find her wrapping a bandage around it. In front of him was a bag of ice. He had only closed his eye for a second, but it may as well have been an eternity.

"You are a tough man," Ruth said, putting the finishing touches on the wrap. She picked up the bag of ice and pressed it to his swollen eye. "Hold it."

Spitting, cringing, he managed to get his arm high enough to hold the ice there.

"There is something I have to tell you about the creature our family swore allegiance to. I can tell that you are a religious man. In the basement, I saw you mouthing prayers."

Had he been? Dario drove the bag of ice harder against the throbbing swell of flesh.

"The creature wasn't just some creature. The orifice in which you saw the Maggot belonged to It."

"You said—" he coughed, "—the creature your family served was... in Europe."

"It is. It is very large and Its domain occupies an even larger space inside the Membrane. It is no creature, though. It is much more than that, Dario Onai. It is God."

He lowered the bag of ice, cheek twitching.

"Not a god, but the God."

It took everything Dario had not to debate with her, but he managed to manage his words. He was a social worker. She was a client. It was not his place to challenge her, not yet.

"The Vermillion God, that is Its name. It had been lying dormant a very long time, until the Ashcroft family caused It to stir and gave It a reason to take an interest in our world. They did not know it was God, but Amon did, and so when Amon and I left Cairn, we left as missionaries, to bring the true God to those who had unknowingly placed their beliefs in false idols.

"For years we crossed the continents, breaking down the barrier between the Membrane and this world."

"How does one… do that?"

"Religion reigns supreme in a world unshackled by science and technology. Amon and I tapped into the supernatural and gave rise to 'monsters.' We planted carnivorous trees, coaxed forth ghosts and phantasms. We unleashed beasts from the Membrane that the people had only read of in books, or heard of in tall tales. We gave life to every urban legend and horror story humans had ever told. In the deserts, we resurrected ghouls. In the mountains, we unleashed wendigos. We supplemented the rituals of Witches, and encouraged the efforts of spellweavers. But most importantly, we spread It where we went. The vermillion veins are Its veins—tangible proof of Its existence. In the soil we planted the veins, and in the minds of others, we planted Its word."

Dario was starting to get his bearings again. "You brought monsters into the world. Are monsters not evil?"

"Are they?" Ruth asked him such a way that she seemed to really want to know. "Are they any different than any other species in an ecosystem? Do you think they think highly of us?"

"Good point," he mumbled. "Releasing these monsters… it broke down the barrier between the natural and supernatural world?"

Cheerfully, she said, "It did. God is easier to accept when those supposedly 'godless' things—" she laughed, lost in a memory, "—are allowed to run free."

"And you planted these vermillion veins…"

"To increase God's influence. To show It how far It could go."

"Did the people believe in what you were saying?"

"Some, but not all of them. This was the early 1900s. People were stubborn, and stupid, and devoted to the god which had a monopoly on the afterlife."

"How do you know It's God?"

"I've seen It. Have you seen your god?"

Dario didn't respond.

"My God has a body and a will, and Its power can be felt and seen at all times. I do not need faith to know that which I can see with my eyes and hear with my ears."

Dario changed the subject: "You and Amon went your separate ways."

Ruth nodded, played with the hammer on the table. "We made our way to the United States and did what needed to be done. We visited a plantation in the South—Carpenter Plantation. It was owned and run by a man named Abel, and he was one of the most powerful families in the South at the time. Amon wanted to use Carpenter Plantation as a portal by which vermillion veins could be harvested and propagated.

"It did not go well." Ruth picked up the hammer and squeezed its handle tightly. "Abel became obsessed with me. He tried to rape me, and when I told Amon he said I should have let it happen, I snapped. Amon and I beat each other to a bloody pulp that night. The next morning, Amon was gone, and I was left alone there. Abel had already started construction on the plantation to turn it into something else; a prison, I think, to keep me there forever.

"He thought I was a child, and because Amon had abandoned me, I did not know what to do. I had no one, and my only purpose in life was derived from his. But in my wanderings of the Membrane, I had discovered something, and with my hatred, I was given a purpose."

Dario's hand hurt badly from trying to keep up with everything Ruth was telling him. At first, he had been jotting it down for the sake of appeasing her, but now, he was invested, hanging on her every word as if they were the ledge from which he dangled about the claws of Death. If he escaped Brooksville Manor tonight, he would have to have something, anything, to explain what'd happened here.

"Alone, in a new country, with someone who didn't respect you, and no family? That must have been so hard for you," he said.

Ruth shook her head, and then admitted: "Yes, yes. But I knew what I had to do. There was a Witch. Her name was Pain, and pain was her game." She snorted. "I summoned her to Carpenter Plantation, told her to go to town torturing the family, especially Abel. Before I left, I filled him with vermillion veins, to make sure he had a long and terrible life under Pain's watch."

"Revenge is important to you," Dario said.

"Isn't it to you?"

Dario could still hear Darnell laying into the children in the sewers, one wet, heavy punch at a time. He thought about the drunk driver who had killed his mother while she was crossing the street. He thought about his father, who he'd bumped into at the grocery store once, and who didn't offer any apology for abandoning him and his mom before Dario was born. He thought about the boy who had groped his daughter in gym class, and how, despite all his fury, he had said nothing at all to the boy's father, because the boy's father was larger and meaner, and head of the PTA.

"I don't know," Dario said. "I let people walk all over me."

Ruth leaned in. "Why do you do it?"

"I used to think I was afraid of what would happen to me if I stood up for myself. But maybe I'm afraid of what I might to do them if I did."

"You can never do enough to a person," Ruth said. "Even if they die, you can always go further."

"What did you do to Amon?" Dario asked.

"For a while I tracked him, but he was always one step ahead of me. He had discovered ways to move around the country that I was not privy to. Once or twice, we did cross paths, but I could do nothing to him. He was still my Amon, and the man who had taken care of me when I had lost everything else."

Brooksville Manor shook; a picture frame fell off Ruth's wall, and the glass shattered.

Raising an eyebrow, she continued. "While I was looking for ways into the Membrane, I tried to live a normal life for a while. I formed many connections, mostly criminal, and made a lot of money off the prohibition. When World War I and II happened, I roamed the cities and embedded myself into businesses, for no reason other than I could, and no one would stop me."

"What about God?"

"Yes, God. When Amon and I had been traversing the Membrane, I discovered an opening into God. An orifice into Its gastrointestinal track. And there was something inside it."

"The Maggot."

"Yes, the Maggot. It had been so very small, then, but it spoke to me, and to me alone. Amon said to pay it no mind, but I always found a way to come back to it. The Maggot warned me of the Vermillion

God, what It was capable of. The God had already consumed worlds and eons, and the Maggot had formed from the corpses and cultures digesting there.

"After Amon left me, and before I arrived here, I spent my time searching for the Membrane, as I said. And I did find it. The openings were temporary, but I was powerful enough to make the most of them. For thirty years, I fed people to the Maggot as often as I possibly could."

Dario's eye fell on the hammer in her hand.

"I counted, once, how many I killed. It was almost a thousand."

"To feed... the Maggot?"

"God slumbered, and the Maggot needed to grow. But it wasn't only me. I had an accomplice."

Dario said, "E.A.973."

"Well, it was only E.A.1 through E.A.612 at that point."

"Edmund Ashcroft."

"It isn't my brother, but a representation of my brother. With the Membrane and the veins, I can mold pathetic recreations of him. They all have kept me company, and they all took the falls for my crimes, so that I could keep the Maggot fed."

Dario had to keep the conversation going, to keep this new surge of adrenaline pumping through his veins. Without it, he'd be done for. "You said you came here because the barrier to the Membrane was weakest."

"I did. Amon and I spent a lot of time in Brooksville, Bedlam, and Bitter Springs. Brooksville Manor had been constructed in response to the United States' government's push to provide low-incoming housing for the poor. With the barrier at its weakest and with an almost infinite supply of... stock—"

Someone screamed outside in the hallway.

"—I knew this was the place I had to be." She paused and said aloud, "Edmund, please, go check what is going on out there."

Out of nowhere, E.A.973 materialized. The gaunt, garish, museum-exhibit of flesh and bones built itself into existence from the living room, until it was standing behind Ruth in its leather apron, with the butcher knife attached to its belt. It had been there the whole time.

E.A.973 nodded, walked past Dario, but not before giving him a pat on the shoulder, and then opened the door and went into the hallway.

"But you... killed Michael." Dario used restraint to shape the tone of his voice, to avoid it sounding judgmental. "And Jam."

"I did, but that is not typical of what happens here. The Maggot's appetite has grown exponentially. For years, I fed it limbs. Pieces of the tenants. We have a system here, Mr. Onai. Would you like to hear it?"

He nodded, and noted how she had let go of the hammer.

Brooksville Manor rumbled again. And again, as he had hours before, he heard something inside the walls.

"The newest tenants live on the bottom-most floor. As people pass away or lose faith, the tenants are shifted. There is a clear distinction of progress in Brooksville Manor. The ultimate goal is to live on the third floor, with myself."

"They do that by sacrificing their bodies?"

"Yes, they do. There is a culture in Brooksville Manor, you see, and it is one that I have created. It is a living building, a country all its own. Everything is provided for, the same way your government supposedly provides for its people. I take their checks, and I take their needs into consideration, and I give them what they need."

"And they go along with it?"

"Most of them do, but it is usually the youth that rebel. And that is fine. I make the most of them."

More sounds from inside the walls.

"I give them everything, and they give everything they have, because to them the Maggot is god. They believe it is the Maggot that provides for them. And whereas your god only seems to answer prayers through sheer coincidence, the Maggot is reliable, and it is timely."

"But it's not god."

"No, it is not, but that is okay. Do you always buy name-brand when you go to the store?"

Dario shook his head.

"But unless you really look for it, you seldom notice the difference between it and generic."

"That's true," he said.

"It is. These are people that are nothing. They are already dead; dead to themselves and this world. They are whores and drug addicts, rapists and murderers. They are a drain to the system, your system."

"How do you know?" Dario asked.

"I know," she said, resolutely.

"If you think so lowly of them and this world, why does it bother you so much what they do to it?"

"I love this world," Ruth said, cocking her head. "Everything I do, I do for this world."

"You've filled it with monsters. You have murdered thousands of people."

"I have."

"Is that love?"

"You would do anything for the ones you love, wouldn't you?"

Dario didn't answer, because he wasn't sure he would.

"The Vermillion God is real. And Amon is going to awaken It. This is inevitable. The Maggot is not God, but it has lived inside God, and it was formed by those that resisted God's efforts. I'm not trying to destroy the world at all. I am trying to save it. When the Vermillion God awakens, so, too, will the Maggot, and it will stop God from enslaving everything and everyone."

The bag of ice had melted in the heat inside Dario's hand. It hung limply over it, like a body bag. "You said you were trying to summon the Vermillion God with Amon."

"I was, but not anymore."

"Do you not believe in It?"

"I do. I believe in It so much, that is why I have done what I have done all these years. It is God, but I do not want It. And neither will you or anybody else, once you see what It is capable of."

More shouting, coming from somewhere on the second floor. Doors rattling; a loud thump; more noise in the walls.

Dario asked, "What is…?"

But Ruth cut him off. "I know that I am a terrible person, but I am still human." She pulled down her blouse, where her breasts were covered in vermillion veins. "Despite every inhuman thing I have done and gone through, I am still human.

"I did not want this. I did not want to become this. I thought I was doing the right thing by trying to bring God into this world, but I was wrong. I thought I was doing the right thing by trying to feed Its nemesis, but now I am not so sure. I found Herbert North the other day, coming home with his partner from a case on the west coast, and killed him, thinking it would make me feel better. And it didn't.

"The people that live in Brooksville Manor repulse me, and I do get pleasure bending to them to my will, and yet, at the same time, I am unsettled. I lie in my bed most of the day. I abuse E.A.973 for no reason other than it is there to abuse. I relish seeing the Maggot, and yet the feedings leave me empty. I have started to drink. I have—" she pointed to the scars on her neck, "—started to hurt myself.

"At first, I only did what I did to get back at Amon. I wanted to show him I didn't need him. Later, I did what I did because I could, because no one would stop me. I wanted fulfillment. Now, I do what I do because it is routine, and because I have done it for so very long, and because I do not know anything else. I am not a gentle woman. I break everything I touch. The God inside me will not let me be anything else, and all I've ever wanted is to be happy. I cannot cope with what I've become."

Dario was able to open his left eye a little. With his vision partially restored, and with Ruth Ashcroft's supposed life laid out before him, he saw her in a somewhat different light. She was fidgeting, and her eyes were large. She had made tiny braids in her hair from the anxiety that had taken to her hands. She looked her age, which was one hundred and then some, as if the confidence she'd lost was the glamour that'd run out. The vermillion veins on her exposed chest were revolting, but like the needle in the junkie's arm, they were also part of the problem. Dario hadn't known who Ruth Ashcroft was, nor had he known Oblita Vesper, but he knew desperation when he saw it. She couldn't go to a priest for guidance, because they would only validate what she'd done. Did she want out? Did she want to convert him?

Another scream from outside the apartment.

Dario went to stand, but Ruth started talking again.

"Can I be helped?"

Dario set down his pen. As a social worker, he had to believe everyone could be helped; otherwise, what the fuck was the point of his job? Even if it was the smallest of changes, it still meant something. Ruth Ashcroft was the most terrifying person he had ever met, but he had seen the Maggot with his own eyes. He didn't, and wouldn't, believe her about the Vermillion God. But the Maggot was real, and as far as he could tell, so too, to her, were the actions she'd made and the reasons that justified them.

"Would you help me? If you could?"

More screams. Something being torn down. This time, Dario did stand, and he looked to the front door, which E.A.973 had closed behind it.

"Ruth... there's something going—"

"I'm your client," she said, standing. "Will you come back to see me?"

"I... you... I have to report you... for everything. You know that."

"It won't make a difference. The police won't come. They never do."

Sounds in the walls, like dirt shaking free from the topsoil and cascading upon a grave.

"I won't hurt you. You know that." She slid the hammer across the table towards him. "I could have, but I did not. You might save them, saving me."

Dario opened his mouth to stutter out some bullshit answer when E.A.973 burst into the apartment, screaming, "Sister, my sister! The Maggot has come for you!"

Ruth backed out of her chair, knocking it to the ground. Mouth quivering out malformed words, she ran past Dario and into the hallway.

Dario grabbed the hammer off the table, pocketed it, and then hid what still showed underneath his shirt. He picked up his bag, dropped it as E.A.973 slipped its hard hands under his armpits and jerked him to his feet. His skin stung where the imposter had touched him, as if it had left behind hairs or nettles. But it hadn't seen him take the hammer, or if it had, it had wanted him to.

"This shouldn't be happening," Ruth was saying as E.A.973 shoved Dario into the hallway.

If the Membrane operated like clockwork, then Ruth's final feeding had sent its gears into disarray. Phasing in and out of existence, the bio-organic plane was taking over the Manor like a timid tide lapping against a shore. Paint-like splatters of meat and fungus grew and shrank on every possible surface. The apartment doors widened and thinned, from gaping holes to bristled slits. The sleep-inducing light of the twelve chandeliers alternated between a heavenly white and hellish red. The diamond tiling on the floor congealed into maelstroms of color that puckered upward like nibbling lips. Fissures appeared in the ceiling—smeared eraser marks from god's disappointed hand—and inside them, belts of stars were wrapped around abyssal bodies.

For all that had changed, one thing had not: the tenants were still locked in their apartments, and every man, woman, and child inside was screaming at the top of their lungs, begging, pleading, praying for any kind of release. Something was inside each of the apartments, and it was doing the kind of things to the tenants that made a human sound like a dying animal. Torture of the most terrible kind, where not even one nerve ending was spared.

"Where's the Maggot?" Ruth asked E.A.973.

It shook its head. "Still… coming through."

Because Dario's body seemed to deem it necessary, he felt the blood draining from his face, allowing his eye to finally open completely. His broken arm, while unusable, became more manageable; and the chunk of flesh on his shoulder that breathed cold fire into his senses had dulled. He felt unlocked, unfettered; all the bats in his battered belfry had spread their wings, and inside his skull, they took flight to chase the ghosts away.

Ruth took off down the hall towards the stairwell. E.A.973 waved Dario on, not threateningly, but as a brother would his own. There was still time, Dario realized as he trailed after them. Time had frozen for them at Brooksville Manor, in the foul amber of Ruth's deeds, but it didn't have to, not anymore, and especially not for him. The larva of lethargy had incubated inside him long enough. He had to learn from hell. He had to do something. It was funny, but it took being on the brink of psychosis and about to collapse for Dario to finally figure out god's purpose for him. But that was how it went, wasn't it? If Ruth Ashcroft had gotten anything right with the Maggot and her designs for deicide, it was that suffering made the most potent motivator.

And his purpose was this: If he could save Ruth, he could save those who lived here. If he could get Ruth out, he could condemn her; turn her in, have her committed. If he could do that, then every problem he'd ever walked away from, every scapegoat he'd shielded himself with, might have actually meant something.

Ruth stepped aside. E.A.973 opened the stairwell door, his butcher knife readied, and told them it was clear. Ruth regurgitated hymns from deep in her breast; a ball of nightmarish green light, like an apple, formed inside her palm.

"There's a part of the first floor the Membrane doesn't overlap," Ruth said. "Lets out to the back of the building, where the dumpsters are kept."

Dario nodded, had looked inside the stairwell. It had taken the form of the metal sewage pipe as it had before. It was still sticky stair after stair connected to the cigarette burn-colored landing. But whereas there had been light shining through the opaque, square windows over the landing, there was now only a shadow; a shadow cast without light, by the shape clinging to the opposite side of the glass. It appeared to be an overgrown moth.

A swell of screams lifted through the stairwell. They carried a force with them that moved through their clothes and hair. Ruth leaned over the railing, cast the light of the orb onto the levels below; searched for stragglers.

"Why're you running from the Maggot?" Dario asked. He could bash the back of Ruth's head right now and end her. But he didn't.

"I'm to be its last meal," she said.

E.A.973 went down the steps, trying to steer clear of the moth's shadow.

"A maggot feeds off the dead and decaying. I've been decaying for a very long time, Mr. Onai, but I am not ready to die. I want to be sure that all of this meant exactly what I told myself and the others it did."

E.A.973 made it to the landing and waved for them to follow.

"You're holding out for something, aren't you?"

Dario wasn't expecting to confess, but if the Membrane was truly, in a way, the gates that guarded her heaven, he figured he might as well. "My wife and daughter. Divorced for four years. Haven't heard from them or seen them since I lost custody in court. They asked me to dinner. Tonight.

"I thought I wasn't going to make it; now I have to."

"Put that on our headstones, Mr. Onai," Ruth said. "It is the mantra of our species."

Dario and Ruth made it to the landing as E.A.973 crept towards the second floor. Thick tangles of greasy hair unraveled from the ceiling and spread their cloying scent into the stairwell. The sounds of scratching came from behind the window to which the moth had attached itself. It sounded like knives were being dragged across the glass. It sounded like it was trying to get in.

E.A.973 started to go around the bend, to make his final jaunt to the first floor, when Dario heard something else. It wasn't the moth, or the knives its fingers seemed to be made of. He craned his neck to look back the way they'd come. It was the wall. It was heaving. The cement was coming apart, melting, as if it were being broken down at a molecular level.

Dario reached for the hammer in his pocket, and then a gout of blood spewed out of the widening crack. Like a spear boring through a body, the Maggot thrust itself into this world and, writhing, dropped into the stairwell. Almost too large for the stairwell, its glistening girth destroyed the railing, crumpled several stairs. But it was here for a reason. And it didn't need eyes or ears to see or hear that what it had come for stood but a few feet from it.

Screaming, they ran for the second-floor door as the Maggot plunged itself on their flight of stairs. E.A.973 threw open the door, and Dario and Ruth hoofed it through.

The second floor was littered with bodies, some still breathing, most barely together. Doors and walls were blown-out; large, dark explosions of blood radiated outwards from the destruction, as if the tenants had been hurled like bombs back and forth along the hall. Those that were alive immediately spotted Dario, Ruth, and E.A.973, and then played dead. Their savior had betrayed them. Her speaker had told them nothing but—

The Maggot slammed through the stairwell's door behind them.

Tripping over the strewn bodies, they hurried down the hall. The Maggot inched towards them, feet at a time. Sick, slurping sounds: Dario looked over his shoulder. Corpses, and those soon to be, were attached, no, hanging out of the Maggot's body. With every tenant it trampled, the creature absorbed them into its body. The men and women and crying children were decayed upon contact; the Maggot's greedy, gulping pores sucked up the stinking melt, sparing not a single drop.

There was a bend in the hallway, but the Maggot was gaining ground. Dario was out of breath; his stomach was flanked by cramps on all sides, and his legs kept giving out, one after the other. Noticing Ruth's stumbles, he grabbed her by the sleeve of her blouse and urged her onward.

E.A.973 made it to the bend first. He stopped, cocked his head as he stared at them.

"What?" Dario shouted, but he didn't need to shout, because the sound of the Maggot giving chase had gone completely.

Ruth had noticed, too. Simultaneously, they glanced back and saw that the beast wasn't there. Where it should've been, there was a flickering patch of the Membrane—a small garden of white and blue flowers.

E.A.973 started to say something. And then the Maggot lunged from around the bend in the hall, slamming E.A.973 into the adjacent wall. It could have driven the butcher knife into the creature, but instead, staring at Ruth, it nodded, dropped the weapon, and let the Maggot break it down, until it was nothing more than a bloodstain in the larva's gore-encrusted folds.

Dario and Ruth wheeled and ran back the way they'd come. Two men and a woman were darting between the apartments, carrying and handing-off TVs, laptops, tablets, and purses and wallets between one another. They weren't taking them out of the Manor; they were taking them back to where they lived for later.

Making it back to the stairwell wreckage, Ruth threw the orb of light into it, to burn away the dark that had gathered there.

"What's wrong?" Dario asked.

The Maggot was seconds away; arms and legs were protruding from it, catching on the ceiling.

Dario slipped past Ruth. The stairwell had transformed again, back into the sewage pipe it had resembled when the Membrane first took over the complex. The orb she had thrown was still falling downwards, its light growing fainter and fainter. The first floor they needed to reach was worlds away.

Dario grabbed Ruth's hand—even now, it was cold to the touch— and ran with her to the stairs carved into the wall. As they descended into the dark, the Maggot bashed into the stairwell wreckage above, showering them in debris.

"Fuck." Dario pawed at his eyes, where bits of stone had cut them.

"It will have been worth it," Ruth said. She stared up at the Maggot as it loomed over them from the second floor. "You will have been worth it."

Groaning, Dario slipped his finger through Ruth's belt loop and tugged her towards him, with him, down the stairs. The Maggot, unable to fit on the steps in the walls, melted like the bodies it had consumed into the floor.

"It's gone," Dario said. He drew a sharp breath and held himself. "How... do we... get out of here?"

Ruth, still staring up at the second floor, didn't answer him.

"What's wrong?"

The Membrane exerted itself upon the wreckage above. The wood and stone and scattered concrete were converted into scabs.

"Ruth," Dario persisted.

"Edmund..." She lowered her voice. "I'll have to make another."

Dario ran his fingers through his hair. He steadied his breathing. The ache was returning to his elbow. The skin around his left eye was getting tighter, hotter. New wetness drooled down his damaged shoulder. In a place without time, his body was the only way by which he could count the minutes.

"Ruth," he rasped. "We have to keep going."

"What's my diagnosis?" Ruth asked, finally addressing him.

He stumbled down the steps, leaving her behind. "What does it matter?"

"It gives me something to work on, when I've finished."

It's too late, he wanted to tell her, but he was a social worker, and it had been beaten into his head that anyone was capable of a change, however small it might be.

"You're psychotic," Dario said.

Ruth's eyes shined with enlightenment. Breathlessly, like a child repeating her parent, she said, "Psychotic."

A white fissure shot across the stairwell's wall. Light, hot and painfully bright, seeped in through the growing cracks and crevices. Rumbling; the deafening sound of heavy slabs crashing against one another. Heaving vibrations rolled like waves through the stairwell, causing the stairs to buck and buckle. Like sand falling through fingers, the stairs at their feet crumbled, and they were left with no place else to go.

Dario grabbed onto Ruth and held her tightly. With their bodies pressed into one another's, he could feel the vermillion veins beneath her skin, nervously winding through her musculature. For what was probably the first time in a very long time, Ruth Ashcroft was afraid of something.

The walls split apart further. Crooked stretches of cement wavered and then fell outwards, into the light, outside the Manor. A watery sound, sloppy and sickening, like a throat gargling vomit, assaulted the stairwell from the bright place beyond. It was the Maggot, Dario thought as he clenched his jaw and waited for it to arrive. It couldn't catch them, so it was going to bring the whole place down—that was the depth of its need to feed on Ruth Ashcroft. An insatiable hunger, one perhaps only the decayed carcass of God could satisfy—maybe there was some truth to what she had said about the Vermillion—

Dario and Ruth fell. The ground gave out from underneath them, and the light outside swallowed them whole. In the few seconds he thought he had left, Dario tried to confess for everything he had done, but before the first sin passed his lips, his ankle hit something hard, twisted, and broke with a loud snap.

"Jesus Christ!" Dario screamed, grabbing at the pulsating site. He rolled onto his side, sucked in the air, which tasted of fish and chemicals. Eyes still adjusting to the light, he could've sworn he was lying on a staircase.

Ruth jabbed her fingers into his side, said, "It's okay, Mr. Onai. We're going to be okay," and then pointed to the glowing orifice that had once been the stairwell's wall.

The Membrane was gone, and so, too, was half of Brooksville Manor. In trying to impose itself upon the place, the Maggot had bisected the building and most of the cliff it sat on. The thousands of pounds of ruin had fallen into the river below, causing the waters to almost stop completely against the blood-dusted dam. Brooksville Manor was exposed now, its insides and the horrible things that'd grown within them out for all the city to see.

And yet the city didn't seem to notice. Standing there, at Brooksville Manor's new, crumbling precipice, Dario didn't see any police cars tearing through the streets, nor did he hear the chilling wail of a cavalcade of ambulances and fire trucks muscling their way through gawking traffic. In fact, there wasn't any traffic at all. Across the river, the cars flowed at a steady pace, and the pedestrians on the sidewalks and crosswalks kept going where they were going, as if nothing had happened at all.

It wouldn't last for long, though, Dario knew, turning around and heading down with Ruth to the first floor. The outcries and the outpourings would come soon enough, when the news story broke and social media said it was okay to care. And that was fine. It was a better kind of attention than what most of the surviving tenants of Brooksville Manor were used to.

Dario and Ruth made it to the first floor without exchanging much other than sighs and side-eyes. Silence was an extremely effective tool in the therapeutic process; it allowed for self-reflection, and for those who were uncomfortable with silence, it sometimes coaxed from them spontaneous, unguarded truths. There was nothing more Dario wanted to hear from Ruth. Today had been her admission, and her discharge. No, this silence between them as they prowled the brutalized halls was one for self-reflection, because they had both ended up here for a reason, selfish as it was. Now the question remained: had it been worth it?

They passed the door to the basement, which after everything, appeared completely unscathed. The picture of the black Jesus with the face-shaped blood drops and maggots in his hands was crumpled against the door, as if it were trying to get in, as if it didn't want to be left behind.

Ruth supporting him, keeping him off his broken ankle, Dario strained his ears as they made for the front doors, to see who was left and who was left alive. And there were people still alive, still behind their locked doors, rummaging through the wreckage that'd become of their lives. But no one was leaving the Manor. Dario had half a mind to knock on the doors, to escort them out of the shock of being freed from Ruth's shackles, but he knew they wouldn't listen to him. That was a job for the police, for the medical professionals; for the politicians who would soon uproot them and transplant them to another Brooksville Manor, in another city just the same.

Ruth pushed opened the front doors. The scorching heat was just where he'd left it, except this time, Dario welcomed it. He was freezing; he'd lost too much blood, and he'd spent too much time in the Membrane. He'd been so close to Death that he felt Death in every inch of him. The ordeal was over, and he was dangerously close to being over himself. His injuries—his left eye, his broken elbow and ankle, and hammer-mauled shoulder—re-activated at once and reminded him of how much they could hurt. The pain hit him like an overdose, and he went stumbling outside, underneath the skybridge, and into the parking lot, where he grabbed the nearest car and dry-heaved over the windshield.

"It began here," Ruth said.

Collapsed over the car, seeing the setting sun in its glass, Dario became aware of what time it was and what needed to be done. He pawed at his pocket, felt the bulge of his car keys through the fabric. Steadying his breathing, he pushed himself off the hood and headed for his car parked in the boonies.

"You were part of it, Mr. Onai."

Dario's foot dragged behind him as he practically hopped across the parking lot.

"You were complacent, Mr. Onai."

He stopped, fished the car keys out of his pocket. Complacent.

Never was there a crueler weapon in an enemy's lexicon. It was everything he was, and everything he hated. It was Darnell, Mark, and Brad, and the blood in their palms from the faces of the children they beat in his stead. It was MichaelIndomitable crying out for his mother as he was hacked to pieces to be fed to the Maggot that'd been grown and guided by Ruth's hand. It was every fight Dario had run from him; every argument he refused to have. It was every lie he told his wife, every smile he faked for his daughter. It was every needle he'd stuck into his veins, every pill that passed through his throat. It was every reason he was here, when he should've been anywhere else. It had never been about the clients, and it had never been about him. It had been about stasis, and the maintenance of mounting madness. Until he did something, right here, right now, it would have all been for nothing.

Silence was one thing, but self-reflection? It was a mean son of a bitch.

"What time next week?"

Dario did some breathing exercises, squeezed his keys as if they were a stress ball. Car a few feet away, and not wanting to turn around to face Ruth, he said, "What?"

"What time is our appointment next week?"

In his other pocket, he had the hammer. He took it out, but still didn't turn around. A foul smell broke over him, probably from the dam breaking in the river below.

"I know that I am a sick woman, and I need help."

"Are you going to stop the killing?" he asked, hearing her approach.

"No, I don't think I will. But I won't kill as many as I have before. And that's progress, isn't it? Every little bit counts, doesn't it?"

Dario squeezed the hammer's handle. Ruth Ashcroft was never going to know the punishment she deserved for what she had done over the years. If he killed her, would anyone care? He turned around and—

Ruth and the Maggot stood inches away from one another, her small frame dwarfed by its viscous mass. Out in the open, out of the Membrane, the Maggot's existence solidified itself in Dario's mind. There was no denying it now. Ruth's god-killer was real.

"I... I..." Ruth stuttered. "Dario... h-help."

Dario glanced at the hammer, and then pressed it into her hand. "A social worker merely gives their clients the tools to forge their own path," he told her.

"Coward," Ruth whispered.

And with that, the Maggot struck. It drove its head into Ruth. She dropped the hammer, didn't make an effort to use it. The Maggot reared its head, and her body went with it. She was stuck to it, like a fly to fly paper. Her flesh liquefied; her muscles turned to mush; her bones broke through her softening frame. Her limbs twisted under and over themselves—her legs over her shoulder, her arms between her legs. Handfuls of organs dribbled like jewels down the Maggot's bulk. Intestines unspooled. When there was nothing left except a bubbling sum of what she'd been, the vermillion veins she'd harbored for over one hundred years exploded outwards, like scrabbling claws trying to find purchase on the clouds of heaven above. But they were no match for the Maggot's touch of decay; like everything else, they dissolved, and eventually, disappeared into the creature's body.

But unlike its previous victims, the Maggot bore the mark of its final consumption. On its front end, above and between the eye-like chevrons there, Ruth Ashcroft was immortalized in an upside-down crucifix rendered in vermillion red.

The Maggot considered Dario, and then, leaving behind hissing secretions, made its way back to Brooksville Manor. When it reached the apartment complex, he thought it might go back inside, to finish off the tenants who'd once and probably still worshiped it. But instead, it went past Brooksville Manor and over the cliff, into the river, where it submerged in the waters and the wreckage and christened itself in the substance of this world.

Dario limped his way to his car, unlocked the door, lowered himself into his seat, locked the door as fast as he could, and broke down. Head to the steering wheel, one hand on the dash, he cried until his dehydration had dehydration, and all the windows were fogged from the airs of his suffering. Snot and spit dribbled out of his nose and mouth like wax from a ruptured candle. He tried to think of one thing, but instead thought of everything, creating a horrifying collage in his mind that made him feel as if he were imploding. He teethed the rubber of the steering wheel, made childish mewing sounds.

Minding his broken ankle, Dario moved his legs to the gas and brake pedals. He pushed the key into the ignition and started the car up. He gave the Maggot a moment to return, and then Dario left Brooksville Manor.

On his way home, Dario passed Ødegaard's Health Clinic, Isabella Ødegaard's, and her husband, Fredrick's, rapidly growing and soon-to-be Brooksville's premiere hospital. He thanked Isabella under his breath for the referral of Oblita Vesper, and then choked down the taste of bile in his throat.

Close to his own apartment complex, Dario began to notice police cars and a single ambulance headed back the way he'd come. They were taking their time.

Dario pulled up to his apartment, parked the car on the street, and fell onto the pavement trying to get out of it. Struggling to walk, he crawled out of the street, onto the sidewalk, and up the steps to his apartment which was, thankfully, on the first floor. A few kids that looked like Michael laughed at him. They would all look like Michael from now on.

Inside the apartment, he left the front door open, dragged himself to the TV, turned it on and to the news, and then, with the help of the arm of the couch, managed to get to his feet. He checked the time on the TV—6:10 PM—cranked the volume, and shuffled into his bedroom.

"Tragedy has struck Brooksville today," the newscaster rumbled from the television.

Dario dropped his head against his closet doors. Clenching his teeth, he slipped off his shoes, unbuttoned his pants, pulled down his underwear, and shook the both of them down until they were around his ankles. He tried to take off his bloodied, dirtied shirt, but his broken elbow screamed at him, and he stopped.

"Brooksville Manor, an apartment complex that housed over one hundred low-income families, partially collapsed for reasons unknown."

Dario's legs were the color of blood and bruises. He could still smell Brooksville Manor in his skin—the stench of the river; fried food, cigarette smoke, and marijuana; and the underlying aroma of incense. It made him feel as if he had never left.

"City Planner, Mark Donaldson, issued a statement moments ago stating that, despite Brooksville Manor's location on the cliff overlooking the river, the land was deemed safe, and the building itself up to code."

Dario opened the closet, found the baggiest dress pants he could find. He dropped them to the ground, stepped into them, and pulled them up, like a clown putting on its costume. He didn't bother with socks. His foot was too swollen for that.

"We will be coming to you live from Brooksville Manor, shortly."

Dario slid the empty hangers aside. Maybe it was because he had spent too much time in the Membrane, but the act reminded him of butchers and how they sent meat on hooks down the line. Finally, at the back, he found a dinner jacket. He hadn't worn it in years, on account of the fact that it still smelled faintly of his wife's favorite perfume.

"Until then, let's touch base with the head coach of the Brooksville Bombers to discuss the big game coming up this Friday."

With nothing in his stomach but painkillers, Dario drove in a daze to the restaurant. The date was at 6:45 PM, and he didn't find a parking spot in the adjacent lot until 6:55 PM. He didn't bother paying the meter. He already didn't look good. Being late would make him look even worse.

After a string of screwed-up faces and scathing comments about his appearance, Dario made it through the throngs of twenty-somethings and into the restaurant. While he waited in the lobby, listening to the clink of silverware and teeth on porcelain and glass, two young women with rainbow-colored hair were standing in the corner, staring into their cell phones, speaking to one another without making eye contact. The skinnier of the two was the more domineering, and she told her "friend" she better not blog about the Brooksville Manor incident first, as she, having the most followers, should be the one to raise awareness and support.

Dario gave his name to the busser. They asked him if he was okay, but started leading him to his table before he could answer. He expected that his wife and daughter would be holed-up somewhere in the back of the restaurant, where the shadows were thickest, so one else would see them sitting with him and get to thinking things they shouldn't be thinking. He was expecting this, and banking on this, but this wasn't the case at all.

The busser made the first right turn around the second set of booths, and there his wife and daughter were, more beautiful and enchanting than ever.

His wife's name was Michelle, and she was sitting with her hands folded in her lap, the black dress she wore sparkling like the stars he'd seen in the deep of the Abyss. It had been four years since he'd seen her in person, and she hadn't aged a day. She looked better than ever. Her blonde hair was fuller, more vibrant. Her skin looked great, and she had lost the weight she always talked about losing.

His daughter's name was Sarah, and she was sitting opposite her mother with her hands wrapped around a cup of soda, and a look of shock on her face. She was wearing a blouse and jeans, and her dark brown hair had gotten so long that it went almost down to her waist. While Michelle looked the same, Sarah looked like a completely differ-ent person entirely. She had been ten on the final days of the split, and now she was fourteen, almost fifteen. Though she still had some years to ago, to Dario, she was a woman. She had that look about her, in her eyes, at the corners of her mouth. She had learned to make do without a father, and now that he was here before her, she didn't seem to need him anymore.

Michelle pressed her fingers to her lips and in that kind voice he'd thought she'd lost for him, on that day when she found the needle in his arm, she said, "Dario?"

Driving to the restaurant, Dario knew that his wife and daughter would see how terrible he looked and ask him what had happened. He had recited what he was going to say, how he was going to say it, and he had promised himself that he would not spare any details, be it about Ruth Ashcroft, E.A.973, the Membrane, the Maggot, or the Ver-million God. Despite how insane or impossible these things would seem to his wife and daughter, he had to say them, because they were the truth, and he knew that, if he didn't, he would bury them in the deepest recesses of his mind, deeper even than where he'd put the skel-etons he'd recently unearthed. Michelle had reached out to him be-cause time had passed and people were supposed to change with time. If he wasn't honest, he wasn't anything. He knew that now.

Sarah finally let go of the cup, condensation dripping off her fin-gers, and mumbled, "Dad?" She looked around—he was starting to draw attention—and said even more quietly, "Are you okay?"

He almost laughed. Instead, he stepped closer to the table and de-bated on who he should sit next to. Already he was trying to avoid the—

"Dario," Michelle said, "what happened to you?"

Sarah. He would sit next to Sarah. Like an old man getting into their wheelchair, Dario lowered himself into the booth. His broken ankle snagged on the side of the seat, and he let out a small, pathetic yelp.

"Jesus Christ." Michelle was losing her patience. There was that harsh tone he remembered and deserved. "Dario?"

"I—" He smiled at his daughter and wanted nothing more than to hug her. "I was working today. I… I was at Brooksville Manor when it… collapsed."

"Holy shit," Sarah said.

"Sarah, watch your mouth," Michelle said reflexively.

That made Dario smile.

Eyes wide like oceans, Sarah said to him, "Do you know what happened there?"

Dario opened his mouth, and on his tongue, he had maggots, faces shaped like blood-drops, and a vermillion woman reduced to the symbol of the faith she wanted to destroy, now crowned atop her wriggling weapon's killing head. He had children screaming in his ears for their mother, and a butcher knife that had severed centuries of families. In his heart he had fear, and in his gut, an anxious mire formed from the run-off of the Membrane. And in his mind… and in his mind, there was a grave. At this grave, he stood no longer alone. His wife and daughter were there, shovels in their hands, waiting for him to make the final call.

"No," Dario said, nearly choking on the lie. "I don't. I got out. I didn't see anything."

Michelle put her hands together as if she meant to pray, and pressed her face into her palms.

Sarah chewed on her lip, and the woman she'd become was lost to the little girl he remembered.

Dario faked a smile, thought up a fake story, and took his memory of the Maggot and buried it deep inside himself; in that dark place beyond consciousness, where women like Ruth Ashcroft reigned supreme, where hells like Brooksville Manor thrived; where all the painful, hurtful, terrible, disgusting, disappointing mistakes humanity and himself tended to make—where the skeletons swam in their soil, the ghosts haunted their skulls, and the bats in the belfry sang madness at the midnight hour; to that shed, where the creeping things keep each other company, that forgotten place, that forlorn place—that necessary place, where the dead go to die.

AUGURS

Lux, Fenton, Ramona, Asher, and Echo sat in quiet contemplation as they nursed their coffees on the Grindout's patio and considered Salinger Stevens, a twenty-one-year-old, white, poor but still over-privileged, cisgender male whom they hadn't cared for in high school, and who they now couldn't stop talking about, as he had been found dead in his apartment last night, his head degloved, with small worm-shaped lacerations on his chest that formed the word 'faggot.' While his death was, ultimately, the centerpiece of the conversation, they kept finding themselves coming back to his sexual orientation, because each of them, with the exception of Ramona, had been completely convinced he was straight. After all, the group considered themselves excellent, if not almost prophetic, judges of character, which either meant the murderer incorrectly spelled the word ('Maggot' was Fenton's suggestion), or that Salinger was actually straight, and that this crime was no more than a message directed at their leader, Lux, and her sidekick, Echo. Begrudgingly, Lux did admit that the murder may have been a sick threat to the whole of the LGBTQIA community in their town, or if nothing else, just their group, being that they were so popular. Nevertheless, they were, each of them, gender-fluid; and living in a place named Bitter Springs, it was, to them, only a matter of time until the waters soured. Or so Lux preached; the others agreed it wasn't the most successful of similes, but Echo liked it well enough. That was generally the way of things.

"Good lord, who do you think found Salinger?" Fenton asked, cringing. "I hope it wasn't his mom. She's a sweet one."

Asher scoffed. "Ms. Salinger's a sweet one? Honey, I saw her wrestle a holiday ham out of Sister Mary Pascal's arms. She was putting on the brass knuckles by the time security rolled up."

"Oh, come on." Fenton rolled his eyes. "Everyone gets a little impatient during the holidays."

"Holidays? That was last week, Fen." Asher laughed into his coffee as he sucked up the drink and the steam coming off it. "That woman gives me the willies."

"Strong women freak you out, huh?" Ramona chimed in, eyebrows raised so high they joined her hairline. "Color me surprised."

"Thought someone already did," Asher said, referencing her makeup. "Or was it you just got into the box of crayons for a snack?"

Fenton, incurably gullible, became concerned. "Ramona, you're not starving yourself again?"

Ramona's face turned radical red, with that waxy, crayon coating to boot, and said, "You're an idiot. Fuck you both."

At the head of the table, Lux cleared her throat so hard it sounded as if she'd been gargling gravel the entire time. Echo, her right-hand woman to her right, pleaded to the others with her wide and permanently watery eyes for them to be quiet. She hadn't always looked that way, but Lux meant 'light,' and she was the one thing Echo couldn't look away from. Ramona had warned her once, when they were both good and liquored-up, that Lux was like the sun—that if you followed her too long, you'd end up blind and somewhere you never intended to be. Good as the advice might've sounded, neither of them had listened to it. They'd been following Lux's path for as long they could remember; there was no safety to be found in the shadows she cast.

"Let's get serious," Lux said.

Echo nodded, echoing her sentiment.

The Grindout's patio was empty today. It was Sunday, and the good people of Bitter Springs were getting their routine doses of godliness at the various churches and chapels scattered across the town and the forest of Maidenwood. Atheism was in right now, so most of the youth had skipped the pews for a seat at their favorite coffee shop, bookstore, or hole in the wall dive that didn't serve anything with a soul. Though the congregated youth would never admit it, these Sunday mornings were their own form of Mass; the multi-syllabic foods and drinks, their host and wine, and the hot-off-the-Internet controversy, their gospel. And just like church, they'd feign kindness, and interest, until the service was over, and they could conjure up with all their shit-talking, a storm of epic proportions that would see them through the week until their next date with drama.

"We're not going to let this blow over like the Brooksville Manor collapse," Lux continued.

Ramona piped up. "Salinger's a white man from the suburbs. It's not going to blow over." Being 1/64th Asian, she felt qualified to make such statements. "Hate crimes are all the rage."

"Don't minimize it," Lux said.

"Yeah, come on, don't," Echo repeated.

"Bitter Springs, Bedlam, and Brooksville are, basically, a microcosm for this whole corrupted country," Lux said. "If we can make a difference here, it stands to reason we can make a difference elsewhere, right? I mean, I have so many followers online."

Echo nodded enthusiastically; Ramona, Asher, and Fenton less so, given that they'd been reminded of the fact almost every day of every week.

"Like the rest of the world, this is something very wrong with our town. A low-income apartment complex collapses and no one bats an eye? And now someone is targeting the sexual norms of Bitter Springs? Come on, now. Everyone else here might be blind—" Lux said this loud enough for everyone on the coffee shop patio and outside it to hear, "—but I know we're not. We see things other people cannot or will not see. We say things people cannot or will not say." She licked her lips and leaned into the table, banging her coffee down on it, like a gavel. "What's wrong with being brutally honest?"

Echo shook her head, and shrugged.

"No one changed the world by asking it nicely to do so."

"We should put that on a banner," Asher said. "In bold, bright, blood-red. We can use Ramona's crayon box for that."

Ramona opened her mouth to yell at him again, but her smile stopped her.

"That might clash with the message we're trying to send, especially in the safe spaces around town," Fenton said.

"Yeah, but how did we get those safe spaces?" Lux asked.

Cringing, Fenton said, "We were a little brutal, weren't we?"

Ramona said, "Got to be with these fat... not shaming, you know what I mean."

Together, the group nodded in agreement.

"Fat fucking bigwigs running the show around here," she went on. "Goddamn. Makes me so mad. Pull up the carpet they've been sweeping everything under and you'll find a full-on graveyard."

"Exactly, exactly!" Lux leaned back in her chair, as the rest of her congregation moved to the edges of theirs. "I don't want to be a victim ever again."

"Neither do I," Asher said quietly.

Fenton shook his head, eyes downcast.

Ramona spit.

Echo kept her attention locked on Lux, and reflected her hard exterior.

Lux took a sip of coffee as if it might be her last and said, "What do know about Salinger Stevens?"

"Salinger Stevens," Fenton started. "A twenty-one-year-old white, allegedly straight male from a middle-class family. His dad left about the time we were in… fifth grade? Sixth grade?"

"Sixth grade," Asher said. "He was the first to get hit badly with acne. Guessing it was the stress of his daddy leaving that aggravated that mess."

"No guessing," Ramona said. "Definitely was."

"His mom, Judy, as we discussed, is a… tough woman," Fenton said.

"Bet you she's a femme." Asher nodded. "The butch act isn't fooling anyone. I've seen her getting fresh with Mom."

"How the hell you know so much about Judy Salinger?" Ramona asked. "Never mind. I do not want to know."

Asher winked at Ramona, and bit into his knuckle.

Fenton continued. "Salinger worked at the Lawn and Garden over on Cadence Street. Full-time. He'd been there for little over a year. No jobs before that. According to his page, he wasn't with anyone, but I'd heard rumors he had been seeing Lauren over in Brooksville after her friend, Beatrice, was found dead in Maidenwood."

"White girl ends up dead in the forest? Damn near national news." Ramona's cheek quivered. "I do get it, Lux. I'm sorry Brooksville Manor never panned out."

Lux waved her off, as if she wasn't bothered. But they all know how much time Lux had spent in trying to raise awareness for the low-income families in the tri-county area. The sum total of her efforts had resulted in five-hundred-dollars from a few, rich, guilty white families and the aforementioned safe spaces—one on the high school campus, and one here at this coffee shop. The idea of having the safe spaces in Bitter Springs rather than Brooksville was to encourage those who were sick of the institutionalized racism embedded in the Brooksville system to come to Bitter Springs, to show their discontent and to be part of Lux's plan of making the town a safe haven for minorities. No one ever showed up the safe spaces, except for a handful of freshmen and sophomores who had recently come out as furries and transsexuals. Bummed by the response, Lux ended up blowing the five-hundred-bucks at a micro-brewery on the riverfront, where she rented the place out and turned it into an echo chamber, to have her beliefs confirmed by her peers and sooth her bruised ego.

When Echo told her later that night the gathering had been a success in strengthening the support network for minorities in the tri-county area—two suicidal teens chose life that night—Lux laughed it off and told her to turn off the lights.

"He was a jock all throughout high school," Fenton said, "but he didn't want to get into college for his sports performance alone. He volunteered at the soup kitchens during the winter."

Asher said, "Aw," and rolled his eyes.

"Smoked a lot of weed his senior year. His group of friends got smaller and smaller. His last girlfriend, before Lauren, if she counts, dumped him the night after prom. Posted on her page afterwards that the only time he could get it up was if he was looking at himself in the mirror."

"And his mom has a wicked rage when it comes to holiday hams," Asher said. "Don't forget that detail."

Echo snorted.

Lux did not react at all.

"He was pretty conservative last time I saw anything from him," Ramona said. "Made some stupid ass comment after the Brooksville thing about how there went more of his tax dollars to pay for the poor's mistakes. Or some shit like that. I don't know."

This time, Lux did react. She had a grin on her face. "He said, 'Everyone's asking for hand-outs, when we should be giving them hand-jobs. That'll shut them up.'"

"Pig," Ramona said, hate-drinking her coffee.

Asher threw up his arms. "Man's got a point—"

Lux shook her head, and the color left Asher's face.

"He was a really nice guy in high school," Fenton said.

"Was being the operative word," Ramona corrected.

"So, what changed?" Fenton chewed on the inside of his lip. "Do you think everything went downhill after his dad left?"

"One less man in the house?" Lux chuckled. "Should've been smooth sailing from then on out."

Echo, who had been so quiet it was if she had faded out of existence, cleared her throat and said, "I went over to his house once, like two years ago, when I was a junior, I think?"

Lux shot her a damning glare.

"I... I was with my mom. She had to drop something off. Ms. Salinger invited us in."

"What'd you see, honey?" Asher said.

"Nothing... Well, I mean, his house seemed normal."

Ramona scoffed. "Don't they all?"

"I had to go the bathroom. I used the one closest to his room. I didn't get a good look inside it, but in the bathroom, I started to snoop."

Lux relaxed and took Echo's hand and started rubbing her fingers.

"There were pills, prescriptions, for depression and anxiety. I... can't remember... the names of them. But, yeah."

"Good girl," Lux whispered, and then to Asher: "You ever see him around Tiffany's?"

Asher thought long and hard and then said, "Few times, yeah, actually. He was with his bros."

"Bunch of fuck-boys, if you ask me," Ramona said. "They all went off to the same college, you know? He didn't get in."

"They hung outside the bar, tried to pick some fights, but they were a bunch of twigs," Asher said. "Salinger never said anything, though. I'd say he looked embarrassed."

"All things considered, I thought he was an alright dude, until that hand job shit," Ramona said. "I think he wanted in on our group. Caught him eavesdropping a few times."

"He did," Lux said.

"Did he talk to you personally about it?" Fenton asked.

"I just knew," Lux said, dodging the question. "He wouldn't have made the cut, though. He never knew who he was."

"He sent you some messages, didn't he?" Echo asked.

Lux's eyes went dark. She took a deep breath, and swallowed it, like a demon might swallow a soul. "Fenton gave us the facts. Ramona?"

Fenton dealt in details, and Asher had his finger on the pulse of Bitter Springs' various scenes. Echo hadn't found her niche, yet. When it came to Ramona, besides her foul mouth and not-so-cheery disposition, she was their psychologist. After all, she was getting a minor in the field.

"Depression and anxiety?" Ramona said. "I bet that started before Salinger's dad left, but when his dad left, it got a lot worse. He was an alright dude, but then he started hanging out with shittier people… probably because we wouldn't let him hang with us."

Fenton looked away, embarrassed.

"He was trying to find acceptance in all the wrong places," she said. "I heard he came to your get-together at the micro-brewery. I bet he was rejected there, being straight and all."

"Had no right to be there," Lux said.

Ramona looked as if she disagreed, but didn't voice it.

Lux sat there a moment in quiet contemplation. She fingered the gaps in the table's metalwork and stared at the clouds that were crawling across the sky. There were so many thoughts racing through her skull, one could almost see the human braille of their being etched into her forehead. She took out her cell phone, considered a message, and then swiped it away. Then, decided, she nodded and began.

"Salinger Stevens was a twenty-one-year-old, white, poor but still over-privileged, cisgender male who had been battling a losing battle with both depression and anxiety. His mom was a push-over when he was a kid. You all might not know that, but I do. Believe me. His dad was a piece of shit. Big surprise. In fifth grade, not sixth, Asher, his dad walked out on him. Judy Stevens butched up, and so did Salinger. He started trying-out for all the teams, started making friends with all the jocks and meatheads. But he was soft on the inside. I always knew he wasn't straight, but I didn't want to label him."

The group simultaneously raised their eyebrows and bit their tongues.

"Salinger Stevens was gay. His ex knew it, and he couldn't have sex with her because of it. He was living a lie. Tried to be tough, but he was a total twink. He wasn't talented enough to get into college for sports, and he wasn't smart enough to get into college with his grades. It's no wonder he started spewing conservative propaganda. Reaction formation. That's the word to use next time, Ramona."

Ramona muttered an enraged, "Thanks."

"Here's what I think happened," Lux said. "He came to my gathering thinking he could come out, but it was too much for him. He was too mainstream. So, he left, but he was followed by a man, obviously, and I bet he brought this man back to his place. Depressed, anxious, he was looking for anyone to make him feel better. But instead he got himself killed by some hateful, white male bigot, age thirty-five to forty, who had probably read his crude hand job message on his page and targeted him for it.

"You know what I think it is? I think someone doesn't like the changes we're making. I think someone thought Salinger was close to us—probably a teacher, or a parent; maybe even his father—and they killed him to get to us. The 'faggot' being seared into his chest is obviously the work of someone who was just as repressed as Salinger. Someone who probably had sadomasochistic or psychotic tendencies. His face had been degloved. I tried to look that up on my phone, what that looks like, but I can't even. Obviously, they want to strip us of our identities. They want to reduce us to 'faggots' and 'queers' and 'niggers.' I think—"

A server, Ansel, approached their table with an uncomfortable smile upon his cleanly-shaven face. In blue jeans and a button-down shirt, he dressed the part of an employee at the shop, but his face, according to Lux, was all wrong. It was a mask, she told the group once, to hide to who he was deep inside, which was a cisgender male who was guilty of cultural appropriation on account of dating a Hispanic woman. According to Lux, he had no business working at the coffee shop; he should've had some bullshit job, like coaching the girls' volleyball team at Bitter Springs High. The only tip she ever gave him was to wake up.

"I'm sorry to disturb you," Ansel said, "but we've received some complaints about some of the things being said at this table. We want this to be a safe space for others, but the aggressive nature of your conversation is making some of our patrons uncomfortable."

Lux's jaw dropped. She stared at him as if he had just spent the last few seconds speaking in a foreign language. Pointing at him, looking at Fenton, Asher, Ramona, and especially Lux, and with a rattle in her voice, she said, "Are you kidding me? Are you fucking kidding me right now? There is someone out there trying to thin out the LGBTQIA community, and we're trying to figure out how to stay safe. This safe space? I know. That's because of us. We're here to be safe. This micro-aggressive shit isn't going to fly. Let me speak to your manager."

Ansel nodded and began to turn away.

"You know what?" Lux stood, nearly knocking her chair over. "Don't bother. We're leaving."

Echo was the first to rise. Fenton second. Ramona, slowly, the third. Asher polished off his coffee, and even then, he didn't stand upright completely. He stayed crouched, hopeful perhaps, that this might blow over.

"You all know what to do," Lux told the rest of them.

And with that, she grabbed Echo's hand, the same way a mother might grab a child's when they dawdled too long in the toy aisle of a store, and stormed off the patio. She was two paragraphs deep into her new blog post before they even made it to their bikes.

Ramona liked working at the library about as much as she liked reading books; that is, she couldn't be bothered with either short of threats of death or dismemberment, or even worse, being fired. She was a closeted dyslexic, and that, in combination with a nasty case of ADHD, made even the sight of words exhausting. Like Salinger Stevens' long-con, working at the library was a front for something Ramona found incredibly embarrassing, because she equated her struggles with literacy to her white trash side of the family, as if she had been doomed to inherit what she so affectionately called their "bum-fuck genes." But as she worked her way through her freshman year of college, another possibility emerged through her coursework: that the dyslexia, ADHD, or both, were psychogenic in nature—that they weren't rooted in anything physical; her wack-ass mind had simply made them up. That presented a whole host of other issues for her to contend with, but she always felt she had a strong control over her mind. It was her body she couldn't best.

The library was in transition today; the head-honchos had ordered more computers, and to fit them in, Ramona and her co-workers had to break-down the shelves and box-up the books that'd been on them. Trading books for computers; the idea made Ramona laugh. Even the goddamn library had gone corporate.

With the coast clear to coast, Ramona ducked into the aisle where they kept the anime DVDs (no one who watched these was going to rat her out) and spent an excessive amount of energy casing the scene for her superiors. If she had even put a fraction of that energy to her actual work, she could have easily had several shelves broken down and boxes filled, without any worries about getting chewed-out for sitting on her ass all day. But that wasn't the point. She knew that. It was a game. If anyone actually did anything, workers and bosses alike, they'd all be out of a job. It was the illusions they maintained that mattered. And at this rate, given her pathetic productivity and her lips firmly pressed to the head-honchos' asses, she'd be running the place in no time.

Tiny sneakers sneaking across the dull gray, blue-speckled carpet set off Ramona's internal alarm. She straightened up and backpedaled out of the aisle, eyes probing for gaps in the DVDs to see who was coming.

"Cool!" a little girl yelled. And then, even though she was alone, in a whisper: "Cool."

Eyebrows cocked and ready to rock a mean consternation, Ramona parted the DVDs, sending a movie about andromorphic owls and their high school lovers one way, and a show about post-modern demonic astrologists the other. With a grin of satisfaction, she rested her chin on the shelf and felt her faith in humanity restored.

There was one aisle clear of the computer-induced construction; or rather, one portion of an aisle—five shelves—that was growing at an inspiring rate. It was Ramona's aisle, or rather, her idea she had planted and, with a little bit of Lux's special brand of brutality, seen to fruition.

The Bitter Springs library hadn't exactly been lacking stories that had been written by, for, or in regards to the experiences of People of Color, nor had there been a dearth of literature written by, for, or in regards to the experiences of the LGBTQIA community. But there wasn't much of it, and it wasn't easy to find. It was hard to say if Lux, or their group, were really responsible for the increased awareness and presence of individuals from minority groups in town, but in Ramona's experience, it was undeniable that the need and interest was there. Although she wasn't a reader herself, she understood the value of books, and words, and the influence they had on others.

So, like an adventurer from a far-off land carrying stowaways from home, she released her foreign beliefs into the local library system and let them build their hives, for inquiring minds to buzz about, when once they'd had nowhere else to go.

And though the aisle had been busy, mostly with people from her age group, it was the little girl she heard and now saw there, crouching down, sloppily pulling out children's book after children's book, that made Ramona feel as if the brutality, the threats, and the not-so-peaceful mid-week protest had been worth it. The little girl was black, with an afro so dense and dark it could've been a moon with its own field of gravity. In her hand, she had a picture book about some black family and some good moral of the story (again, Ramona detested reading), and at her heels, there was another picture book about some white family and, undoubtedly, some good moral of the story. It wasn't that one was better than the other (or was it? Ramona was still trying to figure that part out); it was that the little girl had finally found what she was looking for, and that it was cool.

Ramona watched the girl gather up a gluttonous amount of books to consume and then detached her chin from the shelf. She took a step back, and backed into something. Her heart went haywire. One hearty "fuck you!" on her lips, she twisted her neck. Asher was standing behind her, making a face.

"Fuck you," Ramona said, the words rolling over her teeth like air being vacuumed into space. "The hell? Why're you always sneaking up on people? Poor fucking trigger discipline."

Asher looked around the library, to hear if anyone else had heard her cussing. "I just thought I'd drop in on you. So sorry."

"Why?"

"No reason."

Ramona huffed and rolled her eyes. As she slipped past Asher—

"To apologize."

She stopped, turned around.

"For... earlier. I'm sorry I made fun of your make-up."

Instinctively, Ramona touched her cheek. She had taken all of it off the moment she got to work. People said she looked better without it, but what did that mean? That she couldn't doll herself up worth a damn? It was such a stupid fucking thing to care about, and she couldn't believe she bought into the grotesque bazaar of glam. Sure, she'd entered of her own volition, but now she wasn't so sure. She wasn't sure of many things these days. She felt captive.

"Yeah, well, whatever." She smiled to show that she forgave him. And then, bluntly, she said, "I got work to do," which meant she really hadn't forgiven him at all.

Asher ballooned his cheeks out like a chipmunk's mid-foraging.

"Oh my god, what? What do you want?"

"Can we, like, sit somewhere? This cartoon stuff—" Asher grabbed one of the DVDs—a middle school girl was bent over on the cover, her panties glowing like some ancient artifact before a throng of men—and shuddered, "—gives me the heebie-jeebies."

"You're seriously overusing that phrase."

"Heebie."

Ramona's eye shut, as if she were having a stroke.

"Jeebies."

"Come on!" She grabbed him by the front of his shirt and shoved him forward. "Go sit in one of those oversized chairs, you child."

Ramona led Asher to the chairs, which were properly lubricated with human grease. Grabbing a magazine off the reading table beside it, he laid it down over the cushion, the same way he might toilet paper over a toilet seat. Satisfied with the coverage, he plopped down to a loud, crinkling sound that landed all nearby eyes on him.

"Speaking of children," Asher said, nodding to the library's entrance and the slowly opening, glass doubled-doors. "Looks like the cavalry has arrived over there yonder."

Son of a bitch, it was Sunday, wasn't it? Ramona copped a squat next to Asher, put her best "I'm on my fucking break" look on her face, and watched as one by one, stunted legs after barreled bodies, a troop of kindergartners came shambling into the library. At the head of the procession was their teacher, Ms. Lucy, in loose fitting jeans and with a head of wild hair that screamed "kill me." Holding up the tail end of the sniffling, sneezing, booger-eating brats was a single parent—an over-privileged, overbearing, overweight, and, if you asked her, underappreciated white mother of one who attached herself to these library outings like a tick who never knew when too much was too much.

Her name was Tessa—a name that damned anyone who donned it to a life of mini vans, mini bars, and those mini bibles so often found in the nightstands that accompany one-night-stands. Her child was the one farthest away from her, nearest the teacher, as if he were prey mingling amongst prey, to disappear from a predator. The child's name was Morgan, and Tessa claimed Morgan was non-binary. Like kids with a peanut allergy, pronouns were explicitly forbidden from being administered to Morgan, out of fear the moldable child may take on a form that differed from the one Tessa saw fit. Initially, Ramona supported Tessa's determination, and wished her own parents had been supportive at that age. But when a second child joined the library group a few weeks ago, she wasn't so sure where she stood on the matter.

The second child's name was Zoe, or Zeke, depending upon where Zoe, or Zeke, fell upon the spectrum that week. Today, Zoe was Zoe, and Zoe had on skinny blue jeans, a nicely fitting cardigan, and a choker. Zoe's hair was slicked back like a 1920's gangster (well, as much as a kindergartner could pull off such a look), and on their back, a pink backpack that matched their pink-and-white striped shoes. Zoe looked comfortable, and none of the other kids gave them shit.

It was and continued to be such a stark contrast to Morgan and Tessa-fucking-le Fay (yeah, Ramona had read a book or two in her day) that Ramona found herself feeling better for Morgan. Today, as on most days, Morgan was rocking an aquamarine dress, combat boots, earrings, and rainbow-colored hair that matched the unicorn backpack they wore. It looked good on Morgan, but Ramona imagined it was how Tessa wished she could have dressed, before her stomach started touching her zipper. It was the way Morgan wore it, and the way Zoe wore what they wore, and how Morgan tore at the dress like they had ants crawling over their skin, like a schizophrenic deep in a psychotic break. Ramona had always struggled with her body and the dysphoria it brought her, but Morgan looked downright depressed, and violent, as if they might hurt themselves, or someone else. They looked captive, too.

"Those two the two you were telling me about?" Asher asked.

Tessa closed in on Morgan. Morgan gave her the slip and took off with half of the group towards the computer banks.

"Sure is," Ramona said.

Tessa stood at the doorway, faking a "non-binaries will be non-binaries" face at Ms. Lucy, who shrugged and headed, with the rest of the kids, Zoe included, to the computers.

It was then, with everyone's attention off Tessa, that Ramona saw it. Tessa made a fist and pretended to punch the back of Zoe's head. Her arm didn't go much more than a few centimeters, but the gesture was undeniable. And to add insult to injury, in that way only children know how, Zoe turned around, grinned an ankle-biter grin, and said, wispily, "Bye Misses T!"

Tessa's eyes went small and dark, and she took on all the jittery qualities of an irate amphibian. "Be a good boy," she said, emphasizing the word, as if it were a spear she was wrenching into Zoe's side.

Zoe didn't catch her meaning, or care, because with a skip, Zoe took off.

Asher grabbed the armrest of Ramona's chair and coughed out, "Shit, she hit her!"

"What?" Ramona shook her head. "What're you talking—"

He was talking about the blood, not on the back of Zoe's head, but the patch of bleeding through the pocket of their jeans, where the outline of their small cell phone bulged. Zoe didn't appear to be in any pain. Before Ramona could even think about calling out Zoe's name, they were gone, back into the cozy confines of the other children, to watch videos on the Internet on repeat until it was their eyeballs that bled.

Asher pushed himself out of the chair and came to his feet—the magazine stuck to his ass. "I'm going to say something to Ms. Lucy."

"Stop." Ramona rose and stood in front of him. "Come on. Don't overthink it. It was a stain, dude. See?"

Ms. Lucy had noticed the splotch, too, and holding her nose, she started going at it with a healthy dab of spit and the end of her own shirt.

"Honey, you better get a camel if you're going to try to spit-shine that out," Asher said, as if he were speaking to Ms. Lucy directly. Then, to Ramona: "Okay, I didn't just come to apologize."

"That's what she said," Ramona snapped back.

Dead-eyed, Asher continued. "Lux... was weird today."

"I mean, she's right to get fired up—" Ramona noticed her boss emerging from the back office, his attention fixed on her. "You know? This could be the start of a bunch of hate murders or something. We have to get on this."

"Yeah, I know." Asher noticed Ramona's boss and started to drift away from her. "But the way she handled the server. I know she doesn't like the guy, but damn. Dude likes to get pegged by his girlfriend while watching cartoons. He's got enough on his plate."

Ramona drew a sharp breath, and then, quickly backing away, "Ash, shut up! What's wrong with you?" She saluted her boss, to show she was going back to work. "For real, though, are you serious?"

"Not about the cartoon thing. I don't know." Asher chewed on his lip. "He seems decent. Kind of reminds me of Salinger, and we shit...

pooped… all over him. We're supposed to be more accepting." He scratched the back of his head and turned away from her, to leave. "I don't know."

Ramona heard someone clear their throat behind her. Thinking it was Asher trying to scare her again, despite the fact that he was right in front of her, she stayed her heart and glanced over her shoulder.

There was someone behind her, but the smell of them preceded the shape of them. It was a rank odor; a cloying musk, like that which would lift off the charred remains of a fetid offering. It smelled of ripe fruit, and sulfur—an alluring feast from the sickening larders of hell itself. It made Ramona retch.

"Am I already vegan?" Asher carried on, not seeing what she was smelling, because his back was to her. "I can't remember… Good golly, miss Molly, what the hell is that—" he spun around, "—smell."

Ramona and Asher both saw him at the same time. Ansel, the server from the coffee shop. The one Lux had insulted, and had insulted before, time and time again. In his hand, he was gripping his cell phone, and there was blood coming out of his hand, and the cell phone. The smell was strongest at the device—the technological origin of that very organic stench.

"I…" Ramona started.

But the server shoved past her, his slick arms sliding over her skin like sea-polished stone. And as he hurried towards the exit of the library, Ramona caught a glimpse of something on his cell phone's screen. An image. A symbol. A diamond of light wreathed in tentacles. The very same Lux used as a header for all her blog posts.

The server's name was Ansel, and sure, yeah, when he was in the right mood and with the right person, he'd let a woman fuck him in the ass. Sometimes, he and whoever was strapping in for the night would even laugh about it and say he was taking one for the team. It wasn't something he did often, nor was it something he was all that embarrassed about. That was the great thing about Bitter Springs. Over the last few years, it had become so open in regards to sexuality and "gender roles" and the usual bullshit people debated about on the behalf of those who could just as easily, if only asked, speak for themselves on the matter. No, Ansel could handle someone knowing his sex life as well as he could the toys he used to enhance it. What he couldn't handle, what had him sweating profusely and hallucinating shapes and whispers, was that someone had attacked him and his life-style on the Internet, and stated with the utmost certainty that it was result of latent pedophilic tendencies.

That someone was Lux. And although the post didn't talk about him directly, it was obvious, and it would be obvious to anyone else, as Bitter Springs was a small town. She had written the damnation on her blog two hours ago. It had hundreds of comments, and thousands of 'likes,' and both metrics were increasing steadily by the minute. The overall sentiment of her readers was not good. Lux had never laid a hand on him, and yet she had fucked him in the worst way possible.

Ansel's phone had blood all over it, but he wasn't thinking about that right now. Instead, for the umpteenth time, he read Lux's profile of him, or rather, people 'like him,' and felt his stomach turn, do a belly flop inside his belly—its best dead, beached whale impersonation.

The blog began as all self-important blogs began. With a call to arms attached to a body of hyperbole. It read thusly:

When the gates are unlocked, anything can come through. Something has found its way into Bitter Springs, and I need your help rooting it out, or everything we will have fought for, everything we will have modeled and promised to this country, will have been for nothing.

As you may well know, there has been a death in Bitter Springs, but what is even more insidious than death itself are those things that cause it, for if they have happened once, then it stands to reason that they may happen again. Salinger Stevens was found brutally murdered with the word 'faggot' slashed into his chest. As an involved member of the LGBQTIA community, and someone who knew Salinger Stevens both in passing and personally, I can say with absolute certainty that he was not a gay male, but a heterosexual cis-gender male posing as a gay male. He was killed not for what he was, but for what he pretended to be. I will be called a bitch for saying it, but it is the truth, and I don't care: We are fortunate that Salinger Stevens died, because he died in place of one of our own. That does not make him a martyr, but it does buy us some time, as not only do we need to find out who the culprit behind the hate crime is, but how many more imposters there are in Bitter Springs, as they threaten our very way of life.

Make no mistake, I am not saying that people are not free to do as they choose, but cultural and sexual appropriation as a means by which one disguises their personal issues and inadequacies is deplorable. This is the majority passing themselves off as the minority in attempt to reap the benefits of systematic discrimination. By posing as, for example, asexual, bisexual, demisexual, gay, lesbian, metrosexual, pansexual, skoliosexual, transgender, transsexual, or even as another race or ethnicity, they are effectively minimizing who we are, diluting our community, and stripping us of the few supports and resources available to us. Some may claim that they are merely questioning their identities, but do not be misled. They mean to infiltrate us and see us eradicated. And it is not an eradication through typical means, but a slow decay of our values until we are normalized into nothingness.

Now that I am aware of them, I have begun to see many imposters in our midst. It is not my intention to start a warlock hunt (I can't even get into the misconceptions of witches right now), but it is my duty to warn others of the liars that walk amongst us.

With so many places to begin, let us start with the safe spaces in Bitter Springs, as they mean very much to me, as well as everyone else who uses them as a way to escape from the negativity and the triggers this world seems so desperate to ram down our throats.

I am so angry right now that I literally cannot see straight, so I will begin with Bitter Springs' coffee shop, the Grindout.

There are several imposters at the Grindout, mostly among the staff there, who I now believe have been planted deliberately in those positions to keep tabs on our community. Among them is a cisgender, white male who reportedly has women perform anal sex upon him. Initially, I, too, attributed this behavior to nothing more than a kink, but in interacting with this individual, it became obvious that he was a straight male trying to give the impression that he was gay, or at least, so I thought.

Self-diagnosis is a valuable tool in these days where psychologists, psychiatrists, and social workers are paid to apply labels to groups the general public find undesirable. I consider myself extremely proficient at self-diagnosis, as well as the diagnosis of others. And what I discovered was that this imposter at the Grindout was not only pretending to be gay, but that he was using it as a cover—a cover for latent pedophilic tendencies. Many brave women who have been forced against their will to perform anal sex on the imposter have stated he made them pretend to be children—little boys, actually, age nine to ten. Displacement at its finest.

Can you not see the importance of this issue? Can you not see the weight that it carries? True criminals and delinquents are invading our community and wearing it as a costume, to keep tabs on us and to carry out their twisted fantasies. These repulsive individuals may even find themselves modeling their behavior as acceptable for those of you in the community who do not possess a keen eye such as myself, and you will be led astray because of it.

The imposter begins this way at birth. They are raised this way, and I have seen many children—a supposedly "non-binary" kindergartener, in particular—parading about Bitter Springs, creating confusion and chaos for those other children who are trying to better understand themselves. It makes me sick to see the lengths that the mainstream will go to so as to see us undone.

There is a murderer in Bitter Springs, and though they may be doing us a favor, they will have to be stopped, before those that truly matter fall beneath their blade. Stay vigilant against this malevolent virulence that sickens the straight man's soul. False faces must be unmasked.

Ansel's hand was shaking again, and there was blood seeping between his fingers from the cell phone. The tendons in his neck tented. His eyes went out of focus. His teeth clamped down on the side of his tongue, and his canines carved a place for themselves in it. He tried to steady his breathing, but his breaths were so short, it was as if he wasn't breathing at all; his body was simply going through the motions. Now, it was a vessel, a place to hold an eventual vigil, as anger and fear ripped him apart, inside and out, and made him stupid, and slobbering.

Holding the phone like a beaker bubbling over with a bad chemical reaction, Ansel left his kitchen and went and stood in the middle of the living room. He swiped the screen, to bring himself to the comments section of the post. It made his finger hurt, going down the page like that, as if he could feel the literal pitchforks poking out of the glass.

The comments were curated by Lux, and so almost all of them agreed with and contributed to her narrative. They read thusly:

I think I know who you are talking about at the Grindout, and I am going to report him to the manager. I threw up in my mouth reading this blog. Thank you, Lux, for, as always, being our light of reason.

It's no surprise to me but that the mainstream wants to impersonate us. Whites have been doing it since the dawn of the time. What they cannot understand, they take over.

I know who you are talking about. I'm going to key his car. Let the police try to stop me. Do the Bitter Springs police support pedophiles now?

I want this server out of our town, and away from our children. Gay men have fought so hard to remove the stigma of them being unfit to be around children. This monster is going to bring it back.

Pedophiles and imposters should be killed. The murderer is doing us a favor. For once, it's a hate crime I don't hate.

Your hair looked so good Lux at the get-together.

I say that we organize a meeting to begin tracking down these imposters. Their values are ruining our tradition.

You're so brave, Lux, for posting this. You speak the truth when no one else will. I can't believe you're the only one writing about these things. When I don't know what to think, I find it's best to listen to you, lol.

There were more comments than those, calling for Ansel's arrest, or death, as well as the arrest or death of the supposed imposters living in Bitter Springs. The only comment Lux had bothered to respond to was in regards to whether a woman should shave her body, not because a man asked her to, but because she wanted to. Lux told the poster she had a responsibility as a woman to ignore what she wanted for the good of womankind. To the other posters, she had nothing to say. They were all in agreement with her.

Ansel took the blood-soaked phone and slipped it into his pocket. Standing there, in the middle of the living room, he could feel the gaze of the people outside his windows, passing by on the sidewalk or in their cars. He felt like a wild animal that had been captured and caged and put on display for a depraved audience to see. Everyone was looking at him, judging him; to Ansel, everyone had read Lux's post, and everyone had believed it.

There were the voices in his head, thudding back and forth, like thick, electrified chords flailing in the dark belly of the sea. The voices came from those who'd commented on the blog, except they weren't him simply recalling what he'd read—they were actual voices, with their own gender, tone, inflection, and accent, and each of them was yelling at him, harassing him, calling for his blood. It was as if Ansel were an antenna that had picked up, for the first time in his life, a signal, a small blip, of the Internet's unrelenting, uncompromising ire.

Then, alongside the voices, were his own thoughts. Quick leaps of logic and uncoordinated jumps to baseless conclusions. He was going to school to be a teacher, a grade school teacher, and now that was off the table and buried in the backyard. He was going to be a father one day, or at least he'd hoped he would be, until Lux had socially castrated him. Friends would disown him. Family would disavow him. Ex-girlfriends would take the stand, and prosecutors would press them for facts on every sexual encounter, or any time he'd played with one of their children.

Ansel went to the windows and let loose the curtains. He sprinted out of the living room and made his way around his modest, one-story house, boarding up the place the best that he could in the way a modern man would—with shades and curtains, and the ugliest chairs wedged underneath doorknobs.

Deep down, in the floor of his gut, where the butterflies had yet to settle, he knew he was overreacting, and yet he couldn't stop himself. He remembered the first time he had been stung by a bee as a child, and how he had completely lost it; how no one could calm him down, and how nothing else had existed in that moment except for that moment and the mounting pain.

"Stupid fucking bitch," Ansel said, the blood in his pocket built up to such a point that it sloshed around like an IV bag. He retreated into his bedroom, but kept the lights off.

Sitting on the edge of his bed, he then felt it, a literal sting. He drove his hand into his blood-filled pocket to stop the pain. But nothing had bitten him. There was nothing there. Except for his phone. It was vibrating. Someone was calling him.

Ansel took out his phone. The screen struggled to glow through the gelatinous gore that had congealed on it. His friend, Annette. It was his friend calling him. Or at least, she had been his friend. The voices in his head said that he was a pederast, and that the only friend a pederast deserved was the bullet someone was bound to put in his head.

Feeling that sting in his leg again, Ansel answered Annette's call, but didn't say a word.

"Ansel?"

He grunted.

"What's wrong?" Then, more seriously than before: "Ansel, what's going on?"

"Did you read it?" he asked, whispering in the darkness of his own room, as if he were afraid to wake the beast that might be lying in his bed. "Did you... see it?"

"Your text?"

"Lux's blog."

"Yeah, I mean... is that what you're freaking out about?"

Ansel sat up straight. Outside his room, somewhere near his kitchen, he heard something wet slap against the linoleum.

"Hey, why are you freaking out about that?"

"I..." He strained his ears, but the sound was gone; all that remained were the voices, and their derision. "Did you see what she said about me?"

"She didn't say your—"

He yelled, "You know who she was talking about!"

Annette went quiet; he could imagine her retreating away from him, the distance the same from Earth to Space, with all that suffocating silence they shared between them.

"Sorry," he said.

"I'm not the bad guy here."

"I know."

"No one buys into Lux's bullshit, except the people she pays to peddle it."

Ansel shook his head. "There're hundreds of comments. Thousands of people have seen it. People want to kill me."

"It's the Internet." Annette drew a sharp breath and held it until she couldn't anymore. "They're all cunts; every last one of them. And you know how I feel about using that word."

"It's bigger than you think," he said.

"How? Ansel, she has like two friends in Bitter Springs. The rest she just bullies into submission."

"Not on the Internet."

"So?"

"That's worse."

"You're saying anonymous strangers on the Internet are worse than the flesh and blood losers we have running around our town? Dude."

A creak. Wood bending. Ansel lifted off the bed and, still in the dark, went to the doorway. Holding the molding for dear life, he leaned into the light coming in from the living room and looked around his apartment.

"I'm pretty sure we can report her for this," Annette carried on.

Nothing made a person more self-aware than the feeling that something terrible was about to happen to them. He had stacks of poetry books on his living room table, and he could still call to mind almost every inspiring line he'd highlighted inside them. If the voices were right, then the police would turn his house inside out, and what would they find in those poetic verses? Were there secrets in the letters, in the words? Could they forgo interrogation and simply build an Ansel to their liking based off the misinterpretation of his interests?

And, oh Jesus, there was a picture of his nephew on the wall. It was the two of them at the beach, not an adult in sight. Both of their shirts were off.

"She's never liked you. Anyone who knows anything will see right through this. I promise you."

Ansel moved into the living room, past the ukulele propped up against the side of the couch; there were burn marks on the arm of it, from where he'd gotten drunk and fallen asleep holding his cigarette. The carpet made a squishing sound as he walked across it. He didn't bother glancing down; he figured it must've been from all the blood pouring out of the phone.

"Are you a pedophile?" Annette blurted out.

Ansel stopped, halfway into the kitchen. "Fuck no," he said, while glaring at the linoleum floor. There was a trail of a sticky, translucent substance running across it; it had no definite beginning, nor a definite end. Whatever had caused it existed for that moment, and that moment only.

"No, you're not. If you geek out and act guilty, it's only going to make it worse."

There it was again, that wet sound. It was in the kitchen with him, but where? Ansel went to the sink and fished a steak knife out of the mountain of dirty dishes. It still had last night's supper on it—Chinese take-out—because he couldn't be bothered to learn how to use chopsticks, even though he had a small collection of them in a drawer. That's something else they would find, when they did a moratorium of his life. Leftovers and dirty dishes, and recycling bin filled to the brim with beer bottles. Too much beer for one man, they'd say. Lures, Lux might write, for fish to ensnare in his net.

"What's that sound?" Annette asked.

Ansel turned towards the basement door. "The voices or…?"

"Voices? What voices?"

"Nothing."

Ansel went to the basement door, the knife shaking in his hand.

"Ansel, what voices?"

A loud crash exploded out of the guest bedroom. Ansel jumped and stumbled backwards, catching himself against the kitchen island.

Annette cried, "What the hell was that? Is there someone else there with you?"

The voices inside Ansel's head were getting louder and louder. It was a constant barrage, one after the other, accompanied by tiny, ringing noises, like messages coming in by the tens and twenties in a chat room. They told him it would probably be best for him to kill himself. They told him they were coming for his mom and dad. They recited his address, his phone number. They were talking about his face, and the mask of lies he hid behind.

"Ansel, fucking talk to me."

He whispered, "I think someone has broken in."

"Call the police! I'll call the police. I'm coming—"

"There's so much blood coming out," Ansel said, holding the phone in his hand, which was gushing blood, like a severed artery.

"Blood? What the fuck—"

The cell phone died in Ansel's hand, and when it died, the blood stopped, too. He dropped it, and when it hit the ground, it melted into a crimson puddle.

Another crash, this time from the living room. Turning to the living room, he saw the picture of his nephew and himself at the beach swaying on its hook, recently disturbed.

Heavy thudding—Ansel spun around, slicing the air behind him. There was more sticky, translucent liquid on the floor, and on the cupboards. It smelled salty, and of the ocean.

"Get out!" Ansel hollered. "I'm calling the police."

He backpedaled through the kitchen, into the living room. Someone was in the house. He couldn't see them, but he knew they were there. He could feel them, right ahead, around the corner, near the front door or the guest room; a shape, a shadow; a shade standing in the dark, biding its time, clinging to every corner, stalking his image as it was held in every reflective surface; he could smell their breath, that salty, oceanic spew; and he could hear it, the weapon they had brought—the wet, thick, leathered tails of a whip; they were caressing it, lubricating it; letting it drag across the ground, as if they were marking their territory.

Ansel had his computer in his room and a window he'd "boarded" up with pillows. He could lock the door, contact the police through the Internet, or fit his doughy body through the window. He could do something, anything, other than stand here.

He ran towards his room, flicked the light switch on the wall. As the dying bulb buzzed to life, he threw his body into the door, slammed it shut, and locked it. Turning around to go to his computer, the air caught in his throat, and he dropped the knife.

The monitor, the tower, keyboard, and mouse were weeping blood, like infected sores. Ansel went to one knee, fumbled for the knife. A force from behind pushed him into the desk. His hands skated through the blood, until they gave out, and his elbows cracked against the floor.

"Women… and children," someone whispered behind him.

Ansel reared up, but his attacker was on him again. It took him by the back of the head with hands larger than his head and pressed his face into the blood. It tore Ansel's shirt off, split his pants in half. It

88

grabbed the elastic of his underwear and bunched it up in its slimy fist, wedging the fabric painfully into his ass.

"Please," Ansel cried, unable to hear his own voice over the voices of the Internet inside his head. "Don't do that."

It started to carve into the small of Ansel's back, not with any blade, but its long, stinging fingers. Ansel bucked in the blood, but it pressed down harder on his head, so that he couldn't move.

"Stop, stop!"

It kept carving into his body, one letter or symbol at a time, and when it was finished, it moved onto his sides. The pain was nauseating. He was being branded. He could smell his skin splitting to an impossibly cold heat, wilting into the seething ravines scored there.

When it was finished with Ansel's sides, it grabbed him by the hair on the back of his head and twisted his neck until he could see what had been written into his flesh. The tattoo read 'women' and on each of his sides, the word 'and.'

It bashed Ansel's face into the ground, over and over, until he was about to lose consciousness. When he could barely see, it turned him over and drove its fingers into his stomach, above his pelvis. Both its hands worked together, stirring his skin and muscle into the shapes of letters.

"It hurts!" Ansel cried. Unable to see who or what was doing this to him, he sealed his eyes shut with his tears and disappeared into his mind. As the attacker worked at his stomach, he could see the letters it was cutting into him. A 'c' and then, with the other hand, an 'n.' He was counting on the numbness of shock to save him from this, but in seconds, the message was complete.

Children. It had carved 'Children' above his cock. 'And' into his sides. 'Women' above his ass. Women and children. A place for each of them, when they were his to have.

Ansel felt his eyes being pried open. It was on top of him, pressing its weight into him. It peeled his lids back, and when his eyes were open, it leaned in and kissed his irises.

"It's time for the world to see you for what you truly are," it whispered, a voice that was both male and female.

Ansel begged for his life, but his life had been forfeited the moment Lux had put him up for bounty on her blog.

The attacker closed its hands over his face, slipped its fingers into his jaws, and slowly, carefully, as if to make sure Ansel didn't miss a moment of agony, it began to peel away his face in one complete, glistening sheet of skin.

Ansel didn't die until his face was no more than raw muscle, and his attacker was staring back at him, wearing it.

It was all over the news: the non-binary kindergartner, Zoe/Zeke Crampton, was found dead in the bathroom of their home last night. The word 'Liar' had been burned into their throat; and like Salinger Stevens, their face had been degloved. Ansel Adams had also been found dead in his bedroom with the phrase 'women and children' carved into his torso—his face also having been degloved. Due to recent allegations regarding Ansel's latent pedophilia, social media was already beginning to make connections between the cases, suggesting that Ansel had killed Zoe/Zeke. Some proponents of non-sexual, but intimate relationships between adults and children claimed Ansel and Zoe/Zeke had been lovers, and that they had been targeted for their counter-culture beliefs. The police were still looking for a murderer at large, while everyone else stayed focused on the victims, and what they had done, or not done, to have deserved such a cruel fate.

Fenton liked facts. They never let him down. It was true that facts could be distorted, but they had an almost brittle malleability. If one knew where to look, and if they looked hard enough, they could see the stress fractures in what others wanted everyone else to consider true, and know they had been manipulated. He was naïve, and he approached the world like a child, but only because as a child, he could play his peers' childish games. They were children, too, but they didn't know it. They thought the clothes they wore, the jobs they held, and the sex they had, somehow elevated them above the playground antics they'd never graduated from. He wasn't better than them, but he knew them better than they knew themselves, and that was why he was Lux's principle augur.

But after three murders that could be linked to Lux or Lux's blog, Fenton found himself reconsidering the company he kept. It wasn't because of the others—he'd seen the fractures in their facades since day one—but because of himself. Their "work" as Lux called it, had always been meaningful to him, but unlike Lux and to a lesser extent, Echo, it wasn't the reason he woke up in the morning, or the explanation for why he could sleep so soundly at night. Social justice had been the carriage to carry him to the group, but it was the group itself that carried him. They were his friends, his best friends; and to them, he was a stranger. Because he was an impostor. He had twisted the truth of himself to fit the shape of their claws, and gladly went where they flew. But he could feel Lux's claws tightening, and he could bend no more. If he broke, he would be bare.

Fenton's favorite place in Bitter Springs was the cemetery, where he now stood; the dead didn't bother him, and the living kept to themselves. Also, it didn't hurt that there was a fairly strong Wi-Fi connection being broadcast from the house by the cemetery. The wireless connection had been not-all-that-cleverly named "AshestoAshes." Surprisingly, Fenton hadn't cracked it as quickly as he thought he would've. After trying "DustoDust," he went back and forth between "zombie" and things related to zombies, until he remembered what the owner of the house looked like. He was a thirty-five-year-old white male that lived with his grandmother; he worked out in the basement, and wore expensive jewelry and tracksuits. If the wind hit him hard enough, everything near him would be given a light dusting of protein powder and cheap cologne. His name was David Goldstein. The password had been "Dust2Dust."

Taking out his tablet, Fenton made his way to his favorite spot—a grove near the Goldsteins' house. He sat down, wedged his back into the giant Weeping Willow that had overtaken the other trees in the grove, as if it had pulled them in with its leaves for a huddle, to talk about what should be done about all these meddling corpses in their backyard. Fenton liked to think nature cared about trivial things, the way humans did. It was the same way how two people felt when they came together to share in their bickering over a sub-par waiter, or how complete strangers could find common ground in the aneurism-inducing stress of their favorite show ending on a "to be continued," teasing them until next year's next season. Fenton found most things he did in life to be inconsequential, like someone planting trees to bring beauty to a cemetery. For all the fleeting moments of reprieve the act might offer, reality still waited swathed in the trueness of rot. Being an augur was not much different. They could break down a person's traits and qualities, but in the end, like the caretaker who'd cultivated this grove, it wasn't for anyone but themselves. If anything, it amplified what it wasn't, what it couldn't be.

Augurs of the past used the behavior of birds as ways by which to measure the approval or disapproval of the divine. Who the hell were

Fenton and the others trying to understand? Not god, and certainly not the sad specimens they judged on this decaying orb.

The sunlight left the tablet's screen. While it was booting up, he caught his reflection in the glass and quickly looked away. A stinging sensation drilled his leg at the place where his phone in his pocket was pressed against it. Focused on the tablet, he scratched the stinging until it graduated to burning. Pain was easier to manage when it was of your own making.

The tablet rang like an old rotary phone, and a message overcame the home screen. Fenton thought he'd heard something rustling behind the willow, but he couldn't be bothered to check. This was more important.

The message was from a mutual contact of his and Asher's. The contact's name was Gulliver, and he was, as Asher put it, "gayer than gay… a new species of gay; a color we'd never seen but always knew was there." The augurs had a file on him that expanded with every encounter, like most tabs they kept on their community. It had the usual details—twenty-five-year-old, white (middle-eastern), gay male with the body of a dad, a mildly unhealthy drinking habit, and a free pass to the patriarchy (on account of his wealth, not his skin)—as well as some newer ones, which included reports he had been spotted with chewed-up knuckles, possibly from a roofie-gone-wrong (whether he had been the victim or the perpetrator remained to be discovered). Asher liked him, because Asher liked everything that was bad for him, but Fenton was lukewarm on the worm. And yet he couldn't deny Gulliver made one hell of a snitch.

His message read thusly:

Someone has been seen fleeing each crime scene. Cops are keeping it out of the papers. Reports are all the same. A slender figure dressed in somewhat transparent clothes, except their clothes looked wet, like they'd been standing in the rain for an hour, even though it'd been clear skies after every murder.

What do you think that means? What in gay hell is going on?

Did Asher break his fingers? Tell him to call me. It's been an hour, and I'm growing moss sitting here waiting by the phone.

Whatever. I couldn't care less. I saw Echo storming away from Lux just a minute ago. Know anything about that?

Don't hold out on me, robo-boy!

Love,
Gulliver

More rustling in the trees surrounding him. Fenton glanced up. His heart seized in his chest. There, beyond the grove, a shape stood amongst the headstones. Spindly, vitreous, its body wasn't separate from the cemetery, but a part of it, raised from it, like a crack in the paint on a canvas.

Fenton jammed his thumb into the tablet's screen. The pressure of his fear warped the LCD. He told himself what he was seeing wasn't real, and then it wasn't. The white sunlight sliced through the clouds, like a hammer nailing to the Earth a holy decree. The shape vanished, disappeared into the dull grays and dying greens of the cemetery's tarnished palette.

There was blood on his pantleg; two large drops, and one small, and another, a fourth, that hadn't finished bleeding through the fabric. Fenton took his phone out of his pocket. He almost dropped it because it was so slick, like it'd been covered in jelly. But there was a cluster of notifications vying for attention, and so he ignored it. Because amongst the spam mail, automatic bill payments, and texts from his constantly worried, recently separated mother and father, there was a reminder that Lux had, minutes ago, posted something new on her blog. He tracked her every movement as best as he could, because he didn't trust Echo to do it right when she did. She was too involved. She did it out of infatuation. He did it out of survival.

Except, there was no post. The last thing she had written had been her proposition on impostors. And yet, there had been something. Remnants of a post. A larger gap than was normal between the header and the body of the front page. Something had been there, and now it was—

Fenton blinked as he saw it, the same way someone blinks instinctively, almost pre-meditatively, to keep something out of their eyes. It had been on the site, but it wasn't. Like the languid shape that'd spread itself across the graves, it disappeared into the light. But, damn it, he had seen it. It had been a picture of himself. Where the hell did it go?

Digging his heels into the corpse-fed dirt, Fenton closed out of the browser and sent a text message to Echo that said, "Everything okay?" Not expecting a response, because Lux had a monopoly on Echo's fingers and what she did with them, he slipped the phone into his other pocket. And then, experiencing a rare moment of uncertainty, he fell back on his palms and, for the first time in a very long time, actually considered the world around him—not the one they'd built for themselves, inside themselves.

The cemetery was like all cemeteries: quiet, reserved; a place where shadows bred and the sunlight never seemed to last for long. It was row after row of plot after plot—a stone timeline of friends, families, and strangers dating back to the days of Bitter Springs' founding. The property was small, but the woods that checked it gave the cemetery an infinite quality, as if to promise those that passed that there would always be enough room, even for them. It was these woods, which eventually fed into the larger forest, Maidenwood, that gave the cemetery its sinister atmosphere. You could see it in the air, a slight discoloration of slate gray and muted white. A constant fog, regardless of the temperature or time of day, that crept and crawled, like fingers feeling out the presence of trespassers.

Fenton squeezed the bridge of his nose. Facts were safe, even when they weren't. His imagination was another matter entirely. It got away from him, and when it came back, it came back with worry and shame hitching a ride on its hunched back. The last time he let it have its way with him was the first time he'd come to the cemetery, and the last time he'd been his true self around Lux.

That day had been a day like any other day of that year when he was in sixth grade. A day where he drifted through the sea of students, never uttering anything to anyone, unless called on in class. Up until this point, he hadn't paid much attention to Lux and Ramona (Asher had yet to join the fold, and Echo was in another school altogether), except when he stole glances at them, because they always seemed more attractive than the last time he'd seen them. Up until this point, they had been cute, and somewhat intimidating. And then they gave their presentation in History class, and then they were both those things, and more.

In an oral presentation that was one-part beat poetry and one-part verbal assault, Lux and Ramona laid out the class and the teacher with a caustic retelling of the women's suffrage movement in the United States, and how women were still fighting for rights that should've been granted to them since, and this was quoting Ramona, "The dawn of fucking time."

After the ten minutes it took to, this time quoting Lux, "drop a knowledge bomb" on the class, the students sat there in silence—the guys staring at the girls from out the corner of their eyes, waiting for their reaction to tell them how they should react. Their knowledge bomb had left the whole class shell-shocked, and not because of the content, but because of the fiery impact and the crater it left in their pre-conceptions. All the teacher could do was tell them to take it easy on the language, and when he clapped, everyone else clapped, too. Most of the students had forgotten about the presentation by the end of the week, but for Fenton, it had left such a ringing in his ears that he couldn't hear anything else.

In a haze of Lux and Ramona, a few days later, Fenton, not thinking or caring about where he was going, walked home from school and ended up in the cemetery. His ever-scientific mind had been weighing the pros and cons of approaching the girls, how they would react if he did so, and how he could tell them he appreciated their presentation without seeming as if he had an ulterior motive, when he tripped on a broken grave that looked like it'd been stamped into the soil. The name placard read Fenton Laurent, 1890-1940. And after he did some re-search into the matter, Fenton found out that this man had been a distant relative. The most his father could say about him was that he was completely unremarkable.

"So, I'm not named after him?" Fenton had asked his father that day.

"Just a coincidence," his dad had said. "If I'd known we'd name you after such a waste of space, your mother and I would've come up with something else."

He remembered his dad laughing and shaking his head, and nudging Fenton to make sure he knew it was just a joke. But that was a lie. He knew it then, and he knew it now. His dad had, and continued to have, almost impossibly high expectations. Even compliments were lies. Fenton could see the truth through the cracks in them all.

In his reminiscing, Fenton's body had steered him to that sad and forgotten plot of Fenton Laurent. He stood over it now, the same way a sailor stood over a maelstrom, wondering how they'd gotten here.

But he already knew the answer; that was the downside of having all of them. He was here because he had found a grave that not only shared the same name as him, but also his crippling normality. As a sixth grader, he'd seen his whole life ahead of him. There would be grad school and acquaintances in the place of friends, and he would drink often and alone, and end up marrying someone he didn't love, because they were easy and, for all his supposed smarts, he didn't know any better. Nothing made a person a better augur than having to look up to those everyone else looked down on.

He was here because of the grave, and because of the two girls who'd infected his belief system years ago. Back then, he knew they would've never accepted him as he was, so he became something else, instead. Not because he didn't like himself. He liked himself well enough. He did it to get closer to them, to be something more than intelligent and talented; to have the chance to leave a mark that amounted to more than a dog-eared page in a book only he and a few other nerds could comprehend.

So, he made a mask for himself from the truth of his being and molded it to his liking, making sure to obscure every crack of every lie, until some days, he struggled to find the seam of where the mask ended and his face began. He emphasized his French background, and studied the language in his spare time. He became bi-sexual and re-interpreted every strange encounter he'd ever had with the same or opposite sex as a result of his sexuality. He immersed himself in gender studies, and denounced himself as a man as much as possible. He be-came more childish, withdrawn; he dampened his emotions, so as to emphasize Lux's and Ramona's. And when he had the chance to funnel money into Lux's blog or her projects, he did so without question, be-cause as long as his family's fortune was going to a "good cause," then his over-privileged status could be ignored.

It had been good while it lasted, Fenton thought to himself, catch-ing his reflection in the golden placard of the adjacent grave, but now he'd outgrown his mask, and if he didn't take it off soon, someone else might do it for him.

"Imposters" were being murdered, and it didn't take a seasoned de-tective to see the connection between the cases and Lux's blog. For those in the know, it was obvious who Lux had been targeting with her writing. His first thought had been that she might be the murderer, but she had an alibi for every victim.

His second thought was that it might be Echo, and that thought had been echoing through his head the whole morning. Like the ring-ing in his ear from Lux and Ramona's presentation, he couldn't be rid of it.

Stinging in his other leg now, on the skin underneath his phone.

Annoyed, he ripped his phone out of his pocket. Staring at the screen, he stopped breathing. It was a message from Caleb.

It read thusly:

We need to talk. All of us. This is big. My buddy at the police station has a buddy at the lab where they're checking the evidence over. First off, said there was way too much blood at the crime scenes for the wounds inflicted. Second off, the lab nerd said there's something wrong with the blood. Said it's not just the victims' or the perp's. Said the blood was from a shitload of different people. Like... hundreds. Maybe thousands.

What. The. Fuck?

Echo sat in the greenhouse section of the local Lawn and Garden and her ran hands down her legs, feeling their smoothness, admiring the way her pale flesh caught the light from the overheads. She kept telling herself Lux was missing out. Aside from her head, Echo had shaved every inch of hair off her body. Lux liked her like that. It took a lot of work, but relationships were work. If there was anything to be learned from trashy talk-shows, that was it. Relationships were work, and the payouts didn't always arrive when they were expected to. Echo was still waiting to get hers. Had been all her life.

She leaned back in the metal chair, propped her feet up on the glass table next to it. Her cheeks felt tight in the places where the tears had dried. She imagined she must've looked like one of those washed-out statues at the park, where the acid rain had carved away their faces, leaving them in a permanent state of mourning.

The automatic doors opened at the greenhouse's entrance. A man pushed a cart through, and his wife followed after. They were young, and black. While he leaned over the cart, deflated and defeated, his wife flew back and forth between the various flowers on the shelves and ground with all the energy and insanity of a coked-out humming-bird. Her excitement was exhausting him; his exhaustion was exciting her. They were pulling away at opposite ends, and yet somehow, probably thought this would balance their relationship out, help them meet in the middle.

Echo scoffed and tipped her head back, letting the overheads print their afterimage into her corneas. She hated heteronormative gender roles. The oafish husband who only showed enough interest in his wife's interests to keep the peace, and to make sure he kept getting a

piece. The neurotic wife who kept herself busy at all times, doing everything for everyone, and silently hating everyone for everything she'd
ever done for them. The recently married and the marriage certificate
they practically carried around, like it was the key to the kingdom the
marginalized could only dream of one day entering. The little girls who
only played with dolls, and the little boys who played with action figures. The monotony of monogamy.

Shaking her head, she positioned herself so she wouldn't have to
see the husband and wife, because they were triggering her feelings of
depression regarding the fight she and Lux had earlier. Those two stupid, heterosexual shitheads should've known better than to come here
with that lovebird crap. This was the place where Salinger Stevens
worked before his death. For the straight to come here was like a serial
killer returning to the crime scene. Or, at least, that's what Lux said.

It was so annoying how much she missed Lux. Lux was the love of
her life, the woman she wanted to settle down with. She'd done everything for Lux, been everything for Lux. Damn it, she had even planned
to make dinner for them at the end of the month so she could propose
to Lux. It hurt so badly knowing that Lux was mad at her. It was like
when her Dad used to tie knots or tighten screws so much so that no
one but himself could ever get them undone. No matter how much
she tried to unravel this feeling inside her, the only hands it would
loosen to belonged to the woman who had put it there in the first place.
The only way to feel better was to make Lux feel better.

Echo was secondary; it was the curse of her name. She wasn't the
source, but what came back to it. Lux, Ramona, Asher, and Fenton
didn't have to pay attention to their surroundings, because they simply
superimposed their own worldviews onto it. Echo was her surroundings. She had never been known to have been anything else.

These blacks are pissing me off, Echo thought, hopping to her feet. She
crossed the greenhouse, went through the automatic doors into the
Home portion of the Home and Garden.

The Home in the Home and Garden was a small warehouse jam-
packed with every unnecessary necessity one could ever guilt themselves into wanting for their quaint, suburban getaway. It was shelf after shelf of things for the kitchen and the bathroom, the living room
and the family room; tools and containers; hardwood, lightbulbs; bird
feeders and water fountains; couches, chairs; paint of every imaginable
soccer mom-manufactured color. It was endless, too; stacked to the

ceiling, the stock seemed to be coming out of the ceiling, as if it were being deposited from the corporate mothership hovering stealthily above the store.

Lux had said she always thought the hippie movement was for pussies, but even then, she could see why the Home and Garden and places like it would make them sick. Naturally, Echo agreed.

Remembering why she had come here, which wasn't to sulk around until someone felt sorry for her, Echo dug her nails into the heels of her palm and headed for the paint department. That was where Salinger Stevens worked, and where his last best friend, possibly boyfriend, was on the schedule today. Lux was convinced Salinger, as well as Zoe/Zeke and Ansel, had been impostors of the LGBTQIA community. Echo agreed with her, even though by being here at the Home and Garden, she was sending another message entirely. A message all her own. For a person named Echo, that didn't happen a lot.

Salinger Stevens' main squeeze, Paul Zdanowicz, wasn't at the desk when Echo came around the corner. His cell phone was on the large, wraparound counter, though, and it looked to be sitting in a pool of red paint. Echo looked around to see if there were any other sales associates nearby, but it was just her—her, and all the forty-something, failed high school football stars, eyeing her like a rare dish they hadn't seen, but were itching to try.

Or at least, that's what it felt like to her, when she caught them staring at her.

Echo shivered, as if she was physically ridding herself of their ocular filth, and twisted her mouth, concerned. She needed to find Paul. A friend of a friend of a friend had said Paul was with Salinger the night he had been killed. He might've seen the killer, Echo told Lux, after having shared this information. He might've seen the killer, and he might've seen where the killer had gone, after murdering Salinger.

That's when Lux had lost it.

"If you want to suck Paul's dick, just go ahead and do it!" Lux had screamed at her, her irises rimmed with light, as if something had passed in front of them. "He'll tell you anything you want to hear after that!"

Echo had only been able to shake her head and stutter out, "What a-are you talking a-about?"

And that's when Lux's eyes had darkened, and retreated into the recesses of their sockets. "If you go looking for the killer, he might find you." Her lips had thinned, her cheeks had become razor sharp. "If you think I want something bad to happen to you, then go ahead, you groupie slut."

That's when Echo had shed her subservience, and the two of them cussed each other out and pushed each other around, until Lux locked herself in her room, and Echo, wanting to add insult to injury, left to go find the now mysteriously absent Paul Zdanowicz.

Echo went to the wraparound counter and leaned over Paul's cell phone. The red paint underneath seemed to have spread farther. It looked watered-down, though; less like paint, more like... Echo laughed, swiped the screen. Without a password to prevent her from pursuing Paul's personal shit, she pulled up the last thing he'd looked at.

It had been Lux's blog, and there was a new post.

Echo didn't need to read it. If she was an expert on anything in life, it was of the wills and whims of her love, Lux. Like the light of the sun, she moved in a constant, predictable pattern. In the spring, she gathered her strength and energy, and those who had missed her presence began to seek her out, to elevate her to her rightful place on all their horizons. In the summer, she came into herself; she was the center of everyone's attentions; the searing threat; the harsh wake-up call. Summer saw her in her element, in that harsh in between—in between the rebirth of spring and redeath of winter. It was in summer that all her work was done, and all her projects completed; and all transgressions tilled from the patriarchal field, to make way for the bones of her oppressors. At the first signs of fall, she fell into a depression, and by winter, she was seldom seen; preferring the confines of her "woman cave" and the sex she demanded from Echo to "keep the light inside her alive."

So, yeah, if Echo was an expert on anything in life, it was the wills and whims of her love, Lux. Which meant that was blood coming out Paul's phone. Which meant he wasn't far from here, fighting for his life. Which meant there was still time.

Echo tore down the aisles of the Home and Garden, keeping her eyes peeled for the killer's familiar trail. She dodged customers and carts, and felt herself already getting winded—the consequences of smoking at the ripe age of eleven. Stopping, sniffing, she caught the telling scent pressing into the aisle. The large fans above had carried it here, and the heavy musk of it seemed to be slowing them down. It

THE AGONY OF AFTER

was the killer's scent. Sea salt and sulfur. The forever and the fatal, intertwined; the brood from the breast that'd birthed it.

They should've never gone into the forest.

Lumber up ahead, and a short-lived scream. Echo stopped, stumbled forward. Her knee went out. She grabbed a coil of garden hoses that capped the end of her aisle and righted herself. Another scream. Wet appendages smacking against tile. Then she saw it, that distinct signature: numerous, tightly bunched smears running along the cement floor; crusted over, and reeking; sexual secretions from the promise of sadism. It was here.

Echo crept towards Lumber. The aisle was narrow, and empty. On each side, long, restrained boards towered over the walkthrough. Whitewood, spruce, fir, pine, poplar; amber-like Douglas and technicolor-red Redwood. Wildly different trees that, as Echo walked past them, began to look the same. They lost their individual qualities and shades and shifted into the dark, contorted oaks that formed the dense corridors of Maidenwood. And just like that day, this corridor ended in a faint light, and a beckoning hand.

Echo shook her head, and the memory lifted from the scene. The hand vanished, but the light remained. At the end of Lumber, there was a single-person, unisex bathroom. The door was slightly open, and the light leaking out strobed, as the shape inside moved rapidly back and forth in front of its source. It was driving its appendages downwards into something; a primal display of power; relentless, emotionless; mechanical.

"Stop!" Echo whisper-screamed, taking off towards the bathroom. One arm out, she wheezed loudly, "Stop it! Stop it!"

Echo barged into the bathroom. Paul Zdanowicz was on his knees, his body thrown over the toilet; naked. The killer was standing over him, holding his head up by the hair on the back of his head. In the killer's snaking tentacles, Paul's degloved face hung. Catching the fluorescent light, the skin turned transparent; there were blush-like blood splotches on his ghoulish cheeks; and broken capillaries like purple webs around the ragged eye holes. His mouth was crooked, his lips swollen; they glistened with spit and blood, like two throbbing egg sacs.

The killer released Paul. His lifeless corpse fell raw face-first into the shitty toilet water. It turned to face Echo. As it did, it soiled itself with the substance of its making. That glassy brimstone. The milk of hell.

"Give it to me!" Echo ran at the killer and wrenched Paul's flap of a face from its squirming grip. "I'll take it to her. She doesn't need to know!"

Three members of the LGBTQIA were dead, and Lux wanted to throw a party? As insensitive as this might sound to others, Asher thought it was a pretty damn good idea. What better way to bring an at-risk community together than to bring them together on the same night, in the same place? Together, they could be strong, and safe. Together, they could clash craniums and find the fucker who was thinning out their herd. Lux had given him a list of names of people to invite, but Asher wasn't feeling this new drive of hers for exclusivity. He was going to invite everyone he could get his hands on, and whoever he could get his hands on… he'd save for later.

"Too many lesbians," Asher mumbled, stopping his car at a stop sign to look over the list again. "Too many high school sophomores, too. Lord, Lux. Predatory much?"

Someone honked behind Asher. He looked into his rear-view mirror, blew them a kiss, and then floored it down the road. He wasn't overtly feminine as a person, but if someone pissed him off, he'd be a sassy drag queen in a half a second flat. Nothing disarmed a person faster than a mouthy, muscled man whose hands you couldn't follow.

Asher hauled ass through a yellow light at the next intersection and, peeling out, made a sharp turn into the nearest fast food joint. The line was long, like a-soup-kitchen-on-Christmas-long, so when he pulled up and claimed his spot amongst the rumbling desperate, he put the car in park, and got to work.

With his phone, Lux's list, and his own additions, he had the invites sent out through social media in about five minutes. During that time, he'd barely budged but an inch in the drive-through, but that was fine. Like the sinner in a confessional waiting for the priest to get settled, it gave him time to reflect on this bad decision. This bad decision which consisted of a tub of food and a bucket of soft drink, and a small slice of apple pie. Like the teenagers of today loved to say over a cocktail of pills, cheap beer, and over-the-counter, under-the-covers prophylactics, only god could judge him.

Staring at his phone's screen and the list of eighty he'd invited— most of whom had already accepted—a gnawing hole opened up in Asher's stomach no amount of greasy carbs could fill. He'd known it for a while now, but with the way Lux had been acting lately, it had become unavoidable.

He didn't care. He didn't care about their "work," or being an augur. He was tired of talking, day in and day out, about social justice and the patriarchy, gender roles and the spectrum of sexuality. He was tired of tearing himself apart and attaching labels to each idiosyncrasy, like some retail wretch tagging clothes on a rack. He still liked Lux, Echo, Ramona, and Fenton, but he didn't love them like he wanted to love them. They were convenient, but he'd outgrown them. They didn't make him happy; he wasn't allowed to be happy around them. Happiness denoted compliance. Compliance was, according to Lux, the ultimate killer. The only way to improve something was to flay it to the bone, to be rid of the lies that rode like lice upon the flesh.

Maybe over the years Asher had become a simpleton, but hearing shit like that come out of Lux's mouth without a hint, a morsel, of self-awareness, sounded absolutely retarded. He couldn't be gay without being a statement. And he couldn't be a statement unless it was Lux's statement. Sure, he and the others agreed to their "mission" and what it all meant. But goddamn, what did it all mean? They were fighting just to fight, flaying just to flay. Aside from the occasional hatemonger, Bitter Springs wasn't a bad place to be. Certainly better than other cities he'd gone to visiting family and friends. Lux would say he was giving up. Lux would say he'd lost his way. But he'd only lost it because it was her who'd brought him here.

After waiting a solid ten minutes, Asher rolled down his window and rolled up to the intercom.

"Can I take your order?" the worker buzzed, sounding not much different than the robots that would probably replace them years down the line.

Asher leaned out the window, opened his mouth to order, but the summer air passing through turned cold and he was reminded of fall. This was Lux's last hurrah, he realized. Her dedication to equal rights and social justice was undeniable, but it wouldn't be long until she reached that point in her routine where she became dormant. The collapse of Brooksville Manor was supposed to have been her summer swan song, and it hadn't reached the chilling crescendo she'd hoped for. She was grasping at straws to remain relevant. The auguring would start soon, and they would pass judgment in the court of public opinion. He would have to talk, and goddamn it, he was tired of talking.

"Sir?" the intercom spat out in a garbled mess of letters.

Asher bit his lip. He'd lost his appetite. Laughing, shaking his head, and mouthing an apology there was no way anyone could hear, he turned out of the drive-through and back onto the road. He needed something more fulfilling than the shit he'd been eating these last eight years.

Lights blipped like beacons on the edge of Asher's vision. Slowing with the traffic, he turned his head and muttered, "Fuck me Jesus," as he caught a glimpse of the chaos unfolding behind the main stretch.

The Home and Garden had transformed into the Hospital and Cemetery. Four cop cars and a fire truck formed a perimeter around an ambulance, where paramedics and police, like well-dressed vultures, circled a covered body on a blood-soaked gurney. The vehicles' emergency lights formed a blue and red sphere, and outside it, as if it were repellent, onlookers were gathered, contorting their bodies and straining their necks to have but a glimpse of the corpse that lay blooming under its blanket.

Asher's instincts told him to watch the road. The car ahead of him had come to a stop. With a yelp, he slammed the brakes and skidded onto the rumble strip, narrowly missing a messy fender bender with the car or cars stacked up behind him.

Drivers zoomed past him, honking and flashing, and throwing up middle fingers so hard a few might've even strained their wrists. It didn't matter to them that, for a moment, they'd both been ogling the crime scene with the same doe-eyed glee. That was the way it went in his circles, too, among those who prided themselves on being more open and understanding than the general population.

"An asshole is an asshole," his last partner, Jared, had said.

Asher remembered laughing at him, because just as it had been then as it was now, his mind had been born, raised, and made a man-child in the gutter.

But for once in his life, Jared was serious. "Doesn't matter who you are, what you call yourself, what you've been through; an asshole is an asshole. Even the outcasts have a pecking order."

"I know you're talking about Lux," Asher had said, rolling his eyes.

Jared had been talking about Lux, and when it came down to it, Asher was given a choice to choose between her or him. He chose the Light. He always did.

By the time Asher had made it back to Bitter Springs' Community

College's off-campus housing, social media had already convinced it-self that it was Paul Zdanowicz's corpse the cops had pulled out of the Home and Garden. The cause of death was inconsistent—in a matter of five minutes, he'd been stabbed, skinned, burned alive, beaten to a pulp, and curbed-stomped—but a few details found purchase in the perverted minds of the city's amateur reporters: Paul's face had been degloved, though a piece of it had been found snagged on a hook in the Lumber aisle; and the word "confederate" had been blistered into his perineum—the official term for what quickly devolved in reports into the perennial favorites of taint, gooch, and grundle.

Absorbed in the newsfeed, Asher somehow parked his car, made it to the front door, and down the hall to his apartment unscathed by pushy stoners and clingy frat boys. Entering his apartment, he found the discussion had shifted from Paul's death being the fourth in a hate-crime-spree to the killer's choice of the word "confederate."

Lux was not well-liked, but she was frequently read; her influence was undeniable, and her good favor hard to grow and even harder to maintain. It had been the reason why Asher became one of her augurs. It was one of those us or them situations, and being a sixth grader at the time, nothing sounded better than belonging to an "us." The "them" kept him around because he let the straight girls grope him—"It's okay," they would cry. "He doesn't mind!"—and he wasn't as gay as the other gay guys in their grade. He could almost pass for straight, someone had told him once. Like that was some shit he should be proud of. And shit, he had been. Once. And then some.

It was that us versus them mentality that gave Lux her power. Not necessarily naturally here in Bitter Springs, but on the Internet, which in turn gave her a presence and a voice that rose higher than the usual wails on the wind. It was that us versus them mentality which made Lux more important to most than they actually wanted her to be. It was that us versus them mentality that transmitted Lux's words and actions like signals into the minds of her allies and enemies, allowing them to take root, to take form; to eat away at their patterns of speech until the prescribed discourse replaced their own, like a cuckoo bird taking the place of a pushed hatchling, and being fed to maturity by the very thing that wanted to kill it.

So, confederate. Lux had used the word multiple times in her last blog post, the one that went out prior to Paul's death. And here it was, over and over again, being pounded out on keyboards by kids and adults who probably hadn't used the word since their last class on the American Civil War. It was a good word. A good word to use in auguring. A confederate could mean a supporter, or it could mean a bigoted individual still clinging to racism under the guise of heritage. The difference between the two being whether or not the "C" was capitalized, but that didn't matter. People didn't pay attention to shit like that.

Confederate was a good word. It was a word covered in bristles and thorns, and had a sharp taste other words didn't when they came out your mouth. It was the cornerstone of the monument to come, Asher considered, plopping himself down onto his couch; a throne, really, with Lux upon it; Echo to her right; but who would stand to her left? The augurs? No, the lack of symmetry would make Lux sick. So if not them, then who?

"Blah." Asher lay down on the couch, dropping his phone on the floor. So over-the-top. All of it. So over-the-fucking-top. He grabbed the TV remote and cruised the channels until landing on some glossy, empty, and utterly forgettable horror movie remake from the early 2000s. It was trash, but if trash was anything, it was sweet. Twenty minutes in, he was out.

Asher woke up to rolling credits and some nu-metal song that was playing over them. He couldn't explain it, but he had a mad case of the heebie-jeebies, which, though off-putting, made him smile, because the word made him think of Ramona, and how badly she wanted to punch him every time said it.

It was dark outside. The only light in his apartment came from the TV screen, and the faint glow of the moon just barely pushing through the windowpane, as if the clouds that covered it were in league with the sun. In a building with forty other students, Asher somehow felt disconnected from the world. That which wasn't touched by the harsh illumination of his television or cell phone was lost to the gray dark, where vague outlines lurked amongst the mildewed vapors of the central air.

Asher sat up, broke the crust on his lip with a raspy, "Goddamn," and leaned over on his elbow. He grabbed his cell phone off the floor from where he'd dropped it earlier. He had about one hundred notifications, thirty texts, five missed calls… and why the hell was there blood on his phone?

He went from comatose to practically caffeinated as he sat up, the glaring device oozing a chunk of gore from its charger port. Instead of geeking out and shaking it off, he watched the piece of pink, mushy meat inch down his wrist and forearm, like a slug. His throat tightened, as if to seal off his esophagus from the sick threatening to escape his gut.

And then he did flick it away, as he felt an intense stinging at the spot on his arm where the fetid lump had stained it. And he dropped his phone, too, as the foul ejaculate continued to seep from the seams of the phone's plastic shell.

"Whatthefuck?" Asher's knees shot into his chest and he scooted sideways down the couch, as far away as possible from the phone. "Holy Jesus jumping Christmas shit!"

Damn near asthmatic, Asher stopped breathing and bent over the edge of the couch. The cell phone's screen lit up. A text message ran like a news ticker across its upper half. It was from Ramona. He could tell by the icon he'd used in place of her photo—a pink pig that looked as if it had eaten its way halfway through a make-up kit. A pretty shitty thing, all things considered, but that was the nature of their relationship. After all, the picture she used in the place of his photo was a turd-shaped cock with a rainbow flag planted at the top of it.

"Ramona," Asher whispered. Did he leave the voice assistant thing-a-ma-jig on? "Call Ramona." He clenched his teeth, leaned farther forward. "Call—"

His eyes lingered on the text message.

It read thusly:

Did you see what Lux said about you?

He hadn't. And it was the last thing in the world he cared about at this moment. Because there was something in his living room with him. Something standing on the edge of the shadows, in that no man's land, where perception and reality gave birth to horrible imaginings best suited for purgatorial vaults and breached Membranes.

Asher had always wanted to be a writer, but now, he just wanted to live through this night.

It wasn't human. It couldn't be human. Seven feet tall. Translucent. A billowing, gelatinous bell for a body; from it, countless undulating limbs, thin and thick, unfurled. Not flying, rather, floating; swimming, even; riding on the hidden currents of an uncharted sea.

It wasn't human, but it wanted to be. Its body twisted like a sheet, as if it were trying to wring from its form the telling signs of its morbid symmetry. At first it was male, then female, and then both—a perfect harmony of each manifestation of gender and sex from every point along the spectrum.

Aroused, disgusted, but mostly horrified, Asher leaned in and learned that the vein-like structures that grew along the creature, inside and out, weren't veins, but sentences—vessels comprised of words and punctuations through which a dark oil pumped in short, forceful movements, as if it were mimicking the brutal hammering of a piston. If he forced his eyes, Asher could almost make out the sentences. It wasn't gibberish. Adverbs, adjectives; verbs, conjunctions—their meaning was lost on him, and yet he could feel it all the same; a great, bullying swell of emotions. The same way one might feel if they stared into the sun. To understand, to know anything more than its surface level, he would have to burn out his eyes, and live with their secrets in the lonely dark of his mind.

Asher was certain that this was the killer, and it must've decided this delay had been torturous enough, because with one graceful, eerily silent push, it thrust itself onto him, over him, and laid its stinging limbs upon him.

Its form was male now. Its shoulders, the color of smudged glass, were wider; its torso had folded itself, and used the word veins as stand-ins for pectorals and abs. It had no legs, save for the appendages that waded on the air, but from where a pelvis might be, the limbs wrapped together, forming a penis-shaped trunk that was heavy with the hateful substance that coursed throughout its body. It pressed down on Asher's crotch with a stomach-turning weight, and then split apart, from improvised frenulum to absent scrotum, forming a grinning smile of tissue inside which rows of teeth were fixed—the building blocks of their jagged form also words. Words, such as gay, faggot, hate, pathetic, and sick.

Asher managed to whimper. And whimpering, he said, "Don't... don't hurt me."

The killer had no eyes, but because looking at it was like looking through a window, Asher felt as if he were being watched, being judged, being consumed. He felt the same way he felt when he used to give presentations in class, or once, in the auditorium, when he'd been convinced to run for student president, despite not being nearly as extroverted as the world had decided him to be. He felt thousands of eyes gazing upon him through that gelatinous mesh that gave the killer its shape. It made him want to die, more so than the creature that straddled him, its gasping, grinning cock in his lap.

"Gay men are still men," the killer whispered. Its voice was neither male nor female, but something else, something alien. "They are one of us, until they are done with us."

The killer raised its limbs—a writhing bouquet of glassy tentacles—and pressed them against Asher's clavicle. Hot, shooting pains drove into his flesh, and he drove his body into the couch to break free. But he was harpooned, fixed to the creature; the pain it made and pain he felt the singular bond between them.

"It hurts so bad," Asher said, voice breaking.

His skin bubbled along his neck and chest. A necklace of blisters formed and immediately popped. While their slick, stinking fluid oozed down his nipples, more blisters formed; little domes of rancid filth.

"You mother fucker."

Asher drove his fists into the killer's torso.

"Get off me!"

And when his knuckles would've met the meaty bell of its body, the killer vanished. Or at least, he had thought it had. Asher sat there, reclined, wracked with pain, his mitts ready to bludgeon, and still he could feel the killer's presence. Like a ghost, it haunted the place where it had once hovered. It was still with him, but it couldn't touch him.

A touch of trauma kept him rooted, but after a few minutes, the paralysis waned. He sat up, his shirt drenched in blood and pus. With the harsh light of the TV, he could see it, the killer. It wasn't a hallucination. The thing was in his living room, watching him. At times, there would be a new dimension added to his living room—a portion of its bell-shaped torso, or the faint outlines, like fossils in rock, of its tentacles. It hadn't gone anywhere, and yet it couldn't hurt him anymore.

Asher sat there awhile longer—hours, maybe—staring into that space, searching for signs the same way scientists scoured the stars for life. There were hints, promises, and though he couldn't always see it, he knew it was there. It refused to leave his side. Such a terrible dread filled him when he wondered if it would be this way forever.

With dawn, the living room lost its deathly qualities. The killer hadn't left. It was quiet, contemptuous; hidden like a spider in the folds of reality.

Frozen to his spot on the couch, Asher found with the sun he began to thaw. Muscles aching, drenched in the acidic run-off of fear, he carefully came to his feet. When his body nearly touched where the killer resided, there was a dimensional shift, as if it were making room for him, as if to say he could go where he wanted, but it wouldn't be far behind.

Asher's mouth was hot and raw. His tongue flaked. The blisters on his chest had mushroomed into ripe, pale yellow bulbs. Overdosed on his own adrenaline, his ears buzzed, he couldn't breathe well, and parts of his body had taken on a phantom limb quality.

He remembered his phone had gone off at some point. His phone was his lifeline. Bending down, it felt as if the whole world were going down with him, like the dying in their death throws, yanking a curtain from its rod. He grabbed the phone, forgot how to use it for a moment. Ramona had sent him another text, an image. A screenshot from Lux's blog.

It was as follows:

Gay men are still men. They are one of us, until they are done with us. An ally can just as easily become an enemy. There are impostors amongst us, and they can most easily be found in those that possess male traits or qualities. These are members of the minority who wish to be part of the majority. They want to have their cake and fuck it, too. They will act feminine, or transition to the opposite sex, but they are fooling no one. They are not one of us.

I can think of one gay man in particular. A would-be writer who has formed an allegiance with a group of people with real problems. He is a hyena; a greedy creature content to sustain itself on the scraps of our labor. He thinks that, by being one of us, we will forget that he was always one of them.

In a famous psychology experiment, people were recruited to be both guards and prisoners, and they were encouraged by those involved to carry out those exact roles in a prison-like environment. Those who were guards did as we can expect all pig law enforcement to do, while the prisoners took their beatings. Some even sympathized with their captors. The gay man has taken his beating and aspires to be a guard. He has forgotten what it means to be a prisoner.

Women have raised this world. We have forgotten the value of eating our young.

There were tens of thousands of likes, thousands of comments.

Crying, Asher covered his mouth and swiped farther down Ramona's text to another message. It was from several hours ago, about when the killer had arrived, or perhaps shortly after it had vanished.

The second message read as follows:

Are you okay? Jesus Christ. Look now. She took it down.

The third message had arrived sometime in the witching hour. It read as follows:

If you're still awake, Lux wants us to get together. All of us. She said it's time for us to track down the killer.

After Lux's episode at the Grindout and the subsequent death of Ansel, the server who worked there, the augurs decided to move their operations from the coffee shop to the larger, but far less sexier safe space in the old, unused band room of Bitter Springs Junior High. Depending upon how one looked at it, to call the band room a safe space was fairly ironic. Being that it was an abandoned and relatively unsupervised gathering spot for horned-up high schoolers, it was only natural that, over time, it would turn into less of a place for people to discuss pertinent social issues, and more into a convenient location for people to get laid. Because of this, and because of teenagers' tendency to forsake even the most basic of hygienic practices, the walls of the band room were practically dripping with STDs.

It was an after-school special's wet dream.

Ramona was the first to arrive. She sat in the parking lot, in her car, hugging the steering wheel, as she watched through the dirty windshield the stragglers making their lonely marches across the campus. It was Friday. They should've been high-tailing it home. But she got it. Home was heartache. What was the rush? It wasn't going anywhere; at least, not until they did.

She could still see the both of them, her mother and father. Her mother, and how she used to pinch her stomach and her arms, the same way butchers used forceps to measure the thickness of meat. Her father, her father, and how he used to make inappropriate comments and jokes whenever an attractive girl passed the two of them in public. To understand her, he had tried to emasculate her.

Fenton arrived shortly thereafter and parked one space away from Ramona. He acknowledged her, and she him, but they stayed in their respective cars. He leaned into his armrest, covered his mouth with his hand; he breathed in the dish soap still sticky in the creases of his palm. It'd taken him a long time to wash the blood off his hands. His pants and underwear were taking their fourth tour of the washer and dryer back home. He'd dressed sharply to hide the fact he hadn't slept well these last few nights. Try as he might, he couldn't shake the feeling that something had been standing over his bed, watching him. When he had finally dozed off, he would immediately awake to a tingling sensation on the edges of his face, as if something had been stroking him.

He knew what it was, though. It was the mask he wore on his face. His body was pushing it out finally, the same way it would the deepest of childhood splinters. This had been a long time coming, but being back here at Bitter Springs Junior High had been the final shove he needed. This was the place where his two hard crushes and him sick of being picked last for everything had led to Fenton forsaking himself for the sake of them: Ramona, Lux, and to a lesser extent, Asher and Echo. It was his last-ditch effort to survive the killer at large by going back into the closet he'd never really come out of.

Ten minutes later, narrowly missing a teacher who looked like a nursing home escapee, Asher careened into the parking lot. Not seeing Ramona or Fenton, and yet seemingly drawn to them all the same, he double-parked behind them and immediately got out of the car. He shut the door as fast as he could, locked it even faster. His invisible stalker in the passenger seat caught the light as he caught a glimpse of it through the window. The killer had been with him this entire time.

Having had a brush with Death, it seemed Asher's mind had made up its mind about him living any longer. He hadn't slept; the only thing he'd eaten was the skin off his lip, and the only thing he'd drunk was the bile in his throat. He was sickly, in that numb haze of singeing aftertastes and bad jitters that followed sleepless sleepovers. The world seemed to be moving faster than he could keep up with. He was never meant to be an augur, and now it seemed he wasn't even meant to be here, on this earth. And yet he was. Why had he been spared when the others hadn't? Or had it been following them, too? Where had they gone wrong? What could he do to make this right? Would anyone else see it? Would anyone believe him, even if they could? Was it because he was gay? Or because he hadn't been gay enough? He scratched his chest through his shirt, raking the blisters with his nails. It felt as if he had the world's worst sunburn.

Caught at the light outside Bitter Springs Junior High, Echo stared at the other augurs in the parking lot from the road and wondered if they'd pieced it together yet. She was surprised to see Asher still alive. Lux had put up and deleted blog posts on each of them, Echo included, over the last few days, but Asher's had received the most attention. Lux's lambasting of men, gay and straight, had really resonated with a lot of other true believers out there. The community was spread too thin, Lux had said, and because of this, any justice they managed to raise meant next to nothing, because everyone had their hands in the pot. Echo had agreed. She always did. That was why they had gone to Maidenwood, to meet the Sisters' apostle. If Connor Prendergast hadn't wanted anyone to do that, then maybe he shouldn't have written it in his stupid, misogynistic book, *Black Macabre Occult,* or whatever the hell it was called.

Red to green—the stop light gave her the go-ahead, and Echo made a sharp left into Bitter Springs Junior High's parking lot. She nodded at Ramona and Fenton and parked between the both of them. Glancing in the rear-view mirror, she watched Asher for a couple of seconds as he stared into his car, eyes nearly bulging from his black-rimmed sockets. They, but him especially, had taken Lux's love for granted. They thought it would be easy, and maybe it had been, but things were different now. Extremity was the only way to trim the extremities from the gropers, the fondlers; the cat-callers, the leering; those who took advantage of the things they took for granted; raging hard-ons, soft snivelers; the cocks gathered at all the long tables, and all the cunts who'd willingly taken the short end of the stick. They'd all been there that night, in the black, with the Black, on the pavement, beside her. Hundreds of years of dehumanization and systematic discrimination had paved the path by which he found her and gagged her. Blinded, bleeding, she had called out, and her call had been heard. Until then, all she'd known were echoes of her own, catching on the indifference of the world around her, taunting her like an image in a mirror. Until then, but never again.

Echo took a deep breath and killed the engine. She turned to Lux beside her and said, "Ready?"

Lux, not looking up from her phone, took Echo's hand and squeezed it. Echo noticed there was still blood underneath Lux's fingernails, but didn't bother pointing it out. She wore it well.

Lux led the way into Bitter Springs Junior High, and the augurs followed after, first Echo, then Fenton. Asher was farther back, and noticing this, Ramona stopped and fell in beside him. He smelled ripe, like sweat and garlic, and he was going so slow that, if he went any slower, he'd be going back in time. And that might've been exactly what he was trying to do.

"Hey," Ramona whispered, "you okay?"

Asher didn't look at her on his left, but to something on his right. He side-stepped, bumped into her.

"Sorry," he said.

"It's about—" she waited until the others were farther ahead, "—Lux's post, isn't it?"

This time, he did look at her.

"She deleted it. I don't think she meant it."

Up by the Junior High's front doors, two nerds were leaning against the bricks. They'd said something to Lux.

"Why'd she write it, then?" Asher asked, a single tear in each eye barely clinging to their lids.

"I don't know. I'll talk to her." Ramona squeezed his arm. "Did something happen last night?"

Asher rasped as he breathed his foul breath into her face. "I'm good, girl," he said, smiling a pathetic smile.

"Fuck you." Ramona pinched her nose. "Smell like something the sea shit out."

Asher laughed, and then there were more tears in his eyes. "Can you see what's—"

The nerds kicked off the wall. Like sacks of raw dough, they ambled awkwardly towards the augurs, practically tripping over their sagging sweatpants.

"What'd we do wrong now, huh?" one of the nerds asked, grinning.

The other nerd shoved his hands into pockets and rocked back and forth on his feet. "Not all guys are bad."

"We don't all rape women."

"I don't… mansplain things."

"All we've ever done is be nice to girls."

The nerd with his hands in his pockets was suddenly struck with anger. "People like you make us feel like shit. Everyone reads your stuff at school—"

Lux beamed.

"—all the girls always talk about how bad guys are." The nerd wrinkled his nose. "Most guys haven't done anything wrong! We haven't."

Echo sighed. "Just because you don't do it, doesn't mean it doesn't happen."

Lux smiled, threw her arm around Echo, and planted a sloppy kiss on her lips. The nerds' anger gave way to surprise, and they walked off, shaking their heads, but looking back often, just to make sure they weren't missing out on anything else.

"Everyone loves a lesbian," Asher said, the words coming out with a sling of spit.

"Don't start," Ramona said. "Please." She squeezed his arm harder and stared at Lux as she disappeared into the building. "Please, don't."

A few furries were getting fresh with one another when the augurs came into the old band room and sent them packing with their tails between their legs.

"We have a lot of work to do," Lux said, taking her place at the head of the cheap, plastic table.

Echo and Fenton sat on opposite sides of her. Ramona grabbed a seat in the middle, while Asher sat across from Lux, at the farthest end. He turned, as if he wanted to be ready to get up at any moment. Small glimmers of light danced around him. The others, apparently, didn't think much of it.

"Asher," Lux said.

He gave her one eye's worth of attention.

"Are you okay?"

"Yeah." He frowned instead of smiling. Then, woodenly, like a total try-hard: "It's the room. Can feel all pre-pubescent pregnancies weighing down on me."

"Huh," Echo said, smirking.

"They give out condoms at the nurse's station to the guys. Can't be that bad," Fenton said, naïve as ever.

Ramona kicked Fenton's foot underneath the table. "Girls can get them, too," she said, playing her part as best as she could.

Lux cleared her throat. She pressed her elbows into the sticky soda stains that ran in rings around the table. The yellowed fluorescent light covers buzzed, making the bug carcasses collected inside dance. The bulbs blinked. Outside the abandoned band room, someone laid into a trumpet, blasting out a dooming note.

Eating up the theatrics so much her mouth was moving like an old woman tonguing peanut butter in her partials, Lux leaned in and said, "Who is the killer? They will be at the party, I'm sure of it. Who is the killer?"

Everyone looked to Fenton, their facts man, and so Fenton began. "A white, cisgender, over-privileged male who—"

"A woman," Echo interrupted.

"Yes," Lux said.

Ramona, Fenton, and Asher exchanged looks with one another, the color in each of their faces like the soda stains on the table—faint and sickly.

"A woman," Lux said, echoing Echo. "The killer is a woman, not a man. That is how they go unnoticed. She's defected to the other side. She's taking out the weakest of us, working her way up the food chain."

"Why?" Asher rumbled.

Lux's eyes shone. "Let's figure that out. Together. You're the only friends I have in this town. I know it. You know it. You're targets, for being who you are and for associating with me. I really do appreciate you. All of you.

"I know you've seen some of my blog posts lately. They've been pretty... militant. These deaths have had me thinking about things, re-assessing our mission statement and what we're trying to achieve. I think we created this killer." She paused for dramatic effect. "We were too inclusive. There are a lot of sick people out there. An asshole is an asshole."

Asher twitched. He gave her his full attention.

"Let's put our heads together. Let's figure out who the killer is."

Asher turned in his seat, scooted it closer to the table. Sweat beaded on his brow. He looked tense, the way dead things looked after being left out awhile. A stink rolled off him, as if the air had shifted and unearthed the rot within. It smelled of sea salt and sulfur, and the sweet, eye-watering reek of piss. A black spot spread out along his shirt, where it was pressed to his chest. And then another, and then another.

"A woman," he said, shifting his gaze to Fenton, the facts man. "A young woman."

"Or older," Fenton said. "Someone who could move around unnoticed."

"White," Ramona said. "Obviously."

"A young, white woman," Asher clarified. "Someone who knew the victims. Wouldn't look…" He stared to his left. "Wouldn't look suspicious."

"Twenty-five to thirty, I think," Fenton said. "Gender fluid, I think, and probably someone from our grade back in high school."

"Over-privileged," Ramona said. "If they're tearing people's faces off… they had to have learned that from somewhere. Probably reads a lot."

"I think she reads Lux's blog," Echo shouted over the piercing flutes from next door.

The augurs, unanimous in their surprise, drew their breaths and held them until their bodies made them start breathing again.

Lux remained silent.

But Echo did not. "After every blog post Lux made, someone died. You have a lot of people who follow you."

Lux nodded and said, meekly, "I do."

"A lot of people who look up to you, believe everything you say."

Lux's cheeks quivered as she resisted every urge to smile.

"Did you suspect?" Echo asked, her voice taking on an almost Hollywood starlet type of tone.

"Yes."

Asher twitched.

Fenton and Ramona closed their eyes, opened them again.

"I meant every word of what I wrote, but obviously, someone is trying to use me. They want to twist our goals to fit their own worldview."

Ramona said, "Why didn't you stop writing, then?"

"I won't be censored, not even by slaughter."

As if in slow motion, Ramona fell back into her chair. The rusted metal that kept it together whined, made a crunching sound, as if the impact of her had broken through the pubescent gunk that'd been holding it up, holding it back all these years. She felt all the "I don't knows" unspooling inside her brain. They pressed into its folds and formed the track on which a new thought could roar. And roar it did, deathly, violently, as the mechanisms inside her mind tried to derail it. She didn't want to hear it. It was all she could hear.

"Mentally, she has issues," Ramona said with trepidation.

Lux nodded, said, "Please. Tell us."

"She's… she has no empathy for others." Ramona tightened her jaw, and then pressed on. "She's self-righteous. She thinks her way is the only way. No one is as smart… as her. Narcissistic Personality Disorder. Sociopath" A shiver shot through her body. This was like spitting in the face of god.

"But I think she has an accomplice," Fenton said, stopping the awkward silence before it could start. "People have seen someone fleeing the crime scenes."

Ever since they had sat down, Fenton had felt the straps of his mask tightening around his head, digging into familiar grooves. He had wanted to shed it, shred it, and yet with a few prompts, he was back to wearing it proudly. It was too comfortable, too reliable. Now was his time to unveil himself, to show the others the impostor within the skin they'd grown to know, and hope and pray they'd accept him for who he was, even if who he was wasn't what any one of them wanted him to be. He knew where Ramona was going; he could tell by the pain in her voice she was flying too close to the sun and seeing the truth in its lying landscapes. The truth was important, but not if they were all but ashes in its hands. There had to be a better way.

"Accomplice?" Echo croaked, her cool composure coming off her in an avalanche of sweat. "Really?"

Ignoring Ramona's glare, Fenton said, "Yes. Yep. Supposed to be wearing weird clothes, like see-through plastic?"

"Guy or girl?" Echo asked.

"Don't be so mainstream," Ramona snapped.

"Didn't say." Fenton's heart was beating so fast he could hear it in his ears. "The blood they found at the crime scenes was contaminated, too. My source says it might've come from multiple people, not just the victims or the killer."

"Killers," Asher rasped.

"They may be wearing protective gear to avoid bloodstains on their clothing, or leaving prints and fibers," Lux said. "What was the sex? The gender?"

Fenton shook his head. "Male. Female. Both. Eyewitness testimony isn't very reliable."

Lux nodded and said to Asher, "You've been quiet. You're our social butterfly—"

Asher swallowed his revulsion as he felt the invisible killer's tentacle slide over the nape of his neck.

"—so what do you think? Who did she spend time with socially? Everyone is coming to the party tomorrow. If we can find her crowd, we can find her."

What did Asher think? It was written all over his face, and if these fuckers couldn't read it, well, then he'd tell them what he thought. He knew what Lux and Echo were doing, and he knew what Ramona and Fenton were so clearly trying not to do. He didn't know how this worked, or what the fuck this thing was that kept following him around, but he knew where it came from and why it had been let loose into their town. Lux called him an augur, but all these years he was nothing more than a glorified, gossipy bitch. She wanted to know what the killer was like, labels and all? He'd tell her.

"The killer is a white, twenty-two-year-old, over-privileged lesbian who spends most of her time alone or on the Internet." The words coming out so quickly they began to slur together. "She has friends, but they are more like pawns. She'd been bullied most of her life for being different, so now, anytime anyone is any different from her, she bullies them. If they're not like her, they're an affront to her. She is her beliefs. There's no separating the two. If one dies, they die together.

"No one ever took her seriously. The only time anyone ever listened was when she was pretending to be some anonymous person posing as a man on the Internet. Her parents never listened to her. They were always gone. She tried to tell them she was a lesbian, and she prepared herself for a big blow-out that never came. They didn't care. Hurting others is the only way she thinks she can make others listen.

"A guy took advantage of her. Salinger Stevens, I think."

Lux bared her teeth. Her nails dug into the table. Echo moved away from her, as if she was giving off too much heat.

"That was before... she knew who she was really attracted to," Asher said. "Or... she took advantage of him. Paul, too, from the Home and Garden. She says she's gender fluid, but I think she'll be anything to promote her brand. One time, her heart was in the right place, and maybe it still is..."

Asher felt the killer constrict its grip around his throat. For a moment, he even saw it—and it was like a distorted window through which he saw Lux and his reflection melded into one.

"But it's more than that. She wants a following. Other people like her. A cult of identity. She wants everyone to be dissected. No secrets. No surprises. If everyone is like her, then she'll know she was right all along."

Lux let out the faintest of laughs. Like a queen rising up from her council's table, she came to her feet, arms out, a gesture for the augurs to rise with her. Aside from Echo, they remained seated.

"Who is the killer then?" Lux asked, searching each of them for signs of betrayal. "Asher…" She swallowed hard. "Asher painted us a very vivid portrait. Are we in agreement?"

Ramona shrugged.

Fenton stared at his shoes.

Echo nodded.

Asher swished the spit around his mouth. It tasted of the sea.

"Then who is it? Who is the killer?" Lux leaned forward, pressing her hands to the table, like a general looking over a map of a battlefield. "We seem like we have it narrowed down. Who is it?"

Ramona didn't say anything.

Neither did Fenton, nor Echo.

"Do you know?" Lux said, staring at Asher, while her eyes glazed over. "Please, tell us."

Asher could feel the accusation in his throat. The words were there, fully formed, after such a long gestation. It made him sick to his stomach how badly he wanted to say them. But try as he might, he could not pass them onto his tongue. They wouldn't take. His sentence would be final. There would be no coming back from this, and he could not leave this place alone. Every one of them was a killer in their own way; the invisible creature beside him was the least of his worries. It would kill him quickly. They would destroy him and his reputation until he destroyed himself. He couldn't leave here alone. Alone was what had gotten him here in the first place.

Finally, Asher whispered, "I don't know."

Lux nodded, her face flickering both a smile and a frown. She straightened up, sized up the augurs, and threw one arm around Echo.

"Party tomorrow night at the wharf on the river. The place is rented out. You can see the wreckage of Brooksville Manor from there." She kissed the side of Echo's head. "It's a good place to rebuild."

At 6:00 PM, an hour and forty-five minutes before the party began, Asher got into his car and picked up Ramona from her apartment and Fenton from his parents' house. Neither of them had known they would be carpooling, and yet each of them had been dressed and ready to go, and out their doors before Asher even had a chance to honk his horn. It was one of those rare moments for the augurs were words weren't needed to know the future. The bond between them had been enough to show them what was to come.

"Lux is the killer," Asher said, his voice hoarse, almost gone; deprived due to sleep deprivation.

Fenton finished climbing into the car and closed the backseat door behind him. Ramona was there, too, on the opposite side. Asher had been insistent no one sit up front with him. It was almost as if he were saving it for someone else.

"Let's just fucking say it."

Fenton's neighborhood was so rich it made Asher's teeth hurt. He took off down the street, not watching the road, but his friends in the mirror, who still hadn't said anything.

"She is," he hammered. "And if she isn't, she's fucking getting someone to fucking do it fucking for her."

Ramona kicked at the fast food bags that blanketed the floor in the back. "What happened to you?"

Asher ignored her. "Fenton?"

"I'm not gay," Fenton blurted out uncomfortably. "I'm... not. I'm not at all."

"We know," Asher said.

Ramona gave Fenton a shrug.

"Ramona and I are gay," Asher said. "That's like a fox going into a hen house and talking about all the eggs it's laid."

Ramona snorted. "What the hell kind of simile—"

"Simile? Not a bad word choice for someone who only reads the nutritional facts on the back of snacks."

Ramona lunged forward. Her seatbelt went taut and caught her before her hands could close around Asher's glistening neck.

"You guys don't care I'm not gay?" Fenton's naivety was in full effect, but for the first time, it was legitimate.

"Jesus Christ, no." Asher looked at Ramona in his rear-view mirror. "I'm sorry. Fuck. This shit I've... and that's groovy you're straight, Fen. Doesn't really fucking matter. Still love you."

Fenton could feel the weight falling from his face; each layer of the mask peeling away. He smiled, said, "cool" like the most generic man to walk this Earth, and then: "Did you see Lux do it?"

"I saw the post—" The car slowed down as Asher absently took his foot off the gas, "—and then... something was in my house."

"What?" Ramona pulled the seatbelt aside, sat as far forward as she could. "Are you serious? The fuck? What? I was texting you. Why didn't you...?"

"I couldn't. It wasn't going to let me."

Fenton covered his mouth. "It?"

Asher nodded. "Don't know what it is. But it looked like you—" Could he tell them the truth? "It looked just like you said. I don't know if it's human or... I don't know. But it could've killed me, and it didn't. It just... left." He had to lie about that part. "As soon as she deleted the post about me, it... left."

Ramona was squeezing her hands shut so hard it was a surprise diamonds weren't dropping out of them. Just what the hell was Asher saying? Like a thief raiding a house, she tore the latches off the doors in her mind, hastily rooting through the remnants of coursework she hung on hooks like coats she might wear for the right occasion. Fenton dealt in facts, but he did it coldly; Ramona didn't know much, or so she'd convinced herself, but what she did know she carried around like trophies.

"Blood came out of my phone," Asher said, nearly winded by his confession.

Ramona stared at Fenton, while remembering not only what he'd said about the massive amounts of different blood at the crime scenes, but also the blood she'd seen on Zeke/Zoe's pants and the gore dripping from Ansel's phone in the library. Psychogenic? No, she wasn't her dad. She couldn't make that same mistake and transfer her bullshit onto this. That wouldn't make it make sense. It would just make it make sense to her.

Fenton cleared his throat and said, "Yeah, mine too."

The car lurched forward as Asher tapped the brakes. He sped back up as he changed lanes and headed for the highway.

"When?" he asked.

"Few days ago." Fenton took out his phone—there were red splotches across it; not stains, but shallow burn marks. "I know I should have said something. It seemed so... normal to me, though. Like when you're in a dream and even the weirdest things seem so ordinary. Like... of course there is blood coming out of my phone. Why wouldn't there be?"

Psychosomatic. Ramona tried that coat on, and it almost fit. Physical symptoms that manifested from psychological origins. Jesus, was she really going to believe what she was hearing? But psychosomatic didn't make sense. Fenton wouldn't lie, and she'd seen what she'd seen, so if there really was blood gushing out of everyone's phones, then it couldn't have been psychosomatic. Phones weren't a part of their bodies. And then, seeing the faded outline of her phone in her pocket, she laughed. It wouldn't have been there if it wasn't always there.

"Zoe/Zeke had blood on her pants when I saw her in the library. Ansel had blood coming out of his phone, too," Ramona said. "I saw him."

What were you supposed to do with facts that led up to fallacies? Ten minutes after his admitting he was straight, and here he was again, betraying himself for a place within the group. Nothing about these murders or the killer or killers or the omens involved made sense, but then again, as augurs, did they? They assigned meaning in broad strokes, categorized people with all the intricacies of a finger painting. They jumped from one conclusion to another; they never fell because they never failed. They supported each other and the truths they spewed so that they always landed softly. He saw where this car ride was going, and it wasn't just to the wharf.

Asher merged onto the highway. Going eighty past the sign that read sixty-five, he muscled his way into the farthest lane. The setting sun blasted the windshield with blinding light, but didn't faze him any. He could see past it now.

"If Lux is part of this," Ramona said, "then how?"

"Echo said she had posted about all of us, and deleted the posts later. She had posted about Ansel, Zoe/Zeke, and Paul, too. And I think she posted about Salinger, but deleted that one." Fenton was doing this for them, regurgitating the facts to feed their curiosity. He had to be indifferent. "Everyone she has posted about has died, or..."

Asher looked at him.

"Almost died."

"And blood. First comes the blood," Asher said, jumping into another lane. "Blood, and then the killer, like a shark."

"All the posts about the victims had a ridiculous amount of likes and comments," Ramona said. "Before yours got taken down, Asher, yours did, too."

"I never saw one about me," Fenton said.

"Me, neither," Ramona said.

"But I saw blood." Fenton rubbed his phone. "A little. She must have deleted it before anyone really read it."

"Must be nice." Asher, realizing how fast he was going, took his foot off the gas pedal and cruised. "If she deletes the post, the killer... goes away." He checked the passenger seat for its telling glint. "But if she leaves it up long enough... if enough people support it..."

"Is it like a hit?" Fenton gritted his teeth. "Is someone doing this for her? Why... why would she want to hurt us, though?"

"No, she's doing it," Asher said, the exit for the wharf a few miles away. "It's not human. The thing that was in my apartment wasn't human. She's doing it. They're doing it, the people that read her bullshit."

"Our bullshit," Ramona whispered, repulsed.

"I don't know how, but she's doing it," Asher said.

Everything they were saying finally caught up with Ramona. Scoffing, she said, "What... what the fuck are we... Lux is a witch? Is that...?"

"She's been called worse," Asher said. "I'm not saying I get it. Okay? Honey, I have... no fucking clue. But this isn't adding up in any normal kind of way." He flicked his turn signal to get off on the wharf's exit. "She's doing something she's not supposed to be doing. I don't know if she knows it or..."

"She knows it," Fenton said. "I think she was testing us yesterday in the meeting. I think she thinks we know and wanted to see what we would do."

Ramona's chest tightened. Spit got caught in her throat. How had it come to this? She'd known Lux ever since the fourth grade. Until freshman year of college, they'd still been sleeping over at each other's houses on a near weekly basis. They were best friends. Partners in crime. After everyone'd had their run at Ramona for her weight and exhausted every insult in the book, she had simply stopped existing to her classmates. Too fat to be attracted to and too serious to have fun with, she had been resigned to the back-row corner desks of the class-rooms and all the other places where sharp edges were formed and the forgotten ended up caught on them. The bowers of the cafeteria. The dirt patches behind the bleachers. The ends of buildings, farthest away from doors and opportunities. And that's where Lux had found her, and with Lux, she'd left them behind forever.

"She wanted to see if we would be loyal," Fenton continued.

How did it come to this? This feeling inside her? This stark empti-ness? This gnawing numbness? How long could someone be friends with someone until they were strangers again? She'd taken for granted how much each of them had changed; that is, she accepted without considering if she'd really accepted it. Maybe Ramona wasn't as smart as Fenton (she was certainly smarter than Asher), but was it possible she and Lux had reached their event horizon? That dark place where all the light cannot be seen and cannot follow? Talking about Lux as a killer made Ramona feel like she was killing her, and yet there was a certain satisfaction in the thought she might be rid of her. How long had they been fumbling in the dark like this, mistaking company for clarity?

"Then she knows what she's doing. Echo, too, maybe," Asher said.

Ramona's stomach sank. "She wanted us to die."

"She changed her mind," Fenton said.

"She still tried," Ramona said.

Fenton opened his text messages on his phone and went back to the text from Caleb. He read it aloud. "We need to talk. All of us. This is big. My buddy at the police station has a buddy at the lab where they're checking the evidence over. First off, said there was way too much blood at the crime scenes for the wounds inflicted. Second off, the lab nerd said there's something wrong with the blood. Said it's not just the victims' or the perp's. Said the blood was from a shitload of different people. Like… hundreds. Maybe thousands."

Asher wheeled the car down the ramp. It winded over the outskirts of Bitter Springs, before reaching the warehouses that lined up and down the river that ran between here, Brooksville, and Bedlam. "That from Caleb Jones?"

"Parthenogenic," Ramona blurted out. "Something from nothing. She's… whatever Lux is doing… she can…"

"It's not nothing," Fenton said. "The blood. The belief, loyalty, whatever you want to call it. I bet if they tested it and had all the right samples…"

"It would match everyone who liked and commented on the posts," Asher said, coming off the ramp. He pulled the car over into one of the warehouses' parking lots, parked, and twisted around to face the augurs. "Their blood on our hands." He laughed, stared into the passenger's seat. "Shouldn't it be the way other goddamn way around?"

Ramona took out of her cell phone. She hadn't noticed it before, but it was there, around the charger port: small flecks of dried blood. "Not if they think we deserve it."

Fenton said, "Not if Lux thinks everyone's forcing her hand to do it."

"Salinger, Zoe/Zeke, Ansel, Paul… us… it's our fault for being impostors." Asher slumped down in his seat and dug the heels of his palms into his eyes. "Fuck me sideways, we're not anything but ourselves."

"Aren't we?" Ramona stared out the window, watched the sun slip behind the clouds. "Or maybe we just stopped being her. Like you said, Ash. It's a cult of identity."

"We should call the police," Fenton said.

Asher laughed. "And get her on what? Cyber bullying? She'll just end up with more exposure, more groupies that'll want to suck her dick, then."

He pulled down the collar of his shirt and showed them the festering stretch of boils that'd wept across his neck.

"Fuck," Ramona said, snapping out of her daze.

Fenton covered his mouth. "That smells infected."

Asher covered himself up. "It was going to take my face off. That's what it was going to do next. I've been keeping to myself but… fuck, it looked like a… fucking jellyfish… thing. I know it sounds crazy, but that's what I saw. It wasn't her. But it was there for her. And… yeah… Lux has done a lot of good… and we have, too. I feel like… in some ways… we've brought Bitter Springs out of the stone age and shit… but… whether she knows what she's doing or not… or even cares… if she doesn't stop… I don't think it will or can… or… I don't know.

"But she was testing us, like Fenton said. I don't know if we passed her dumbass… but Echo looked fucking smug, didn't she?"

Ramona and Fenton nodded.

"She was testing us… and… and now she's having a party? Getting everyone together? She's got something planned." He turned away from them, settled into his seat, and took the car out of park. "I want to be wrong. Lord baby Jesus, do I." He looked at the passenger's seat again. "We got to catch her. I don't know what we'll do when we do. Call the police? Fucking tackle her? I don't know. But I love our community. Even the lesbians."

Ramona huffed, kicked the back of his seat.

"If we don't do anything, then we're just as bad as her. As bad as all of them. All the fucking patriarchy and the misogynists and homophobes and the little bitches that package our image and sell it and… Can we do this?" He didn't look back, but he asked it again. "Can we do this? Please? If we're wrong, then we're fucking crazy and wrong, and that's fine. That's fine with me. But that thing… or Lux… they're going to come back for us, eventually." He sniffed his nose and started to cry. "I'm so fucking sick and tired of not being enough of something. I'm so fucking sick and tired of giving a shit about it, too."

Ramona slipped her hand through the gap in the headrest and pressed her hand to Asher's cheek.

"I wish I wasn't straight right now," Fenton said, laughing and shaking his head.

Asher wiped his nose on his sleeve. "I wish it didn't matter." He started the car up and headed out of the warehouse. "Put a magnifying glass on anything long enough, and the light will always find something to burn."

The Wharf was as much as of a wharf as it was also a restaurant. Since the foundation of Bitter Springs back in the 1800s (then known as Tranquil Springs), the wharf served an important point on the tri-county river where goods could be loaded and unloaded between Tranquil Springs, Brooksville, and Bedlam, and migrant workers would show up to shore up their failing farms and families in the counties and states north and south of here. As time went on, the wharf expanded, and multiple berths were built to accommodate the increased naval presence. Behind it, warehouses were erected, and they changed hands more times than those hands could count, until the great wars came in the 1900s, and they were transformed into munitions factories. With death on the other side of the world, life in Tranquil Springs couldn't have been any better.

But then the wars ended, and the soldiers were sent home. They came back haunted, possessed by the creatures they had to become to survive the battles they fought and still fought in the theaters of their minds. Many were kind, many were quiet, but those that were not sought violence and bred it when it wouldn't bear. The munitions factories became bars and brothels, and criminal elements more reactionary than any on the periodic table settled in and set up shop. The Wharf fell into disrepair; its berths broke and turned in with a blanket of dirt on the riverbed. Prostitutes and contraband began to be loaded onto the ships. Brooksville and Bedlam were known as nice places to live, until the waters had turned bitter in Tranquil Springs and corrupted everything they'd touched.

Eventually, the warehouses and the Wharf itself were abandoned, and the pimps and self-proclaimed drug lords moved south. Migrant workers were replaced by the migrant poor, many of whom were the men who'd survived the wars. The upper class pretended this part of the riverfront didn't exist, while middle class missionaries made frequent trips there, to silence their guilt and stuff bags of socks like presents under the homeless' trash bag pillows. It wasn't until the lower-class quarantine broke that Bitter Springs' politicians turned their attentions to the riverfront. Outrage had made them swivel their chairs around to the issue, but it was the corporations that came calling that made the mayor and his council motivated to do something about the issue.

With gentrification, the Bitter Springs elect set off a bomb that sent the lower-class and homeless scurrying like rats across the river into Brooksville. The warehouses were converted into small, disposable, flavor-of-the-month shops with expensive apartments above them. And the wharf transitioned from a historical hellhole into the Wharf, a bar and grille that, as of two years ago, had dropped the grille part of its name, as the cooks hadn't been able to keep up with the home-grown, cage-free, cruelty-free, microscopic portions of food that sounded more like a cafeteria dare a than full-course meal (grilled snail served on river rocks with a light coating of shredded seaweed and a side of paste). Expectedly, there was an outrage, as there always was, but in the end, the young, rich yuppies that'd moved in to or frequented the riverfront didn't mind. The less money they spent on food meant more could be spent on drinks, which worked out for everyone, as most people hated one another, and it was only through alcohol, selfies, and the latest crowdfunded activity that they could find common ground.

In the Wharf, the minorities were the majority; or rather, the majority of the minority stayed the majority. The young and rich were the only ones who could afford, let alone stomach, the scene. The lower-class gays and lesbians had their own haunts on the edges of the river-front, where the old warehouses met the new whorehouses. For a place that that was the antithesis of everything Lux supposedly believed in, it was surprisingly, but not all that surprisingly, her favorite place to spend her time. She was close with the owner, closer than Echo liked, and her business brought business. There was good money to be had from social justice. Anything could be bled if you squeezed it hard enough.

There was also something else about the Wharf Lux undoubtedly enjoyed. From its docks, one could see, down and across the river, the ruins of Brooksville Manor, the back half of the building jutting out of the water like a stone fin. It was even visible at night, because the construction crews left their lights burning through the dark hours, to scare away squatters and thrill-seekers. It didn't matter what the time of the day was, because from the Wharf, everyone could see society's failing. There was going to be a performance art piece about the collapse next weekend. The show was already sold out.

As Asher, Ramona, and Fenton pulled into the Wharf's parking lot, it became obvious there were far more than eighty people at Lux's party. One-hundred-and-fifty to two hundred, maybe, but not eighty. Every parking spot was taken, and every meter on the street working overtime. People had parked their cars in the grass and on the sidewalk, and some were even braving being towed from the heavily monitored lots of the shops and apartments. They had come out in skinny-jeaned and flannelled droves. They might not have all been there for Lux, but something told the augurs that wouldn't last long.

Having decided he had more important shit to care about, Fenton cruised the parking lot until he spotted some hoopty held together by tape and prayers and parked directly behind it. Whoever owned it wouldn't be moving it again until the sun came back up.

"Okay," Asher said, getting out of the car, Ramona and Fenton quick to do the same. "Let's just lie low and keep an eye on things."

"No new posts," Ramona said. She'd had Lux's blog pulled up. "Not even about the party."

"I don't think she'd be caught dead inviting anyone to a party," Asher said, leading them through the lot to the Wharf.

"It might be hard to stay together," Fenton said. "She always divides us up to cover more ground at these things."

The closer they got to the Wharf, the more people they began to see lingering in the dark, chatting, taking pictures of themselves, or occasionally, digging for China in each other's pants. Some smiled at the augurs, while others gave them anemic nods. Every letter from LGQTBIA appeared to be in attendance tonight, though none of the augurs would necessarily publicly admit that, as it was dangerous to assume someone asexual when they were actually quite sexually active, as long as someone could appreciate their appreciation of scantily clad video game characters. Everyone here and in the Wharf ahead wore their labels on their sleeves; the only problem was the words were often written in a language only they could understand.

The augurs passive-aggressively commented their way through the throngs of people clogging up the stairs to the dining area of the Wharf. Inside, people were so tightly packed they were spilling drinks down the backs of those in front and beside them. Over the speakers fixed to the supports, non-threatening pop music thumped out repetitive lyrics about the price of ass these days, like there was a stock market for that kind of thing.

Ramona got on her tippy-toes and, pushing down on Asher's shoulder for support, searched their scene for signs of its leader.

"I don't see…"

"Um, excuse me!" A woman said sharply.

Fenton turned around to find a twenty-something woman unironically wearing a United States flag shirt and shorts patterned with sickles and hammers standing behind him. Her arms were folded over her breasts, and she squeezed them tighter against herself when Fenton noticed this, as if she thought he was leering at her.

"Oh," he said, "sorry. I didn't see you standing there."

The woman squinted and pushed past him, never lowering her arms from her chest.

Behind that woman, a second emerged. She wasn't wearing anything special—just jeans and a band's shirt. She appeared to be transitioning, most likely from male to female.

"Sorry," the second woman said, her voice husky, "Zhe's been terrible lately."

The first woman spun around, the red, white, and blue of her shirt turning her into a patriotic tornado, and belted, "Don't listen to zher. Rodney—" that must've been the second woman's name, "—don't embarrass us. I don't need zhim—" she pointed to Fenton, "—or zher—" she pointed to some random redhead in the crowd, "or anybody else ruining my night tonight."

She huffed, finally lowered her arms, revealing the outline of her bra behind her shirt. In the stars and stripes of the American flag, Fenton could see she'd stuffed her bra. And by the smell of it... it smelled like hamster shavings.

"Zhim? Zher? Zeriously?" Rodney dropped her jaw and rolled her eyes. "Zhem and zher have nothing to with any of this!"

Fenton looked at Ramona and started to laugh. It sounded like two vampires fighting about who'd get to drink the blood next. No wonder people never took them...

Echo came out of nowhere and ushered them into the Wharf and into a corner, behind where the busser stood.

"Hey, oh good, hey." She smiled and let out an exasperated sigh. "Where were you guys? I thought you weren't going to show. Lux was so worried."

Asher's boils began to throb. "We got stuck in—"

Echo cut him off. "Ramona and Fen, can you do some meet-and-greet?"

Ramona stammered.

Fenton said, "Sure," without even really thinking about what he was agreeing to.

"Lux asked if you could be our DJ, Ash," Echo said. "This music sucks."

Asher snorted. "Of course, she did."

Echo pointed at the stairs that led up the second floor. "Lux is over there somewhere. She'll... tell you what she wants."

A couple of meatheads meandered by and gestured for Asher to follow after them.

"Sorry, he's mine tonight," Echo said awkwardly, shooing them off.

Asher said, "I..."

But again, Echo interrupted. "I forgot all the stuff in my car. I got some lights, and my phone, I think, fell between the seats. Can't find it. Can you help me?"

Ramona and Fenton shook their heads, but Asher mouthed "It's fine," and let Echo lead him back out of the restaurant.

Following Echo down the stairs and into mosquito-laced dark, Asher couldn't recall the last time he'd actually been alone with her. They all had their relating Lux back to the sun thing going on, but there was some truth to the idea that people who orbited her the closest tended to burn up the fastest. Lux was covetous, and Echo loved to be coveted. These days, given how much Lux entrusted to her, Echo was less of a moon and more a star. Something to be stoked. And as Asher trailed after Echo through the parking lot, he realized how well Lux'd groomed her. Echo was the ideal the augurs had failed to achieve.

"How are you, Asher?"

"Alright," he said, checking the parking lot for signs of the killer. His pocket was dry. That was a good sign. "Lux's killing it lately."

Echo looked over her shoulder. "With her get-togethers? Yeah. My car's just over here."

Echo started walking faster, towards the end of the lot, where a few feet from the cars, the wharf was sectioned off with guard rails, to prevent anyone from driving into the river below. She raised her keys and pressed the button on them. The car at the farthest end, right against the guard rail, blinked its brakes. She hit another button and the trunk clicked, and then rose up slowly. The brake lights went out. He heard something splash against the cement.

Thinking he had a text message, Asher reached into his pocket, but his phone wasn't there. Cold sweats in the hot night. His boils breathed their rank perfume. He tried his other pocket and came back only with lint and a receipt for fast food. He spun around, glanced back the way they'd come. No one was nearby, and he couldn't see his phone anywhere.

"Shit," Asher patted himself, like the police officer he'd once wanted to be. "Shit."

Echo, almost to her car, turned around, grinning. "What's wrong?"

"I can't find… my fucking phone."

"I bet you left it in the car. Here, help me drag this stuff out of the trunk and I'll help you find it."

Asher wandered towards her, but he wasn't looking at her. He was focused on his peripherals, where he could've sworn he'd seen a re-fraction of light. He tried to sniff the air, but it wasn't any good. The river always smelled like sulfur.

Lowering her voice, Echo said, "I think we need to have a talk with Lux."

Asher's attention snapped onto Echo. "Why?"

"She said some nasty things about all of us on her blog. I know she deleted it, but... that doesn't mean it didn't happen. I worry about her." She leaned against her car. Something sloshed nearby. "All these murders have her all messed up."

"She's always been messed up," Asher said, going to her.

"You know, when we have sex, she doesn't do anything for me? I have to go down on her for hours. I know that's probably too much information—"

Asher stepped up beside the car and looked into the trunk.

"—but I feel like I do so much for her—"

What the hell? Maybe it was because it was so dark that his depth perception was off, but what the hell was wrong with Echo's trunk? It looked completely shallow, except there was a phone in there... and... how the hell was it floating?

"—and she takes it for granted."

The phone's screen turned on. The trunk wasn't shallow, but filled completely with blood. On the screen was Lux's blog, and a new post. There wasn't much to it. Just a picture of Asher, and below that, a poll with one word. It read: "Impostor?"

Yes and no were the only options. Over ten thousand had voted yes. A little less than thirty had voted no.

Shaking, Asher looked up at Echo.

She said, "How can you call yourself tolerant when you routinely insult lesbians and individuals with mass consumption issues?"

"I... I..."

"Exactly," Echo said. "It was us or them. And you choose I."

The blood exploded out of the trunk and crashed into Asher. It flooded his eyes and mouth, and filled up his ears. It smelled and tasted of sea salt and sulfur, and he could hear thousands of voices inside his skull, chanting. Spinning, he dug at his eyes and vomited blood and chunks of food all over his feet.

When he was able to see again, he saw it. The killer. In a blur, it sprung like a spider from the dripping trunk and latched onto him.

Asher screamed, and the killer shoved several thick tentacles down his throat. Muffling his cries, they winded down his esophagus into his stomach, and everything they touched erupted with a horrible burning sensation. Asher heaved, choked by the limbs stirring inside him. He threw his fists into the killer, but its other tentacles took his arms and bent them back until they broke.

Asher bawled. He sank his teeth sank into the tentacles. Hot bolts of pain drove into his gums and sliced through his nerves. The killer drove its bell-shaped trunk against his face. In that gelatinous bulb, he saw not his face, but hundreds, thousands of other faces, laughing at him, sneering at him. He didn't know any of them, and yet he recognized all of them.

The killer made itself heavier and heavier. Asher backpedaled; he hit the guard rail. Smaller, hooked limbs wound out of the creature's torso and found Asher's face. They pierced the skin around his eyes and mouth, and behind his ears.

Asher tried to speak, to beg for help, but the tentacles down his throat ballooned outwards, so that he couldn't breathe.

"Once all the impostors are unmasked, they'll never trick us ever again," he heard Echo say.

The killer's hooked limbs went taut and then, slowly, it began to peel. The skin of Asher's face ripped away from the muscle. A curtain of blood poured down his face as his forehead separated from the meat underneath. He shook and moaned, but the killer would not, could not, stop. Loose flesh flapped around his eyes, near his jaw. The air got into the tender, glistening patches and called forth greater agonies. He could hear the skin pulling away with stomach-churning clarity—the subcutaneous fat coming apart with sticky, snapping sounds.

By the time his face was loose enough that he could feel it bunching up on his lips—the thick of his cheek prickling his tongue with its sweaty, coppery heft—Asher went into shock and then, seconds later, died.

The killer handed Echo the hunk of flesh that had been Asher's face, and threw his lifeless corpse into the river.

By friends and family, Asher would be remembered as having died tragically at a young age. For the weeks and months and even years to come, they would recall his big personality and his even bigger eating habits. His mother would be steadfast in her assertion he could've made it as a writer one day, while his father would throw-in all the work Asher had done for the gay community. A man Asher would've married would end up married to a woman instead, and the son they would've adopted years down the line would stay in foster care, to be beaten and abused.

By the Internet, Asher would be remembered as a cisgender, black, depressed, self-harming, fat-shaming homosexual who pretended to be gender fluid as a way by which to garner sympathy and quick fucks from otherwise uninterested parties. His writings would be unearthed by anonymous sources and reinterpreted to support the narrative that Asher hated women, especially lesbians, because they stole attention and resources from gay men. As an overweight man, Asher's interests in nerdy activities would have him eventually labeled as a neckbeard that spent most of his time stuffing his face and masturbating to violent porn. He would be outed as an impostor and an informant to the straight community. Rumors would spread that he had AIDS, and supposed former lovers and flings would state Asher had been abusive towards them. He would be held up as a shining example of how gay men are not supposed to be by the vocal minority of militant feminists and white knights abroad. The Internet would forget Asher by the weekend, but his death would be one coal after another in the fires of outrage that would burn for validation for years to come.

Ramona and Fenton stood in front of the table beside the stairs to the second floor and, together, shouted over the music, "She wants us to do what?"

Sitting at the table, behind a battlefield of fallen glasses and puddles of swill, sat Jessie and Cole, a small, wooden box that held index cards between them. The two looked three sheets to the wind. Jessie's eyes were glazed over, going different directions, while Cole kept stroking and smirking at the rope that blocked off the stairs, as if he were trying to get digits from it.

"Sit here," Jessie slurred, "and when it's the right time, r-read the next c-card."

Cole gave the rope a nod—clearly, they'd come to some sort of agreement—and joined in the conversation. "Yeah." He dug around in his crotch under the table.

"Fucking hell. You two are blasted," Ramona said.

"Hiroshima-style," Jessie squeaked. She turned her hands into guns and shot at them. Then, to Fenton, said, "Sorry."

"Sorry, my dick got in the way." Cole laughed and heaved a microphone onto the table.

An ear-splitting screech shot through the Wharf from the speakers on the walls. Those inside crouched and covered their ears and started hurling insults and peanuts at Cole.

"Read into this," he said, turning the microphone off. He opened his mouth, trying to catch some nuts. "And... goodbye."

Sprier than he looked, Cole backed out of the chair, knocking it to the ground, and melted into the crowd.

Jessie, too drunk to get up, simply reached over to the nearest table, grabbed an empty stool, and transplanted herself onto it. "I'll stay... here. Make sure you... jokers... do it..." She fell asleep. And then woke up. "Do it right."

Fenton glanced back at the speakers on the walls.

Ramona noticed and did the same.

They both turned to the Wharf's entrance and searched it for signs of Asher and Echo. Fenton thought he'd seen Echo, but it was just a scene girl with gauges in her ears large enough to have a picnic on who'd walked in. Ramona could've sworn she'd spotted Asher, but it was actually Billy, a gay man who wore colors so loud they wouldn't even let him into the library.

Two thick basics that reeked of pumpkin spice pushed past Ramona and Fenton, grabbing at each of their asses as they passed.

"Hey, get the fuck off!" Ramona cried, forgetting about Asher.

Fenton shook his head and waved them off. He went around the table and sat where Jessie had sat. He grabbed the small, wooden box and took out a handful of index cards. There were names on each of them, and times. The ones that'd already been called were crossed out. And looking at the clock over the entrance, they were supposed to be calling a name here in the next five minutes.

"What is this?" He held up the next card—Gulliver Grandin, his contact.

"Lux's got some... exclusive shit going on... upstairs." Jessie closed her eyes and leaned so far forward, Ramona had to rush to push her upright. "You know. You... should know. You're her besties." She burped, and then licked her lips at the semi-decent looking dude who she'd noticed a few feet away. "Some big... to-do. It's... whatever. Cole and me were just... filling in... since you niggers were... late."

"Jesus fucking Christ." Ramona came around the table and took

Cole's seat. "Jessie, is Lux upstairs right now?"

Jessie slid off the stool. "She's in the… kitchen. She's… going to make some… big entrance. Just… keep sending them up. She said… she'd get you… soon." She waved her hand and then disappeared into a fog of candy-flavored vaporizer.

Fenton leaned into Ramona and said, "This might not be a bad way for Lux to throw together a ton of alibis."

Ramona wrung her hands until the itch of mutiny left them.

"If we do our part, she might give us everything."

"Did we fuck up?" Ramona checked the entrance for Asher. "Should we have been watching Echo?"

"They might need equipment for upstairs." Fenton picked up the microphone. Before switching it on, he said, "Text Asher."

"Yeah." Before reaching into her pocket, Ramona grabbed the box. "How many names did they go through already?" She flipped through one crossed out name after the other. The party had started about thirty minutes ago. Fifteen names had been selected since then. "Damn."

Fenton turned on the microphone. Nervously, he rattled, "Gulliver Grandin," and then quickly turned the mic off.

"Fuck, where's my phone?"

Fenton stared at Ramona. "What?"

"I can't…" She turned her pockets inside out. "Fuck. I don't have it."

Fenton reached into his pockets, too. His phone was missing as well.

"Dude." Ramona stood and stared out into the crowd. "What the fuck? Who lifted our—"

Out of the wall of designer clothes and carefully maintained grunge emerged Gulliver Grandin. He was wearing a sharp looking suit and a hickey on his neck. Without a second thought, he went to the stairs, moved the rope aside, and started up them.

"Gulliver," Fenton called. "What's going on up there?"

Gulliver threw up his left hand and shouted, "Bye bitches!"

Ramona slumped into her seat. She grabbed the next index card in the box and gasped.

Fenton, still focused on Gulliver, watched him walk the top of the stairs, where he disappeared into the stacks of tables and chairs.

From the speakers, a new song blared. Thudding bass and a crisp snare with some awkwardly placed, looping sample from an obscure '80s movie. Over it, the rappers repeated money and family ad nauseum, as if they'd had a stroke mid-recording. One rapper was a white, art school dropout, the other an Asian refugee. It was a big hit with the Wharf's crowd.

"Fen, what is she doing here?"

Ramona slipped him the index card. The name it bore was Geneva, and she was due for her appointment with the Light in the next two minutes.

"Was she even invited?" Fenton clicked on the microphone, muffled it against his shirt.

"Let's not kid ourselves, not everyone is here for Lux."

"Does Lux know that? We need to get up there." He pressed the microphone to his mouth and shouted, "Geneva!"

"No. No thanks," a woman cried.

Only a few feet away, in the center of the circle that'd formed around her, was Geneva. She'd had a last name once, but her fame on the Internet helped her ascend beyond such trivial things. Fenton and Ramona had no choice but to be familiar with her. She was a cisgender, straight, white woman; age twenty-four; average Body Mass Index; offensively normal. According to Lux, she was over-privileged, but most agreed she came from a modest background. If Lux was the sun, then Geneva was the moon; her opposite and her equal. Lux may have shone brighter, but Geneva's pull was greater. She could make oceans move, whereas Lux could only dry them out.

Geneva stomped her way to the table, shaking her head as she did so. "I'm not here for whatever she has planned. I'm not here to do any social 'work.' I just want to hang out and get a buzz." She smiled. "You two are too good for her."

Ramona shrugged.

Fenton gave her a subtle nod.

"Sorry social 'work' isn't fun for you anymore," Ramona snapped.

"Is that what you're having right now? Fun?"

Fenton groaned. "It does get old."

"I'm putting together a fundraiser for the victims next weekend," Geneva said, "not recruiting an army." And with that, Geneva turned away from the table and slipped back into the center of her inner circle.

Ramona punched the table, and sprung to her feet with the impact. "Fuck it. Let's go up there."

"An army?" Fenton reached over and undid the rope blocking the stairs. "Wait, look. There's Echo."

As the smell of rain hit her, Ramona turned to where Fenton was pointing. A dark, hooded figure was slinking along the edges of the room, moving in and out of the human roadblocks that stood in its way. Fenton said it was Echo, but no, that wasn't Echo. It was Asher. He was in a rain slicker, holding something underneath it.

Thunder rocked the Wharf. The lights flickered. Everyone lost their shit for a moment, and then laughed hysterically.

"That's Asher, dude. What the hell's he doing?" Ramona started after him, but Fenton inched past. "What are you doing?"

"I'll grab him," Fenton said. "He looked bad, like Echo might've…"

A table and several chairs fell over on the second floor. Ramona backed towards the stairs, trying to get a better look at what was going on up there.

"I'll get him," Fenton said. "Get up there before Lux comes back."

Ramona said, "Okay," and took off up the stairs, her self-diagnosed ADHD in full-effect.

Fenton didn't like being separated from Ramona, but he had a better chance of running into Lux this way, and if he could do that, he could keep her distracted long enough with his confession of heterosexuality to give Ramona time to figure out what was happening on the second floor.

Trailing Asher, Fenton pressed himself into the human waves that swelled and crashed all around him. It wasn't intentional, but as he ducked and weaved and went sideways through the crowd, he found himself auguring everyone that he went past. White male. Black, no African American, no black lesbian. Able-bodied. Hearing-impaired. Nerd. Dweeb. Neckbeard. Over-privileged catholic. Brave Muslim. He saw scars on wrists and assumed self-harm. He spotted an overweight woman standing by herself and presumed asexuality. A hipster with a moustache large enough that he had to go sideways through doors triggered Fenton's misogyny meter. A college girl with a Brooksville University tank top had the voice of Lux whispering into his skull that she was a slut. A zhe. A zhe. Quirky white trash with barely eighteen written all over them. A bald man at a table by himself, nursing a glass and staring at nothing in particular, probably planning his next nightly rape.

A business woman sitting at the bar, her pants suit hanging low in the back, probably scoping the scene for easy money. An Asian. A Latino. Latinx. A drag queen reaping laughs, smashing their cheap heels into all their, no Lux's, efforts to promote equality for the transgendered. Cisgender. Queer. A non-binary punk forging a new link in the chain of sexuality by rocking a yellow star-shaped badge on their jacket— victimsexual. Two gays. An African American, no Black, no African American with a cowboy hat. And then, in a mirror on the wall, some asshole: Him: Fenton.

Fenton called out to Asher as he slipped down the hall towards the bathrooms, but Asher didn't stop. Lubricated with sweat, Fenton squeezed past the last few tables and the server serving them. He hurried down the hall, barely catching a glimpse of Asher as he went into the women's bathroom.

Fenton looked around to make sure no one was watching him—it was cute, he realized, that he thought anyone would be—and followed after Asher.

There was nobody else in the women's bathroom except for Asher, or at least, who he'd mistaken for Asher. Her back was turned, but even then, he could tell it was Echo. The rain coat was down around her ankles, and there appeared to be some discoloration around the sides of her face.

"Echo?"

Fenton looked at the lone mirror in the bathroom—a small piece of smudged glass—and crept closer and closer—

"Hey, Echo, are you... what's—"

—until he could see her profile in it.

On her face was another face. A black face. Asher's face. Stretched and held in place by pieces of duct tape. Watery trails of blood ran down her chin and neck, as if she'd taken a bite out of some strange fruit. She looked into the mirror, too, and Fenton could tell she was smiling behind his friend's ragged lips. She liked what she saw. Spinning around, that smile beneath Asher's flesh turned from joy to hunger, and Fenton knew she wanted more.

"I walked right in here, and nobody said a thing." More blood cascaded down Echo's heated skin. "Right under their noses. An impostor posing as an impostor. Ha."

Fenton's body shook violently. His mind was desperate to reconcile the sight of Asher's face over Echo's own, but it was no use. Every time it did, his skull swelled and his gut churned, and years-worth of memories begged, no, pleaded to differ. Asher was dead. They had killed him. That was the truth of things now, and Echo was the lie masquerading as otherwise. He had to stop her.

Fenton ran at Echo. Two feet from her, and outside the bathroom, someone belted out a Scream Queen wail. He stopped. Over the howling came words, just as loud. "Are you hurt?" and "Blood?" and "Oh my god, where is all this blood coming from?"

Echo laughed so hard the duct tape that kept Asher's ear fixed to hers came off. "Dumb trust fund baby, I told her to dump your phones in here."

Fenton remembered the two basic bitches that smelled of pumpkin spice, and how they'd gotten all handsy as they pushed past him and Ramona.

"Doesn't matter." She pointed behind Fenton. "Hate finds a way."

Fenton didn't turn around. He didn't need to. Before he knew it, he was on the ground, on his back, staring into a bulbous, marbled orb—captivated by the captive audience within. Each face inside the orb was as small as a speck of salt, and they were elevated by roiling plumes of dark smoke. He could feel their hate and see its discharge; throughout the orb, veins in the shape of sentences ushered along an uncanny liquid that triggered every painful, shameful memory within Fenton's shrinking mind. He could feel the hate of thousands coursing through his arteries, picking him apart like ants at a picnic; so as to be taken back as easy to digest tributes to their faceless, nameless queen.

The killer's bell-shaped body split open and hundreds of pale fingers shot forth and clamped down onto Fenton's arms and legs; hands and feet; chest and neck; ass and genitals. The fingers pinched his skin and broke through, teasing out red rivulets. Between his legs, he could feel the greedy digits forcing their way inside him, and then stopping. They didn't know what to make of the layout. He hadn't either, and now it didn't matter.

Pinned beneath a nightmare, Fenton no longer found comfort in reason. He dipped his head back, his eyes meeting Echo's within Asher's sockets, and spouted, "You won't get away with this!"

Echo laughed at his last words. "Did Lux teach you nothing? Feelings Trump facts. Every time."

Silently, gracefully, the killer pushed itself off Fenton. The pale fingers drove into him, through layer after layer of skin, blood, veins, and arteries, and hooked their nails into the musculature spasming across his body. Precisely, effortlessly, the killer tore Fenton's flesh off in one uninterrupted sheet. Blood exploded across the bathroom in every direction. Echo took the gory blast without blinking, her arms and legs spread. Behind her, on the wall her body had blocked from the spray, was the outline of her, like an angel left in snow.

The killer dropped Fenton's skin at Echo's feet, on top of her rain coat. She smiled and started to get dressed.

By family and former professors, Fenton would be remembered as having died horribly at a young age. For the weeks and months and years to come, they would recall his quietness, and how incredibly intelligent he was. His mother would seek retribution on the augurs and blame herself for not having seen this coming sooner. His father would disappear into his work and think of the procedures and if they could have, in some way, saved his child; he would remember things Fenton used to say and wonder if they meant more; unfinished sentences, and small moments of bonding—laughing at a bad a movie, long drives on summer nights—the both of them outrunning sleep with '70's rock on the wind. Fenton would have gone on to be a prominent speaker for intersexed individuals. He wouldn't have married, but he would've dated often, and those he might've loved, for all their fights and incompatibility, would think of him fondly later. He would not have been remarkable, but he would have been something.

By the Internet, Fenton would be remembered as a transsexual Asian with Autism and Gender Dysphoria who displayed sociopathic tendencies due to his high intelligence and ability to read and manipulate social situations. Many would claim that Fenton had originally been the killer due to his inability to cope with whether or not he wanted to undergo sex reassignment surgery, and his reported belief that he was sparing those from a life as troubled as his own. Former classmates would recall how he used to leer and do vaguely scary things when no one was looking. Rumors would spread that he was blackmailing others in return for his services as a snitch as well as a financier. Gulliver Grandin would write a video diary about his interactions with Fenton and how he was forced to share confidential information with him from Bitter Springs' police department. Because of the allegations that he was a serial killer, as well as his struggles with being transsexual, the Internet would remember him—not for who he was or what he might have done—but because of how the hardcore conservatives would turn him into a scarecrow and hang him in all their fields, as a warning to all those who were not as god intended.

Lux's stomach was in knots. It'd been awhile since she'd felt this way. It reminded her of when she had first started blogging. She would pour all her thoughts and efforts into a post and go over it several times, liking it more and more with every pass. Then, in a euphoric cloud of certainty, she'd publish. Doubt would settle in as soon as she saw her creation on display, on the great, distorting window of the world—the Internet. Suddenly, the words she had written would seem so childish or ill-informed. She would begin to see their faults and where they could be exploited by others. In a sea of opinions, the meaning of her words and sentences could be drowned, taken under by the neurotic pull of dissent. Unlike a lot of people, what she wrote was who she was, not who she wanted to be. So it wasn't until she posted what wasn't just her thoughts and feelings, but a snapshot of herself, she'd realized that she might be wrong; that not only her beliefs, but herself as a person might be wrong. The two were bound to one another, like the double helixes of DNA strands. To separate one would reduce the other to something indescribable.

In those earlier days of her career in social justice, she had aborted a lot of posts, because she had wanted others to like her. Over time, her skin had hardened, and she felt as if she had a duty to thrust herself onto others. It wasn't about being right or wrong; it was about being Lux, and no one had the authority to judge a person's character as unfit for life. No one, that is, until as of late, when she'd been granted a boon from the Sisters' apostle in Maidenwood. With their teachings, Lux's abilities as an augur had been augmented and she had started to see humans as mathematical problems—unsolved equations in a perpetually unbalanced state. To bring harmony, to reach her life's mission statement, she had to solve these equations, stop them, be it through death or indoctrination, from giving rise to other unbalanced beliefs that were giving rise to discord in the System. The apostle warned that Lux might feel badly about her actions, but in all that time, over all these bodies, she wept nothing but tears of joy; for in the dead, her words would rise above the daily cacophony, and she wouldn't be judged for what she was, but by what she'd done. And for those out there who had half a brain, it was immediately obvious that what she'd done had not only been right, but necessary.

However, the euphoric cloud that'd been following her since the death of Salinger Stevens had begun to disperse. Now, as she sat in the party room on the second floor of the Wharf, staring out at what she'd written and wrought, sensing that all of this was about to reach both its beginning and its end, Lux pressed her hands to her stomach and began to doubt. Would they understand? Would they get it? Could they see past what it was to what it actually meant? She knew what she would look like to them, and it was hard to say whether that was a good thing, or a bad thing. They would want to call her a villain, but when everyone came to their senses, they'd immortalize her as an anti-hero, instead. Someone who had done what no one else had the clit to do. Let them hate her. Hate was everything to her.

Lux was decided, and then, staring at the laptop, watching the 'yes' votes come in by the hundreds for Fenton, she was not. Okay, sure, when this had all started, she'd fought for all minorities. Everyone had been accounted for. But over the years, she began to wonder, as the majority had wondered, if everyone was deserving of equal rights, of having a voice. It was something she would never admit, but when Ramona had suggested they use their abilities as impeccable judges of character to better understand how to help their own community, it seemed like the perfect opportunity to discover the true nature of people.

And she did. She and Ramona, and eventually the others, honed the art of being an augur. But Lux? Lux learned the skills of a social surgeon. Being an augur was easy. Society had embraced being an augur. In a world where memories were recorded with cell phones rather than brain cells, it was inevitable that people like Ramona would change the conversation from the masses to the minutiae. It was all adjectives and nouns, and cheap threats that made people move for the sake of money. But being a surgeon? A social surgeon? It required a steady hand and a keen eye, and the willingness to make cuts, to excise. People wouldn't need to move. All you'd have to do was step over the bodies that'd fallen to her scalpel.

These days, Lux had settled on supporting women. Men were fine, all things considered, but that's not what the people who supported her wanted to hear. They wanted easy answers, boogeymen. What was the patriarchy but some amorphous threats to which there was no method of attack? What were women's rights when some women had some of them, and others did not? There were sluts, and then there was female empowerment. There were heteronormative gender roles, and then there were just some women who genuinely liked cooking. Everyone had an idea of how things were supposed to be, but no one knew how things were supposed to be.

Lux did. She knew. She knew it, because she'd seen it. She'd dissected the soul and seen the things lurking within. She was how things were supposed to be. How could she not be? You need only look upon her works to see the support of her patrons. Salinger Stevens, Ansel Adams, Zoe/Zeke Crampton, Paul Zdanowicz, Asher Jones, Fenton Miike—they had all been impostors, and through Lux's operations, she'd revealed them for what they truly were. But that's all they were. Lies lying on the slab. It was the Internet, the People, who had decided they needed to die. And die they did, in spectacularly surreal ways. Death sentences from the other side. Scissors snipping stalks in the under-Garden. No one else was capable of this. No one else besides her. If she wasn't meant to do this, then why could she? And why couldn't anyone else?

The knots in Lux's stomach started to unravel. She pressed her fingers to the laptop's sticky keyboard and pulled up a picture of Ramona. She hesitated. For as long as they'd gone back, she could only remember yesterday. And yesterday, Ramona had an opportunity to call her out, to stop her. She hadn't. It wasn't like Lux had wanted her to, and it wasn't like it would've made a difference, but still… if she had… With Echo echoing everything she said and did, it might've been nice to hear something else for once.

Lux loaded up Ramona's picture with the poll into her blog, but didn't post it. Someone knocked on the door that led into the party room, and smiling, Lux said, "Come on in."

As someone started shouting about blood downstairs, Ramona stepped into the party room and closed the door behind her. It smelled badly in here, like a locker room and a meat shop. It was almost pitch-black, too. The only light was the light coming off the laptop, which shone on Lux's face, who was seated behind it. She was smiling. Her hands were wet.

"Hey, Ramona."

Ramona's eyes struggled to adjust to the dark. It was like it was a new kind of darkness, an alien blackness that moved like fog might move. There were things in the dark, though, that much she could tell.

How many had Jessie and Cole and Fenton called up here? Fifteen? Sixteen? She strained her ears for breathing, for shuffling feet and cracking knuckles; muffled laughter, slow sips. There were things in the dark, but what?

Ramona took a few steps forward and then stopped. "Lux?"

"Yeah?"

"What's… going on?"

Lux put her hands behind her head and leaned back in her chair. "Celebrating."

Ramona took a few more steps. The toes of her shoe nudged something lying across the floorboards.

"Do you want the light?"

"Uh." Ramona wrinkled her nose. It smelled as if someone had shit themselves. "I… don't know."

"What are you doing up here, then?"

"Can we talk?"

A white sliver crept across the floorboards. As Ramona realized the door was opening behind her, the lights were suddenly switched on. Ramona recoiled.

The room was drenched in blood, the floor covered in hunks of flesh and chunks of gore. Bodies were scattered about Lux's desk, each one a link in a chain that ran unbroken and endlessly around her. Sixteen in all, they had been stripped naked and completely ravaged. Their backs were cavernous; their faces stew. Where their spinal columns should've been were empty holes where gallons of blood stagnated, and a single cell phone, one in each corpse, floated. Ramona didn't read much, and she didn't know why she thought it now, but the phones reminded her how people used to place coins on the eyes of the dead to pay the Ferry Man.

The door slammed behind Ramona. She jumped and spun around.

Asher stood behind her, his chewed-up face peering out from the hood of a rain coat. Ramona started to run to him, and then stopped, noticing his hands. They looked gloved, but they weren't. They were white, and fleshy. And then he spoke.

"They didn't notice," Echo said.

Ramona screamed. She stumbled backwards, her ankles going sideways as she nearly slipped on a tongue.

Echo unbuttoned the rain coat and dropped it on the ground. Underneath, she was naked, except it wasn't her body, her skin. It was…

It was… Ramona's eyes traveled from the bloody color of the body suit to its crotch, where ambiguous genitalia were cradled. The face was Asher's but… the skin… the skin was Fenton's.

"What the fuck did you do?" Ramona belted.

Echo ignored her, addressed Lux. "Didn't even notice."

"Of course not," Lux said. "Like that, you're one of them. All those liars down below."

The room began to spin. Ramona's throat constricted, and then a gout of vomit exploded out of it. She gasped, tasting the rot in the air, and vomited again. Crying, whining, she moved back and forth with short strides, not trying to escape. Not trying to go anywhere at all, really.

Echo took off Asher's face, and shook of Fenton's skin. The costumes crumpled around her ankles, and she stepped out of them, in her own, albeit blood-soaked, clothes.

"Didn't notice?" Ramona drew her fist back. "Didn't notice?! You were…" She looked at the pile of flesh that had once been her friends. "You… were in a fucking coat. You fucking freak. You fucking fuck!"

Echo rolled her eyes and leaned back into the door, her hand on the knob.

"Ramona," Lux called.

Ramona ignored her. She was burning up on the inside. A hazy darkness was closing around her vision. Crying so hard she was smiling, she crouched down and screamed, "Help! Help me!" Globs of spit fell out of her mouth. It tasted of sea salt and of sulfur.

"Ramona," Lux said.

Finally, she turned to face Lux.

"They won't hear you over the music."

"Why?" She drove the heels of her palms into her eyes. "Why?"

"They were liars. They were part of the problem you and I promised to fix all those years ago."

"No! No! I have nothing to do with this!"

"Sure," Echo said.

"It doesn't matter. You can't… you can't just…"

Lux held up her hand. "That's the thing. That's the thing, Ramona, I can. I shouldn't be able to do this. No one should be able to do this. But I can. That means something."

"That means something," Echo parroted.

Ramona heaved. Making growling sounds to clear her throat, she bent over and hacked up phlegm.

"So many in this world are on life support, needlessly sucking up resources they'll never really deserve." Lux stood up. "Even our own. That's the thing. We gave the gays and the lesbians and the intersexed and the mentally ill and the minorities a pass, and all they've done for us is give us a bad name."

"Are you fucking… kidding me?" Ramona shook with rage. "They're human-fucking-beings!"

"That didn't stop you from judging them."

"I didn't kill them!"

"We did, in our own ways," Lux said. "Condemning people based upon a few traits and observations. Making it public for everyone to see. It wasn't wrong, but it was rudimentary. There are better ways."

Echo said, "We have to be strong together. If there is any weakness, they'll use it against us. Asher and Fenton weren't strong. They had turned against us. They made us look bad."

"Made us look bad?" Ramona gestured to the gory remains. "Made us look bad?"

"I know what's best," Lux said. "Echo does, too."

"Because she just does what you fucking tell her to!"

Echo snorted.

"I think you are wonderful. You've been a great friend to me. But if it's meant to be…" She spun the laptop around, so that the screen was facing Ramona. "…then it's meant to be."

On the screen was Ramona's picture, and beneath it, a poll that read yes or no.

"What the fuck is that?"

"That's you." Lux's finger hovered over the Enter key. "And if that's really you, then you have nothing to worry about."

Ramona's body stopped shaking. She stopped breathing. Everything inside her sank. The sweat on her skin retreated. She looked at the bodies on the floor, their backs broken open, their innards drained—the cell phones circulating the bloody lakes of the hateful—and saw herself amongst them.

"Don't," she said.

"I wouldn't worry." Lux hit the Enter key, and the post was uploaded. "I know you better than anyone else. I wouldn't worry."

Ramona said nothing, did nothing. Paralyzed, her eyes were fixated on the poll counter.

Echo opened the door, poked her head out, and said, "Police are here."

Ramona snapped out of it. The poll was still sitting at zero. She still had time. She turned around, threw herself at Echo.

"It… won't matter!" Echo caught her.

Ramona slammed into Echo. She kneed Echo, took her by the face and bashed her head against the door.

"Ramona… Ramona," Lux said.

Echo swung at Ramona, smashing her fist into Ramona's cheek. It didn't matter. Nothing hurt as much as how she hurt right now. Ramona elbowed Echo's throat. Echo wheezed, dropped to her knees. Ramona ripped the door open. It smacked into Echo, sending her sprawling, mouth-first, into a pool of entrails.

"Ramona," Lux said, sweetly.

Ramona didn't know why she turned around, but she did. Maybe she was expecting something else. A monster, or an answer. Or the seams to what should've so obviously been a horrible dream. But it was just Lux and her laptop.

"You're at zero," Lux said, relieved. "You're real."

Ramona's jaw dropped.

"Oh." Lux pressed the Enter button. "Sorry. I forgot to refresh the page."

Backing out of the room, Ramona's eyes fell to the updated numbers.

"It's strange how something can be both true and not true at the same time," Lux said. She sounded as if she were going to cry. "Do you think it would've mattered if I hadn't pressed this button?"

By family and friends, Ramona would be remembered as having died a cruel and unnecessary death at a young age. For the weeks and months and years to come, they would recall Ramona's tomboyish behavior, her wicked sense of humor, and her deep dedication to the LGBTQIA community. Her mother would visit her grave every week, and there she would have a private conversation with her daughter, telling her how beautiful she was, how proud of her she had always been—things she wished she'd said and never did. Her father would immerse himself into the LGBTQIA community of Bitter Springs in an attempt to pick up where Ramona had left off; he would be welcomed with open arms, but his efforts would never amount to much, because he would seldom be able to keep it together long enough to see a project through. Those who would reject Lux's ideology would paint a mural to Ramona on the walls of the safe space at Bitter Springs Junior High, though it would later be removed to make room for a mural of the football mascot. Ramona would have become a local politician in her later years, and much to her own surprise, she would have written a book on her experiences as a gender fluid lesbian. It would be a national bestseller. Many would have been inspired by it. She would have lived until she was one-hundred-and-one. Grandchildren would come to know her as the foul-mouthed grandmother who always gave the best gifts at Christmas. She would've made a lot of mistakes until her eventual death during the Trauma, but that's how these things go.

By the Internet, Ramona would be remembered as a gender fluid, Caucasian lesbian with ADHD, Depression, and Intermittent Explosive Disorder. Due to her heavy involvement with the augurs and the statements by Lux and Echo upon the police arriving at the crime scene in the Wharf's party room, the general consensus amongst the general public would be that Ramona played a part in the murders, and may have even taken part in the killing of the sixteen men and women found in that room. Diligent self-taught detectives would track down where Ramona worked and lived, and they would harass both her employer and her parents, for no reason other than they were undoubtedly responsible for what Ramona had become. Former male classmates would call Ramona a tease, while others would claim that she slept with anyone that looked at her. Former female classmates would say Ramona had done everything she did because she had been overweight most of her life, while others would simply refuse to comment. Men on the Internet would dig up pictures of Ramona when she had weighed three-hundred-pounds and digitally alter them, making garish nudes. Whether or not the Internet would remember Ramona simply depended upon how many women were in the headlines that week. Two was one too many.

Seconds after Ramona's death, the police uncovered the crime scene and arrested both Lux and Echo.

Echo was sentenced to three years in a mental health hospital, and would be released pending the unanimous agreement of several of the psychiatrists there that she had recovered. Despite the court's decision that Echo had been manipulated by Lux to be an accomplice and that the wearing of the victims' skins was clearly a sign of mental illness, the Internet disagreed and turned on her. Because she was a woman, the Internet had decided the judge had taken it easy on her and that the only appropriate sentencing, despite her young age and obvious psychosis, was death. Every once in a while, Echo's echo would be renewed by those interested in the case—those people who spread around terrible trivia like candy; candy to be consumed, and forgotten. She would never be released from the mental health hospital, though. She would be found dead in her room the night before her hearing, a phone in her hand and a pool of blood around her body. The cause of death would be decided to be a poison of some sort no lab in the country would end up being able to identify.

Due to Lux's blog posts coinciding with the deaths of the victims, as well as having been placed at the scene of the sixteen deaths at the Wharf, Lux was arrested and charged with twenty-three counts of first-degree murder. After a long trial and a media circus that went on for years, Lux was given life in prison. There, she continued to blog and gather followers, who, after subsequent deaths following Lux's imprisonment, began a movement to bring evidence to light that Lux had been framed. No DNA evidence had been uncovered, nor was there any true eye-witness testimony. Several alibis were unearthed that were irrefutable, and no links were made between Lux and any hired hitmen.

After eight years, several documentaries, and a recently released web series that people binged and theorized over for months, Lux was granted parole. The deaths continued, and while links could be made to Lux's speeches, blogs, or videos, the links were inconclusive, and the sights of the killer or killers too fantastical in their reports to take seriously.

Lux eventually shielded herself with religion, and she adopted her militant beliefs about feminism to a more conservative approach. She began to incorporate god into her works and appealed to the White Supremacists who'd begun to support her of late, due to "cleansings" that continued to happen all around Lux. Shielded by faith and Southern Politics, Lux continued her work without harassment for several years, where she put out five books, and also five children, as she had been "cured" of her lesbianism.

It wasn't until shortly before the Trauma that Lux abandoned her conservative beliefs and returned with a more liberal-slant. "Don't Assume My God" was her slogan, and it was printed on stickers, shirts, posters, pins, and spray painted across the surfaces of cities all over the world. There was a time when it was believed she had the power to overthrow Lillian. And then that time passed.

Lux's family would do their best to forget her.

The Internet would remember her for as long as it existed. She would be simultaneously loved and loathed, and although many would call for her blood, it would be their blood by which her work was done. To kill her, they would have to ignore her, but she was worth too much exposure, too much attention, too much ad revenue; too many clicks, too many likes, too many hearts, too many thumbs-up; too many conversations, too many debates; she was too easy a scapegoat, too convenient a punching bag; she was too much like them; and not enough were like her. The Internet bled Lux dry, and Lux bled dry the Internet. People to come might say it had all been for naught, but not Isla Taggart, who sits down at this very moment with a battered copy of Lux's last book in her hand.

On the cover is the image of a jellyfish. The species is known as the turritopsis dohrnii, or the 'immortal jellyfish.' It is one of the few animals that are capable of living forever, as it is capable, after reaching sexual maturity, of returning to a polyp state, where, if allowed to flourish, it will once more mature and, again, revert. As long as the conditions are right, this biological immortality can theoretically go on forever.

Isla Taggart does not know these things yet, but soon she will, and so, too, will those she shares Lux's teachings with, and so on, and so on, and so on, and so on…

A CHILD IN EVERY HOME

SUNDAY

The last thing Linnéa wanted was to be like her mother, who had worried so much while she'd been alive that she wouldn't be surprised to hear Mom was still at it beyond the grave, giving Death a hard time, making sure to remind It to put on a coat before going out for the night. It wasn't that Linnéa didn't care about her daughter, Filipa; it was that, for a ten-year-old, Filipa was smart, smarter than most of the mouth-breathers, children and adults alike, on this block, and she wasn't going to learn anything about anything if she spent most of her formative years in a fallout shelter of hand-holding, finger-wagging, and fear-mongering. That was how you ended up with fourteen-year-olds with two kids, and sixteen-year-olds with rap sheets that read like grocery lists ("One aggravated assault and two burglaries will hold us over 'til the weekend."). Linnéa knew this. She'd done her fair share of stupid things to herself and others in the pursuit of independence. She didn't want that for Filipa, and she didn't want Filipa to be her or her mother. She just wanted Filipa to be Filipa. And if that meant getting dirty, getting bruised; getting picked on or getting a detention—then okay, alright, so be it.

Today, though, today was different. Because Linnéa and her husband, Stephen, had been in the backyard since there was enough light to work with, doing this or doing that, and during all that time, the white, unmarked van across the street had not only never moved, but the person inside it hadn't gotten out. They were still in there, somewhere beyond those tinted windows, waiting for something. She knew they were in there, because sometimes the van would dip, as if the driver inside were rummaging around. It was easy to imagine the worst, especially with Filipa not far from the street herself, sitting against her favorite tree, reading from her favorite book, not a care in the world, because her stupid mom had told her she had nothing to worry about.

"Filipa," Stephen called from the garden, his hands green and neck red.

"Filipa, darling."

Linnéa watched the scene from behind the grill she was stationed at. The heat coming off the sun and the coals had reduced her to ratty jean shorts and a bathing suit top. She gave the burgers a flip. Filipa was doing her best to pretend she hadn't heard her dad. It wasn't going to work, though. Stephen was legendarily persistent. He made car salesman cry and telemarketers consider suicide. He was the gnat all other gnats would look at and say, "Chill, bro."

"Filipa," Stephen said, not looking up from his lilies. "Fili—"

Filipa dropped her book in her lap and shouted across the yard, "Oh my god, Dad. What?"

"Get your daddy a beer." Stephen turned around to Linnéa and held up two fingers.

Linnéa nodded and said to Filipa, "Two beers."

"I can't." She opened the book and drove the pages to her nose. "My legs aren't working."

Stephen fell back on his haunches. "Well, isn't that something?"

Burger grease leapt up and splattered across Linnéa's hands. She didn't notice. There was movement coming from the van again.

"Guess we'll have to cancel your birthday party next month."

Filipa lowered the book ever-so-slightly. "Guess so."

Stephen went back into the garden, this time with a spade. "Guess you won't be able to see that movie this weekend with your girly girls."

Filipa shot a look at Linnéa.

Linnéa said, "What? We can't afford to get you a wheelchair."

"The cost," Stephen said.

"It's ridiculous." Linnéa tried not to smile as she threw a few buns on the grill to toast. "We're going to have to sell you."

"To get enough money for the wheelchair," Stephen added.

"And then I don't even know how we'll afford to get you back."

"She'll be deeply discounted, I'm sure."

Linnéa nodded. "Even so. I don't know how much a girl who can't fetch her two poor, loving parents some beers go for these days."

"Not much," Stephen said. "I mean, that's like half the reason to have a kid."

Sighing dramatically, Linnéa launched the buns onto a plate. "Well, shoot. I guess it's good it's summer time. You're going to be under that tree a long while. Least the nights aren't so bad."

Filipa, with her annoyed smirk, not wanting to give in, said, "You could get me a blanket."

"Could," Stephen said, tearing out some strangely colored, almost vein-like roots. "But suddenly, my legs feel a little hinky."

Linnéa made her knees wobble. "I'm going down."

Filipa snapped her head back and hopped to her feet.

"Praise Jesus!" Stephen said, making the sign of the cross. "Our little girl is healed."

Filipa stuck out her tongue as she marched towards the back door.

"Truly, a miracle," Linnéa said, deadpan.

"You guys are alcoholics," Filipa said, pointing at the two of them.

"Hey now," Linnéa fired back.

Stephen murmured, "Don't talk about your mother that way."

Linnéa cried, "Stephen!" and hurled an oven mitt at him. It didn't go but a few inches from the grill.

"I'm getting a beer for myself," Filipa said, as she slipped into the house through the back door. "Going to get lit." And then, with that, their little goblin was gone.

Linnéa didn't bother arguing with the girl. She knew she wasn't serious. Filipa was smart, which meant she was also a smart ass. The two didn't always go hand-in-hand, but in Filipa's case, Linnéa was glad they did. It was that little edge her daughter needed to round her out from being a total square.

The erratic movement in the van stopped. Lunch made and plated, Linnéa stepped away from the grill and drew closer to the white trope that never lost its touch.

"Hey Steve?"

"Yeah?"

"I'm going to go say something."

"Huh?" Stephen pulled his head out of the weeds and stared into the street. "There still people in there?"

"Think so."

He came to his feet, brushed off his knees, and wandered over to the grill and grabbed his veggie burger, which had been marooned to its own maroon-colored plate. "Surprised Joyce hasn't said anything." He chomped down into the burger and moaned. "S'good. S'real good. If only I had a beer!"—he hollered at the house, "—to wash it down."

Linnéa checked her phone. "True. Joyce has the fastest fingers in these parts when it comes to texting out suspicions."

"A life of penny counting will do that to a person." Stephen took another bite. "Got stuck behind her at the store once. Swear to god, that woman only shops with coins. Had to get out of line and buy spider repellent by the time she'd finished, had so many webs all over me."

Linnéa pretended to laugh. "I don't know. It's been out there all day. Jesus, this is stupid." She went back to the grill and grabbed the still-hot spatula. "God forbid we hurt someone's feelings by being rude. I'm going to go talk to them."

Stephen stepped out of her way. "Just don't hurt them, alright?"

She took the spatula in two hands, like a sword. "My mother would be proud."

Stephen shrugged and shuffled back to his spot in the garden.

More movement in the white van. Linnéa picked up the pace, wanting to catch them in the middle of whatever it was that they were doing. Reaching the sidewalk, she became aware of herself and cased her surroundings.

It was Sunday, and church was over, and though their subdivision wasn't large enough to be its own little country like, say, Maidens' Grove, which straddled the tri-county lines, their neighborhood, Six Pillars, it still had some size to it. Sizable enough, that, on a Sunday, after mass, in summer, there should've been more folks out, farting around and making good use of their porches and stoops. But there was no one. No teenagers tearing down the street in their souped-up hand-me-downs, the bass of their music pre-and-proceeding them, like the modern-day drums of war. No old timers sitting catatonically by their windows, behind their windows, befriending the local wildlife, or looking for ways to go messy-up their family's day. No thirty-somethings, like herself and her husband, cranking out chores or taking a crack at long-standing and ultimately forgettable projects.

But most importantly, there were no kids. None of their yelling, nor that distinct smell of their sweat, which read to the nose like spit and nickels. Linnéa searched the front yards and backyards for little bodies bashing into one another. She searched the tallest trees for skinny stowaways. The sounds of gunfire and creative cussing were a good way to track couch-dwellers, but even that was missing.

Granted, this wasn't the worst thing in the world. Linnéa loved her child, but she wasn't a fan of children in general, especially the kind her generation was responsible for squeezing out. It wasn't their fault—the kids; it was their parents. The men and women who let the Internet teach their boys and girls everything, and wanted nothing more than to be their either their bosses, or their best buddies. Children raising children. Narcissistic dollmakers. That was how you ended up with that blowhard, Lux, over in Bitter Springs. And they had the nerve to give her, Linnéa, crap about the way she—

The van. Apparently, she was the only who cared, because she was the only one paying it any mind. And no, that didn't mean she was being overly paranoid. Spatula at the ready, she crossed the street and got right up on it.

Stephen was tonguing his gums, getting the last of his burger from out between his teeth, when Linnéa returned from her reconnaissance.

"Two teens fucking," she said, shaking her head.

"What?"

"Yep."

"This whole time?"

"Guess so."

Stephen scratched his cheek. "Think we should offer them some water?

It's awfully hot out, and they've been going at it for hours now."

"Why here?" Linnéa snorted. "The hell?"

"I mean, got to give them credit. Minus the van, it's pretty incognito. They at least got a window rolled down?"

Linnéa shook her head.

Stephen cringed. "Resale value's shot to shit now."

"It's weird."

Stephen's eye widened. "Hey, want to actually see something weird?"

Linnéa wandered over to the grill and dropped off the spatula. Pointing to the van, she said, "That's not weird to you?"

"It'd be weird if they weren't fucking around in there. Look." After rooting around in a pile of weeds, he took out a handful of the strangely-colored roots Linnéa had seen him yank up earlier. "Now, that's weird."

She reached out to touch them. "What are those?"

But he pulled them away before she could. "I have... no idea. It's really pissing me off because they weren't here the other day."

Linnéa twisted her mouth, raised an eyebrow. "Steve, don't get all obsessive about this."

"Little vermillion fuckers. Look at this." He tore one in half, and a creamy, red fluid sputtered out. "Look at that!"

"You're loving this," Linnéa said.

Stephen had slipped into botanist mode. Mumbling, rumbling, he rambled and ambled back to the garden and started looking for the growth's culprits. He'd be unreachable for the rest of the day, lost in a blur of message boards and poorly-designed web pages. And once he figured it all out, he'd act as if it hadn't been a big deal, and that he'd known, basically, what he was dealing with all along. Linnéa looked forward to teasing him about it later.

And looking forward, Linnéa noticed Filipa hadn't taken her lunch off the grill.

"Hey, Filipa come back out yet?"

Stephen smacked his lips, like a parched traveler deep in a desert.

"I'll take that as a no?"

"Yes. I mean, no. I mean." Stephen smiled. "You know what I mean."

That girl. Linnéa marched across the yard and went to open the backdoor, but Filipa had left it open. The central air was slipping through the cracks. They were literally throwing their money away. Groaning—how many times did she have to tell her?—Linnéa pushed into the house, into the kitchen, and shut the door hard behind her.

"Filipa?"

Linnéa wandered around the kitchen, touching up this, straightening out that, as she waited for her daughter to respond.

"Filipa?"

She opened the fridge and found the five beers in there where they'd left them. She shut the door, strained her ears. The central air clicked off. Pipes hissed. Water was running somewhere.

She sidestepped her way out of the kitchen and into the hall. The bathroom door was shut, but the light was on.

"Filipa?"

No answer. Linnéa knocked on the door. She wedged her fingers between the door and the molding and slowly, creepily, started to open it.

"Answer, or I'm coming in."

No answer. Linnéa gave her five seconds and then barged in. The toilet had urine in it, and the sink was still on. A few squares of toilet paper were spread across the ground. One had a dirty shoe print on it.

"Ungrateful." She shut off the sink and flushed the bowel. "Filipa, I swear, if you don't answer me, you're grounded until your next reincarnation!"

Filipa was learning about world religions in school. She was, as she put it, "all about that reincarnation game."

Getting angry, getting anxious, Linnéa stomped her way down the hall, around the corner, and mountain-climbered up the staircase, calling her daughter's name with every forceful step.

Maybe good cop would work, so: "Hey, Dad found something funky in the garden. Come check it out."

Not a peep from Filipa's room.

So, she switched to bad cop: "I saw a switch outside with your name written all over it. What the heck are you doing?"

Linnéa skipped the last few steps, vaulting onto the second floor. She was winded, and her heart was beating something fierce, but that had nothing to do with the stairs or that little bit of weight she couldn't shake. It was the silence of the house, and the silence of her daughter, and all the voices inside Linnéa at this moment, all sounding off, all at once.

Panic quickening her pace, Linnéa made it to Filipa's room in no time flat and elbowed the door in.

Filipa's room was Filipa's kingdom. An aquamarine court of velvet and frills. Aside from the band posters and corkboard of print-off cut-outs of inspirations, aspirations, hotties, and hotties that inspired aspirations, the room could've easily passed for one of those roped-off, price-tagged 'slices of life' you might find in some antique shop, in some antique town. A four-poster bed with a canopy made of stars; a chest of drawers covered in trinkets and odd, little boxes; several trunks stuffed with all sorts of pre-teen treasures. There was a typewriter in one corner, and a vanity in the other. And on one wall, all by its lonesome, a bookcase stood stuffed and buckled with novels whose spines were so worn you had to write their titles in with the dust that'd gathered there. It was all junk from Linnéa's mother, stuff she'd left behind when she'd left them all behind. She'd been gone awhile now.

But she'd just seen Filipa. Where the hell was she?

Pits turning into sweaty swamps, Linnéa went red in the face, and then went down on her hands and knees and looked under Filipa's bed. Not there. Linnéa hurried to her feet and opened the closet. Not there.

Shouting Filipa's name, Linnéa ran into her own room and searched every corner and crevice, but she wasn't there.

Crying Filipa's name, Linnéa checked the second-floor bathroom and spare closet, but she wasn't in either of them.

Jesus Christ, where the hell was she? Linnéa doubled back to Filipa's room, gave it a once-over, and then bolted down the stairs.

"Stephen!" she cried, going into the living room, going into the family room.

"Stephen!" she screamed, going into the kitchen, going into the basement; hating, for the first time since they'd moved in, how small it was, how there were so few places someone could hide in it.

"Steph—"

Stephen met her at the top of the basement steps, taking on her terror almost instantaneously.

"I can't find her."

"What? Did you check her room?" Stephen moved aside as Linnéa bashed past him, back into the living room. "Filipa!"

"I checked everywhere, Stephen!" Linnéa shot him a damning look. "Go check that fucking van!"

Stephen nodded and hurried out the back door.

Linnéa told herself that Filipa was fine. That she was either hiding, or that she had gone back outside. The girl was quiet. If being a Brainiac didn't work out for her, then a life of thievery surely would. But as much of a pain in the ass as she was, Filipa would've responded by now. She wasn't mean like that, wasn't cruel. She wouldn't—

Linnéa stopped in the living room. Her nose twitched. She smelled something. She couldn't place it, but it had no place here. She sniffed the air. Something earthy, almost creek-like. That faint sewer pipe water smell. And then... oil. And rubber. Dirty smells. Manual labor smells. It was the kind of smell she associated with a certain kind of man. The kind that spent their Sundays at the bar, and their Mondays on the floor.

Linnéa crept towards the front door, but for all her efforts, she never seemed to close the gap between it and her. It was like the house was recoiling, or she was from it. Something was wrong about it, like there was something wrong about the air inside it. Someone'd been here.

She looked back up the stairs, and every hair on her body stood, as if just around the corner, someone was waiting. She glanced towards the first-floor bathroom, and couldn't remember if that light was supposed to be on or off. Through the hardwood floor, she felt subtle vibrations, from her soles to her soul. She leaned farther, caught half the kitchen in her gaze—half the table with it—and her stomach flopped as she imagined someone sitting at it, just out of sight.

"Filipa!" Stephen's faint shouts carried in from the backyard. Each one was a cold confirmation of Linnéa's fears.

"Filipa!" His voice was getting quieter and quieter, as he undoubtedly drew nearer to the street, to the van.

Linnéa started towards the kitchen again, but stopped. She'd heard something else. Shouting, but not Stephen's shouting. It was a woman's voice. Or maybe a girl's. Yes, maybe a girl's.

Linnéa ripped open the front door and ran out onto the porch. "Filipa?" she wailed, looking left, looking right. "Filipa?"

But it hadn't been Filipa screaming.

Down the street, Ellen Cross was standing on her porch, shouting "Darlene," which was her daughter's name.

On the opposite side, farther down, Bethany Simmons was doing a tour of her house's perimeter, calling out for Jimmy, her son.

And then, as each teary-eyed woman acknowledged the other in communal horror, two houses over from Linnéa's, Trent Resin hurried down his driveway and shouted to her, "Hey, Lin, have you seen Charles? I can't find him anywhere."

SUNDAYMONDAYTUESDAYWEDNESDAYTHURSDAYFRIDAYSATUR**DAY**

She had not seen Charles, nor she had seen Darlene Cross or Jimmy Simmons; nor had any of their parents seen Filipa. It was Sunday when the four children had gone missing. And now it was Sunday again, one month later, and none of them had seen their children since.

Dario Onai, the social worker who Ellen Cross had sought out for today's and the previous weeks' group therapy sessions, slipped into the room and gave each of the parents gathered here a neutral smile. He was on their side, it seemed to say, but he wasn't their friend.

Linnéa rubbed the crust out of her eyes and polished off the coffee in her thermos. Before she could ask, Stephen, sitting next to her at the conference table, took the thermos, got up, and went to refill it. He was always doing things like that these days—anticipating her wants, fulfilling her needs.

Ever since Filipa had gone missing, an eternal winter had fallen over their lives, and it was in trivial movements they kept the fire burning in their bones. There were things that needed to be done that had nothing to do with finding their daughter, like paying bills or taking baths, or remembering to laugh at the television. But to do anything that didn't involve bringing their baby girl home didn't sit right with them. How could they go to work when, instead, they could take another tour of the neighborhood, or the outlet mall the unmarked van had been spotted at hours after the children had vanished? How could they kiss one another, hold one another, when it was Filipa who needed all the kisses and all the hugs? So everything they did, even something so simple as a husband getting his wife some coffee, was, in essence, tiny tributes to the altar of Filipa. Small promises that they'd go on living, doing as the living ought to do, but only because that was the only way in which this could all come to an end. If they breathed just to breathe, then it was settled; might as well be over. They'd freeze before this summer's winter's end.

Mr. bigshot social worker, Dario Onai, would applaud Linnéa and Stephen for their "self-determination" and "healthy, coping skills." The other parents, though, didn't seem to be faring as well.

Trent Resin, single parent and proud taxpayer, wasn't big on talking these days. He'd never been much of a chatterbox, but by the time the town threw together a second search party to scout out Maidenwood, there was nothing a scowl couldn't get across that some fancy word could do better. Those woods were dense and dominated the north, northeastern, and northwestern stretches of Bitter Springs, Brooksville, and Bedlam combined. Even with the tracking dogs having a nose full of Charles, Darlene, Jimmy, and Filipa no one expected to find much out there. But they did. They found Charles Resin's pool pass impaled upon a deadfall. Inside the pile of rotting tree limbs, they discovered a pile of clothes—T-shirt, jeans, socks, boots, and underwear—similarly speared. After Trent had stopped screaming, he finally managed to mutter to the party and the sheriff that those'd been the clothes Charles had been wearing before he disappeared.

Now, for group therapy, Trent Resin was generally posted up by the coffeemaker, getting fat on caffeine, sugar, and stale snacks. Sometimes, he'd talk to Stephen about football or gardening, but the conversations never lasted more than a minute or two. Neither man cared enough about what the other had to say to carry on longer than what was needed.

"Good morning, everyone," Dario said, settling in at the head of the conference table. He glanced at Linnéa and Stephen, Ellen and Richard Cross, and Trent. "Anyone spoke with Bethany today?"

On cue, the hot mess that was Bethany Simmons spilled into the room. She looked like a coat rack, and everything fit on her like it would on a coat rack. A rabid subscriber to all catalogues "Mom," she was as basic as milk, and yet her enthusiasm couldn't have been any more acidic. It ate through situations, etched out outliers, until only her and her opinion remained.

"I am... so sorry!" Bethany smiled at everyone and waved vigorously. "God, so sorry."

Dario waved off her apology.

But that didn't stop Bethany from stealing the spotlight and giving the group a full update on how she was doing, what she was doing, and what she was going to be doing once this session of therapy was over.

Linnéa tuned her out. She'd heard it all before, and she'd just as soon not hear it all again. Bethany Simmons wasn't a bad person, but she was like one of those old TV shows doomed to an eternity of mid-afternoon reruns—enjoyable in small doses, until you can tell the time by it. The script might change, but the story was always the same. Two days after Jimmy's disappearance, she'd aligned herself with Geneva, a self-proclaimed social activist. Using the girl's online influence and her husband Todd's checkbook, she launched a campaign to "Bring the Children Home." Flyers. TV spots. Ads and blog posts. A hotline for people to call into with tips or sightings. T-shirts, pins, patches, and even raincoats, with countrified blue jeans in the pipeline. Bethany tended to be the one the local and national reporters spoke to. Sometimes Stephen would joke that people knew her face better than the faces of the children. Sometimes, Linnéa would laugh; other times, she'd just be glad it was Bethany brute-forcing their cause into the social psyche, and not her.

"Todd couldn't make it." Bethany rolled her eyes in that kind of men-will-be-men sort of way.

Todd couldn't make it, Linnéa knew, because Todd was busy putting together the projects Bethany would eventually take credit for. During the first search of their neighborhood, and also their town of Bedlam, Todd had broken down into tears and started punching his fists into windows, until he fainted. His act of self-mutilation had been the catalyst for this group therapy business, but like most men who needed help, he wasn't here to get it. Just the woman who loved him. Vicarious healing.

Powering down, Bethany gave the floor over to Dario.

"How is everyone?" he asked out of formality.

Trent detached himself from the coffee maker and sat a few seats down from Stephen.

Bethany started, "Well, I'm—"

Linnéa cut her off. "Just taking it day by day."

"Day by day," Dario reflected back at her. "How about you Stephen?"

"Been writing in my journal," Stephen said.

"Has that been helpful?"

Stephen's mouth twitched. His personality would have him pried open, to prattle on, in detail, about the details of his journal. But his journal wasn't his journal, but also Linnéa's. And the journal wasn't a journal, but one wall of their house completely covered in notes, pictures, print-outs, and a map of Bedlam. For a few days, they'd gone the second-rate, movie detective route and thrown-up string all over the place, too, to show connections. But it was more of a mess than it was worth. And it cheapened the whole thing.

"I hate how quiet it is at home," Linnéa said, bailing her husband out.

"Have you tried playing music like we discussed?"

A single tear slid down Linnéa's cheek. She quickly caught it.

"Does it remind you too much of Filipa?"

Linnéa nodded, said, "Yeah," and then: "I don't know." She pretended to play the guitar with her hands. "That's okay, I guess. Just… can't listen. She used to play her music 24/7."

"Keep playing, then," Dario said. "It's a good coping skill. Do you ever play for Stephen?"

"Can't afford her concerts," Stephen said. "Have to listen from the nosebleeds."

The other parents laughed, probably because it seemed like the right thing to do.

"I used to play a mean recorder back in the day," Bethany said. "Lin plays guitar? Didn't you used to do the drums back in high school, Rich?"

Richard Cross looked at his wife, Ellen, before saying, "Uh, yeah."

Beaming, Bethany belted, "We ought to put a band together!"

Linnéa squeezed her hand, until the tear she'd caught in it evaporated.

Dario nodded at Bethany, but to Ellen, said, "The last time we spoke, you shared with us that you hadn't been sleeping. You look tired."

Ellen rubbed the rosary around her neck. "We didn't stay in a motel like I said we might."

"That's good," Dario said. "I know that must have taken a lot strength and courage for you to do that."

Richard shifted beside her. Either he disagreed, or he had something to add to the conversation.

"You could stay with Todd and I if you wanted," Bethany offered. "We have a lot more room now."

Stephen stared at Linnéa.

Trent shook his head.

Bethany cringed, and for a moment, she lowered her guard. With it, went the color from her face, and she bit her lips until her teeth had red #5 all over them.

Dario wasn't an idiot, though. Linnéa could give him that much. As a social worker, he was a human filter that caught the bullshit that often made it through for daily consumption. So, he rewound time on the lot of them and let out: "Richard—"

Richard looked at his wife again, with daggers.

"—were you going to say something just now?"

Ellen and Richard Cross were their group's resident holy rollers. Though they weren't local missionaries like some of the zealots from their church, they were comfortable enough in their beliefs to interject them into every conversation; the same way someone might say "like," "um," or, "uh"—it was, for them, fulfilling filler that, to others, bordered on gibberish. While Bethany was busying herself with the material world, Ellen and Richard had turned to the spiritual for guidance and support. Linnéa couldn't complain. Church-folk could get something done something fierce when they put their mind to it. She didn't know what she was going to do with all their prayers, necessarily—as her father used to say, "If you can't even wipe your ass with it, then what's the point?"—but she appreciated the extra eyes and ears in the tri-county area. The donations were decent, too, but when she and Stephen started turning a profit off the food and cards they were getting, it felt awfully indecent.

"Well, go on and say it," Richard said, folding his arms over his pregnant belly. "It's what he's here for."

Ellen seemed like the kind of woman who'd seen her fair share of brimstone before turning to the other side. Maybe it was the darkness under her eyes, or the way her freckles came together in blotches, like Rorschach blots. Or maybe it was because she was as severe as stone, and her skin was lightly fuzzed, as if molded. Her hair was always blown back, and her tongue was always white from dehydration. Crazed would've been the best way describe to her, but she was kinder than most anyone else. Sure, she looked as if she'd crawled out of hell through a twenty-year-old vent of bad stints, but that was alright in Linnéa's book. At least she wasn't the holier-than-thou type like her husband was.

Problem with Ellen was you couldn't tell how she was taking all of this. When you're already eroded to the core, not much else damage is going to show.

And then she said this: "I'm starting to hear voices."

Trent Resin straightened up. It was the first thing to have gotten his attention in the last two weeks.

"Voices?" Dario asked.

Ellen said, "Yes. I hear Darlene. She talks to me. It's not my thoughts. It's really her. I thought it was god at first, but it's her. I know that sounds crazy—"

Dario shook his head.

"—but I think she's trying to reach me from… wherever she is." Ellen started to cry. "She feels so close, it's killing me I can't find her."

"It's nerves," Richard said, like every shitty doctor in every old school, Hollywood thriller. "That's all it is."

Ellen, rubbing her rosary, shook her head, like a stubborn child.

"Whatever it is," Dario said, "if Ellen is hearing it, then it's real to her. Ellen, what does Darlene say to you?"

"I can't make it out yet. I get bits and pieces—"

Richard huffed and fingered his bellybutton.

"—but it's like… another language."

Linnéa raised an eyebrow and glanced at Stephen.

Bethany was biting down on her lips, either enthralled, or about to laugh.

"Where?" Trent asked, his voice walloping the group with its baritone blast. "Where at do you hear her?"

"Everywhere. Home, mostly. I think it's too quiet for me, too, like Lin said."

Dario hummed and asked, "Darlene was just in the other room before she went missing, wasn't she?"

Richard stared at his wife. His face had turned to putty, like most bullies' faces when faced with the harsh truth of things.

"Yeah," she mumbled.

"You feel guilty," Dario said.

"Yeah."

"She was so close. You feel like you should've heard something."

"God was trying to tell me," Ellen blurted out, "but I wasn't listening. He sent his servants. Angels on the walls." She closed her eyes, seemed to take herself back to that moment. "I can hear her now, what she was saying, then; when she was trying to get my attention." She wiped her eyes hard enough to knock them from her sockets. "She wasn't talking right. Like… she had something in her mouth. That's what I keep hearing these days."

Richard threw his hands into the air, started to get up, and then, checking for and not getting permission from his wife, he kept his pumpkin ass planted.

"I don't think it was a… gag." Just saying the word 'gag' made Ellen gag. "It was like she was drunk."

"Drugged," Stephen said.

Linnéa stared at her husband. He'd been here a moment ago, but not anymore. She could smell the heat coming off his synapses. He was working things out, running yarn from one theory to another, seeing what connected, finding what was a stretch.

"Tell them why you didn't go into the other room," Richard said, spit webbing his mouth like a kamado's maw. "Even the blind can see god's light," he quoted. And then: "Tell them."

"I was drunk," Ellen said.

Bethany clicked her tongue against her teeth.

"The second I gave in…" She wailed. "I lost her! Maybe for good

156

this time!"

"For good?" Stephen asked.

But before Ellen could explain what she meant, Dario took the con-versation down another avenue. While he went on about grief, loss, and trauma, Linnéa, Stephen, and Trent formed an unspoken agree-ment between the three of them that something wasn't adding up. By the end of the session, Bethany had successfully stolen the spotlight from the rest of them to apologize, at great length, for the absence of her husband.

Linnéa and Stephen had taken separate cars to therapy. These days, they did most things alone. For them, it was a way to cover more ground, to see more of what needed to be seen. They had convinced themselves they were just as strong together as they were apart. But as Linnéa crossed the parking lot of Brooksville Community Health Cen-ter, going her way as Stephen went his, her stomach took a turn for the worse, and it felt like the hot, trampled pavement she traipsed upon. She wanted to go to him, and she wanted him to go to her. She didn't want to debrief over the phone, or wait until dinner, when these thoughts and feelings were so covered in dirt they might've well been part of the scenery.

She started to call out, but before she could, Trent Resin drove up to him, window down, and started speaking to him. Too far away to hear to him, Linnéa drew closer, keys rattling in her hand, when—

"Hey, Lin," Bethany said, rolling up in her SUV, blocking her path to Stephen.

Bethany's SUV smelled of hairspray and winter fresh chewing gum. Each cupholder was filled with plastic diet soda bottles, the dregs of which still sat at the bottoms. The passenger's seat had a black blanket draped across it. Sloppily sewn into the blanket were stars and planets, and a single spaceship in that lonely, linty dark. "Jimmy" was embroi-dered in a corner, though most of the name was unraveled. Bethany had one hand on the steering wheel, but the other was over her arm-rest, holding onto the blanket. She looked pacified.

"That was a good session today," she said.

Linnéa nodded. Hearing a door shut, she looked past Bethany to see Trent was gone, and Stephen had gotten into his car and was about to take off.

"Can I tell you something?"

"Yeah," Linnéa said, following her husband's car until the horizon swallowed it whole.

"I've been seeing things, too."

Now, Bethany had her full attention.

"At night. Once or twice." Bethany turned on the radio to some steel guitar, country croon fest. She fiddled with the knob, and then switched the radio back off. "When the police were still outside the houses, doing surveillance." She turned the radio on again, kept the volume real low. "In the front yard. I thought it was Jimmy, or…"

"Did you tell the cops?"

"Yeah. They checked their cameras. They were pointed directly at the house and didn't pick up anything. Just shadows. Guess that's what I saw."

"Yeah, but…" Linnéa cocked her head. "You saw something else, didn't you?"

Bethany smiled. Her cheeks were bright red. "I think I'm going crazy. Aren't you?"

Linnéa didn't respond.

"Oh well." Bethany grabbed Jimmy's blanket again. "Do you ever wish this would just… be over?"

"How do you mean?"

"Closure, or something."

"I want to find them," Linnéa said.

Bethany's body went stiff. "Well, yeah, so do I, Lin." She shook her head, blinked hard. "I have to go."

Linnéa didn't go straight home after therapy. She and Stephen each had their own beat. They'd been patrolling it every day for the last few weeks. Initially, they recruited the other parents to help them cover Bedlam, but they hadn't been consistent, and no one got anything done half as well as they could themselves. Because of the way Bedlam was divided by the river that ran through it, Stephen took the western half of the town, while Linnéa covered the east. To the west went the well-off, and to the east, everyone else. Heaven and Hell some people called it, except it was flipped. Hell was where the high-browed browsed; heaven was for the poor—middle-and-lower-class alike. Closest to the tri-county river, east was where the forgotten had washed up from the dockyards of Bitter Springs and the low-incoming housing of Brooks-ville. It was the working class and those who worked you over that lived there. East was where Linnéa and the other parents lived, and though it may have been dangerous, especially on the waterfront, it was home.

Stephen had insisted he work the eastern front, but he had supple lips—perfect for laying a wet one on all the pampered asses across the river—and no capacity for violence. Linnéa, however, had hands that still hurt from time to time; it was that old pain from when she'd been young; bones hadn't grown up right, but then again, neither had she.

It was Sunday, but she gave Detective Mills a call, anyway. It went to voicemail. She didn't bother leaving a message. He knew what she wanted. She considered calling Stephen, but aside from asking him what Trent had shared with him, what was there to talk about? What they wanted for lunch? Yesterday's lunch was still sitting on the table. The flies liked it well enough, though. Waste not, want not.

Linnéa made her way through Brooksville and crossed the bridge that spanned the tri-county river. Going under the sign that read "Welcome to Bedlam" made her feel as if someone had just walked over her grave. No matter where she went, she was never far from her problems, but coming back to Bedlam was like trying to live a life in a burned-down building. Everything recognizable had been rendered in the hard bark of char and blanketed in the cruel snow of ash. And to sleep and eat and go on, you had to lie to yourself; say that things had always been this way.

She cruised the town for killers and kidnappers. She became a talk show host, a PTA mom; an augur searching for auspices in the clothes people wore, or the way they stared at her as she drove by. Like a doctor, Linnéa made her rounds. Her patients were the parks, the public and private schools; the corner stores and the hole-in-the-walls; the sprawling shopping centers and scattered Mom and Pop's; the tucked away neighborhoods and the overflowing state-sponsored housings. By car or by foot, she carried a clipboard, flyers of the children pinned to it, and doled them out like diagnoses.

Now that you know their faces and their names, she tried to get across to those she came across, they are your responsibility. Treat them well, she wanted to say, and you can go on forgetting them again when this was all over. These four burdens were on Bedlam now, and why shouldn't they be? Someone here or near had done this to their children. Someone who'd fallen through the cracks and bided their time there. Bedlam-begotten. Begotten of Bedlam. Some young man known for making inappropriate comments to female co-workers, maybe once caught hurting a stray. Some young woman with bright teeth and dead eyes, and dreams of motherhood from a nightmarish childhood. Some old couple with soft hands and pinching fingers, and a hunger they didn't need dentures for. Some… someone… some… anyone. Opportunistic vultures on a heroin high. Fat necks in sweaters and sweatshirts—rosacea-wracked clowns who got their laughs from others' miseries.

Or maybe, just maybe… Filipa, Jimmy, Charles, and Darlene were lost. Maybe they'd been unhappy. Maybe they'd formed a pact, and like a pack they roamed Maidenwood, to get away from the unhappiness their young, ten-year-old minds couldn't yet express, or to chase dreams in the same way Linnéa used to chase dares.

Or maybe the Earth had seen four children unattended and it opened itself up and took them away. That'll learn you parents, Linnéa imagined the cosmos saying, in her mother's voice, with that shrill, lilting tone.

By the time Linnéa got to the waterfront, she had to pull over, because she couldn't see past the tears in her eyes. Truth be told, that was why she and Stephen did these things on their own. She didn't need him comforting her, spoon-feeding her lies, the same way hot soup was forced upon the sick. She didn't want his "Everything is going to be okay," or, "We're going to find them," or "We have to be strong for them." She knew why he said it, because she'd said it to him more times than she had fingers and toes, but it wasn't any help to either of them. It just gummed things up; fat wads of false hope that got in the way of a good cry.

Facts were her anesthetic, but the well had nearly run dry on those about a week and a half back, and she was jonesing. Before, as she was now, she replayed what she knew over and over in her head, until like tape, it warped and wobbled; became distorted by need and reaching theories.

And what did she know?

She knew that at 11:45 AM, Filipa had gone into the house to fetch her mother and father beers. At some point between 11:45 AM and 12:30 PM, she had gone missing. Forensics had found a muddy work boot print, size 9, in the bathroom, semi-imprinted upon the squares of toilet paper on the ground. They had also found dark hairs, not unlike an animal's, in Filipa's room, despite their family not owning any pets of any kind. There were no signs of break-in or forced entry, and nothing appeared to be missing from the house. The police did note the strange smell circulating the house, but were unable to pinpoint its origin. They had yet to receive a ransom note or any calls from the local crazies laying claim to the crime.

Trent Resin's son, Charles, was estimated to have gone missing at 11:15 AM. Trent noticed his son's disappearance from the backyard, but thinking he might've been in the shed playing, as he was known to do, Trent thought nothing of it. Coming off third-shift like a runaway train, he crashed on the couch until 12:20 PM, until awaking to a strange odor, which he described to the police as earth and rubber. There had been a loud thump, too—a car door shutting, he had thought—and scurrying in the basement. At 12:45 PM, he asked Linnéa if she'd seen Charles. At 1:00 PM, afraid and feral, he took out his pistol, loaded it, and in a sleep-deprived haze, searched the neighborhood up and down for his son. To this day, he's still searching.

Bethany Simmons' son, Jimmy, had been playing in his room all morning. He ate breakfast with her and her husband around 9:30 AM. Pancakes and toast. At 10:15 AM, she checked in on him, and seeing that he was absorbed in his video games, locked him in his room via the outside lock. From 10:15 AM until 10:25 AM, she admitted to having a quickie with her husband. Afterwards, she lost track of time in a social-media binge. Until 11:50 AM, she hadn't heard from her son, which wasn't all that surprising given that he played shooters for hours a time. She made him lunch around noon, and when she went to his room and unlocked it, he was gone. There was a single window in his second-floor room, and it was open, though it'd been open all day and the night before. The only trace of evidence the police were able to find was a crushed tablet next to the boy's controller that was later identified as Rohypnol.

Ellen and Richard Cross' reports to the police of their whereabouts between the times of 8:00 AM, when they claimed to have woken that Sunday, and 12:45 PM are inconsistent. Richard reported during those hours to have spent the majority of his time at home, or running errands. Ellen claimed to have gone to church, but had no witnesses to verify these claims. Their daughter, Darlene, was last seen by the two of them at 11:15 AM, when she came up from her room in the basement for donuts and a glass of orange juice. Ellen had told the police her daughter's eyes were red. Richard had told the police that his daughter looked uneasy. Both of them reportedly thought to themselves it was merely a combination of allergies and anger—Darlene had been grounded that weekend for poor grades. At 12:40 PM, Ellen, after calling for Darlene and not hearing from her, went down to the basement to check on her daughter. She found plaster on her pillow.

As for the unmarked, white van, the two teenagers who'd been inside it were found at 3:30 PM. They were juniors, and were so high at the time of their interrogation, the police might as well tied string to their legs to stop them from floating away. Their story was the same as the one Stephen had suggested that morning: two horny hellions getting their rocks off in the most conspicuous, inconspicuous way. Their names were Brad and Chelsea; they were from the west side of the town, and their well-off parents were none too happy with them when they came to collect them later that day. Brad had seen nothing, but that wasn't all that surprising for a boy his age, when girls were his world. Chelsea, however, had told the cops she did notice someone in Ellen Cross' yard. They had been too dark to make out, though. The police quickly added the suspect might've been black.

As for the neighborhood itself, due to local construction and a few road closures, it had become a popular midway point for traffic to pass through. So when the police asked the parents if they had noticed any strange cars or out of place people that weekend, there was no one thing they could point to. Everyone who had anything to do in that part of Bedlam inevitably slithered through Six Pillars. A lot of it was the construction company responsible for tearing up the roads that led to the detour. But Linnéa did remember seeing a truck or two pass through on occasion that seemed out of their way. None of the other parents, Stephen included, knew what she was talking about. And maybe she didn't, either. If they weren't so damn negligent…

Linnéa snapped up in her seat and wiped her eyes. Negligent. The word burned like a brand in her hand. She held it with a fist. Negligent. What had Ellen Cross blathered in therapy today? Something about losing Darlene… losing her for good. Like Ellen she might've been in danger of losing her once before.

Linnéa drew her cell phone like a six-shooter and loaded Ellen's name like bullets into the search engine. Nothing.

"Dario knew what you were talking about," she mumbled to herself. "He didn't want you bringing it up."

Linnéa searched for Bedlam's Clerk of Courts. There, she searched

Ellen Cross. A list of Ellen Crosses came up, but she clicked the first on there. The birthday checked out, and so did the address. And at the bottom the count read: Child Neglect. Disposition: Charges Dismissed.

Before the information could settle, Linnéa was punching in another name. Bethany Simmons. And there she was. Her count? Child Endangerment. Disposition: Charges Dismissed.

Trent Resin. He was there, too. With a count of Child Abuse. And once again, the disposition read: Charges Dismissed.

Linnéa didn't need to type her name into to know what was waiting for her there, and yet, as she started to…

Stephen sent her a text message.

And it said: Come home. Trent's found something.

By the time Linnéa made it back home, she'd broken so many driving laws that a judge wouldn't be able to help but give her an A for effort. She threw the car into park before coming to a stop in the driveway and vaulted out of it. Stephen was sitting on the porch stoop, turning his cell phone over and over in his hands. There was no sign of Trent, though; just the wake of his revelation, and what it'd done to her husband.

Stephen looked renewed. Compared to the drifting ghost he'd been lately, he was damn near radiant. Linnéa's first thought was that they'd found Filipa, but she tempered her expectations. Stephen wasn't moving from where he sat, and he hadn't glanced up at her, either. Excitement was something they kept at a slow drip; only enough to keep them going. Too much of the stuff and they'd become the Bethany Simmonses of the world. High on lies and the ease of ritual.

Linnéa settled in beside Stephen and rubbed her shoulder into his. "What's going on?"

Biting the inside of his lower lip, he said, "You know that root I found in the garden that morning?"

At first, she didn't, but then the memory was there, bleeding through the bandages wrapped around her traumatized mind. "Yeah. The red, vein-looking thing."

"Trent had one in his yard."

She sighed and stopped herself from shaking her head. These weren't the kind of facts that she'd been hoping for. These were dead-ends that never ended—busy work for the bored.

"Ellen and Richard did, too. Trent said he remembered seeing Darlene tearing them out of the backyard."

Linnéa raised an eyebrow. "What about Bethany?"

He shook his head. "I don't know."

"Didn't you post a picture of it to all your plant buddies?"

"Just did—" he tapped the phone on his knee, "—but nothing yet." He turned on his phone, checked the post. "Nothing."

Linnéa didn't want to say it, but it needed to be said. "I'm not sure this is help—"

"There's a few things out there on it. It's…"

He paused, stared at her. Eyes wide, mouth mouthing phantom words; like Richard Cross, he seemed to be asking her permission to keep speaking.

She didn't say anything. She didn't want him to hear the reluctance in her tone. It would devastate him.

"It's hard because I don't know what to call it or how to describe it. There's nothing special about it, but… it's like I said, Lin. It's weird. I found a few discussions on a few websites about it, but they get shut down real quick. No one's interested, or allowed to be interested."

"If it's a weed, I suppose I can't blame them."

"I don't think it is." He stood up, extended his hand for her to take. "Come inside. I want you to try something."

"Okay," she said, noticing the red stains on his fingertips. It looked like he had blood on his hands. All parents did in a way, didn't they? She had to tell him about the dirt on the others, but he had to get this out of his system first. Saving their daughter couldn't be a competition.

Linnéa let Stephen lead her into the house. Walking through it without her usual blinders on made her realize what'd happened to the place. Old clothes like breadcrumbs were scattered throughout every room. On every surface, dust was gathering dust; framed pictures of the family were nothing more than television static—favorite channels that, for the sake of their sanity, had to be tuned out. The police had found evidence in the form of a muddy work boot print in the bathroom, and now there were footprints all over the place, most of which ran in circles. The house smelled like a hangover, too; armpit sweat, oily hair, and the fumes of partially digested food. The home wasn't a home anymore, but a hideout.

And day by day, it was stripped of little things—picture frames, towels, or coffee mugs; neither of them could remember moving or disposing of the items, but they didn't much miss them. Wherever they were going, they were better off.

Stephen took her to the kitchen, and on the kitchen table, two clumps of red roots lay segregated by an empty paper towel roll. Both of them had been cut into. Small drops of vibrant liquid dotted the tabletop. They were the same color as the faded wash on her husband's fingertips, and the meaty chunks underneath his nails.

"One on the left is from our garden," he said. "One on the right is from Trent's backyard."

"Is that all of it?"

"All that we could find, yeah. It wasn't growing out of anything, though. It wasn't attached to any system. Came right out of the ground. Trent said the same for his."

Linnéa approached the table and sniffed the air. Her nostrils tingled. Her eyes lost focus temporarily.

"I think someone put them there," Stephen said.

There was a sour pocket underneath Linnéa's tongue, as if she'd bit into a mouth-puckering piece of candy. She drowned it in spit and backed away from the table.

"It's more than red, isn't it?" Stephen took her place at the table and prodded the root from their garden. "Been trying to break it down to search for it better on the Internet. Sent a picture to Mom."

Linnéa steadied her breathing. Before she knew it, she was back at the table again beside Stephen. It wasn't the sight of the roots that was setting her on edge, but the liquid puddled around them. It had a power over her.

"Vermillion, that was her read on the roots' shade. Woman can't paint for shit, but at least knows her colors."

Needing to change the subject, to break the hold the strange growths had on her, Linnéa said, "Stephen, I found something, too."

His eyes dulled. His face went hard. He seemed to want to tell her to go ahead, to share what she knew, but the consideration wasn't there, not like it'd used to be. It wasn't a matter of competition. It was just that he'd finally brought something new to the table, and she didn't even bother taking the time to try it out.

Stephen pressed on. "They're not roots, either."

"What are they?"

"Veins." He nodded at them. "There're no hairs, and the epidermis is all wrong. The structure…" He drew a sharp breath. "They're veins.

It's like they were ripped out of something."

Linnéa's jaw dropped. "Are they human? Are they…?"

"We found them before Filipa went missing." Stephen smiled. "Yeah, my mind went there, too."

There was something wrong with Stephen's smile. Linnéa hadn't noticed it at first, but just now… Yeah, there was something on his tooth. She leaned, caught a glimpse of a red-capped canine past his pursued lips.

"Did you… eat them?" she asked, incredulously.

"I took a bite," he said, as if chowing on some creature's veins was an everyday thing for him. "I don't—"

"Stephen!"

"—know what they came from, but they're a hallucinogenic."

"What?"

Stephen ignored her and took out his phone.

"What the hell?" Her neck and her cheeks grew hot. She went to push him, but stopped herself at the last second. "Steve, what the hell?"

"Read this." He pressed the phone into her hand. "It's a lot of bull-shit, but it's the only concrete thing I've been able to find on these vermillion veins so far."

Black Occult Macabre. That was the name of the website. It was so minimalistic in design, it barely registered as existing. The background was pure black, the font a dim white that straddled the line between readable and repulsive. Centered at the top of the page, below a row of non-descript buttons, was a picture of the very same vermillion veins that lay bleeding on Linnéa's kitchen table, albeit coming out of the stonework of a ruined keep. Below the image, there were words; and they read:

The Agony of After: Crime Scenes in Vermillion
By Connor Prendergast

On the eve of the 19th century, in seldom visited English countryside known then as Blackwood Marsh, two events occurred that have since been almost completely scrubbed from the annals of history. At first, there was a viral outbreak in the town of Parish that either killed or drove away the entire population living there. And then, a month later, in the mining village of Cairn, the same virus passed through, but not before driving several individuals living there into a murderous rampage that claimed over thirty lives.

Connected by proximity and the presence of a pestilence, Parish and Cairn's fates were not decided by the disease that infested both the people and the land they lived upon, but by the house of horrors that loomed over them physically and financially for centuries.

The outbreak that ravaged Blackwood Marsh was preceded by the literal collapse of the Ashcroft estate in the area. In the stygian bowels of the ancient mansion, a foul growth emerged. Sentient and seeking subservience, It consumed the Ashcroft line and bent them to Its will, causing them to spread Its pulpy, palpable influence throughout Europe.

The sordid details of the Ashcroft line and their lineage of insanity can be found elsewhere on this website. For now, the focus will remain on the vermillion veins that sprouted forth from the carcass of their fouled family tree.

Like most things supernatural and of the Membrane, little is known about the vermillion veins. Oral accounts speak of their presence prior to the collapse of the Ashcroft estate, but it wasn't until the growths were unearthed in Blackwood Marsh that their nefarious purpose became clear.

At first glance, the vermillion veins appear to be roots. Despite their vibrant coloring, they are, for all intents and purposes, unremarkable, and can easily be mistaken for the garden variety invasive plant. It is a clever form of camouflage that, in combination with the veins' rare appearances, conceals them from the public eye and inquiring scientific minds.

The vermillion veins are not roots, but self-aware structures that exist as part of some still unseen hive or mind. They are human-borne, propagating through the heinous deeds of a carefully selected few. Like parasites, the vermillion veins are indebted to their hosts, and their hosts are violence, and the violent individuals that sow it. They appear where traumatic events have taken place, as if to sop up the sorrow that stains the fabric of that point in reality.

However, recent evidence has suggested the vermillion veins are not being spread by their human conscripts as a means by which to see the writhing masses fed. Rather, it is that those who have sworn themselves to the vermillion veins are finding or creating traumatic tears in the human experience to coax forth the veins from the eldritch muscular that surrounds our world.

The vermillion veins are not thriving off our suffering, but using it as means by which to measure and mark various points on the Earth. The growths are crime scene chalk; and the empty space inside the outlines? Doorways, perhaps, for greater, more terrible things, waiting for the signal to come through. For ages, strange beasts have been crossing the threshold, carving their names and legacy into our folk tales and horror stories. It is not unreasonable to assume their journey and genesis was made all the easier by those fertile gateways.

If the vermillion veins are as dependent upon those who carry the seeds of their will as time would suggest, then who are these individuals who would see our lives unspooled? Amon Ashcroft, for one—the vein-riddled embodiment of the last head of the estate. His appearances are few and uncon- firmable, and yet, if he still exists, like any sadistic master, it is likely he has slaves operating beneath him, carrying out his intent.

Random crimes and seemingly unconnected suspects have made it difficult to determine if there is an organized effort to spread the vermillion veins; however, several sources and documents have pointed to an unnamed cult. Whether they are the perpetrators of the crime, or simply scavengers, the scenes in which the vermillion veins are present have been known to take on an almost religious tone.

Eastern Europe, 1931: an abandoned convent was discov- ered to have been the killing grounds for a prolific serial killer who kidnapped tourists. No ties were made between the serial killer and the rumored cult, but vermillion veins were discovered at the crime scene several weeks after it had already been examined by the authorities, as if a group had arrived later and gave rise to them there. The veins, in combination with the candles, incense, carvings, and incomprehensible scrawling, was said to have mirrored mementos left upon headstones.

Central Africa, 1967: the Onai tribe's village was consumed, in a similar manner, by the vermillion pestilence that afflicted Parish and Cairn; that is, people were overwhelmed with madness and a distinct dissociation of the self; and the very land became infected, rotting all that it touched. Catholic missionaries in the area were sent to the village with medicine and religion—the most potent of anesthetics—to assist. When they arrived, they found that the matriarchal society had been overtaken by a mysterious man dressed in black. Both the missionaries and the tribe were never heard from again, though they were occasionally seen by acquaintances in the neighboring cities, and that they were wearing robes bearing a strange symbol: an eye wreathed in tentacles.

United States, 1992: A freshman at Springwood High opened fire on a psychology class, killing all twenty students, the teacher, and his aide. The shooter, having bought himself time with bomb threats, then preceded to arrange the slain into crude, geometric shapes. When police finally entered the building and discovered the classroom, 'strange, bright red flowers' were seen growing out of the victims' chests. Arrested before successfully committing suicide, the Springwood Shooter now serves out the rest of his days in a long-term psychiatric hospital, where he has convinced the staff there to allow him to maintain his own personal garden. Reports state that, in the right light, under the right circumstances, the shooter's eyes are said to have flecks of red in them, and that occasionally, root-shaped things are said to move beneath his skin. He is currently engaged to a groupie who's been writing him letters for the last twenty years. Five years ago, she created a social media group in his honor. Fifteen strong, they go by the name "The Disciples."

The aforementioned three are but drops in the vermillion wave that threatens to wash away life on this planet. Like many movements, though, the narrative has changed in regards to the vermillion veins. As was discussed earlier, the growths may not be thriving off of torturous moments, but rooting themselves in them and unlocking their potentials—splitting, perhaps, their agonized atoms.

Lately, dead or disembodied vermillion veins have been found at crime scenes. Rather than being drawn forth, they are being harvested and left like offerings at our altars of death. There are several theories as to why this may be the case.

The vermillion veins have become commercialized in the realms of the cult-like behavior. Individuals unaware of their impact or power are digging them up and repurposing them for their own rituals.

The vermillion veins and the hive or mind to which they are connected is dying. The growths have lost their hold over this world and they are unable sustain themselves any longer. As it does with all things, entropy has found a way to combat that which we could not.

Or the vermillion veins are continuing to be used as markers, but rather than marking weak points between here and the Membrane, they are being used as indicators for very real, very natural, earthbound beings. Returning to the religious symbolism, it is not impossible to see the vermillion veins as the lambs' blood the Israelites painted upon their doors to spare their firstborn. However, if this is the case, it begs the question: Is someone being spared, or sought out?

Linnéa looked up from the cell phone at Stephen and, laughing in disbelief, said, "This is… Steve. This is bullshit. Come on."

"What did you find?" he asked, every cuss word and insult in the corners of his mouth.

"I…" She sighed, had a look at the site again. Really? No, she couldn't entertain this, not even if it paid her to. "I looked up all the parents. They've all been taken to court for abusing their kids."

"Well, there you go." Stephen took the phone out of her hand. "Listen, Lin, I don't buy the spooky monster crap, either. It's B-movie bullshit. What did the others do?"

Linnéa strained her mind to recall the details. "Ellen for child neglect… Bethany had child endangerment. And Trent… his was for child abuse."

"Then there's us," Stephen said.

"Yeah."

"Four kids are missing from four families that'd had run-ins with the law back in the day." He jammed his finger into the cell phone's screen. "What if we've been marked?" He nodded at the vermillion veins. "Those things were fresh, but they hadn't laid roots. They were placed at our houses. All of them, I bet. Not saying it's monsters. I'm not. Just crazy sons of bitches."

Linnéa's stomach turned. "What about this guy? This Connor guy? You said this is all you can find on the veins."

"He's local," Stephen said.

"Shut up."

"He is. He's from here."

"How do you know?"

"I've heard the name once or twice. He did that story on the murder of the Zdanowicz family awhile back. Released it in his own rag. He's from Bedlam."

Biting the inside of her lip, Linnéa's said, "He's a suspect."

"Got to be."

She looked at the vermillion veins and the tantalizing blood they'd shed. "Did you really drink from one of them?"

Stephen hesitated, and then said, "Yeah."

Linnéa asked, "Why?" but only out of formality—these kinds of freakish scenarios demanded Whys and What fors. She knew why, she knew what for. Even she wanted to take a chomp out of the things.

"Guess I thought it might help me figure out what it was." He didn't sound convinced with himself. "We should tell Detective Mills about this Connor Prendergast."

Linnéa had a bad taste in her mouth. It was the death of the false hope she'd been harboring this last month like an immigrant; that ostracized emotion that had no goddamn right to be here, or so claimed hate and its equally ignorant brother, retribution. If their houses had been marked by some individual or cult, and if their children had been taken for the sins of their parents' pasts, then that was it. Then it was decided. Filipa was in the hands of some cruel, violent, and depraved entity, and had been for thirty days. She wasn't off experimenting with her peers in Maidenwood, testing the limits of their burgeoning pubescence. She wasn't across state lines, empowered by how embittered she'd become by the parentarchy. She was just a ten-year-old prisoner in a cell just shy of hell.

She wrinkled her nose at the smell that seemed to linger about them.

"You okay?" Stephen took her hand in his.

"Let's talk to Connor first."

"You sure?"

"He sounds like a nut. I don't want him to clam up, especially if he knows something. Can you email him?"

Stephen smiled, said, "Sure," and went in for a kiss. Linnéa tried to meet him halfway, but both their aims were off. He got her nose, and she, some of his chin. Another day, they might've laughed about it, but not today. Couples who were together long enough followed a script, and their interactions were like well-rehearsed scenes from the longest running play.

Linnéa gave Stephen a quick kiss on the lips, but it was too late. There were curtains everywhere they looked.

Later that night, Linnéa, alone, read through Black Occult Macabre once more. From possessed jewelry, astral terrors, to a giant mosquito affectionately known as Mr. Haemo, the website should have been nothing more than clickbait trash, and yet all the information was compiled together as professionally as this low-rent shock blogger could probably muster. She was excited to meet Connor, in the same manner one gets that sadistic glee when they're holding a shoe over a cornered centipede.

By the time she'd finished reading about the Black Hour, it was the Black Hour, and she was in her daughter's room. Or was it Linnéa's mother's room? Ninety percent of the items inside it had belonged to Agnes. Did Filipa's disappearance belong to her to?

Linnéa lay down on her daughter's bed and pressed one of the pillows to her chest. She breathed in the smell of Filipa in the fabric. Whether it was there, or it was in her mind, it was hard to say. But like life support, it kept her alive.

Agnes—Linnéa's mother—had kept a close eye on everyone but herself. Aside from those nine months when she'd been pregnant with Linnéa, Agnes had always been a heavy drinker. That, in combination with the medications she took to treat a chronic case of "mental unbalance," had transformed her from the scrawny, scuffed-up, postcard-picture-perfect youth, to the transient waif that waited in all corners and on all thresholds, ears pressed to plaster, plastic, wood, and brick for thunderous words and stormy rumors. Her "mental unbalance," as Linnéa would learn when such a thing was obviously not normal, was, in fact, self-diagnosed. And the doctors treating her? They were the rich from west Bedlam who she rubbed elbows with until they were hot and raw.

When Filipa was born, that made Agnes a grandmother, and like all grandmothers, the need to see her granddaughter, to squeeze her cheeks and hold her high and relive those fabled days long gone by, bordered on mania. Linnéa, not having seen her mother and wanting to believe she had changed, relented. A bad mother could still be a good grandmother.

And Agnes had been a good grandmother, for a while. But as Filipa got older and older, Agnes hid her habits less and less; again, as always, doing the opposite of what she should have. Until one day, Agnes picked Filipa up from pre-school. High on pills, sloppy-drunk on a forty-ounce, Agnes nearly ran down Filipa as she ran to her. Before the teachers could put two and two together, Agnes floored it off the school property and, ten minutes later, drove her car through the front of a restaurant.

Surprisingly, no one was injured or killed inside the restaurant, but Agnes was found with a concussion and Filipa with a mouthful of blood from a busted lip and a few sprung baby teeth. The restaurant ended up turning into a hoity toity spot where the well-off ordered pictures of food and imagined how good they tasted, while Agnes got a lengthy inpatient stay, followed by rehab, followed by promises and the shattered beer bottles that broke them. Filipa got a social worker, a caseworker, more ice cream and cards than she knew what to do with, and a lot of people who "cared" about her as they buttered her up to get her to break down about Linnéa and Stephen and all the terrible things they had to have done to her over the years.

Filipa had given them nothing, because there was nothing to give them, except a stuck-out tongue and snot rockets. The courts came after Linnéa hard. They slapped a child endangerment charge on her, on account of Agnes being a prolific piece of shit. Instead of doing time or losing Filipa, though, Linnéa and Stephen did parenting classes and supervised sessions with Filipa until everyone involved was sufficiently convinced they did love their daughter, and that what had happened with Agnes would never happen again.

It didn't. Filipa never saw her grandmother again after that. Linnéa tried to get her mother to come around for a holiday get-together, but Agnes refused. The whole incident had led her into a deeper, darker, drug-fueled, alcohol-drenched hole from which she never did emerge. Her last words, which she gave to Linnéa over the phone the evening before she killed herself, were these: "Mirrors mean nothing when you won't see yourself in them."

Agnes hadn't much, but what she had, she left behind for Filipa, and for Filipa alone. The sum total of Linnéa's mother's life was two thousand dollars, her house, and all the spotless antiques she kept inside it. The two thousand dollars was sitting in Filipa's savings, the house now belonged to another family, and all those antiques? They were here in Filipa's room, gathering dust but getting used. It had been her grandmother's penance for everything she'd done. Stephen sometimes joked that Agnes only gave Filipa all that furniture to spare her from all that "cheap, made in China crap," she was always going on about.

Linnéa pressed Filipa's pillow harder against her face. Readjusting herself, the mattress gave and, for a moment, she thought Filipa had climbed back into bed with her. She turned on her side. Her daughter wasn't there, but a picture of her was on the nightstand. A picture of her, Steven, and Linnéa at Bleak's Holdout—the so-called "haunted" forest of the much larger state park it joined up with.

"That was a good day," Linnéa said, trying to mimic Filipa's toothy, troll-like smile. "It was a good day."

Linnéa passed out for a half an hour, and then woke back up recharged, as if a bolt of lightning had struck her in her sleep. Too anxious to go back to bed, she went downstairs, grabbed her electric guitar and amp. Before heading back to Filipa's room, she took a detour into the kitchen, where the vermillion veins lay like dissected specimens on the table.

She flicked the low E string on her guitar. While its dooming note rang out in the moonlit dark, she grabbed the vein from their garden and took a hunk out of it with her teeth. The texture was tough, and there were tiny bumps all over it she hadn't noticed before. The taste was sweet, almost like wine, but at the same time completely different; it was a complex combination of flavors and tones that constantly evolved, escaping any classification her country bumpkin brain could manage. What was most disturbing, however, was how dirty it made her mouth feel. It left her tongue chalky, and her teeth became heavy.

The liquid inside the vein lingered on the edge of her throat, like a finger run around a glass rim. She choked, and because this was the music the fluid was apparently trying to conduct, it then slid satisfactorily down her esophagus.

Linnéa felt dirty, the same way she used to feel after coming home from a party and remembering the men who'd gazed and grazed her like wide-eyed cows with oblivious intent. And then, Linnéa felt unworthy, the same way she had when she went to church with Stephen's family every Christmas and partook in every communion, not because she wanted to or needed to, but because she didn't want to let the big guy on the little cross down; he looked sad enough as it was.

Linnéa lapped at the water sputtering from the kitchen sink until her mouth was as right as it was going to get, and then she got going. Hallucinogenic? She wasn't so sure about that. But by the time she was back in Filipa's room, her ax plugged in and the amp squealing out feedback, she was definitely Anges' daughter—jitters and grinding teeth and all.

In high school, Linnéa and three other girls had a black metal band named The Sisters of Ungoliant. Since her and Stephen were about to kick-up a satanic panic in the next ten hours, it seemed fitting to her she should rock out a few riffs to the Prince of Lies. Dario Onai would understand. When it came to coping skills, how could this not take the cake?

She was two choruses into their most requested song, *Vistas of Evil,* when the vermillion veins kicked in and caused the room to start to spin. Tremolo picking slowing to a sluggish strum, she strained her ears to hear the movement in the hall. It was Stephen, hobbling like a hunchback down this house's lonely corridors, searching for sanctuary in the fruits of persistence. She didn't need to see him to know where he was going; he'd spent most of the night in their office, fiddling with his phone, wondering aloud if Bethany Simmons had vermillion veins in her yard, too.

The front door slammed shut downstairs. It seemed they'd know soon enough.

Linnéa thought about going to the window, but the glass looked as if it were melting, and she figured it would be best if she stayed put. Hallucinogenic? Yeah, alright, maybe so.

The high was short lived, though. As she chugged out the funeral waltz gallop to *The Mares of Bedlam,* she realized what she was doing and where she was doing it, and started tearing up. She dropped her head hard against the top of the guitar—a clang of discord burst out the amp—and shook. Her mother's last words had warned her of not seeing herself when she looked in a mirror, but all she saw was herself, and how desperately she wanted to be anybody but Agnes. Who the fuck was this impromptu concert for? Not Stephen, and not Filipa, and maybe not even Linnéa. Was she coping, or just trying to be cool?

"What's more metal than shredding in your missing daughter's room in the middle of the night?" Linnéa snorted and let her pick fall to the floor. "Fuck, I hate this. I don't—" She sucked up spit and clicked the amp over to 'clean.' "I don't want to do this anymore."

She plucked aimlessly on the A, D, and G strings. With each note came a memory of Filipa. She saw her on the floor, on all fours, plodding along with her baby food-encrusted baby blanket. She saw her at school, at recess, combing the recesses of the building with boys who looked up to her as if she were some punk queen. She saw her in her room, through the crack in the door, face in another book, mind in another world. She saw her and Stephen asleep in the living room, her smashed against her father's arm, the fabric of his shirt wrapped around her clutching fingers. She saw her in Linnéa's closet, blending in with the dresses and shirts hanging off the hangers, and holding them up like swatches to herself, to see what she may look like in five years' time.

Linnéa continued to pluck on the A, D, and G strings until, unknowingly, she'd made something out of them. Voice hoarse and stinking of vermillion blood, she started to sing:

You were there,
And then you were not.
All that I am,
Is all that I've fought.
I see you sometimes,
Under that tree.
I wonder sometimes,
If it was me.
If they touched but a hair on your head,
I'll kill them all.
I'll kill them dead.
Whatever it takes to bring you back,
To under that tree;

Where you aren't.
But where you should be.

Linnéa screwed up her face and dropped the guitar against the side of the bed. Needing Stephen in a way she hadn't needed him before, she stood up and sprinted out of the room. She ran down the hall, stomped down the stairs. She could hear the crickets coming in loudly through the banisters, like they might've kept a window—

The front door stood open. The summer wind set it a-sway.

"Stephen?" she cried.

Her voice carried through the blackness that had filled her house; that eerie, almost solidified stillness; nocturnal amber.

"Steve!"

Heart beating fast enough to give a black metal drummer a run for their money, Linnéa took two large strides and grabbed the front door. But before she could shut it, a scene she'd seen before played before her with a distorted sense of déjà vu.

To her right, Ellen and Richard Cross stood, and as had happened before, Ellen's figure was standing on the porch, waving her arms.

To her left, there was Trent Resin's home, and hurrying down the driveway was the shape of Trent.

Except that wasn't Ellen on Ellen's porch.

And that wasn't Trent in Trent's driveway.

And, panicked, Linnéa looked farther down the street to Bethany Simmons' house, where not one shape, but three were standing on her manicured lawn, staring up at Jimmy Simmons' window.

"S-S-Steve!" Linnéa stammered, backpedaling.

The stair light flashed on behind her.

She spun around.

At the top of the stairs, a dark shape stood against the wall. It laughed like a little girl would laugh. And then slowly, it stepped around the corner, out of sight.

Paralyzed, Linnéa stood there, listening to the invader's footsteps on the second floor. She tracked its movements to Filipa's room, and then to hers and Stephen's.

It shut the door. It was waiting for her to follow.

Linnéa started towards the stairs when—

"Lin?" Stephen whispered behind her.

She stopped, snaked her neck around like a feasting snake to face him.

He was holding a handful of vermillion veins. "The Simmons had some in their... What's wrong?"

"There's something in the house," Linnéa whispered. "Didn't you... Didn't you see..." She pointed outside to the other parents' houses. "There's something upstairs."

Stephen stared past her, into the house, at the staircase drenched in yellow light. His eyes wandered away, met hers. Hand slipping into his pocket, he nodded, pulled out his keys, and said, "Okay."

Linnéa and Stephen went to the driveway, unlocked Stephen's car, and jumped inside. He started it up, backed it down the driveway; meeting the street, he forced it into park, locked the doors, and together, they stared into their bedroom window.

"Call the police," he said, handing her his cell phone.

She took it and started to dial 911.

"Who was it?"

"I don't know," Linnéa said. Before she sent the call: "I tried one of the veins."

Stephen glanced at her. "Eh?"

"You said it's a hallucinogenic. Fuck." She dropped the phone in her lap. "If you didn't see it... maybe it wasn't..."

Stephen grabbed the phone and called 911. "We're not taking that chance."

The phone clicked over. On the other line, the emergency operator buzzed out a question.

Linnéa turned her attention back towards the bedroom window on the second floor. As the effects of the vermillion veins began to wane, her imagination took over, and she conjured creations behind the glass. Shadowy figures with elongated limbs and pointed teeth. Sinister silhouettes brandishing knives and fistfuls of candy. She didn't tell Stephen what she saw, because there was no telling if it was real or not. Looking over her shoulder through the rear window, there were no signs of the other dark shapes she'd seen earlier; but there was the vermillion vein Stephen had brought home from the Simmonses'. Seeing it, she wanted to eat it whole.

The police arrived fifteen minutes later. They searched the house thoroughly and found no one inside. Linnéa left out the detail about the other shapes on the lawns, but in the end, it didn't matter, because though the police hadn't found anyone, they had found something.

A message written in ash on the ceiling over Linnéa and Stephen's bed. It read: A Child in Every Home.

SUNDAY**MONDAY**TUESDAYWEDNESDAYTHURSDAYFRIDAYSATURDAY

Monday morning lurched drearily into Six Pillars. Fat, black clouds wandered across the sky—a funeral procession of elephantine shapes—and made miserable those below. A steady drizzle swept back and forth across the neighborhood, giving rise to just enough mist to make at home any wayward mariner. There was no sun in the sky, and with the moon still riding high, there was no guarantee it had bothered to rise. This world of heel-dragging corporate drones was one lit by porch lights and brake lights, and cell phone screens, like star maps, casting today's course by social media's inconsequential constellations.

Worse than clouds, than the rain, than the mist and the attention-starved machines, was the air. When the authorities had arrived in Six Pillars and discovered the warning writ in ash, the chief of police interpreted it as a threat to the other children in the neighborhood and dispatched most of the force there. Now, at 7:00 AM, as they had been at 2:00 AM, the cruisers were cruising the streets, polluting the air with their exhaust and the sleep-deprived babble that broke from the officers' coffee-stained, gingivitis-drenched mouths. It wasn't just that it was hard to breathe; it was that you couldn't breathe. Sure, all that nitrogen and carbon dioxide from the exhaust would do that to a person, but it was the babble, too; the banter from the boys-in-blue—their professional indifference and sick speculation they basically belted for all to hear.

"Dumbass kids," one cop crooned, playing a tune on his dash. "Better not let me be the one to find them."

"You know, it's the parents," another cop said to his partner, rolling, with the windows down, past. "This is fucking ridiculous."

"I'll buy whoever finds a body a drink," a cop cried into his radio. He floored it down the street, spinning out at the stop sign.

Other police officers on patrol were less vocal, but their non-verbals all said the same thing: Fuck this.

Linnéa pulled away from the living room window and closed it. She wiped the layer of rain off the sill, grabbed her phone out of her pajama pocket, called her boss, and left a message to let him know she wasn't coming in the rest of the week.

A break in a quickly cooling case should've roused the community and the local enforcement, and yet aside from her and Stephen and the other parents, no one could've cared less. Fatigue was setting in, the same way summer was dying, and the rot of change was spreading through the season. Like all things, if she was going to get something done, she was going to have to do it herself.

When Stephen came down ten minutes later, he told her he had taken the week off, too.

"Did you sleep on the couch?" he mumbled, scratching himself through his boxers.

Linnéa looked at the couch and the mess of blankets left on it.

"I didn't sleep," he said. "Just stayed up all night on the computer."

"I didn't sleep, either." Linnéa went back to the window and cracked it open. "Feels like there's something still in the house."

"Can't let anything stop us," Stephen said. He came up behind her and started rubbing her shoulders. "This is our house."

Linnéa turned around. She pressed her body into his, and then threw her arms around him. She absorbed his heat into her chest, and he absorbed her tears into his shirt.

"We have to do everything together from now on," she said, nudging him with her head. "This isn't healthy. We're not covering more ground, just putting more distance between us."

Stephen pressed his nose to her hair, kissed her scalp. "Let's go look at it, then."

Forensics had flayed their bedroom. The bed had been stripped; the closet picked clean. The chest of drawers had undergone an autopsy: the drawers had been ripped open, and the clothes inside torn out. The curtains lay crumpled on the ground, while the picture frames sat askew upon the wall—dirt squares outlining where they'd once been. In the adjoining bathroom, faint remnants of fingerprinting powder dusted the sink and toilet; and with the right light, you could even see the luminol on the tile, along the baseboards.

But it was the ceiling above Linnéa and Stephen's bed that'd seen the most attention. A Child in Every Home. The phrase had been written in ash with a finger, or as the officers so chillingly put it, "Someone's finger." It hadn't been small, either. The phrase ran just as long as their queen size bed did, and the words had been written in a clichéd, childish scrawl—the same way a kid writes when they're referencing their parents' examples. The distance between the bed and the ceiling wasn't small, either. The intruder would've had to have been at least eight feet tall and on the tips of their toes to begin to have a chance at touching the ceiling.

Now, the words were gone. All that remained of them were two black, half-dollar sized smudges a few inches apart from one another. The police had forgotten to scrub them away. Linnéa and Stephen hadn't even really realized they were there until this moment, when they were staring up at them, almost into them.

"It stinks in here," Linnéa said. She held her nose. "It doesn't smell like our home anymore."

Stephen nodded. He grabbed a pillow off the bed and hurled it at one of the black smudges. They didn't budge.

Linnéa grabbed the pillow before he could lob it again. "It's fine. Leave it. I want it to be the first thing I see in the morning, and the last thing I see at night. I'm not fucking around anymore."

"Yeah," Stephen said. Furrowing his brow, he seemed to search inside himself for something, and then: "Yeah. You're right. We've done the 'you're doing everything you can' approach. They were in our house."

Still staring at the smudges, she asked, "They were in our house the night after we found all that out about the vermillion veins. Is that a coincidence?"

Stephen shrugged. "I… I don't know."

"Maybe I did hallucinate the others I saw outside, but someone was in here."

"Right. Obviously."

"Under our nose. Maybe the whole day. Whoever took our baby… they're still in town. They're getting around without drawing any suspicion."

Stephen shuffled his feet. "Lin, they got four kids. Seems like they're intending on nabbing a few more. One month and… if they are… that's a long time to care for that many kids. With no ransom, either."

"Filipa's alive," Linnéa belted at him. "She's alive."

"She is," Stephen said, nodding.

Linnéa didn't like her husband's reluctance. It mirrored her own in ways she couldn't yet articulate. She sat down on the bed, lay back until she was propped up against the headboard. She kept her eyes fixed on the two black smudges. In this moment, they were everything. They were a confirmation that they weren't crazy, that their daughter was truly missing. They were a validation of all her fears and parental paranoias. They were her, and they were her mother: two misshapen omens, identical despite their differences. Someone could've told Linnéa the smudges had always been there, and she would've believed them. You didn't see darkness when you spent your whole life staring into the light. Coolness has its costs.

"You found out all manner of things last night, didn't you?" Linnéa said, finally focusing on Stephen.

"I did."

"Why're you holding back on me?"

"Because…" He sat down beside her, pressed his hand over her knee. "Because you're going to agree with me. And I think I've got my mind made up. And I feel desperate. I feel like… hurting someone."

Linnéa sat up. "You found Connor Prendergast."

"I did."

"We should track him. See where he goes."

"I know."

"None of the other parents even bothered showing up last night."

"They're keeping their distance."

Linnéa's cheek quivered. "We come together, they move away. Bet you they think we're marked."

Stephen shifted. "Are we?"

"It's someone in the neighborhood," Linnéa said, sure of herself. "Living here or staying here."

"You think its Trent, or Ellen, or Bethany?"

"I think we're two parents who've lost their little girl." She covered her nose from the smell. "We're marked already, you know? It's all over us. People either get sympathetic, or sick of us—"

"But they get out of our way," Stephen said.

"As long as we didn't do anything wrong, for now, we can't do nothing wrong." She swung her feet over the side of the bed.

A piece of the ceiling chipped away and fell on Stephen's hand. He wiped it off and said, "Okay. Get dressed, then. Connor will be waking up for coffee in the next hour."

With Linnéa behind the wheel, she and Stephen navigated the clogged streets of Six Pillars. Police cruisers and news vans formed frustrating barricades that only a good deal of honking and middle fingers could break. Towards the entrance to the neighborhood, where the detoured traffic rumbled bumper-to-bumper, Linnéa noticed not only several trucks from the construction company, Hannover, but also an ice cream truck, a school bus one month too early to be picking up kids, and a blue truck with the logo "Price Homes"—the company that was responsible for building and expanding Six Pillars.

She made a mental note of what she'd seen, and then, as they pulled out of the neighborhood, noticed a white van at a stop sign. The traffic was too congested to get at it, so instead she took a picture of the license plate, and they kept on going.

By 7:45 AM, Linnéa and Stephen rolled up to Connor Prendergast's house and parallel parked themselves in between two beat-up junkers.

It wasn't much, this stakeout, but it felt like a lot; at least, it did to Linnéa. For a month and some change, they'd done the missing child routine. They worked the community, hounded the police; they did their interviews, made their public pleas; they went on with their lives, even though their lives had long since left them behind; they played detective from the comforts of their home and cars; they bared themselves in therapy, brutalized themselves in private. And what did they have to show for it? Less weight, more weight; dark circles under their eyes, wrinkles where there hadn't been wrinkles before; sleepless nights, aimless days; an empty bedroom at the end of the hall; photographs of a girl they'd once known—her name had been Filipa, and who knew when she was due back home.

Maybe nothing would come of this, but nothing was better than the empty something they kept sustaining themselves on. That Internet prescribed diet of happy thoughts and keeping busy and avoiding blame and letting yourself move on. It was the kind of diet made to make you look good to others; fancy robes to hide the skeleton inside.

A light came on in Connor's house. She and Stephen shot up in their seats like two dogs hearing the garage door go up.

"Did you take a bite out of the vein this morning?" he asked her.

She didn't say anything.

"Me, too."

Linnéa glanced at him from the corner of her eye. Whatever the vermillion veins were, whether they were hallucinogenic or not, they made her feel renewed in ways most over-the-counters couldn't. Besides, if they were truly left as markings or offerings, then eating them was, in a way, like glimpsing the culprit's state of mind. She wanted to walk around in their shoes a bit, before she knocked them the fuck off their feet.

Connor came out 8:07 AM dressed like a hipster going as a hipster to a Halloween party. His legs were two twigs stuffed into even skinnier jeans; he wore a white collared shirt underneath a brown vest; and his hair was an oily rat's nest stuffed into a red, knit beanie that hung off the back of his head like a nutsack. The only thing he was missing was a thick pair of glasses and... there they were; Connor produced them out of thin air like a magician might a handful of flowers and put them on.

The so-called supernatural investigator triple-locked his front door and did a double-take of the street. Securing the messenger bag slung over his shoulder, he hurried to his car, got in it. It took a few turns of the key before the engine came to.

Then he was off.

And they were off with him.

As Stephen had predicted, Connor drove downtown to a non-corporate coffee shop and retreated to the back, where he sat from 8:30 AM until 12:00 PM on his laptop, hitting the drink hard. Linnéa and Stephen watched him the entire time and kept track of who he was chummy with (the silver-haired waitress, the dark-haired waitress, and the redheaded patron—a Neapolitan ménage à trois, as Stephen called it).

At 11:59 AM, he got a call on his phone, and fifteen minutes later, Connor, with Linnéa and Stephen camped out behind some bushes, was out snooping around a low-income housing complex not but a stone's throw away from Six Pillars. He was there until 1:19 PM, and when he came out, he came out covered in dirt, and sweating. He pockets looked stuffed, too, and soaked through. Trailing behind him was a rough looking, thirty-year-old-or-so woman in a kimono. She tried to hand him a wad of bills that must've been tips from the club she probably worked at, but, with a smile and a laugh, he refused and hurried back into his car.

"What's that about?" Linnéa said to Stephen.

"Start looking closely into anyone's life and shit's bound to get weird."

He took out his phone, called the police, and reported a 'suspicious person' at this address.

"Just in case," he said, trailing off as a man in a business suit walked past their car, waving at them.

1:42 PM, and Connor was at one of Bedlam's abandoned-for-summer grade schools, Magdalene Middle. On his way to graduating from possible kidnapper to full-on pedo, Connor crept up on a group of five boys monkeying around on the monkey bars. The boys, ages 12 to 14, pushed Connor around, pretended to throw punches at him, and then tossed him a bag of weed. Connor threw a fistful of ones to the wind, and the boys scattered after them, all awkward limbs and cracking voices.

Around 2:00 PM, Connor made a trip to the grocery store. This time, Linnéa and Stephen did get out, and they stalked him through the aisles. He didn't buy anything of note; just a bunch of snacks for the night to come.

A uniformed police officer noticed them mid-stalking, and made the sign of the cross in their direction.

2:40 PM, he was back home, and Linnéa and Stephen were back between the two junkers, watching Connor through the windows. They waited there until 5:00 PM.

"I don't know how much longer I can do this today," Linnéa said, rubbing her ass. "I got to pee."

Stephen said, "Yeah," and then bit into his thumbnail. "You want to just go knock on his door?"

"Eh, let's come back tomorrow night. One more go round."

"I just don't want to waste too much time on him if he's not our guy. What he might have to say could be helpful."

"Then go knock—"

Stephen waved his hands. "No, no. You're right. You ready to go back?"

"Yeah." She wasn't going to say it, but before she could stop herself: "I kind of hope there's another message in our bedroom."

With a blank face, Stephen said, "Yeah, I do, too."

"The more time they're fucking with us, the less time they're with Filipa."

"She could get away," Stephen said, voice trembling.

Linnéa smiled. Her thoughts drifted to that dark place in her mind, where her daughter was crucified to cruel statistics. "Alright. Let's—"

Her phone buzzed. She took it out of her pocket.

"It's a text from Ellen," she said.

Stephen started up the car. "What's she want?"

Linnéa laughed and stared at the screen, confused. "She, uh, wants me to come over tonight."

"You?"

"Yeah." She held the phone up to his face. "Girls only. That's what she said."

The Crosses had lived across from Linnéa and Stephen for the last eight years, and still Linnéa couldn't help but feel like a stranger as she crept up their rickety porch. Bearing a cheap bottle of wine and a boring ass salad she'd thrown together as soon she got back, she twisted around before ringing the doorbell and had a measure of her surroundings.

The police presence had died down for the night, though there still appeared to be two or three cruisers on patrol in Six Pillars this evening.

No one else, however, was on the streets. Just as it had been the day the kids disappeared, there were no sounds or signs of children outdoors. They were sealed away in their homes, in their rooms, under the watchful eyes of their parents who now could reap the benefits of Linnéa's and the others' sufferings.

To her left was Trent Resin's place—that small, economy sized home that looked as if it'd been cobbled together from the leftovers of the houses surrounding it. Though the lights were off inside it, and the sun was falling fast, Linnéa was certain he was at the window, watching her.

To her right was Bethany and Todd Simmons' makeover—that mid-sized, middle-class two story that wanted desperately to be one of the mansions from west Bedlam. Painted yellow and green, it stuck out like a gangrenous limb covered in the trashy, overpriced, supermarket jewelry. Everything on, in, or around the house—the doors, the windows, and the American flag; the televisions, tablets, and smartphones; the yard, garden, and swimming pool, and the SUVs on lease—were new, except for the house itself. The house was a forty-year-old overdose, overlooked and looked over, and left to rot in a perpetual, high-school-was-the-best-years-of-my-life daze.

And Linnéa knew Bethany was watching her. She was in the backyard sucking down a twelve pack. She waved when the two of them made eye contact.

Linnéa hadn't always paid attention to these people or the things they surrounded themselves with, but those days were over for her.

Now, she had to watch everything all the time and strip it down with the sharpest of cynicisms. Agnes would be proud.

Going to ring the doorbell, Linnéa took a step back as Ellen flung the front door open and pushed the screen aside.

"Oh, Lin, thanks for coming." Ellen did a hover hands-like hug and then waved her in. "Richard's not home."

The Crosses' house wasn't much to look at from the outside. It wasn't a derelict like Resin's, or dolled-up like the Simmonses'. But on the inside? On the inside, the Crosses had settled on a decade, the 1970s, and hadn't budged since. It was all dark wood and brown carpet and leather furniture in odd places. The lightbulbs in the ceiling and lamps burned dully—dimmed by the motes that floated around them like tiny moths. It smelled, too, like rotting eggs and garlic, but who was to say that wasn't coming off Linnéa? It was all she smelled these days, wherever she went.

"Richard's not home?" Linnéa said as Ellen shut the front door behind them.

"He went out." Ellen flashed a smile. "Yesterday. Kitchen's this way."

Linnéa followed Ellen through the house. A TV stand without a TV stood out to her; mostly because there were fresh TV dinners in front of it.

When they passed the door to the basement, Ellen stopped and lingered on it.

"Darlene's room's down there," Linnéa said.

Ellen fumbled with the knob. "I wash our clothes by hand in the bathtub up here. Washer and dryer are down there."

"When's the last time you went into Darlene's room?"

Ellen shrugged.

Linnéa handed Ellen the bottle of wine. "If we polish this off, we could go down together."

She tapped her fingers against the glass, sloshed the red inside. "Got any more?"

Girls' night at the Crosses' wasn't so much as a girls' night as it was Linnéa and Ellen sitting at the kitchen table, tagging one another in on the wine, while the salad Linnéa'd brought and the pasta Ellen'd made gathered fruit flies on the counter. The bugs complimented the faded yellow, sticky trap-looking curtains well.

After bullshitting for a good twenty minutes, Linnéa leaned back in her chair, wiped the wine off her lips, and said, "No Beth?"

"To be honest, I didn't ask her."

"How come?"

Ellen's eyes went dead. In that moment, she looked everything like the wasteland scarecrow she resembled.

"She'd make it all about her," Linnéa said.

Ellen came to and laughed. "How do you do it, Lin?"

"What's that?"

"Stay cool through all this."

Linnéa twitched. Was it so obvious? Had it always been? What did she look like to the rest of them? She tongued her teeth and tasted the sticky remains of the vermillion veins from this morning. Doing that, she then wondered: Why am I the only parent here?

"I'm not cool," she said. "I can barely stand it most days."

Trying to sound innocent, Ellen said, "You and Stephen were gone all day."

Linnéa cocked her head.

"Did you… find anything?"

"No, we should probably leave the police work for the police."

Why did she feel as if she were on trial all of a sudden?

Ellen poured herself another glass of wine. She took a few deep, heavy, nervous breaths and then: "Was there really someone in your house?"

"Yes," Linnéa said without hesitation.

"Did you see them?"

"In the house? No, not—"

"The angels," Ellen said. "On the yards. Last night"

Linnéa put the glass to her mouth and said into it, "Did… did you?"

Ellen nodded. "What was Stephen doing in Bethany's yard?"

Linnéa scooted her chair back. She glanced over her shoulder, half expecting to find Richard Cross in the corner, a hammer in his hand.

"I'm sorry," Ellen said. "It's… it's been so long." She wiped her eyes. "God's not answering my prayers."

"Stephen found something strange in our garden. A root. Trent had one, too, and so did Bethany." Linnéa didn't like where this was going, and her voice reflected that. "Heard you had one in your yard, too."

Ellen's guilt etched itself into her face. "Oh, those?" she said, non-chalantly. "Darlene used to rip them up. She said they made her feel funny."

"Do you know what they are?"

Ellen glanced away, said, "No."

Linnéa saw the basement door in her mind's eye, and then she slid the wine bottle closer to Ellen.

Ellen took the bait and filled her glass to the rim. Some spilled over, and she quickly drank it up before it hit the checkered table cloth.

Linnéa knew a drunk when she saw one. Again, Agnes would be proud.

"Tell me about Filipa," Ellen said, her words slurring.

Deflecting, Linnéa whispered, "Tell me about Darlene."

Now, Ellen was leaning back in her chair, holding her wine to her chest. The rosary around her neck slipped into the cup; the crucifix turned blood red.

"My Darlene? Oh, my Darlene. My beautiful, wicked girl. She's... she's a quiet thing. Even when she was little, she always kept to herself. I think she's going to be smarter than her old mom here—" Ellen cleared her throat, "—but I don't know. You have to watch out for the quiet ones, you know? Your Filipa's a sweet girl. She's quiet, too, isn't she? You ever wonder what she's thinking? Girls like them don't always say what's on their minds like you and I. We found ourselves through others..."

She downed her glass and poured herself another. "You know what I mean, right? I remember your mom. She was a lot like my mom. The two would've made good drinking buddies at the nursing home if they would've made it that... Sorry. My mother never prepared me for the world. She just... called it shit and then called it a day."

Ellen took another drink and held the wine in her mouth for a moment, savoring it. "I can't remember if I ever prepared Darlene for something like this. I spent so long turning my life around, I think I might've forgotten about her sometimes. She knew not to talk to strangers, but did she know she could talk to me if she knew something was wrong? She was so quiet. Sometimes, I'd forget she was even here. We prayed more than we talked. I guess that was my doing.

"I'm sorry. What am I trying to say? I don't know what I'm trying to say. Darlene is... Isn't that sad? That we could live across from one another all these years and not know each other's girls? Or Charles or Jimmy? Did you know them? I didn't. But it's like... whoever took... them all... knew us... knew them... better than anyone else. They came at the perfect time… right under our noses."

She took another drink, made a fist with her free hand until her knuckles popped. "I want to say it was the angels. I want to say it was god who took them. Wouldn't that be nice?" She settled into her seat, like she was going to fall asleep. "But it was a demon. Maybe a demon we made. Or I made. I'll take the blame. Something from way back, a long time ago."

Linnéa mumbled, "We all did something wrong, didn't we?"

"Did we? Did you? Figured you would find out. You and Stephen are trying. I don't know what I'm doing these days, except just doing what Bethany says. You know about the neglect? I was neglectful. I won't hide it. I was a bad mom. Richard was a bad dad. It's our shadow, following us everywhere we go. Just a shadow to you and everyone else, but we know.

"Darlene was four. I was relapsing. Richard was out of town with some… whore." Ellen ground her teeth. "It was a Saturday. A young man came to the door. The door was open, and he saw Darlene on the floor, playing with a kitchen knife. And then he saw me, a hypodermic needle still in my arm. He reported me to children's services."

"I didn't know that," Linnéa said.

"Yeah. Yeah… yeah, I know." She grabbed the wine bottle and emptied it into her cup. "We got a second chance. That young man? He was from my church. He saw me at my lowest, and then lifted me up. I got my shit together… again… and then I got right with the lord."

Linnéa leaned forward. "Your church is non-denominational, right?"

Ellen hiccupped a 'yes.'

"What's it called again?"

"The Disciples…"

Linnéa squeezed her wine glass so hard it cracked.

"…of God."

"Oh." She thought back to Black Occult Macabre, its article on the vermillion veins, and their place in occult rites. "Oh, that's right. Hey, you called Darlene wicked. I know you're a spiritual woman."

"Not when I drink," Ellen said. "Isn't that strange? When I'm sober, I recite verses non-stop. When I drink, I don't feel the need."

"Calms your nerves, I guess."

"Takes me back."

"I'm sorry," Linnéa said. "I shouldn't have brought the wine."

Ellen held up her hand. "No, no. A little sin goes a long way. I'm okay. You were going to say something about Darlene?"

"Oh, yeah." Linnéa pretended she had forgotten. "You called her wicked. You're a spiritual woman. I take it that means a little more than she's a brat."

"Oh, my Darlene's a brat." Ellen laughed. She looked at the ex-wineguinated bottle, and then looked under the sink, as if more alcohol was hidden there. "Darlene never took to the church. She's quiet, but she broods. She thinks I'm a hypocrite. She knows what I was like years ago. She won't let god in. Sometimes, she would spend some time with the other kids from the church. There was a boy… I think she liked him. But he was one of those rich types from west Bedlam. He wouldn't give her the time of day."

Linnéa nodded, while she remembered the white van that had been outside her house the day the kids went missing, and how the teenagers inside had been discovered to have been from west Bedlam. Were they from the church, too?

"You said in therapy yesterday you heard Darlene speak to you sometimes."

"I guess I do. From her room."

"I thought you didn't go in there."

Ellen's eyes were glazed over. For a moment, it looked as if she were going to pass out. She swayed where she sat, lost in either a drunken bliss, or a holy reverie. Linnéa watched her intently. As soon as she was gone, she planned on jumping out of her chair and booking it down to the basement, to see Darlene's room for herself. Ellen was hiding something and—

Footsteps on floorboards; dry creaks echoing in the stuffy dark.

Ellen snapped out of it. Sobering up at the speed of light, she said, "I doze sometimes. It's nothing."

More footsteps, stickier than before, and a handrail rattling against a wall.

Linnéa cocked her head. "Ellen?"

"Hmm?"

"Who else…"

A metallic screech from a twisting doorknob.

"Who else is here?"

Ellen looked at Linnéa as if she were crazy.

A door slammed open inside the house, bashing against a wall.

Linnéa jumped out of her seat, just as she thought she would, and stammered, "E-Ellen?"

Richard Cross stepped into the kitchen, his button-down shirt draped loosely over his girth. He had a hammer in his hand.

Linnéa went around the table, peered down the hall he'd come from. The door to the basement was open. He'd been down there the whole time.

SUNDAYMONDAY**TUESDAYWEDNESDAY**THURSDAYFRIDAYSATUR**DAY**

Stephen woke Linnéa up in the middle of the night to show her an email. It was from Connor Prendergast and it read: If you really wanted to talk that badly, you could have just knocked.

It was three in the morning, Connor was apparently still awake, and Linnéa and Stephen were still dressed, shoes and all, in their clothes from the other day.

They were in the car and coasting out of Six Pillars before they even had a chance to second-guess themselves. At this time of night, the neighborhood was row after row of disembodied facades all set aglow by street lamp's coppery light. Bodies were few and far between; and voices rode like banshees through the hollow dark. Sometimes, there were cars; they were all strange, out of place. Visitors from abroad, bearing gifts of second-hand smoke and rattling speakers.

On their way out, they noticed a police cruiser parked catty-cornered to the neighborhood pool. He flashed his warning lights and then, drowning their car with his floods, turned them off and waved them on. Linnéa and Stephen were distraught parents caught in a perpetual fog of loss. As long as they didn't break anything along the way, who was anyone else to say they couldn't wander? They got a free press. They were celebrities. Someone would want their autographs soon enough.

Orange detour signs and blinking construction lights grew out of the hill as they drove up to the entrance to Six Pillars. Near the large, graffitied sign that marked the neighborhood, the blue truck with Price Homes' emblem sat on the shoulder. It was the same truck Linnéa had seen yesterday when they left to tail Connor. It was in a different place today, but it was still here.

She slowed to a stop and pointed to the truck. "Remember that?"

Stephen unstuck his sweating back from the seat and said, "Yeah. What do you think that's all about?"

"I don't know." She took out her phone, took a picture of the truck and the license plate, like she had with the white van she'd seen earlier, too. "Don't see why it would be here."

"Me neither." Stephen rubber-necked it as Linnéa started up the car again and turned out of Six Pillars. "Let's look into it." He took out his phone and phoned in another "suspicious person."

The operator on the other line greeted them cheerily, like a close friend, and said they'd get right on it.

By 3:26 AM, they pulled into Connor's driveway and walked up to the front door as if they owned the place. Stephen, making a fist, bashed the door three times, as if he were the police. Linnéa jumped, laughed—the late hours always did make her skittish.

Thump, thump, thump—heavy footsteps thundered behind the front door. As they drew closer, Linnéa and Stephen drew back.

The movement stopped. To their left, a window looked out into the yard. The curtains swayed behind the glass. There was a sigh, a muffled "You fucking kidding me?" Then, one after the other after the other, the three locks were undone and the front door pulled open.

Connor stood in the dark, in his ghoul-print pajamas, staring at Linnéa and Stephen as if they'd just run over his dog.

"Seriously?" he said, barely able to keep his eyes open. "I'm way too stoned for this."

"We need to talk to you," Stephen said, making his voice intentionally deeper.

"Oh, is that it? And here I thought you were going to ask me if I knew your buddy, J. Christ. Please, come on in!"

Connor groaned. He turned and walked away, letting the darkness inside the house swallow him whole.

Stephen started forward. Linnéa grabbed his shirt and shook her head. It was three-thirty in the morning, and they were standing outside the house of someone who could very well be responsible for their daughter's kidnapping. She wasn't about to step foot in there without enough light to blind a blind man. She wanted to see everything, and everything that might be coming. She wasn't ready before. She was now.

"Oh," Connor said, somewhere inside the house. "Sorry, I forgot. As you can imagine—" two clicking twists, and a lamp turned on in the living room, "—I am a little tired."

"Well, Mr. Prendergast, we don't mean to be such a burden to you." Linnéa stepped inside. "But we got questions that need answering."

"Yeah," Connor said. "Well, you guys want some coffee?"

Annoyed, Stephen, coming in behind Linnéa, said, "It's three in the morning."

"I don't think any of us are going back to bed after this."

Connor slipped into the kitchen, which ran directly into the living room. Linnéa nodded at Stephen to keep an eye on him. As he hung out in the kitchen's doorway, ready to put his supple, ass-kissing lips to work, Linnéa gave the strange, but admittedly predictable living room a once-over.

It was small, and packed from wall to wall with horror paraphernalia. Posters from horror movies were framed alongside posters from horror novels. Sagging shelf after sagging shelf were filled with the horror movies and novels themselves—thousands of them, undoubtedly—and they ran around the perimeter of the room in a multi-colored band of spines shouting "blood" and "kill" and "dark" and "terror" among other clichéd titles. There was a decent couch, two chairs, a coffee table, and a very nice television, but even they weren't given enough room to breathe and be what they had to be; beside them, on top or in front of them, were horror figures and other collectibles that ranged from machete-wielding slashers, to grotesque, resin abominations that probably cost more than her and Stephen's car payments.

Any other day, Linnéa would've loved the stuff, but today, it didn't do much for her. When everyone is a suspect, shit like this was too easy to read into; rather, too easy to warp into something you could read into.

"Did you know we were following you?" Stephen asked.

Connor dug in his cabinets for his coffee cups.

Linnéa kept a close eye on the kitchen knives not far from where he stood.

"Yep," Connor said, taking three cups and going back to the coffee maker. Doling out the steaming, human fuel, he said, "I take it you read the website and now think I have something to do with your daughter's disappearance?"

Stephen rubbed his arms, shook his legs. It was far past his bedtime. Finally, he said, "Yeah."

Connor came into the living room, handing a cup to Stephen and then a cup to Linnéa before finally dropping onto the couch. A bit of coffee splashed up and splattered the armrest, but judging by the other coffee stains there, it wasn't an issue.

Linnéa sipped the coffee and sat in one of the chairs near couch, and Stephen, wearily, descended onto the chair on the opposite end of the couch. Between them was Connor, and his coffee table covered in sketches of material for *Black Occult Macabre*.

Stephen laid into him first, and that was how Linnéa wanted it to go. Her husband had been docile. He hadn't gotten to bug the shit out of anyone in a long while. It was good for his health.

"So, why didn't you say anything?" Stephen leaned forward, elbows on his knees, cup between his hands and covering his face like a settler round a campfire. "Why did you wait? Were you just leading us on? You got my email before then, didn't you?"

Connor licked his lips. He had the look of someone who'd been grilled a fair share in his life, scorch marks and all. "I don't. I don't know. No. Yes." He laughed and then: "Okay, guys. You know what I do. You know what I believe in. You obviously don't buy it."

"You think?" Linnéa snapped.

"Yeah, yeah, but we are here," Stephen said, ever the mediator. "You know our case."

"Yep." Connor chugged his coffee. "Kind of hard not to. I know I'm being an ass, but I am very sorry."

The apology washed over Linnéa and Stephen with about as much oomph as air.

"I did follow it for a while. It's awful. And really fucking strange, right?"

They didn't need to be told how strange four kids disappearing in broad daylight on a Sunday morning all at once, in their own homes, was.

"You found vermillion veins? Do you have them with you?" Connor cringed. "Did… did you bring them here?"

Linnéa shook her head, but Stephen nodded and reached into his pocket and pulled out a clump of veins. They were the ones from Bethany Simmons' yard. Linnéa didn't know how she knew that, but she knew it.

Connor twitched. "Yep, that's them. That's… not good."

"Hey, Connor—" Linnéa leaned out of her seat, "—don't give us the vague fortune teller routine."

Stephen took over. "Why isn't it good? What's going on? You're the only one who seems to be writing about these things. I consider myself a botanist and—"

"It means someone or something has been and is still watching you and the other families. I did read your email. If they weren't growing there, then they were put there. You know, for the freaks that buy into them, that… shit—" he pointed his finger to the veins, "—is like gold. They're not going to just dump and run. I'm not trying to be vague. I'm trying to put it in… Whoever did this… they're either living in your neighborhood, or visiting it enough that they might as well be."

"That doesn't make sense," Stephen said. "They took Filipa. They got what they wanted."

"Did they?" Connor glanced between the both of them. "Is it about the kids? Or the parents? Filipa could be a means to an end."

Linnéa's stomach turned. "Is there a cult?"

"In Bedlam? I've looked, but…"

"What about the Disciples of God?" she pressed.

"They're just your standard, pay-to-win, non-denominational, please-donate-in-denominations-smaller-than-fifty, rich people religion. Bunch of shmucks with a headquarters in west Bedlam roping in a bunch of shmucks over here in east Bedlam."

"Darlene and Richard Cross follow them," Linnéa said.

"And you wrote that there is a cult out there called The Disciples that have something to do with the veins," Stephen added.

"I think it's just a really annoying coincidence," Connor said. "I've never come up with any connections between the two. But… there is something."

"What?" Linnéa and Stephen said together at once.

"You don't notice it until someone else does, but there's been new people in Bedlam. Not from Brooksville or Bitter Springs, either. People from afar. Different states. Different countries. Not a lot of them. But they're all gathering here. I don't know what that's about."

"Before or after the kids went missing?" Stephen said.

"After, I think. I'm not sure. I started seeing out-of-state license plates, hearing accents from across the Atlantic. A lot of unfamiliar faces hanging around the motels off the highway.

"Did some sneaking around. All the ones I've found so far have been here only for the last week or two. You can have the names. I figure you're going to make me give them to you, anyway."

"You think they're part of the cult?" Stephen persisted.

"That'd be nice. Cults are great. Catch a bunch of wackos gathered together in some basement or warehouse. So much easier than tracking individuals down. But, man, I don't know. I don't think so. Something's going on, but I'm not sure it has to do with the kids."

Linnéa tightened her gaze on him.

"Alright." Connor stood up, set his cup on the table. "This won't make you trust me completely, but let me give you a tour of the house. I can tell you guys aren't telling me everything, either, which is understandable. But I think you and I have the same problem. Maybe we can help each other."

"Same problem?" Stephen stood up. "Same problem? What do you mean? Do you have a child?"

Linnéa came to her feet. There were no pictures of children in the house as far as she could tell, and Connor didn't seem like the fatherly type.

"Black Occult Macabre was my own thing, at first. A magazine I put out digitally back in the day."

Connor led them into the kitchen. It was a tight fit with the three of them in it, but was even worse when he started opening every cupboard and drawer to show that there were no children hidden inside. Linnéa wanted to tell him that wasn't necessary, but in a way, it was. Not one stone left unturned, because the one they didn't flip would be the one chained to their necks for eternity, giving poor Sisyphus some much needed company.

"It was mostly bullshit. Horror stories based around Bedlam. Then I started noticing weird stuff in our town." He opened the refrigerator, the garbage can. "But it wasn't until I met up with this old man for a story that I realized it wasn't all bullshit. There were other things out there. He showed me. The Zdanowicz murders years back? Monster did that. Saw it with my own eyes." Connor went into the hall, turned on the light, and waited until they joined him. "That old man's name is Herbert North. He's... he's my boss. Don't tell him I told you so."

Connor continued down the hallway, stopped at the first door, which was a closet. He opened it up, stepped away.

Inside, there were toy boxes and Halloween decorations; old shoes, a vacuum cleaner; and a creased picture of an old Siberian husky on one of the shelves.

"Go ahead," he said.

Linnéa and Stephen moved the boxes aside, checking for a

trapdoor. They pressed against the inside of the closet for a false wall.

"Herbert is missing," Connor said when they'd finished their search. "He's been gone for a month. I can see what you're thinking. He didn't take the kids. But feel free to look into that, too, if you want."

Going farther down the hall, Connor stopped at where it dead-ended. On one side of the room was one room, and on the other side, another. He chose the one on his left and went in, flipping the light switch on behind him.

"He didn't live with me," he said, as Linnéa and Stephen caught up with him. "So, his room isn't much to look at it. Just… don't mess up anything."

Connor wasn't lying. Herbert North's room was an old person's room if she'd ever seen one. Minimalistic as the website which they'd built, the room was one bed so tightly made it almost seemed a shame to sleep in. Other than that, there was a writing desk that had been kept in immaculate condition. The room had no closet, or access to the attic. It had no real hiding places, and yet, again, no stone left un-turned.

Linnéa and Stephen swept across the room. They checked under-neath the bed, searched every nook and cranny for any kind of trace evidence. The room wasn't dirty, nor did it smell as if it'd been scrubbed clean recently, but in a way, a mother can sense the wake of their child, like aftershocks from an earthquake. Filipa hadn't been here.

"He was investigating a lead. He got wind Ruth Ashcroft was some-where in the state."

"Amon Ashcroft," Stephen mumbled.

"Yeah, his niece. He went and tried to find her and… he had a couple different places he was supposed to be looking and then… a month ago, he didn't check in." Connor stood in the doorway, fighting every impulse he had to cry. "I've been trying to… find him."

Connor crossed the hall into the room opposite Herbert's and turned on the light there.

Linnéa and Stephen followed.

"I have no idea where he is."

Connor's room was like Connor's living room: a hoarder's paradise; systematically arranged, and stuffily efficient. There wasn't much floor space on account of the shelves and statues and glass cases filled with more action figures. Like Herbert's room, there was a writing desk, but on this desk, there was actually something: a laptop, and beside it, stacks of papers and drawings being held down by external hard drives operating as weights. His room smelled like weed and other things she couldn't quite place. Ancient things, earthy things. Packaged and powered things you might find in old timey stores; natural remedies to fight unnatural maladies.

"Your case is messed up. There's something there. But I've been spending all this time trying to find Herbert that I haven't been able to look into you and yours."

Stephen scoured the interior of Connor's bedroom, while Linnéa worked her away around the exterior, consulting every case and shelf—saving the desk, his writing, and laptop for last.

"But you found vermillion veins in your yard. That wasn't in any police reports."

"Didn't seem like anything," Stephen said.

"That's the point, I think. But, I didn't know about them. If they're in all your guys' yards, then either Ruth is here, or Amon, or one of their shithead followers. If you're going to run with me on this, then some, one, or all of them took the children. But I don't think it's just about your daughter. Maybe it's the house. Everyone inside it."

"We had a break in," Linnéa said. She went to the desk, started rifling through his papers.

Connor didn't say a thing.

"Last night. Someone came into our bedroom and wrote in ash on our ceiling 'A Child in Every Home.'"

Connor furrowed his brow. "Did you get a good look at them?"

Linnéa shook her head. The papers were nothing but cryptological crapshoots. "Just saw a dark shape. Saw a few of them outside."

Stephen made a sound as if he thought Linnéa should stop speaking.

But she carried on. "Ellen Cross has seen them. Bethany Simmons, too, I reckon."

"Shadows," Connor whispered. Then, serious as a heart attack: "Have you been eating the veins?"

Linnéa and Stephen's silence said it all.

"Uh, yeah, don't do… that anymore. It wants you to. But then you see things. Like what you saw. The shadows. We're not sure what they are, but eating the veins makes you more sensitive to seeing them. It's like shining a light on yourself, or leaving your door open, inviting whatever happens by in. They can influence our world, but not much else. 'A Child in Every Home'? That sounds like a warning. Herbert had this theory the shadows might not even be bad. They may be helpful. But… don't eat the veins. That's like eating raw meat. There're things inside it… and it's going to totally discredit you and what you have to say if people find out."

Linnéa opened Connor's laptop. Expecting him to tell her to stop, instead he sighed; she swore she could almost hear his eyes rolling in their sockets.

No lock screen. A black wallpaper with *Black Occult Macabre Productions* written across it. No icons on the desktop. She went into his web browser, checked his history. It consisted mostly of sites used for pirating music and movies, and other generic websites that were to be consumed in this day and age's food pentagram. She gave his email a cursory glance, but only found a few back and forths between the women he'd been presumably talking to at the coffee shop. That, and 'work emails' from desperate souls requiring assistance in being liberated from their monster problems.

"That woman you helped out the other day?" Linnéa said. "What'd you do for her?"

"Heh." Connor rubbed the back of his head. "She thinks her house is haunted. I think she's just lonely. But we both get something out of it, regardless."

"You're scamming her?" Stephen said, red in the face from all the kneeling he was doing.

"Since when do the jobs that matter ever pay the bills? It's the bullshit that keeps us afloat."

"You like black metal?" Linnéa sidestepped away from the desk to a milk crate full of records. She flipped through them, one incomprehensible logo following after the other against a backdrop of nature's cruel beauty. "Nice collection."

"Thanks," Connor said. "Uh, all that's left is the bathroom and the basement. You guys good in here?"

They were, and so they kept at it, going deeper into Connor's ticky-tacky home. The bathroom was clear, and clearly owned by a man; there were driblets of piss all over the toilet seat, and the towels were so used that, given another week or two, they could probably stand up on their own and escape from this place.

"Alright, coffee aside, I'm fading, homies." Connor yawned and brought them around, through the living room, to the basement door. "I'll help you in any way that I can. But tell me: Did you or the other parents do something that might make someone think... think being the operative word here... that you deserve this?"

Linnéa and Stephen exchanged glances. For a moment, the play was back on—the curtains were drawn, and the story they'd been performing in almost perfect synchronicity since the day they'd met so many years ago started up once more.

"Yeah," Stephen said. "We've all been taken to court by Child Protective Services. We didn't—"

Connor's eyes lit up. "Every single family?"

They nodded.

"There's your intent. Or, at least, the reason you were chosen. Let's stick with the human angle for now, but let's say someone knew this. Someone who either has it out for people like you—"

Stephen tried to butt in.

But Connor kept going. "Maybe they are repulsed, maybe they have a history themselves. Or maybe they think you're not worthy of your children. You guys seem pretty keen on the cult thing. If there is a cult, then maybe they took these children because they saw them as damaged. Right?

"The idea with the vermillion veins is that they mark some sort of change. An emergence about to happen. Or a literal change to the person they've marked. Alright? So, if we run with that, who are they trying to change? Are you being tested? Or are the kids? They're watching you. Whether you buy into the shadow thing or not, someone was in your home, right? You said Helen Cross—"

"Ellen," Stephen said, close enough to Connor to kiss him.

"Ellen Cross, yeah. You said she was part of the Disciples of God. Could be a place to start, but that seems obvious. Who was the other one who ate the veins? Bethany? I think I remember her. She's on the TV all the time. The trash bag with bleached teeth."

Linnéa tried not to laugh.

"I'd look at her. Her husband has ties with west Bedlam. I know that for a fact. I wouldn't be surprised if she's in some way connected to the Disciples."

Connor went a little farther and opened the door to the basement. Lost in his thoughts, he went down first, tugging on each chain connected to the suspended light bulbs along the way.

"The detour for the construction runs through your neighborhood doesn't it?" Connor asked, coming off the stairs and circling the basement, illuminating more bulbs. "That's good cover. A lot of people that shouldn't normally be there can go through without raising too much suspicion."

In the basement, Linnéa and Stephen split up, even though there wasn't much ground to cover. It was nothing but stone and cement marked by drainage grates and stress fractures. There was a washer and dryer, a fuse box, and a small storage space which they went over several times, finding nothing of importance.

"There was a white van with two kids from west Bedlam fucking in it," Linnéa said, matter-of-factly. "Outside our house. Broad daylight."

Connor belted out a laugh and said to Stephen, "I like your wife."

Stephen made a fist. "So do I."

"Alright." Connor rubbed his hands together. "You got a bible-thumper following a rich people's religion, and a person who wants to be rich possibly connected to that same religion. Isn't there another parent?"

"Trent Resin," Stephen said. "Don't know much about him."

"I'd find out more, then." Connor shook his head, smiled. "Yeah. You got those two. Mystery man."

"Ellen and Richard couldn't get their stories straight the day Darlene disappeared," Linnéa offered.

"Okay, yeah. There's that… them… You've got a white van outside your house with two kids from the west. I wonder who their parents are, you know? You got them being… very good distractions. You got vermillion veins. And I've got people coming in from god knows where to stay in the town for god knows what."

Linnéa drifted back towards Connor. "There's a truck I keep seeing, too. A work truck for Price Homes. They built Six Pillars. I've seen it twice now parked in different places in the neighborhood. Never anyone inside."

"Price Homes." Connor scratched the side of his head. "They're working on a new project over on Merrin. That's like… fifteen minutes from here? Forty from you guys? Dude seems out of his way. That's something, I'd say. Hey, were you, or all of the families, some of the first to move in?"

Stephen nodded. "We were. We live near the entrance. They built the rest over the years."

"Taking four kids while the parents are home and all at once?" Connor clicked his tongue against his teeth. "Wouldn't hurt to have some knowledge about the house. I imagine running around with a work truck like that, you could come and go as you pleased."

Linnéa's heart started to beat faster and faster. She looked at Stephen and took his hand. Squeezing it, she asked, "Connor, say we're not just keen on the human element. If you were us, what would you be looking for?"

Connor's mouth dropped open. The dark circles under his eyes appeared to grow larger. He started for the steps out of the basement and then stopped, resting his weight against the railing.

"Honestly, I don't know. This would've been Herbert's area of expertise. He's the brain and I'm the... well, not the beauty or brawns. The snarky sidekick he gets to boss around, I guess? The son he never had, maybe? You'd have to ask the old son of a bitch yourself."

Connor quickly wiped his eyes. "Shit. Guys, I don't know."

"Take a guess," Stephen said.

Connor bit his lower lip. "I think something inhuman came into your house and is using your history as a means by which to transform either you, your daughter, or all of you into something else. Something horrible, or maybe just offerings for whatever the veins are connected to. But let's say—"

Linnéa's phone started to ring.

"—the people who are coming to Bedlam are somehow part of this."

Ring, ring.

"Then maybe it is organized. Maybe there are a lot of players involved."

Ring, ring.

"If... if that's so, then they want to see what's going to happen next."

Ring, ring.

"Why?" Stephen whispered.

Ring.

Linnéa took the phone out of her pocket.

"So they can say they were there."

Ring.

"So they can be the first to the front of the line."

Linnéa looked at the screen. It was four forty-five, and Detective

Mills was calling. She flashed the phone at Stephen. His face flashed dread.

"But, uh, that's the problem with this small, Podunk town. You have to be sure. You start loading these cops—"

She answered the phone.

"—down with suspects and theories and everything slows to a crawl... Is everything okay?"

Linnéa held up her hand. "Detective Mills?"

"I'm sorry to call you at this hour," he said, shouting over the voices in the background. "But we found something."

"F-Found something?"

Stephen and Connor moved towards her.

"A book," Mills said. "A book with your daughter's name written in it. The one, I believe, you said she was reading that day."

"Yes..." Linnéa said, not breathing, not thinking; barely being.

"We found it in the junkyard." He paused. "It's covered in... someone's blood."

Copper pool. Burnt rubber. Creased sky. Leaking light.

Linnéa pushes the gas pedal to the floor, and then pushes it farther, harder.

Swerving cars. Fuming high beams. Stale AC. Fogging windshield.

Stephen has been shouting at her to slow down, but now, he just wants her to go faster.

Green time ticking rapidly in the dashboard. Thoughts of books and that day, and lies to make it all go away.

Linnéa nearly spins out taking a turn, as the scene takes a turn for the worse. The junkyard sits on the horizon, a shattered skull of once-cherished memories. Its sockets shine blue, its teeth bright red. There are pigs in its mouth, rooting for tiny, child-shaped truffles.

Shadowy figures flagging her down. A news van circling for scraps. A muddy puddle lapping at her ankles.

Out of the car, forgetting she had been in the car, Linnéa runs. She and Stephen break through the police barricade like a battering ram. No one can stop them. No one could stop them.

Police tape. White coats. Black hats. Gibbering mouths. Plastic sounds.

Detective Mills spots her. He cuts through the officers crammed around the crime scene. Framed in that patriotic, emergency glow, he comes to them with condolences and weak assurances.

Connor's words. Black metal howlers in her forgotten fjords. Price Homes. A price on her home.

Mills is carrying an evidence bag. Inside, there's a blood-splattered book. The blood is fresh enough that it pools in the corners. The book's cover is lost to the red wash, but Linnéa's seen it enough to know what it's about.

It's a book about faeries, and in particular, changelings.

Stephen is crying. He reaches for Linnéa, and she holds him until it hurts. Detective Mills gloves his hands, opens the bag, and flips to the front to show the inscription and Filipa's name.

Something breaks inside Linnéa's head. One eye goes dark, the other isn't far behind. Something breaks inside Linnéa's chest. She stumbles into Stephen and gulps for breaths that never make a difference.

A whirlwind of questions. The smell of metal and earth. The promises of lab tests and hopeful possibilities.

Eighty-five at five in the morning, and Linnéa is shivering. She looks at the bag and book inside, and the blood—the first contact she's made with her daughter in over thirty days—and shakes her head.

"That's not my daughter's book!" she belts.

She has everyone's attention. But all she wants is Stephen's. The play must go on; he has to play his part.

"It's not," she repeats herself. "I swear to god it's not."

She thinks of Connor. She thinks of the truck always abandoned on the outskirts of Six Pillars. She thinks of grilling out on a Sunday morning, not a care in the world, because her world was small and only ten years old.

"That's not her book. It's in her room. I saw it. I saw it."

Fevered, Linnéa swipes at the bag, but Mills is quick to pull it away.

"That's not her blood." She digs her claws into Stephen, puts her teeth to his cheek. "That's not her blood. I know my daughter's blood. That's not her blood!"

White towels. Dark coffee. Thoughts of death in this Black Hour.

They are ushered away. They are offered a stay. Somewhere, anywhere, but everywhere is not there, not home, where they ought to be.

Backseat fabric that still smells faintly new. The rising sun coming through. Jittery dreams. Pothole reveries.

Stephen is a blur as he helps her out of the car. The world is a dark smear like the two on their bedroom ceiling. Across the way, Ellen and Richard Cross are running down their driveway, screaming about Darlene and how her bra and underwear had been found under the bridge to west Bedlam.

"Her photo," Linnéa hears Ellen cry. "Church photo. Her… clothes were around it. Like… like a wreath."

Richard is hitting things. Linnéa thinks he might be hitting Ellen. She knows fist on flesh. Stephen doesn't say anything. Stephen doesn't do anything.

He takes her inside, into their bedroom, and lays her below the black smears. She thinks of Price Homes as she peers into those two distant nebulas, and when she sees her daughter among the plastered stars, she knows what she has to do.

Linnéa and Stephen fall asleep with their eyes open, and do not wake again until Bethany Simmons is screaming bloody murder at their front door.

SUNDAYMONDAYTUESDAY**WEDNE**SDAYTHUR**SDAY**FRIDAYSATURDAY

Linnéa shot up out of bed, a wad of phlegm in her throat. She glanced over at Stephen and shook him until she was certain he wasn't dead.

"Is that Bethany?" she croaked.

Stephen jumped to his feet. His legs gave out and he crashed into the wall. Pushing off it, he ran out of the room, Linnéa in tow.

In yesterday's clothes, which were the clothes from before that, they rumbled down the stairs like repugnant tumbleweeds.

Reaching the landing, Linnéa retched. Her mouth tasted like stale coffee, and her insides were hot, almost sizzling. She made her eyes go wide until they righted themselves. She felt, and felt like she smelled, like microwave-nuked shit.

And then she remembered the junkyard and the book, and the blood inside the bag.

Stephen ripped open the front door.

Bethany jumped backwards, surprised. She took a second, and launched forward, bracing herself against the molding.

"Trent!" She caught her breath. "He barged into my house. He won't leave! He has his fucking goddamn gun with him!"

Bethany became a blur of workout shorts and a crop top as she sped across their front yard, back to her own.

"Stephen, I…" Linnéa started.

206

But Stephen was already out the door, chasing after Bethany.

For a moment, the smell of rot left Linnéa's nose, and in its place, there was Filipa. She was rose vanilla lotion. She was fabric softener and sugar; warm grass, old ink. She was here, somewhere, or maybe nearby. Linnéa breathed her in, held her in; locked her in, deep within. Filipa was here, in what needed to be done, in what was bound to come. Her little devil in the details.

Linnéa caught up with Stephen and hurried to Bethany's house. Bethany was waiting for them by the garage door, already shakily chain smoking her way through the pack crumpled in her fist.

"Did you call the cops?" Stephen asked.

A piece of furniture exploded in the house against a wall.

Bethany screamed. Stephen ducked. Linnéa kept at it into the garage itself, passing like a pirate between the beached SUVs inside. Some deliberately applied mud broke off from them and rubbed into her jeans.

"Lin, hold on!" Stephen whisper-shouted.

Bethany dropped her still smoking smokes and went after Linnéa, who was now camped out by the door into the house.

Stephen met up with them. "Did you call the cops?"

Bethany shook her head.

"Why the hell not?"

"He's just a drudge," Bethany spat.

Linnéa cocked her head. Drudge? There was a word she hadn't heard in a while, and not one she expected to come out Bethany's menthol-flavored mouth.

"We have to stay focused on the children. If the media finds out, they'll eat it up. They'll forget about Jimmy."

"And Filipa," Linnéa said.

"Yeah, and Ellen and Charles." Bethany's mouth twisted like the cinnamon roll it resembled. "I know."

Stephen stumbled forward. Awake only ten minutes, and he was already crashing. "What happened? What's Trent want?" He smiled at Linnéa to show he was okay. "Do you know what started this with him?"

"He heard about what they found at the junkyard. And Darlene's stuff under the bridge."

Stephen stared at Linnéa, the same way the waking wake to realize the dream they'd had was the nightmare they lived. Had he forgotten the book and the blood, too?

He kept it together as his words fell apart: "His... boy's... belongings... were in Maidenwood... a f-few weeks backs."

"He's blaming me!" Bethany cried. "He's pissed because they haven't found anything of Jimmy's! He thinks they're sparing me!"

Connor's warning of strangers visiting Bedlam darkened Linnéa's gray matter. "Who's sparing you?"

Bethany cocked her head back, chin to throat, like an offended ostrich. "Excuse me?"

The play would go on, and so Stephen took the lead: "Are you part of the Disciples of God, too?"

Bethany's tongue pressed against her teeth and forked around them. "I dabble." Then, good and pissed: "Trent's in my house with a gun!"

Linnéa opened the door and hollered into the house, "Trent! It's Lin! Stephen, too! Can we talk to you?"

No response.

"Why didn't you call the cops, Beth?" Stephen asked.

"Why didn't Ellen invite me over the other night?" Bethany snapped back.

Linnéa's disbelief drilled a hole through the bitch's forehead. "Are you fucking kidding me?"

Stephen held up his hand. "Where's Todd?"

Linnéa slapped it down.

"West side," Bethany said. "You know what? Fuck you two. I'll get—"

At the top of his lungs, from the second floor, Trent boomed, "Alright."

Bethany, instantly triumphant, tried to get through the door first, but Stephen barred her with his arm.

"Don't," he told her.

She let out a death rattle rasp.

Linnéa and Stephen went inside the house, crouched and covered with sweat. Thumping noises like tumbling bodies thudded from the laundry room to their left. Unlike the Crosses' place, they'd been to the Simmonses' a few times in the past, for dinners and bake sale bullshit. The decorations were different, but the layout was the same. It was always the same for all the Price Homes. Carbon copied corpses that could be carbon dated back to one uninspired board meeting where a bunch of bald men and bitch-faced women wondered what it might be like to have another comma or two on their paycheck.

"What're we doing?" Stephen asked.

They moved away from the door to the garage to the kitchen.

"Getting more answers," Linnéa said. "He knows something is up."

"He has a gun."

"Get behind me, then."

She and Stephen went around the kitchen island. On top of it, in a bowl, rotting fruit had caved in upon itself.

There was a note on the fridge. A to-do list that read "Missing" and below that, a list of small items, like pots and pans, and underwear, and inspirational picture frames.

"You do the talking," Linnéa said. "He likes you."

"She didn't call the police."

"Something's up with her, too."

They slipped into the hallway, headed towards the front where the staircase was.

Before reaching it, Stephen grabbed Linnéa's arm. "Are they all in on it?"

Linnéa conjured the smell of their daughter and said, repeating Bethany, "She dabbles."

From the top of the staircase, Trent said, "That you?"

"Lin and Steve," Stephen said, taking the lead, inches away from where the wall let out to the banister. "It's just us."

There was another thump, then tapping. The sound traveled down the stairs, one stair at a time, until—

A pistol rolled past the banister and hit the floor.

"Wasn't loaded, anyways," Trent said, still out of sight. "Just wanted to get in Jimmy's room. She wouldn't let me."

Stephen scurried past the stairs, grabbed the pistol, flipped it over, and found no clip inside. He checked the chamber. No bullet there, either.

"Look at you, Army Boy," Linnéa said. "Dad would be proud."

Stephen turned the gun over in his hand. "It wasn't Filipa's blood."

Linnéa shook her head. "Sure wasn't."

With that finally decided and Trent seemingly disarmed, they, high on the thrill and numbingly ill, hurried up the staircase.

Trent was waiting for them in the hall, one hand in the pocket of his cheap, cowpoke knockoff jeans, the other clutching a balled-up T-shirt. Reading his expression was like reading a rock's—it simply wasn't there. And if it was, you couldn't see it. A thick, crimson paste clung to his lips and cheeks, and it dripped off his chin, down his neck, to where it created with a banded stain an image of a priest's collar.

He'd been in the veins.

He started to dip back into the room beside him—Jimmy's room—when he stopped himself and, holding out the balled T-shirt, said, "The dumb bitch. She did it on purpose."

Trent threw the shirt at Stephen.

He caught it as if it were bomb and straightened it out.

It was a white T-shirt with three semi-exaggerated faces—Filipa's, Darlene's, and Jimmy's—centered inside an ejaculation of color. It looked like something you could get done by an acne-wracked, would-be artist working for minimum wage during their summer break at an amusement park. Beneath the children's faces floating in the rainbow regurgitation were the words "A Child in Every Home."

Linnéa couldn't help but laugh. "Son. Of. A. Bitch."

"Flip it around," Trent said.

Stephen did just that. On the back, there was a butchered, strung together quote from the bible that read: "Whoever welcomes this little child in my name welcomes me… For the kingdom of God belongs to such as these…"; this was followed by Bethany's own invention which read in bubble print: "Keep 'em close, keep 'em safe; keep the Faith."

Rage and revulsion washed over Linnéa. She didn't know if she should pitch a fit, or simply spit.

"She forgot Charles on purpose," Trent said.

It was true: Resin's boy had been spared the shirt, and that might've been for the best.

"Trent, you didn't bust in here just because of this, did you?" Stephen asked.

Linnéa took the shirt out his hand and threw it over her shoulder down the stairs.

Trent wiped his mouth. "Found more in my yard, Steve."

"Yeah, I see that."

Trent shook his head. He started to speak, and then slipped into Jimmy's room instead.

"What are you doing in there, man?" Stephen asked.

He and Linnéa crept towards the room together, bound at the hip by the worry they shared.

"I heard about what they found in the junkyard. I'm sorry," Trent said to them.

"Appreciate that," Linnéa said, "but it's not what it seems."

"All the same—"

She and Stephen filed into Jimmy Simmons' room.

"—there's you, and then Darlene, and... Charles' things in the forest—"

Jimmy Simmons' room had been ransacked. The bed had been flipped, and the closet turned inside out. A flat screen lay face-up on the floor, while the video game system against it hummed annoyingly as it tried to eject the disc tray. There were holes in the wall, too; bloody, crumbling craters that left the room looking like a decayed honeycomb. For all their random placement, the holes couldn't have looked any more deliberate.

"—but where's Jimmy in all of this?" Trent slouched, like a deflating balloon. "I thought he might be here. That fucking bitch never seemed all that broken up."

He wiped his nose, cleared his throat. "I don't get calls from the cops. I don't get cards or well-wishes. I don't get strangers in my home, leaving me clues. I wish they'd never found Charles' things in Maidenwood. They might not have written him off if they hadn't."

"You two have been coming and going at odd hours." Trent's tone changed. "There were the veins you came to me about—"

"Which you've been into," Stephen said. "Did you find—"

"—and the break-in. And the coming and going. I saw you at Darlene's, Linnéa."

"We're not hiding anything, Trent," Stephen said. He shook the pistol in his hand. "What's really going on here?"

"What do you think I'm trying to find out?"

Linnéa asked, "Did you ever do anything with the Disciples of God?"

"I heard her call me a drudge," Trent said. "That's what they call working class people like you and me. Drudges."

"Why?" Stephen said.

"We're a means to an end." Trent went to hit a wall, but his fist fell short. "Got roped into going to one of their get-togethers a few years back. That's the kind of shit they were spewing." He grabbed his head. "Is that what this is about?"

"Where did you find the growths? Same place?" Stephen said.

Trent nodded.

"You see anything after eating them?"

"Yeah."

"What… did you see?"

"Shapes. Ellen's angels, I guess."

"Shadows," Linnéa clarified.

Trent nodded. "They were all crowded around your house."

Outside, a car peeled down the street. Linnéa went behind Stephen to the window.

"But they were all coming out of here. This house."

Linnéa breathed on the glass. She wiped away the smudges Bethany had undoubtedly placed there fidgeting with the thing, trying to recreate the kidnapper's point of entry.

"I understand why you wanted to come here," Stephen said, doing his best Dario Onai impression.

Linnéa gasped. She turned away from the window, grabbed Stephen's hand, and hauled him out of the room. He dropped the pistol, winced when it hit the ground.

"What's wrong?" both he and Trent asked.

"The truck," she said. "The Price Homes truck. It just took off down the street."

As Linnéa and Stephen came out of Bethany's home, so, too, did Bethany come out of theirs. Too caught up in the moment to ask what the hell she was doing, Stephen asked her to grab his keys off the table by the stairs. She nodded, smiling, and when she came back out with them, Linnéa and Stephen were already at the car, itching to go.

"Your phone went off," she said, chucking Linnéa the keys. "It was Detective Mills. He said the blood on Filipa's book wasn't human. Isn't that great?"

Great? It was the best goddamn, mother fucking thing Linnéa had heard in a long time.

She said, "Yeah," got in the car and started it up.

"Hey," Bethany said, closing the gap between her and them. "What about Trent?"

"He's harmless," Stephen said, and then waved her goodbye.

The truck didn't have but a two or three minute head start on them, but where the hell had it gone?

Linnéa peeled her eyes and pressed her face to the glass. Six Pillars wasn't a sprawling neighborhood, but a dense mass, like a dying star. Its pull pulled people in and seldom let them go. Intersections were cross-sections that gave telling glimpses into the cramped and wanting lives of this intergenerational hoosegow. At every stop sign, she had to stop and stare, and process, as a computer would, the cluttered chaos of their decayed suburbia. The background and foreground flattened; prospects fattened in the skewed perspective. Every driveway taunted, every garage door threatened; any car on the roadway, truck or not, made her heart pump something fierce. In every road, distant or near, she saw shadows and shapes and, with her mind, wrought them into something more. But they were never what she wanted; only distractions.

The truck could be anywhere, but where it wasn't was where it ought to be. So with that in mind, Linnéa left Six Pillars behind and made her way through Bedlam to Merrin Street.

By the time they made it to Price Homes' newest construction site, Linnéa had chewed her lip to pieces. Getting out of the car, she spat out the dry skin like chew and flagged down the first worker she found.

"Sir? Excuse me, sir," Stephen said, heading off the worker. "Just a moment of your time, my man."

Something clicked into place inside Linnéa. A gear, maybe, that'd be unaligned. She was the muscle, he the mouth. Brute Force and Beauty. That was going to be their band name, they'd decided once in the late hours, when sleep was second to Filipa's baby monitor.

The worker was a lean, freshly shaven—bloody nicks and all—man in clothes that didn't fit and a hardhat with as many scuffs as he had second chances. The shell of the house he stood by was infested with others just like him, and when they asked him what was going on, he waved them off, rubbed his stubble, and said, "What can I do for you?"

Linnéa put her hands on her hips, to give herself that demanding mother-like figure men always seemed so afraid of.

"We need to speak with the foreman," Stephen said.

The worker stared in silence and said, "You... You two. Oh my god, I'm sorry about your little girl."

"It's about our little girl," Stephen said. "Can you point us in the right direction?"

The worker pointed past a house further along, to the squat, mobile can of an office all bosses seemed to be stationed at these days.

The worker took off his hat and shielded his mouth with it as he said, "Is Mr. Reynolds involved?"

Linnéa nudged Stephen. Parked beside the office was a blue truck with the logo of Price Homes fixed to it.

Stephen swallowed hard and said, "Whose truck is that?"

"Mr. Reynolds'," the worker said. "I'll take you to him."

"That's good of you," Linnéa finally said, a fire building in her belly. "Did he just get back?"

"Mr. Reynolds? No, ma'am. He's been here all morning. We'd know." He laughed. "That's when we cut out, when he's gone."

The worker led them across the dug-out, mud covered, gravel-choked, corporate no man's land and left them standing outside the office, their hate in their hands. Stephen asked if the worker would wait outside. He obliged.

They entered without knocking, and at first, the foreman, Mr. Reynolds, lost in an air conditioned, cell phone game coma, didn't realize. Sideways and bent, a full moon at high noon at the back of his pants, he smashed his pudgy thumbs into the cell phone in his hand, racking up points with complete indifference.

Stephen cleared his throat.

Linnéa let the door close with a sharp smack behind them.

Mr. Reynolds jerked up in his swivel chair and spun around, losing the phone to his breast pocket and his breath to the movement in a few seconds flat.

It smelled rotten in the office, too. Even the foreman noticed, twitching his noise as he did so. Had he rushed back in here? Did he just beat them here? Was this their guy?

"Mr. Reynolds?" Stephen said.

"Mm." He grumbled as he half stood and shook Stephen's hand. "Sorry." He sat back down. "I wasn't expecting any visitors today."

Stephen's breathing settled. He approached the desk like a lawyer would a witness on the stand. "Is that your truck out there?"

Mr. Reynolds glanced at Linnéa.

She crossed her arms.

"Company truck. Why?"

Ignoring him, Stephen continued. "Mr. Reynolds, I know a decent man when I see one. I used to think of myself as one, too, but when I look in the mirror, I'm not so sure anymore. You might know my wife and me from the television…"

Linnéa found comfort in the tone of his voice, the cadence of his words; that downhome drawl that'd disappeared in their own Great Depression. It was funny how sadness could do that to a person; rob them of who they are, like plucking notes from a song, until they were nothing more than a monotone drone. Sums of their symptoms.

"Our daughter, Filipa, is missing, along with three other children from our neighborhood. And of late? Of late, we've seen a truck just like that one outside in our neighborhood, day in and day out, at all hours. I don't know what that means, but we need to speak to whoever's been driving it. Please. We're at the end of our—"

Mr. Reynolds held out his hands. "Okay, okay. I got you. But that's the only truck—" He punched the table, shook his head, and pointed at the door. "Someone standing out there? Would you mind?"

Linnéa opened the door and gave the worker waiting outside a nod to come in.

The worker came in with his cap in his hands, like an animal with its tail between its legs. He smiled at Mr. Reynolds in the same way something small smiles before a shark. The foreman wasn't their guy, but someday, he'd be someone's.

"Hollis. Is he back yet?"

Hollis didn't need reminding. He knew who exactly what Mr. Reynolds was getting at. He shook his head.

"Son of a bitch. He's done. You see him pull up two hours from now and send him straight to me. He's done. Go on, then."

Hollis nodded, tapped out a tune on the top of his helmet, and backed out of the office.

"Someone else drive a blue truck like that one out there?" Stephen asked.

Linnéa took out her phone. With three percent of its battery left, she carried it like a guttering torch to the desk and shoved it into the foreman's face. Flipping to the picture she'd taken earlier of the blue truck, she said, "Those his plates?"

A handsy person, like strangers who have to touch everything in a new room, the foreman pawed for the phone as she took it away. "That's his, but that logo shouldn't be there. I told him not to..." He got out of his seat. "Listen, I can't just share employee information with you. I understand where you're coming from. I'll deal with this, but... I can't."

Linnéa backed up as Stephen stepped into the ring. He said, "You fired him," and then: "He's not an employee anymore."

"I—"

"Sir, I don't know if you're a father or not."

"I'm not and—"

"Filipa's been missing over a month now. When it comes to statistics, she's in the negative. The chances of her…" Stephen stepped away, wiped his eyes. "This right here? This is all we've got. The cops don't have anything. Whoever did this is leading them in circles. We could send them here and maybe they could talk you into giving them a name and an address, but that would take time. Minutes. Hours. Days, even. Those kids? They've been gone hundreds of hours already. You know what a person can do with just a few minutes. A person can destroy a life in a few minutes. We can't wait any longer. Filipa can't wait any longer, and neither can Darlene, Charles, or Jimmy. Those're the other kids who were taken. That's their names, Mr. Reynolds.

"We're not going to tell anyone what you did for us. But if we find those kids because of you… you'll have saved their l-lives." Stephen was crying again, but this time, he didn't bother with the tears. "And… if we find them… and you could've helped, but it was too late. I… I won't hold it against you—"

"I will," Linnéa said, darkly.

"—because you were just doing your job. I get that. But no one job is worth the lives of four children, is it?"

Mr. Reynolds shifted uncomfortably, as he sweated through his shirt. "You're sure it's him?"

Stephen shook his head. "No, not at all. But if we're wrong, we're wrong, and that's all right. So, what do you say?"

The owner of the blue truck's name was Ved Matcira, and he lived at 707 Meridian Avenue—a short, crooked road that began at and dead-ended into the same, crescent-shaped cemetery. It was a place where all the houses were built on the same side; four one-story monuments to expired aspirations; broken gutters, missing siding, and for-sale signs from centuries past; and no sounds or sights of life, save for the headstones across the way, where lives were written, not splattered, across stone.

707 Meridian Avenue was hidden in the way that all obvious things were hidden. They'd passed it or the cemetery more times than they could count, on almost a daily basis, going to work or going for groceries. They might've noticed once, when they'd first moved in, or when Filipa was old enough to point it out, but beyond that, it was no more than a blur—blended brushstrokes of disposable memories.

Things like that were bound to happen, especially when you lived as close as they did to 707 Meridian Avenue; that is, ten minutes away.

Linnéa and Stephen parked the car in the cemetery and hurried to its edge, where it met Meridian Avenue, and hid themselves amongst the frail trees there.

Ved wasn't home yet. The blue truck was nowhere to be seen. Linnéa lay in wait, waiting for the sounds of a struggling engine, or the sticky sound of tires on cement, but even after several minutes, there was nothing. Despite being so close to the construction and the detoured traffic, there was no noise here at all. The street was like a scene underwater—muffled, unreal.

Seeing the home of the only true lead they'd had in weeks, Linnéa's vision went blurry and her face burned. Dizzy, nauseous, she pressed her forehead into the nearest tree. When had she truly slept? When had she last showered? When she pissed, it stank, and what little she'd eaten of late was wedged inside her bowels, pressing against her side. Smelling herself, she could smell a part of all the places she'd been: the old carpet from Dario Onai's office; the rotting food of the Crosses' home; the hairspray and tar of the Simmonses'; and Connor's place, which smelled of hot coffee and that late-night outside odor not unlike a dog's coat. And then there was her own house, deeper in the fabric of her shirt, in the pores of her flesh. Unwashed sheets, oily pillows; overflowing garbage, clogged sink; the build-up beneath the toilet seat, the cold, dull chunks of hardened mud on the floor; plaster, and trapped musk; ash.

She pulled away from the tree. The world pulled away from her. She righted herself and fought back the encephalitic swell of exhaustion building in her skull. She and Stephen had sworn to one another they wouldn't fall apart, for their daughter's sake, and yet the closer they came to her, the more they unraveled.

Even though she looked like something that might've crawled out of the cemetery behind them, truth be told, she hadn't felt more alive. Where her body bucked and begged for a bed, it simultaneously stung and sparked. Her hands shook. Her calves tightened. Her mind wavered and wandered, and yet its focus was a drill boring through the center of her forehead. Fight-or-flight gave way to fight-or-fight, and soon she was imagining the floorplans of Ved's house and the things she might do to him out of need or want.

She thought of everything, but she did not think of Filipa.

"Phone have any battery left in it?" Stephen asked.

"No," she said, without checking.

"We're on our own."

"Haven't we always been?"

Linnéa licked her lips and took the lead. She hurried across the road and ran up Ved's yard. The soil squelched; tufts of recently cut grass climbed into the air and scattered with the wind. She looked to her left and right for nosy neighbors, but there was no one. There might not have been for years now.

Slowing down, Linnéa and Stephen crouch-stepped up the porch. She went to the front door and pressed her ear against it. Nothing.

"Is it locked?" Stephen asked.

She hadn't tried, but when she did, it was.

Hearing that, they broke apart, going their separate ways across the porch, overturning every rock and empty flower pot for the possibility of a spare key.

Getting discouraged, Stephen said, "Lin, Six Pillars is right around the corner. We should get one of the cops to come and…"

Linnéa toed a loose board. "Why? They can't do nothing without a warrant or probable cause." She pressed into it harder. The board turned upwards. Taped to the underside of it was a grimy key.

"He might not be our guy."

She grabbed the key and hurried back to the door.

"He's got to know something. Seen something."

She held her breath and pushed the key into the lock.

"Could be a decent man for all we know."

She turned it. The bolt gave itself to her.

"We have to do this."

Stephen closed his eyes, nodded, and pushed the front door open, and together, they stepped inside, closing the door behind them.

Whatever gore-stained, semen-slickened slaughter they might've imagined Ved's house to be, it was not. It was, if nothing else, quaint. It was warm and smelled like apple cinnamon. The hardwood floors, though old, were spotless. The walls were a calming blue and covered in cheap, offensively normal canvases with inspirational quotes written in cursive on them, such "Live Life to the Fullest" and "A Happy Wife is a Happy Life." Something Bethany might hang up.

Pressing farther into the house, they found the living room with white carpet and a single couch draped in knitted blankets of kittens and puppies. There was an old tube TV with a wood paneled encasing, like something the Crosses' might own, and bent bunny ears covered in foil atop it.

Heading into the kitchen from the living room, Linnéa stopped Stephen with her hand and sniffed the air. There was another scent here. It was faint, lingering like smoke does above a candle. She breathed it in. Rose vanilla. Rose vanilla lotion. The same kind Filipa would wear.

A surge of adrenaline shot through Linnéa with such strength she almost fainted. She sniffed the air and hunted for its source. It grew stronger and stronger as she went back across the living room, muddying the carpet with her shoes.

Then she found it, the source. On a coffee table tucked against couch, in the corner. It was a picture in a bronze picture frame. The picture was black and white, and of a woman she never really knew, but still had come to know all the same.

It was a picture of her mother, Agnes.

Linnéa reached for it, and then turned away. She tore through the house. In the kitchen, she found a nice table with a red and white-checkered cloth draped over it. A plate with a spoon and fork were set there, with a mug, too, that read across it, *Bethany Simmons' Consulting*.

She started ripping out the drawers in the kitchen, unsure of what she was looking for, but finding things all the same. Mismatched cutlery—three forks, three spoons, four butter knives, and four ceramic knives—and mail. Junk mail, mostly, but mail; not addressed to 707 Meridian Avenue or even Ved Matcira, but to Six Pillars—to Linnéa and Stephen, Ellen and Richard, Bethany and Todd, and Trent.

Stephen, taken aback, whispered, "Is this all from our…?"

Linnéa grabbed one of the ceramic knives and, seething, cut down the hallway.

She kicked opened the bathroom. There were four half empty bottles of shampoo in the shower, and four crumpled tubes of toothpaste on the sink.

She shouldered into a bedroom. Ved's bedroom. Inside was a child's bed that looked as if it had spent some time on the street, waiting to be collected by the garbage collectors. A pink pillow crowned it, a child's blanket depicting camouflaged soldiers covered it. In the middle of the bed was a book. Filipa's favorite. The one about changelings.

"Oh my god," Stephen choked out.

Linnéa turned out of the room, nearly stabbing him, and made for the last door at the end of the hall.

She gripped the knife until it hurt and opened the door.

Three descending stairs.

And darkness.

She flipped the switch with her knife-hand. She braced herself for the cries of children, but they never came. She told herself they were here, and then she went looking for them.

Linnéa went slowly at first, but the harder her heart beat, the faster she went, until she was nearly tripping over her feet to get to the bottom of the stairs.

"Lin, wait," Stephen cautioned her.

But she threw caution to the wind, banished it for good and all time, and plunged down the last of the steps. The cold basement floor met her feet and she caught herself.

The basement could've been a dead ringer to Connor's, but whereas his had been basically a cave, Ved's was a workshop. A long, wooden bench stretched most of the length of the basement under a series of still-burning and loosely suspended lights.

Beyond the table were a small chair and a small TV. It was still on, and it was playing recorded footage of someone driving through a neighborhood. Their neighborhood.

Stephen grabbed Linnéa's free hand, but she wouldn't let him have it for long. There were things on the table that needed her attention. He would have to wait. For just a little bit longer, he would have to wait.

First, she went to the pictures. The pictures of Filipa. The pictures of Darlene, Charles, and Jimmy. Pictures of them outside, or inside, having been taken through a window. There were pictures of them going to school and going to bed; of them in towels, their tiny bodies still wet from their showers.

Linnéa punched the table. Stephen took the side of it in both hands and gripped it hard enough to crack it.

Then she went to the pictures of the houses. Of all the entrances and exits. And the blueprints. There were windows and rooms circled and arrows pointing to walls.

Trembling, barely able to contain herself, her hands dragged more things across the table towards her. Pamphlets from the Disciples of God. A napkin with the name Chelsea—the teen in the white van?— and her number on it. Another decal with the Price Homes logo on it for the truck. A few empty, unmarked prescription bottles atop it. A bible with the Disciples of God's branding on the front of it. A drawing of Brooksville Manor with illegible notes scrawled in the margins. More pill bottles. Files. Files on the children. One for each of them. But they began with images and descriptions of their parents.

Filipa. There was Filipa's. And there was Linnéa and Stephen. And under their names... one word: Unworthy.

"Lin," Stephen whispered.

With such tunnel vision, she hadn't noticed what he was holding.

In his hands, he had a thick bundle of vermillion veins. They writhed in his hands, and reached up to drink the tears from his cheeks.

But then she realized that wasn't what he was talking about.

There was something else.

Someone else.

Someone standing behind her.

She spun around, knife out, slinging the evidence out in front of her.

Ved Matcira stood on the basement steps, both hands in his corduroy's pockets, neither impressed nor surprised. A strand of blond hair swept across his face, catching on his thin, crooked glasses. There was a scar on his lips, and scars on his wrists where the skin was exposed. He stood to one side, not intentionally, but because one leg was shorter than the other.

When he opened his mouth, a few of his teeth were missing, and those that weren't were stained red.

But before he could say anything, Linnéa and Stephen screamed, "Where are they? Where the fuck are they?"

"Where we left them," he said, laughing.

Linnéa ran up to him, grabbed him by the shirt, and shoved the knife into his stomach, into his bellybutton, barely breaking the skin.

Ved winced.

"Where?" Stephen cried.

"At home," he said. "There's a child in every home now."

Holding his arms behind his back, Linnéa shoved Ved out of the house, while Stephen led the way. He didn't drag his heels or try to fight back; he went calmly, willingly—his pursed lips passing no protest. To Linnéa, his silence was maddening, and she made him suffer for it, by twisting his arms and applying a crushing pressure to his wrist.

She drove the ceramic knife into his spine and made superficial carvings there. He bled, but he was not bothered.

"Are they okay?" Linnéa screamed into his ear. She noticed his truck wasn't here. Had he parked it elsewhere? Did he have an accomplice?

Crossing the street, reaching the cemetery, Stephen wheeled around them like a caged animal. "Answer her!" he shouted, stabbing his finger into Ved's boney side. "Answer her, goddamn it!"

"Yes," Ved said.

Linnéa and Stephen looked at one another, their faces going red from holding their breath.

"They're taken care of."

Stephen wrenched Ved by the collar of his shirt.

Linnéa drove the knife deeper into his back, steering him across the grass and graves.

Stephen hurried to the car, opened the doors. "They're still alive? They're at home?"

Ved nodded.

Linnéa slammed him into the car. "Use your fucking words," she said, pushing him into the backseat, going in after him. She pinned him, her knee in his stomach, the knife to his neck. "Talk!"

Stephen dropped into the driver's seat and started up the car. The smell of burnt rubber poured through the vents as he peeled out of the parking lot.

Ved swallowed hard; the knife threatened to impale his Adam's apple. "What do—" he coughed, "—want to know?"

"Did you touch them? Did you hurt them?" She drove her knee into his stomach, until he looked as if he might vomit. "I swear to god…"

Ved's eyes shone vermillion. "You will, soon enough. And no, we did not lay a hand on them, except to take them."

"We?" Stephen stared into the rear-view mirror. "We? How many?"

"Hundreds," Ved said, laughing.

Linnéa spit in his face. "Don't you dare."

"Every one of you had it coming."

Stephen jerked the wheel to the left, slinging Linnéa and Ved across the backseat.

Before he could think of going out the door, Linnéa was back on top of him again; this time with the knife's blade bearing down on his cock.

"What do you mean?" she said, giving everything she had to stop herself from castrating him right then and there.

Like most men, the threat of losing his balls got Ved talking. "You weren't good parents. You don't deserve your children. You'll turn them into you."

The accusations hit Linnéa harder than she expected.

Honking horns blasted the car as Stephen sped through a stop sign. "God will take care of them."

Stephen cried, "Are you with the Disciples?"

"Absolutely."

"Did they make you do this?"

Ved tongued the scar on his lip. "No one makes me do anything anymore. Not anymore. Not anymore. But they did ask. They asked a lot of us. Us like me."

Linnéa pressed her weight into him. "Who? Who did? The people from your church?" She paused, overworked her brain. "The kids in the van? The police? The people coming in from out of town?"

"All of the above," Ved said.

Stephen whipped around a corner. The entrance to Six Pillars was no more than twenty seconds away.

"The… other parents?" Linnéa whispered.

"In their own way," he said.

She slapped him, stabbed the knife into his scrotum.

He whimpered and tried to shake her off, but there was a new fear that had a hold on him. A dormant fear. An unresolved fear. Not weakness, but instinct. His body went hard all over, and she imagined it a shield behind which his mind could hide. He'd been here before. She wasn't the first mother to do this to him.

Stephen turned into Six Pillars and hauled it towards their home.

"I don't think you'll have anything to worry about," Ved said, admiring the houses on the street as they ran past the glass in a muddled blur. "Filipa was the favorite."

Stephen rolled down his window, shouted to neighbors on the street, "Get help! Call the police!"

Whatever hope Linnéa had felt before was gone. "What are you talking about?"

"They tried to tell you."

The shadows, she realized.

"A month is a long time," Ved said. "I would know. God, I would know. But I wouldn't worry."

The car bounced up. Stephen hopped the sidewalk and drove through half their neighbor's yard before screeching to a stop in their own driveway.

"Wouldn't worry?" Linnéa's throat constricted. Her mouth filled with spit. "Wouldn't worry?"

Stephen got out of the car, opened the rear door.

"Your house does smell, though," Ved said. He started to laugh. "Do you think something might've died in the walls?"

A child in every home.

Linnéa grabbed him by his throat and backed out of the car, dragging him with her. When he hit the ground, she kicked him in the face. His lip popped open; a bright geyser of blood shot across the driveway.

Leaving him there, she grabbed the keys from Stephen, unlocked the trunk.

Seeing what she was doing, Stephen grabbed Ved underneath his arms, barely lifted him to his feet.

Together, they pushed Ved into the trunk, slammed it shut, and locked it.

From across the street: "What's going on?"

Linnéa turned around. Bethany Simmons was standing at her front door. Ellen and Richard Cross were next to their car, about to leave. And Trent Resin was checking his mailbox.

"Did you hear about Brooksville Manor? It just collapsed out of nowhere!"

She tried to tell them what was going on, but the words were lodged in her throat, held back by their impossibility.

"The kids," Stephen cried. "The kids are in the houses!"

While the other parents stood there dumbfounded, Linnéa and Stephen rushed into the house. Hand shaking, it took Stephen a good ten seconds to unlock the door. When he did, they spilled across the threshold—an avalanche of scrabbling desperation—and bounded up the staircase.

They ran down the hall, into their room. Linnéa jumped onto the bed, outstretched her hands to the two black smudges on the ceiling.

"Filipa? Filipa? Baby?"

She stood on the tips of her toes. She focused as hard as she could on the smudges.

A gust of wind. That foul smell of rot. And a fleck of plaster.

The smudges weren't smudges, but tiny holes.

Peepholes... for the person on the other side.

"No, no, no!" Stephen ran out of the room, came back a minute later with a mildewed 2x4 he'd used to line his garden. "Watch out!"

He stumbled onto the bed.

"Filipa, we're coming!" Linnéa said.

And then he drove the 2x4 into the ceiling, bashing through the eggshell-like plaster. It slipped into the darkness inside the walls, came back out covered in a black, viscous material.

"Honey!" Linnéa dropped off the bed, ran into Filipa's room, grabbed the stool from in front of her vanity, and came back in and dropped it on the bed, so she could get closer to the ceiling. "You have to move. Daddy's going to get you..."

Stephen, grunting, crying, rammed the board into the ceiling again, faster and faster, harder and harder, carving it away with a frenzied intensity.

First came the cloying smell of decay.

Then pieces of ceiling covered in piss and shit.

"I see something," Linnéa said, on top of the stool. She reached for the gap in the ceiling, sinking her hands into the fleshy mush that rimmed it. "I see..."

The ceiling buckled, and in a cradle of rot and ropes, Filipa fell through. In that morbid moment, time slowed to a stop, as if to taunt Linnéa and Stephen, to show them what couldn't possibly be.

To show them their daughter's raw, meat-red body, bloated and dried-out; to show them where the hair had fallen from her head, where the teeth had dropped from her gums; to show them the flesh and muscle ripping away from her bones as she plummeted to the floor; to show them her empty eye sockets, and all the times she must've watched them at night; to show them her twisted mouth, and all the times she must've wanted to call out, to tell them how close she was, how easy she would've been to save.

And then time was done with them.

Filipa's body burst apart when it hit the ground. Putrefied organs leaked out of her orifices in a rancid stew. Her flesh pulled apart and her bones drifted. She split down the middle, like two continents separating, and between them, an ocean of gore in which only Linnéa's and Stephen's images were captured.

Shock sent Linnéa careening through the house. Off her rails, she was out of her mind, screaming and beating her chest as she ran, crawled, and ran down the hall, down the stairs.

She cried out with words that weren't words, making silent sounds only the loneliness of stars might know. She threw herself through the front door, tripped, and fell onto the stone walkway. The rocks bit her knees, bled her hands. She vomited all over herself.

She rocked back and forth, back and forth, grinding herself harder and harder into the stone, searching for some horrible sensation to steal away this inhuman feeling inside her.

Back and forth, back and forth, she heard Ved in the trunk, trying to kick and punch his way out.

Back and forth, back and forth, she heard Stephen coming down the stairs, wailing so hard he might never speak again.

Back and forth, back and forth, she began to lie to herself about the body in the bedroom, about having had a daughter at all, about—

A gunshot exploded through Six Pillars.

Linnéa reared back and fell on her haunches.

Trent Resin lay dead on the front lawn of his house, a trail of smoke pouring out of the hole in his head. Before him, the body of Charles Resin lay, all bones, but for the face attached like a mask to his skull.

Then she looked to the Simmonses' house and she saw Ellen sitting on the porch, a cigarette in one hand, the blue baby blanket of her son, Jimmy, in the other. Everything she held was covered in blood, and she was smiling.

And then she looked to the Crosses' house, where at first there was nothing, and then, there were three men coming up to it from the down the road. In their hands they held multi-colored stones and neck-laces. When they reached the house, the front door opened and Ellen and Richard Cross emerged, their hands folded in prayer, their eyes cast to the ground. They were shouting about something, but Linnéa couldn't make sense of the English language anymore.

At least, not after what she saw; after what came behind Ellen and Richard. A frail shape. Bound in rope. Covered in blood. A little girl of eleven or twelve. She wore a cloak of vermillion veins and walked upon a carpet of them, too. They moved when she moved. They were her, and she was them.

Before Linnéa and Stephen hanged themselves in their living room, they watched the news report on the whole thing. Darlene Lillian Cross claimed to have survived only by listening to God's will. She told the reporters she would only answer to the name Lillian, and that she would only listen to the word of the true God.

For she was the only one on this world who could hear Its message, and for this world, It had a message.

TRAUMAS

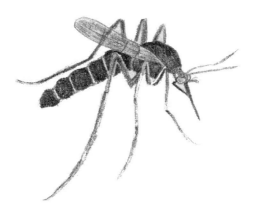

Judas remembers more than he should, and no one else can know that.

He remembers Lillian from the television; all the fire and brimstone she spewed; all the fire and brimstone she'd brought.

He remembers when the ground opened up and out of Hell, Heaven came—a winding maelstrom of veins and blasphemous germinations.

He remembers the well-dressed corpses in their gleaming coffers; the lies they told, the lies they sold; the parishioners they purchased by the millions, while they salivated over the property and prospects in the loaming Deep.

He remembers when the bombs fell and the bullets flew—a unified wave of killing hate stirred and sown and grown to drown the discord and discontent that surrounded Lux, Earth's self-proclaimed last hope and savior.

He remembers, as he looks to the horizon, that once there'd been a God, and now It is no more.

Abandoned by his Creator, he remembers no greater pain.

That is, until that dreaded day, when everything was taken away.

11

Judas has been following this river beside him for as long as it's been here. He knows its every bend. Though the water changes, the river remains the same. Its history is in the soil, and in the shape it has taken, despite the shapes it might take. Judas admires this about the river. He sees himself in its waters, hears himself in the strange syllables they speak. If others were to stand beside him and see him reflected as he does, they would understand. But along this river, he walks alone, for he is a needle passing through the fabric of time, undoing what others have done, sewing himself in where he does not belong.

Ahead, ruin. Against the smeared horizon, a piece of a town stands. Uprooted, overturned, and hurled into these wetland wilds, jagged shards of cement protrude from the ground. Beyond them, at their center, two homes have been fused together by Heaven's heat. There is also half a bakery. Having been there before, Judas knows there is no food to be found—only the remnants of those who might've tried to steal it. The walls, floor, and ceiling of the bakery are caked in large, dried explosions of gore, as if the building, when it had been picked up, had been shaken violently, the same way a child would shake to snuff a box of bugs.

Judas is not here for the ruins. He is here to eat.

He takes the knife out of his belt and goes quietly towards the wreckage. The slippery mud of the riverbank gives way to gurgling grass. Skinny mosquitoes looking to get fat fly about his head, but he doesn't dare swat them away. He knows better. Everyone in these parts does.

At this early morning hour, the clouds appear curdled, but for a moment, as Judas approaches the ruins, they loosen and part. Not much light comes through—the sun is slow to wake, and most days has its back to the world—but there is something. A glimpse of the sky, and the landmasses in it, weeping rubble. From the underside of raw earth, massive vermillion veins hang; some are even long enough to reach the ground. People are said to have had climbed them, and gone with the islands into the stars. Judas has had people try to tell him that the landmasses are from Europe, but he's never left this country before. All he knows is that everything is coming apart; nothing wants to be here anymore.

The distraction disappears. Judas puts it out of his mind. He hurries to the cement shards and passes between them. The smell is strongest at the fused houses. Like most these days, he follows his nose as if it were the Word of God. At least when it came to the syllables of starvation, they didn't need an interpreter like Lillian to tell them what it all meant.

Minding the rubble, Judas moves to the houses and presses himself against the charred seam that'd brought them together. God's unification hadn't been of people, but of the things they'd created. That which hadn't been swallowed down Its throat had been smashed together. Even the continents were changed. This world hadn't been good to God, so God had Its way with the world and molded it into something that it might be in the eons to come. But like the river behind Judas, this world was still the world he knew, unrecognizable as it might be; somewhere beneath the scar tissue, the rotting flesh, the putrefying organs, there were bones.

The smell makes Judas' stomach rumble. Battling with his hunger, he twists his body until he looks like a twisted tree. He squeezes the knife, catches his reflection in the rusted blade. He was a tree, wasn't he? Skinny, bare. Pale, coarse; sad. He'd ignored his roots for so long, and kept them moving when they needed to take. But things were different now. He can settle, and settle in for the long nights to come. He doesn't have to go at it alone.

Salivating, Judas climbs into the house through what might have been a window. He crosses what might have been a living room. If he has learned anything from all this, it was that everything you could ever need could be found in the dark. The shadows were small sanctuaries. If the Lillians had ever taught him anything, it was that Heaven was in the low places.

He goes as deep as he can into the house, letting his nose guide him, and then goes deeper still. Not touching the piles of wreckage in the house's furthest corner, he searches for fissures and, finding them, slips through. That's where most people were these days. In the cracks, waiting to die as they waited things out.

Coming out of the fissure, Judas finds no one in the dark pocket on the other side. His eyes don't need much light to work with, so he leaves the wreckage where it is and picks over the blackness.

There are a lot of cans of food. All of them are empty. The labels have been torn off and probably eaten. There are plastic soda bottles; most of them are filled with piss. Animal feces cultivate a small kingdom of flies in a recess. Stained cardboard and soiled linens stand in place of a bed. A few magazines about women's health, do-it-yourself home improvements, and musical instruments are splayed out along the ground; pleasure, purpose, and past-time.

Judas can't find any weapons aside from the sharp edges of the aluminum cans. He takes a seat in the makeshift room of a makeshift life.

It wouldn't be long now. It couldn't be long now.

He dozes off. He dreams of the families he's known. They offer them his faces. It was nice to know they still fit.

Judas jerks awake. There had been a noise, either in this world or the one inside his head, but there had been a noise. He knows what he wants it to be; his mind goes elsewhere.

North of here, deep in the swamp, there is a village called Traesk. Hundreds of Night Terrors are said to live there. To Judas, there is nothing more frightening than them. Pretentious, entitled, and narcissistic, the semi-organized tribe of sociopaths have dedicated their entire existence into "balancing" the human race by engaging in the very same behaviors they supposedly condemn in the "Corrupted." At night, they sneak into towns and villages and rape and murder humans by the handfuls. Those women that are raped but are not fortunate enough to die afterwards sometimes give birth to demonic offspring that have been known to eviscerate entire families before being put down.

People call them Night Terrors, but Judas prefers to remember what they were called in the Old World: flesh fiends. It is important to him not to forget these things. A terrorist is a terrorist until it is on your television, at your table; accepted, celebrated; normalized.

The movement softens. Judas draws to the fissure and listens. He hopes it is a Night Terror. Some have chosen to wear the skulls of Lord animals rather than the skulls and flesh of humans. Those animal skulls fetch a nice price. Even in a world as hopeless as this one, oversized beasts and beautiful mutations can open mouths and wallets.

The hunger finds him again. With the knife in his hand, he thinks of cutting out his stomach. He has to stop doing this to himself.

The sounds draw nearer to the house. Footsteps. Long nails clicking against cement. He hears panting—two kinds—and rustling. Someone speaks. A man like himself, or so they all say. A Night Terror, perhaps. It could be a Lillian, which is not an issue, except the Lillians tend to move in droves, like locusts, eating away their host's good will until nothing is left but prejudice and discrimination. Judas has killed his fair share of Lillians, but anyone more than one body wouldn't do him any good. He has others waiting on him. Their mouths are not meant for human meat. Not yet, in any case.

They are inside the house, outside the fissure. Judas hears mum-

bling. Something heavy and filled with metal is set down. More panting, and a high-pitched whine.

Guided by hunger, Judas forsakes patience and pushes into the fissure. The knife leads the way, as it always has. The smell is overwhelm-
ing. He weeps.

A gasp. Bare, dry feet sounding scratchy on stone. Snarling.

Judas stops at the fissure's midpoint. He's been spotted.

On the other side, an old man stands in sweat pants and a grey
hoodie. There are holes in his clothes from where he's been hurt; the
bloodstains around them are proof of that. He had been obese once;
curtains of loose skin sag from his frame. Judas can't see this, but he
has before.

At Judas' feet lie what might be his most prized possessions.

To his right, a stuffed sack of canned goods topped off with a rod
of skewered squirrels. Winter wouldn't be long now, and this was
meant to see him through hibernation.

To his left, a dog. A mangy thing with greasy, matted fur. A quivering thing with wet, lifeless eyes and a pink, snarling mouth. It snaps at
its master, perhaps out of confusion, or simply out of disappointment.
It knows what's coming, and the old man, by fire and stars, had promised otherwise.

Judas keeps pushing through the fissure, his eyes locked on the old
man's.

The old man turns to run, but makes fists instead and stays where
he stands. There is nowhere else to go. There is nowhere better for
him and his but this.

The knife scrapes against the fissure, issuing knells. It catches on
the edge and then, as Judas moves free from the wreckage, it stabs
through the air. Like a magnet, the blade is drawn to where it belongs.

Through flesh, in bone.

One for him, one for them.

The journey home is long. Judas goes by sun, and when he gets
there, will be greeted by moon. He steers clear of the northern swamps
of Traesk and dares not go farther south than needed to avoid drawing
the attention of the Lillian sentries outside Cathedra. His place is in the
east, far from the black city of Vold, where once he lived and now lives
again. In that day, they called it Bitter Springs. Nowadays, they call it
nothing at all.

Judas carries the dead dog in his arms and the sack over his shoulder. It is slow going on a stomach so stuffed. Through the fields and forests, he is vulnerable, but he knows no other way. There are things he can do to protect himself if needed, but he'd rather not. Some masks worn too long tend to crumble when removed.

This wasteland is one unending rupture. Where once there had been roads and cities and countless neighborhoods, there are now only the gaping wounds from which God's wanting veins came through. After all these years, Judas still finds these scenes too surreal. Some say God did not die, that It slumbers. And if that is true, then the Earth left behind is one of Its nightmares. Or, perhaps, Its most stirring fantasy.

Judas sees the forest and makes for the trees. Dark things dwell in the heart of the Heartland. Not just Night Terrors or Lillians, but inhuman things. Fanged beasts, winged terrors; skittering hordes. Ancient horrors from myth and Membrane, ready to find their place in a world once cut-off from them.

But hostilities remain. Judas reaches the trees and slips into their wooded embrace. There is a heat in the air, like a wick quickly burning down to the wax. An inevitable clash is coming; something to swallow this rallying fire of freedom whole. He is not alone here.

Shouting. Gunshots.

Judas looks back and sees a lone truck struggling up and down the ruptures outside the forest. Gathered round it is a camouflaged gang of angry men and women. Those in the truck's bed have the guns; those around the truck do not. They have torches and stakes and sharp pieces of silver fixed onto sticks, like spears.

Judas runs faster. The Corrupted don't know they want him, but they will, and if they don't, they'll find a reason.

Their game isn't far, and realizing that, Judas sees their victims in the northern part of the forest, not walking or running, but dashing between the boughs.

He sees the twenty or so vampyres in their conservative school uniforms. They are aged between five and twelve, and their hands are split from finger to wrist, as the mouths inside their palms plead with gnashes and hisses to suck dry the flesh bags that trail them. But the little girls and little boys show no sign of stopping. Combat is not their concern. They are desperate, and of late, endangered.

The lamias are slower. They slither from tree to tree on their serpentine bellies, while their feminine top-halves exert every muscle beneath their coppery skin to hurl them through the canopy. Unlike the vampyres, there is no question as to whether they are considering standing their ground. A lamia's scales, colored in accordance to their temperament and toxicity, fetch a fetching price in the right markets. Judas expects that most of the fleeing lamias are responsible for the deaths of the mob's many children. They will not be killed. They will be taken alive, first to be raped, then to be flayed, and then, when thoughts of revenge and acts of posturing have lost their taste, the lamias will be discarded, left to the cruelness of nature for their cruel nature.

Judas goes his own way. The Great Hunt will go on whether he does something or not. The Corrupted have decided that creatures such as the vampyres and lamias are the ones responsible for the Trauma. Even now it is easier to make fists than to point their fingers at themselves.

A lamia is sniped from the boughs. It cries out and hits the ground. The mob and pick-up truck close in. Its brethren do not stop, nor do the vampyres with which they've aligned themselves. Because the Nameless Forest is farther still, and for now, their only sanctuary.

Judas makes it home with a pack of strays trailing him. They smell the blood on his breath, and are desperate for the corpse of their own he's been carrying. He sets down the old man's dog like an offering. When the strays move, stiff and scared, Judas takes off his mask and does what needs to be done.

Mary's heard the commotion. It would've been strange had she not. Their home is underground, beneath the shattered remains of Bitter Springs, but you don't have to hear pain to know it's near. You develop an organ for it. It makes you itch, like an allergy; on your neck, on the back of your hands. She's scratching at herself when she flips the fallout shelter's door back and comes halfway up the ladder.

Judas gets dressed and glances back. She is a pretty thing, framed by ruin or not. He would be lucky to have a wife like her, but for now, he's just a guest in her home, with her two pretty daughters, Harper and Jane. They don't know yet. His shape is the same, and they can't yet see behind his eyes.

Surrounded by the broken bodies of "man's best friend," Judas laughs. He starts to drag the dogs in by their legs, and she comes out to help. He hands her the bag of canned goods with the skewered squirrels and she goes back with it under the ground, like a pilfering goblin.

They will eat well tonight. She, lonely and with needs of her own, will still be hungry when the fires have gone low and coals have begun to cool. He will have to think of something to keep her away. He is running out of excuses.

Judas drags the last of the dogs to the metal door and drops them down into the dark. He looks up to the sky and sees a green mist like a halo around the moon.

There is a sickness in the stars tonight. Or maybe there always had been. You see what you want to see.

God should've known better, he considers, closing the door over him as he descends down the ladder. It's troubling that It didn't.

10

They had dog for dinner, and dog for breakfast. Seeing Harper and Jane tear into the animals with their grubby fingers didn't surprise Judas as much as it used to with the others. Pets were things of the past. Companionship didn't count for much where a life could be lived from sunrise to sunset. Mary's daughters had never known anything different, and never would. They, their mother's only dreams, had been born into this nightmare.

"It's such a nice day out," Mary says to them.

Judas laughs.

She does not.

Harper and Jane have not seen the sun in some time. Like flowers feeling the first drops of rain after a long drought, they straighten up, and take off around the fallout shelter. There is not much room down there to run, so it is only a few seconds before they are swarming Judas, tugging on his shirt, jumping on him.

They smell like wet fur and blood as they whine in unison, "Please, daddy! Please!"

Judas is not their father. And if he were, he would not allow either of them to set foot outside of here. But he has a part to play; not to hide, but to pay for this gift in which he hides.

Mary sends Judas up the ladder. He tells the girls to be quiet while they put on their coats. Unlocking the hatch and pushing it back, sunlight floods the shelter, sending Harper and Jane scurrying for the comforts of dark.

"Find some shade," Mary calls after him.

They want to go outside, and the first thing they ask for is to be out of the light. Before stepping off the ladder, Judas glances back and sees Mary's preparing for a picnic.

He lowers the shelter's door slowly. It clicks rather than clanks into place. Sound carries in the wasteland, and when it echoes back, he doesn't want anything coming with it.

Bitter Springs, or what remains of it, is hard to look at. Having been so close to God, the town could not hold in Its presence. There is little left, and even less to recognize. Most buildings simply disappeared. They, along with almost every sewage pipe, power line, and other utilities, had been ripped off and out of the ground. What's left is piles of rubble and hills of dirt, and the blighted and hewn forest they once called Maidenwood. It does not offer much in the way of cover, and yet because of where the town is, it is almost invisible.

Fifty miles from what used to be Bitter Springs' outskirts, and across the soured, stagnated Tri-County river, is Bedlam, the birthplace of Lillian, God's speaker and the leader of the Lillians. It is a holy site caught in a constant conflict between the religious order and those who have decided to live there. Some say they fight just to fight, while others say the aggression is being stoked by Vold to keep the Lillians scattered and stupid. Either way, with everyone there, or held up in the much closer ruins of Brooksville, it leaves Bitter Springs ignored.

Judas goes out a quarter mile from the fallout shelter and circles it. The wind howls in his ears with sharp warnings he has yet to heed. "Go back inside," it seems to say some days. And on others, "You should not be here."

Farther on, the morning fog clings like cotton. It is dark, though, and putrescent in color. The Putrid Prince had passed through these parts last night. Its taint lingers. Judas isn't sure of the creature's intent, but like the Night Terrors, the roaming cloud of disease appears to be targeting humans exclusively; more specifically, those Corrupted who do not bear the crimson defect. It used to kill them, but now it consumes them, repurposes them into contagious colonies. Mary, Harper, and Jane have Corruption, but Judas still insists on being precautious. It seems like something he would do, and therefore, something he should do.

Judas makes his way back to the fallout shelter. For a moment, he slips off the mask and trains his eyes and nose on his surroundings. He smells the pack of dogs he killed last night, and sees their blood blinking in the soil. He takes his senses farther out into the wilderness, probing every piece of debris and detritus that he can see for shapes and smells. Animals, rodents mostly, and stinking bones stand out to him in his stomach's eye, but nothing of the human or humanoid variety. For now, they are alone here.

"Dad—"

Harper's voice breaks likes a violin string.

On the ladder, holding the door over her head, she's seen him without his mask.

Judas turns away from her and calls forth the flesh. Like clothes in a closet, they hang silently in the dark, waiting to be put on. His closet has gotten so full, he loses track of what he's stolen over the years.

Harper persists. "Dad?"

She's climbed out of the shelter. She's coming towards him.

Judas walks away from her. The pressure slows his perusing. The flesh is here somewhere. He has to choose the right one. He can't do this to them.

"Dad, what's wrong with your—"

He's found it, or thinks he has. She's close enough to touch him, and she will, with those small, warm, dirty hands of hers, because she is a child, and eight, and like the blind, she has to feel something to truly understand it.

He needs to see his reflection, but everywhere he looks, there is only overgrown destruction. His mirror is behind him.

So, heart beating and nearly breaking, he turns to face her.

Harper stops. She grinds her heel. One eyebrow arches after the other. "Dad?" she whispers.

He doesn't say anything.

"Never mind." She smiles and grabs his hand. "Is it okay? Can we? Please?"

Judas would rather wait until the fog lifts to be sure, but by the confused happiness on Harper's face, he's not sure he can. She's his confederate. She knows what she saw, but for their sake, she's willing to forget it.

When God left, it was the children who learned the quickest about how to survive.

"Well, I don't hear your father yelling up there," Mary says from inside the shelter.

Jane, seven, comes from the ground with a basket in her mouth.

"So, it must be okay," Mary finishes, emerging from behind her daughter. She has a tarp folded over her arm and a bottle of wine in her hand.

Judas wishes Mary hadn't brought the bottle of wine. It was special to her and her husband, and he has no idea as to why.

Mary drops the fallout shelter's door. It clanks loudly, breaking this sad serenity. She tightens her shoulders, cringes, and says, "Oops."

Judas spins in place. He searches the fog, but in it, nothing stirs. Only the dead world he once knew. Day by day, it's breaking down. Sometimes it's so loud, you might even think it's raining. Jane, sentimental as ever, told him once that the sound was the planet crying. He liked that, but he didn't like knowing why it wept. Because it was falling apart? Or because others wouldn't let it?

"Are we okay?" Mary asks.

Judas nods. "Good as it's going to get."

Harper and Jane turn to one another like two cowboys in a standoff. Their excitement bubbles over into red blotches on their faces. But they are quiet. They know better.

Judas picks a place for their picnic. It's farther away from the shelter than Mary might have anticipated, so when he points it out, she doesn't say anything. And when he realizes he's not acting himself, she can't stop talking.

"I'm so sick of the shelter," she says.

Mary holds one end of the tarp.

Harper and Jane share the opposite end.

"Same," Harper says.

"Same," Jane confirms.

Judas, left holding the basket of food and bottle of wine, watches as they lay out the tarp. Its crinkling sets his nerves on edge. He glances at the trees they're under—three bulbous, conjoined trunks with clumps of hair for leaves—and then back at the shelter. There's about thirty or forty feet between them.

"Hey, Jude," Mary says.

Judas snaps out of it. He smiles at her as a tune plays in his head. She'll never understand, so he doesn't bother to tell her.

"Sit, sit. Come on." Mary waves him over as she and the girls plop down on the tarp.

"Sit, Daddy," Harper says.

Jane points at the ground and growls, "Sit."

Judas does as he's told. Harper plods towards him and sits in his lap, while Jane does the same but with Mary. He's been with the family for a month. This is the way it's always been. He also knows that Harper likes hugs, whereas Jane likes kisses on the cheek—and they both can eat and cuss like sailors when their stomachs are empty and their patience has run out.

But they are children. They are mercurial. A fraction of the person they will be in ten year's time. He knows how to love them without having to know them, because he had girls of his own once. Harper and Jane are not substitutes. He would not do that to them.

It is the woman across from him he has to understand. Mary's wedding ring is a faded tattoo of interlocking shapes. His wedding band was a piece of copper, the skin underneath very faded. They had made the effort to have the ceremony, however small it might have been. That says a lot, and for Judas, not enough.

Mary reaches for the basket and says, "We have… honey—"

Harper and Jane wiggle.

"—and stale crackers!"

Harper claps.

Jane is less than impressed. "I'm tired of stale crackers," she pouts.

Mary bounces her up and down with her legs. "I'm tired of ungrateful girls. Maybe we should just eat you."

Jane squeals in anticipation of the tickles to come.

Judas quickly changes the subject. "We have wine."

Harper licks her lips like a regular lush.

"For Mommy and Daddy," he adds.

Now, Harper is pouting; arms crossed across her chest so tightly it has to hurt.

"Maybe just a little for the girls," Mary says, slyly.

Judas tries to read the situation, but he's tired. He's been reading situations for weeks. If he's going to keep this flesh, he has to let himself be comfortable in it.

"A little," he says, gesturing with his fingers. "Only a little."

Mary doles out the honey and stale crackers in equal portions to the girls, and then to him; then to herself. While Harper and Jane are crunching away, Mary takes out four thimbles. Judas figured out Mary used to be a seamstress for a community she and her husband lived in years ago on the west coast. She can stitch with just about anything, and can make clothes out of nothing. In the past, she would've been a social media darling. Now, all she has is all she is.

"One for Jane," Mary says, filling a thimble.

Harper huffs.

"So sorry." She smirks. "One for Harper."

Harper lifts her chin. "The oldest."

"We know," Judas says, rolling his eyes.

Mary hands Harper the wine-filled thimble.

She goes to down it.

"Wait. Wait until we all have one. Then we'll toast."

Jane grabs her mother by the shirt. "We have toast?"

"No, we'll toast." Mary fills a thimble for Jane and hands it to her. "Words can mean different things. You'll see."

"That's dumb," Jane says, taking it.

"Used to be a lot more words," Judas says.

He doesn't know Mary's age. Things get older quicker in this world these days. Without her clothes, after a wash, she looks like she's in her early forties, but Judas isn't sure. He didn't look for long. But if she is, then there's a chance, as a child, she knew what it was like to lose God.

Harper tips her head back and says, "What happened to them?"

"The words?" Judas puts his arms around her. "Stopped needing them. If there's no more trees left in the world, and everyone forgets about them, do you need the word 'tree'?"

"Yes," Jane says, resolutely. "What if someone finds a tree?"

"Guess we'd have to call it something else."

"Then it's not a tree," Harper says.

Judas smiles. "Guess not."

"That's dumb," Jane repeats.

Mary gives a thimble to Judas. She holds his hand as he takes it. There are designs in her eyes. This means a lot to her. He doesn't yet know why. It feels like the end of something. It's a good feeling. He feels it in her fingers, the way she caresses the bones in his wrist. It sparks. It's sensual.

Judas is the first to break the bond and holds the thimble up. "Ready when you are."

Mary pours herself a thimble. "Before we toast. Not eat toast…"

She rubs her face against the top of Jane's head and growls like a monster.

"We should pray."

Judas lowers the thimble and holds Harper tighter. Sometimes, he forgets that Mary is a Lillian, or some crack of that fractured church. She doesn't pray nor bring up God often, but when she does, she glows. Her eyes go wide and her mouth shakes, and she speaks in quiet, caustic tongues. Her belief is bottled up. Either she's too embarrassed to let it out, or she's too afraid of indulging too much, as if by doing so, one day it'll be gone for good.

Harper and Jane squirm out of their respective parent's lap and find a place for themselves on the tarp.

Judas has another look around. The fog was clearing. He can see clear into the distances beyond. If anything had heard the shelter door closing, then they'd know where to find it.

"Bless us, from the Deep, our God and these gifts we are about to consume from Your offering," Mary says, voice rising higher and higher.

Judas moves to interrupt her, but her eyes are closed and she is closed to him. Even without his senses, he is sure something is watching them. It isn't far. Maybe where the clouds cling like mold to the sky; beneath them, in that bramble of rubble. Twenty feet away.

"We give thanks to Lillian, God's Speaker, for she is Its voice and our guide. Though we have sinned, we will soon sup at Its table." Mary had added that last sentence herself. "Bless us, forgive us. Amen."

"Amen," Judas says, glad to have the prayer finished.

"Amen," Harper says, drawing the thimble to her lips.

Jane is staring into the trees, like she's seen something.

Mary nudges an "Amen" out of her.

"To us," Judas says. He extends his thimble. This picnic has run its course.

"Is that the toast?" Jane asks.

"Not a very good one," Mary says.

Harper agrees.

Judas glances behind them to the fallout shelter's door. Past it, he makes out the black slit of the Tri-County river. Just beyond it, in the vapors, a holy war rages. He can't see it, but he knows it's there, and then he wonders: Why did they really choose this place to settle?

Playfully, anxiously, Judas says, "Go on, then. Show me how it's done."

Mary licks her lips and lingers on the thimble in her hand, in all their hands. Is that the tremor of an old addiction that moves through her?

"Tell them how we met," she says.

"Yeah!" Harper and Jane shout.

Judas glances around to see if anything has heard them. But there is nothing, still. Just the quiet crumbling of the bones of the earth around them.

"You want me to tell it?" she asks.

He looks at her and sees disappointment. This is a well-rehearsed story to which he knows none of the lines. They might have even talked about this day, before the girls came to be. He's going to have to let her down.

"I'm sorry," he says. "Get us started, and I'll fill in where you get it wrong."

Mary snorts. "I'm sure you will. Well, your father and I met when we were very young."

"Most beautiful thing I ever did see," Judas adds. You can't go wrong with something like that.

Mary shakes her head, smiles. "He was and is a charmer. My mommy and daddy didn't like him very much."

"Why?" Jane asks.

"Because he was a charmer. They called him a snake charmer."

"What's that?" Harper leans in.

"A liar of sorts."

"You were a liar?" Jane asks him.

He shrugs.

"We all lie to get by, sometimes," Mary says. "But you two won't."

"Because it's bad," Harper says.

"Butt kisser," Jane snaps.

Judas nudges Jane, nearly spilling his thimble.

Mary straightens up at this, then relaxes when not a drop falls.

"Your daddy and I used to live on the other side of this land. Really far away. I thought he was cute, but he was shy. He wouldn't talk to me."

Judas says, "You intimidated me," and that seems to work.

"My family did a little better than his. That's also why they didn't like him. But I watched him a lot, and I knew he was sweet."

"And I was sweet on you."

Mary touches her neck, like she's checking for a pulse. "Your daddy saved me from a bad man."

She has Judas' attention.

"The bad man… wanted to hurt me." Mary pauses. "And your daddy saved me. He pushed him off the Tower."

The Tower? Judas pretends to be strong.

"You killed a man, Daddy?" Harper asks.

"I suppose," Judas says, eyes locked on Mary's.

"That day, we promised never to let the other one get hurt." Mary raises the thimble. "A toast to no more hurting. A toast to the happy days in Heaven."

Judas raises his thimble.

Harper and Jane do the same.

"This is a good day," Judas says.

Now, there is something shambling in felled Maidenwood. He doesn't want to cause an alarm. He can't have the girls panicking.

"Good as they can get." Mary draws the thimble to her mouth.

Everyone follows her example.

"A promise is a promise, Jude."

Judas nods, thought to what, he isn't sure.

Mary downs the wine.

Harper and Jane down the wine.

Judas tips his head back, lets the wine run down the side of his face where they can't see it. Human food and drink don't sit well with him on a full stomach.

Harper and Jane act dramatically, coughing and grabbing at their throat. "Ew," they say, and "Gross!"

Mary shushes them. "Thank you for this, Jude."

"Yeah," he says, and then: "I hate to do this, but we should get inside."

"Right here's fine," she says.

"No, I think there's something out there." Judas stands. "We…"

Jane coughs, grabs at her throat.

Harper laughs at her, and seconds later, she's doing the same.

"Hey, hey. Girls, quit it." Judas goes to his knees.

They are rolling on their backs.

"S-stop it."

Jane is spitting up blood.

Harper is clinging to her little sister while her eyes roll back in her skull.

"Oh, god." Judas picks up Harper. She smashes into his body with violent tremors. "Mary. Get Jane. Get her inside!"

Mary doesn't move.

Judas steps off the tarp, turns when he realizes Mary isn't moving, and Jane has stopped altogether.

Harper goes limp in his arms.

Mary starts to tremble.

"Mary?" He's breathing hard. His lungs hurt. His face stings from where the wine stained it.

Mary shuffles forward on her knees, pulls Jane's dead body against her. "It's okay, Jude. It's okay. It's done now."

Judas' mouth drops open. "What did you do?"

"Me?" Foam comes out of her mouth. "We promised each other. On a perfect day, after so much hurt, we wouldn't hurt anymore. We wouldn't let them hurt. It's okay. God understands. We'll see It soon and explain everything!"

Judas drops to his knees. Carefully, he lays Harper out. She's cold and covered in blood and spit. Her eyes are lightless. She stares into the heavens for the God from below.

"The wine..." he whispers.

Mary coughs. She grabs her stomach and buckles over. One hand after the other plants onto the tarp. Sweaty palm prints are left behind.

"You didn't forget, did you?" She leans over Jane's body, coveting it. "We p-promised." She falls. Her face hits the tarp. She groans. Blood oozes out of her mouth.

Judas rises. He backs away. He didn't know. He didn't know. He tried to understand each of them the best he could, but it had never been like this before.

"Where... are you... going?" Each word is a monumental struggle for her to speak. "Don't... let me... go without... you."

This was their moment. This was their moment, and he's taken it from them. Judas keeps going backwards.

Mary looks up, her face covered in blood, one eye shut, the other bloodshot. She hates him, and she will hate him, until she makes it to Heaven and finds him there.

And then she slumps over, and she dies.

Judas gasps. He tears off the mask and takes on his own rigid flesh.

"I'm sorry," he says to the girls. "I'm sorry. I wouldn't have let her if I had known." He grabs his stringy hair, picks at the scars on his scalp. "If I had…"

Buzzing breaks from the last of the fog.

And the figure he heard shambling comes shambling nearer.

Mosquitoes, nowhere and now everywhere, descend upon the dead like he might have and start drinking.

The shambling shape, closer now, is cloaked and hooded, and out of its cloak, wings explode. The shape lifts off the ground and flies towards him.

The ghoul closes his eyes and waits. All the blood he has he's stolen. But it's blood all the same.

9

The six-foot, skin-cloaked mosquito buzzes past the ghoul and lands beside Mary, Harper, and Jane. Its gangly legs seem too skinny to hold its engorged frame, and yet the severe, black limbs do just that. A sloshing sound, like that of liquid in a barrel, emanates from the creature's yellow-splotched belly. A prehensile proboscis uncurls from the dark shadows inside its flesh hood and extends until it's two feet long. Then, laughing, and with clawed hands, the mosquito throws back its hood, revealing the massive, ruby-like eyes that encompass most of its head.

Mr. Haemo, rubbing his stomach, nods at the corpses and says to the ghoul, "You going to finish this?"

The ghoul makes fists.

Mr. Haemo throws a hand into the air with dramatic flair. "Waste not, want not!"

Mosquitoes form overhead like storm clouds. The ghoul wants to tell him to stop, but he has no claim to these corpses, and no right to try and leapfrog his way up the food chain. Ever since he clawed his way out of the ground, the ghoul has been trying to avoid encounters with inhuman things. They want allegiances he can't give, and they remind him of what he can't be.

The bloodsucking swarm forms a funnel not unlike their draining appendages and dives for the woman, for the girls.

The ghoul reaches outwards, as if to stop them, but he does not. He wonders if he could have, and then, as the insects stab thousands of weeping holes into each body, he wonders if he should have. Inside him, he keeps the skins of his sins. There are many, and despite how many lives he eats, he is never full. Just this once, it may be okay to let these three go for good.

He turns away. Mr. Haemo, in his silence, seems satisfied. Those in the area, especially those from the swamps around the Night Terror's village of Traesk, are said to pay blood tributes to the giant mosquito. Let this be his tribute. He can't die just yet. He hasn't figured out what he's living for.

"Where are you off to, sourpuss?" Mr. Haemo calls after him.

The ghoul doesn't turn around. He hears the mosquito lift off the ground with its massive, ragged wings. He's offended it.

"Moving on," he says.

The mosquito draws nearer. Its shadow swallows his. No matter where he goes, which way he turns, he can't be free of it.

"You're going the wrong way," Mr. Haemo says.

The ghoul stops inches from the fallout shelter. Mr. Haemo's two-foot long proboscis sticks into the side of his throat. It doesn't draw blood, and he doesn't draw a breath.

"All the talent is back that-a-way."

Mr. Haemo's words rattle down the proboscis in terrifying vibrations.

The ghoul was a human once; he still has a heart, he still can feel. Aside from his appetite and appearance, and his cannibalism-induced chameleon abilities, he is much the same as he had been that day his killers put him in the ground. He knows Mr. Haemo only by name and reputation. Either one is enough to make him quake, and to make him pray to God to come back and do him this one last favor.

He turns.

Mr. Haemo drops to the ground, steps to the side. His wings ruffle as they slip back into the slits of the skin cloak.

The ghoul knows what the mosquito is getting at, but his eyes stop short of that sight and rest on Mary, Harper, and Jane, instead. On the tarp, pale and covered in red polka-dots, they are at peace. Their eyes are pearls; their lips a slight shade of vermillion. Wine and honey surround them. The ghoul hopes they got to where they were going.

He looks past what might have been his family, into the distance, where a field of tree trunks are host to pink parasitic growths, and farther still; to the Tri-County river and the dismal stretches beyond, where the land is a like watercolor palette: a hard crust of indescribable mixtures, old and new, painted overtop by the fresh red that runs in rivers and rivulets all around it. He can't see it from here, but he knows it's here.

Bedlam.

The ghoul says to Mr. Haemo, "Are you the devil?"

And Mr. Haemo says to him, "Don't I wish."

The blood-drunk swarm of Mr. Haemo's children lift from Mary, Harper, and Jane. Lazily, intoxicatedly, they fly over to their master.

"You have something better to do, ghoul?" he asks.

Ghoul? He has been called many things, but seldom what he actually is. And what is he exactly? His needs and their machinations are primal, instinctual. He doesn't have to know them to know them. Like breathing, eating human flesh is just something that he has to do. Putting on the appearances of those he's consumed is no different than how he used to get dressed before going into the office every morning. It just makes sense.

"Didn't think so," Mr. Haemo says.

The mosquitoes land on Mr. Haemo by the thousands until his shape is lost and theirs becomes his.

Like the presence of Bedlam, the ghoul can't see what the mosquitoes are doing, but by the way Mr. Haemo jerks and moans, he understands it well enough.

They're feeding him. Pumping the blood into his body, one tiny proboscis at a time. Now, when the ghoul hears the sloshing inside the giant mosquito's body, he realizes what's making the sound.

Mr. Haemo's children quickly make their deposit, and then they are gone, as if they were never there.

The giant mosquito puts his hands on his hips and says, "All this blood makes me bloaty. It's going straight to my ass!"

Mr. Haemo laughs. It sounds like two trains colliding.

The ghoul searches his closet for any skin that might, at this moment, save his own.

"I've been in the need for company," Mr. Haemo says, throwing his hood, which is stitched together from tens of human faces, over his head. "Come back to my haunt with me. It's not far from here."

The ghoul steadies his breathing. He glances at Mary, Harper, and Jane one last time and promises them he'll do better next time, with the next family.

"Coming?" Mr. Haemo says, taking the lead.

The ghoul gathers his courage and asks, "Do I have a choice?"

"No," Mr. Haemo chuckles. "Not at all."

Mr. Haemo didn't lie. His haunt wasn't far from the fallout shelter. It was an old, hollowed-out tree that stood alone and apart from the parasite-infested trunks the ghoul had spied earlier. The tree isn't like anything he's seen before. It doesn't belong. It sits against the misted space like a paper cutout pasted into this world from another. Yet when the ghoul moves closer, the innards of the tree recoil, springing deeper into the dark dimensions contained within.

It isn't until the ghoul reaches the exposed roots that he sees light. Hundreds, no thousands, no millions of pinpricks of light that stab through the red, shadowy film inside the tree, at its end. They remind him of the stars, and staring at them, a suffocating weight forms upon his chest. Like the day God woke, and the night that God died.

A shadow passes over the ghoul. In the sky, a massive raven flies, beating its molting feathers in slow, hypnotic movements. The Lord animal's head jerks back and forth with spastic paranoia. It is searching the lands for Night Terrors. They'd just as soon worship it as they would kill it. The raven knows better; the Night Terrors should, but will say they don't. It makes the ghoul sick to his stomach.

Mr. Haemo stands beside the ghoul and says, "Every day there's always something new in this world. If all it took was a good, old fashioned genocide to open the gates, it makes you wonder who was holding who back."

In silence, they watch the raven turn southward, until it is no more than a black speck set against the volcanic mountain range that rises and falls on the rim of the horizon.

The ghoul stares at the mosquito. His heart slows. His pulse becomes a whisper rather than a pleading thud. He stares at the skin on his hands and arms. It is his skin, his true skin; no one else's. He touches it; the texture of it, like burlap, is strangely satisfying. His fingers probe the hole in his stomach. The bullet casing is still in there, lodged between bones. He keeps it as a souvenir, and he keeps it as a reminder that once he'd been human; not always this way.

"Something on your mind?" Mr. Haemo asks.

The ghoul nods. "This is the first time I've been myself around someone and not killed them afterward."

"Lucky me. Feels nice, doesn't it?"

"It does."

"It's a new world we live in." Mr. Haemo climbs into the tree and beckons the ghoul to follow. "The Old World's gone. Go on, set that proverbial torch down. You let it guide you, you're going to get lost."

The ghoul grips the tree's opening. It's rough, scabby; healed once, maybe, but torn open again, like a surgical scar. It isn't wood, either, this tree, and that isn't bark that covers it. He can't place the material, nor its scent, but the feel of it calls to mind the inside of passion fruit: hard seeds, like imprisoned insects, encased in viscous cells. The tree shouldn't be able to stand on its own given what is made of, and yet something keeps it together. Science surmounted by sheer will.

When the ghoul steps inside the tree, he is in another place entirely. The red, shadowy, light-pricked film he'd seen at the back of the tree is now above. Where there should've been bark, there were vistas. Sprawling fields of golden grass splattered with crimson from the bleeding sky. Rolling hills checked by bottomless pits. When he looks closely, he can see that this place is like a honeycomb—its walkways narrow, its pitfalls numerous. And when he looks even closer, he realizes they are not alone here in this alien world. Across the fields, crowning the highest hill, sits the eerie image of a convent against a twelve-moon sky; each one in a different lunar phase.

He's forgotten Mr. Haemo beside him, but the bug can't stay silent for long.

"Have a seat," he says.

The ghoul turns. Between him and the portal he came through is a small, crackling fire surrounded by large, smoothed boulders—primitive chairs.

Mr. Haemo takes a seat by the fire. He throws the skin cloak over his sick, insect body. The flesh it's made of is much thicker than the ghoul realized. It runs four inches deep, and the stitching between the discolored patches varies from new to old. The mosquito has had this cloak for a very long time, and it hasn't stopped adding to it ever since.

For two years, the ghoul has been so careful, so cautious. He wonders how he got here, if he would've got here, regardless. Staring through the portal that lets out into his world, a part of him sinks, like an eroded cliff finally falling into the sea. Ever since he woke, he's been carrying on as if this New World were the Old, moving from family to family, from flesh to flesh in search of purpose and peace. He accepted and adapted but he never appreciated this cruel, phantasmagorical way of things. If he had, his own skin cloak wouldn't be so thick, like Mr.

Haemo's. If he had, Mary, Jane, and Harper... Elizabeth and Mitch-ell... Cary... Sarah and Dillion... Jasmine... Erin... Bailey and Ayleanna... Setsuko... Luciana and Paulo... Katie... Christina... Mark; Ava, Zoey, and Faye—they might still be alive.

The ghoul sits opposite Mr. Haemo. The boulders are more com-fortable than he would've thought, but sitting on them, this close to the fire, he is shivering. He crosses his arms, moves closer to the flames, but it does him no good. The fire is freezing. The only heat that comes from it is the itching heat he feels spreading across his body like lichen; that warm omen of frostbite to come.

But Mr. Haemo does not move.

And neither does the ghoul.

The engorged bloodsucker wiggles his feet like he couldn't be more comfortable here. Smaller mosquitoes phase in and out around his head. Thousands of different lights play out across Mr. Haemo's eyes, as if he's looking at a thousand different scenes all at once.

The ghoul glances back at the portal and finally says, "Where are we?"

Mr. Haemo jerks awake, as if he'd dozed off. His proboscis grows like an erection. His gaze lingers on the ghoul, like he's forgotten he was here and now only sees prey.

"Where is this?" The ghoul starts to stand. "Where—"

"Exuvia," Mr. Haemo says. His eyes go black, and when they open, they shine with only the light of the blood-red sky above. "What do you think?"

The ghoul shakes his head. "What is that? French?"

"Latin, you mongo."

"Is this where you're from?"

Mr. Haemo nods.

The ghoul moves closer to the cold fire and says, "Why'd you bring me here?"

"Boredom," Mr. Haemo says.

But the ghoul suspects it may be closer to loneliness.

"I'm a blood keeper. Every drop is a record. Lives aren't long these days, but you've fared well enough, especially for a ghoul. Your kind is almost extinct."

"You've been watching me?"

The mosquito's compound eyes flash a multitude of lights and col-ors. "I watch a lot of things, guy."

"I, uh, thought only female mosquitoes sucked blood," the ghoul says.

"That's right," Mr. Haemo says. "But looking at me, is my gender really the worst of your concerns right now?"

"No."

"Smart ass." Mr. Haemo leans back and laughs. His laugh is like razor blades sawing teeth. "Why are you still alive? For me, there's always blood to keep, but just what are you doing?"

"I'm sorry, Bug, but we just met. You really expect me to bare my soul to you?"

"I always get to first base on the first date." Mr. Haemo makes a fist; blood leaks out of it. "That's good you have a personality. Here I was, worried you were a drip. But answer my question."

Black smudges, like eraser marks, begin to form around Mr. Haemo. They are not his children, but something else. Appendages, almost, reaching in from another plane.

Another piece of the ghoul sinks inside him. The black smudges boil on the air, like tar. He feels words being teased from his mind, dragged up his throat and across his tongue—hooked on a line that runs from his mouth to the reeling unreality bubbling around the bug.

"I d-don't know," he stammers. "Just g-getting by."

Mr. Haemo shrugs. The black smudges vanish.

The ghoul gasps and falls back against the boulder. His brain itches from where the words were wrenched from it. Despite having eaten last night, he is ravenous. He sees the blood in the mosquito's hand and wants to take it off at the wrist.

"As long as a ghoul hibernates, it can live almost forever," Mr. Haemo says. "You planning on getting by forever?"

The ghoul stifles his hunger. "I thought it was eating people that did that."

"Poor thing. You don't even know what you are."

"When I sleep, I forget things."

"That's the price of a long life. You keep the flesh of those you eat, but you forget why they're there." Mr. Haemo snorts. "Everything has a price."

"What did you just do to me?"

"I demonstrated my power. You got uppity. I had to put you down."

"You're toying with me."

"Duh," Mr. Haemo says. He leans forward on his knees. "And I have a soft spot for rare things. They have the best blood. I'd like to see you succeed."

"At what? Being a family man?" The ghoul shakes his head. "Is that what you want to be?"

"It's what I was."

From the distant convent, a bell tolls. The sound pulsates across Exuvia. The golden grass parts, flattens; and parts of the honeycombed fields fall away into the red cavities below.

The ghoul sharpens his senses; he smells flesh from the convent, oiled and incensed. He asks, "What is this? Really?"

"A moment in time," Mr. Haemo says, cryptically. "Pay the nuns no never mind. They're going to be doing the same thing for eternity."

"Is this where you're really from?"

Mr. Haemo nods. Blood sloshes inside his belly. "Are you the first to come here, ghoul? No, I've had many."

Survival instincts kick in. The ghoul slips into his skin closet and begins looking for a life to hide behind.

"Something is happening in Bedlam tomorrow. The fighting there is going to end."

"A lot of talent," the ghoul whispers, about ready to put on his Judas suit.

"Exactly. A lot of corpses. A lot of blood. A little for me, a little for you. That's a lot of disguises. Hey, ghoul, does the blood speak to you when you drink it? Does the flesh make promises to you when you eat it?"

The ghoul shakes his head. "It tells me nothing."

"Do you want it to? No more guessing. No more slipping into lives. You can possess them."

Did he want it? The ghoul considers the mosquito's offer. In truth, he wants nothing more than the life he had, before the bullet in his belly and the three corpses in the hall. He asks himself what he's been searching for this entire time, but he can't say. He had slept for so long that some memories were lost to him, and others refused to form. He searches inside himself all the lives on all their hangers and sees no patterns in their fabrics. He's told himself time and time again he was a family man, but in the end, was he nothing more than a hungry man? The need to eat had always taken precedence over the need to live. He lived out of guilt.

"Alright," the ghoul says. "Okay. I'll go with you."

Mr. Haemo says, "Good," and throws the skin cloak's hood over his head. His wings push out of his back with a pained struggle and flutter until he's flying. "Get out."

The ghoul doesn't question him. He quickly stands and heads towards the portal. Reaching it, his world just out of reach, he stops and stares at the bug over his shoulder.

"What happens to you when there's no more blood left?"

Annoyed, Mr. Haemo says, "The same thing that happens to you."

"Are you too weak to feed on your own?"

Mr. Haemo strokes his proboscis in silence.

The ghoul nods, satisfied, and slips through the portal.

On the other side, back in the wasteland of Bitter Springs, he hurries to the corpses of Mary, Jane, and Harper and drags the tarp they're laying on back to the fallout shelter.

He spends the rest of the night crying as he eats them.

8

The ghoul wakes in the dead of night and decides to run. If he stays, he knows what he'll become: a blood slave. The stories around the human settlements are too consistent to be anything but true. If Mr. Haemo doesn't kill you, he'll conscript you to do his bidding. Those he chooses are injected with infected blood and made puppets to carry out a series of ritual murders. When the task is completed, which can take from days to years, the slave is abandoned. Even so, they still continue to kill for their master, because the tainted transfusions leave them irreversibly insane.

The ghoul has done well enough so far on his own. If he's going to kill, it's going to be on his own terms.

There isn't much left of Mary, and Harper and Jane are bones. He'd binged like a bear winding down for a long hibernation. As a result, he is sluggish, both in movement and in thought, and wired. He stumbles around the fallout shelter in the dark. He breaks things, steps on their shards. The pain will come later, when this sugar-high-like-shield comes down.

He takes nothing. He needs nothing. His memories are in his mind, and the girls in his heart with many others. He leaves no footprints so he can't be followed. It keeps him safe, even if he keeps going in circles.

The ghoul climbs the ladder, gets to the top, and stops. His stomach sloshes like Mr. Haemo's had. Stomach acid and clumps of partially digested human push up his throat. He stifles the urge to vomit and swallows the meat. He overdid it. He didn't even have to.

Carefully, the ghoul unlocks the door at the top of the ladder and pushes it open. If there was one good thing to come out of God's wrath, it was that it made the nights dark like they were supposed to be. There was no saw-toothed skyline to flood the night with its millions of beaming, blinking, begging lights. There were no clogged highways awash in pools of red and amber. Gone were the billboards. Gone were the televisions filling up living rooms and bedrooms with commercial-stuffed filler. Gone were the pale faces in the shadows, their eyes illuminated, their minds inundated by the phones in their hands— too focused on the distilled world to pay the one around them much mind.

The forty-year-old man the ghoul had once been would've appreciated the technological scourging. He climbs out of the shelter, shaking his head at himself. If only his wife could see him now, she'd say he'd gotten everything he ever—

The dark is dark, and then it's not. Fire sweeps across the north, arcing over the crest of the ridges there. One swell after another, it grows, until the fires lift into the sky in spasming orbs.

There are vibrations, too, in the ground. He bends down and puts his hand to the cold soil to feel them. They thud in his fingertips, and chase one another around the bones in his feet. The vibrations are slow, the deep decibels of a funeral dirge. He knows them well.

The ghoul stands. Beneath the raging orbs, there are figures. It's torches they are holding, but they stand so close to one another, the fires are feeding off one another, creating an unbroken stream of flames. They are marching eastward, following the rumbling, wheeled contraptions that the ghoul can only catch in shadowy glimpses.

He listens for prayers on the air, thinking they may be Lillians, but instead hears:

"Woke me up, too."

The ghoul goes sideways.

Mr. Haemo is standing beside him, his skin cloak pulled tightly around his severe, and yet swollen frame.

"The early bug gets the blood, that's what my mother used to say."

The ghoul curses himself for not having left sooner.

"That's a lie." Mr. Haemo clicks his claws together. "I don't have any parents. Crawled out of the same womb all of this did."

"What's…" The ghoul steadies his breathing. "What are they doing?"

Mr. Haemo points to the torchlight-drenched multitudes. "Those sorry bastards are Vold's most and least wanted. The sons of Vold's fat cats convinced their fathers to let them mine the Nameless Forest. The entitled shits haven't worked a day in their lives, so naturally, they're going to get the poor to do it for them."

"There're so many," the ghoul whispers, the river of flame never drying up, as more and more cross the ridge.

"Thousands," Mr. Haemo says. "A good chunk of Vold's population. We're not that far into the Trauma and the rich are already back to trying to kill the poor."

"The Trauma…" The ghoul had forgotten the Corrupted… the humans… were calling this time period that.

Mr. Haemo shrugs. "Your kind kills me. You name your wake-up call the Trauma. Boo-fucking-hoo."

"Some people still believe in God," the ghoul says, childishly.

"Have you ever seen a longer lasting abusive relationship?"

The ghoul doesn't say anything.

"Trauma, my ass." Mr. Haemo's wings lift him into the air. "They love it. What good is a God you can see, touch, hear, and smell? You can't find salvation if it's staring you down every day of your life. You'll have to actually take responsibility for once."

The ghoul, somewhat offended, asks, "Why do you care?"

"I'm tired of waiting."

"For what?"

"Exuvia."

"Isn't that…" The ghoul wonders how far he can run before the mosquito catches up. "Isn't that in your tree, though?"

"Everywhere can be Exuvia," Mr. Haemo says, dreamily.

"It's Latin? What does it mean?"

"Things stripped from a body."

The ghoul doesn't ask any more questions. It's dangerous to ask questions about dangerous subjects. Mr. Haemo's intentions are clear to him, however muddled by madness they might be. If the ghoul becomes too enlightened, he'll become indentured.

The damned march on into the morning hours. When the last of them disappear into the ridges, the clouds begin to glow, like a piece of skin through which a strong light is shone. The ghoul doesn't know why the mosquito made him watch the whole procession, but when Mr. Haemo tells him it's time to go, he does as he's told.

Bedlam is fifty miles away.

"I can get us there in five," Mr. Haemo says.

The ghoul follows him back to his tree. The portal inside it is sealed, but amongst the roots is a boiling pool of smoking blood. The hot, sludge-like cruor creates crusts on the crimson surface in the shapes of fingers and hands and screaming faces. It is a surface in its purest, most elemental form.

"Hop on in," Mr. Haemo says.

The ghoul stops at the edge of the pool. The blood reaches for him, but its forms cannot hold, and they stop short of touching him. This has gone on for far too long. Though he's a ghoul, he's still himself, whatever that might've been, whenever that might've been, a century or so ago. He has to be something. Like the blood begging before him, he cannot be hollowed. He must be hallowed, like the flesh he keeps. He is ugly and repulsive and a cannibal, but he is not a monster like the monster beside him.

Defiant, the ghoul steps back and shouts, "No!"

Mr. Haemo rolls his thousands of eyes. "Tough titties," he says.

And then he shoves the ghoul into the blood well.

End over end, the ghoul plummets through the blood. When he thinks it can go no deeper, it goes deeper still. From a puddle to a lake to an ocean, the blood expands at an exponential rate. He squeezes his eyes shut, but the blood peels his lids back. It worms its way into his irises and pupils and stains his ocular nerves. The blood seeps into his veins and arteries, replacing his own, and invades his heart. It fills its chambers like a cuckoo bird would another's nest and forces it to foster the filth in its throbbing chambers.

The ghoul cannot breathe. The ghoul cannot think. He cannot hear or move. He can only see. Surrounded by blood, his vision is blood, and by blood, he sees.

It comes to him in a blur, but it is there, at the bottom of this darkening Abyss: stars, and the massive moth drawn towards them, and farther still, beyond the grey place in the corner of his eye, Exuvia.

It's there, and then it isn't. A claw sinks into the ghoul's shoulder and jerks him out of the blood. He flies out of the blood well and slams into a pile of concrete and bricks. His thick skin bears the bashing well enough, but from where the claw had punctured him, he bleeds.

Kneading his shoulder, the ghoul, with not a drop of blood on him, rises shakily to his feet. He blinks his eyes until they are able to adjust to light.

Mr. Haemo's here, but that's no surprise. What surprises is where he's brought them.

Bedlam. The heart of Bedlam. He knows it's Bedlam because they are standing in the remains of a gymnasium. The ceiling is gone, most of the walls have collapsed, and the bleachers have been scattered and smashed, but on the tiled, maple floor, surrounded by murals of blood and shit and blackened bones, is that telltale logo of the town's local basketball team: a man in a straightjacket, his tongue out, his eyes bloodshot—the Bedlam Madmen.

Except madmen had been crossed out and replaced with "madpeople" with black paint.

And all around the logo, painted, drawn, carved, and sprayed, were the words "Don't Assume My God."

He remembers them well. Before he died, they were written everywhere, in every color and every font. At the time, Lillian had taken to the television and declared with utmost certainty and irrefutable proof the existence of the one true God.

At the same time, Lux had taken to the streets, a born-again liberal, and on the backs of her devoted followers, was thrust into the limelight, where with nothing but short-term sweet nothings, she gave the Internet a slow, repetitive, ultimately empty drip of dopamine in the form of balled fists, nasty letters, poorly edited videos, and the promises of a better god, a universal but personal god.

Don't Assume My God. The ghoul stares at the slogan, which had been on so many bumper stickers, right next to the ones celebrating pastafarianism, and his heart starts to ache. Don't Assume My God. His daughters had written the words on the front of their three-ring binders. They hadn't even known what it meant, but goddamn if it hadn't been 'in.'

Mr. Haemo whispers, "You remember Lux?"

The ghoul looks up at the mosquito, then at the bubbling blood well behind him. It's closing up with awkward, jerking movements, like a stop-motion video. There's no getting away from the bug now. He's going to have to see this through. He wonders: did a part of him want to, regardless? If the flesh he kept could keep its history and share it with him, would that be worth whatever atrocity Mr. Haemo is going to ask him to do? Would it stop the eating? Slow it down, if nothing else? Did he really eat out of hunger, or embarrassment?

Mr. Haemo tucks in his wings, closes his skin cloak tight like a shivering grandmother, and goes forth into Bedlam. The ghoul goes after him.

The gymnasium lets out to the pulverized suburbs of what once was Bedlam's largest suburb, Six Pillars. It hadn't always been that way, with Six Pillars barely registering on the county map; but after Lillian emerged from her home there, the suburb was expanded and consumed all neighboring ones.

The gymnasium was supposed to be connected to an expensive, privately funded Lillian school built shortly after God's arrival, but all that was left of it was a crater and some piping.

Six Pillars wasn't much better. There had been hundreds of identical houses here once; now, there was only dirt and debris and the dead vermillion veins wrapped around them. It looked like a garden you might find behind a dilapidated house: dry, rigid, and blackened; covered in weeds and fungus; abandoned by the thing that'd created it; cursed by the thing that'd demanded it.

It was a battlefield without bodies; a warzone without a war. The destruction stretched on for as far as the ghoul could see in the fog, but where were the Lillians? Where were the Bedlamites who were supposed to be fighting them for the right to live on this land?

The ghoul turns to ask Mr. Haemo what is going on, and then his answer comes to him, not from the mosquito, but from the west.

Prayers. Slow, melancholic prayers from phantoms in the fog. They come to him one utterance at a time, each speaker's contribution weak and wanting, like a begging child. When the words wash over him, they reform behind him in a unified drone. It was as if the prayers and those praying them were, for a moment, speaking directly to him.

"Serial killers often return to the crime scene," Mr. Haemo whispers. He nudges the ghoul. "Follow me."

They cross Six Pillars without making an effort to hide. Mr. Haemo knows there's nothing here, and if they do find something, who's going to challenge him? The ghoul feels a kind of sickening safety as he trails the mosquito's shadow. It's exciting; he hates it.

Reaching the wall of fog out of which the prayers pour, Mr. Haemo puts a single finger to his proboscis, and then pushes forward.

The ghoul plants his feet. He watches the fog swallow the giant bug without spitting it back out. He could run. Now is the time to do it. They are out in the open, and clearly whatever Mr. Haemo has come to see, he has no intention of letting it see him. The distraction might be enough for the ghoul to get away.

He starts to turn, but stops himself. Where will he go? Who will he go to? Who will he go as? He can't be himself, looking like the corpse he is, in a world where monsters are being hunted down and slaughtered to secure a place in line at the front of heaven's barred gates. He is the river he's walked so many times along. But is he worth the erosion he brings to those around him?

Mr. Haemo clicks for to him follow.

And, like a lapdog, he follows.

They wander through the fog for minutes, the ground becoming less uneven, the debris becoming more recognizable. Then there are patches of grass, and the foundations of houses. Every thirty seconds or so, Bedlam's Six Pillars is put back together before him, until the fog finally parts and they find themselves standing at the end of a road, where ahead, four houses are completely intact in an otherwise obliterated field.

Between each of the houses runs a network of dead, dried out vermillion veins, but looking closely, the ghoul sees that all the veins seem to have the same origin—one of the four houses, and the same house the prayers are coming from.

Mr. Haemo shoulders the ghoul to the side of the road where one house stands alone from the three opposite it.

"Inside," he whispers.

He and the ghoul go around the vein-choked driveway, up the porch, and through the front of the house, where the door has long since been torn from its hinges.

He tries to get a good sense of the inside of the house, but before he can, Mr. Haemo spins him around and pushes him towards the window in the living room.

"The house in the middle of the three," Mr. Haemo says, nodding to it, his proboscis plinking against the busted glass.

The ghoul's attention drifts to the mantle, where graffiti reads: "Never Forget Filipa."

Near it, there are two holes in the ceiling. Nubs of rope dangle from them.

Mr. Haemo stabs his finger into the ghoul's stomach, right through the bullet hole that killed him so long ago.

The ghoul gasps. The cold pain squeezes his gut, and he retches.

Mr. Haemo rips his finger out with a sucking sound. "Pay attention," he says. "The house in the middle."

The ghoul tells himself he should have run. He closes his eyes, puts on his Judas suit out of reflex, and wears it for a while. Coming to, he takes it off and says, "Yeah. What about it?"

"The 'Holy War' here has been over for weeks," Mr. Haemo says. "The Lillians killed every Bedlamite here."

"I thought..."

"News doesn't travel as fast when you can't put hashtags in front of it," Mr. Haemo says, snidely.

The ghoul presses his forehead to the glass. "Aren't we here for the bodies?"

"No, I'm here for the holy rollers in that house. You're here for what comes afterward." Mr. Haemo purrs; blood dribbles down his lips. "I've seen a lot of shit in my time, but this is exciting."

"What's about to—"

Mr. Haemo shushes him. "Don't get fussy on me ghoul, or I'll tuck you in for the long, dirt nap."

Movement in the middle house. Men and women in hooded white robes with rope sashes emerge from it, one at a time, and file down the steps to the front yard. There, the six spread out, forming a circle. In each of their hands, they hold a silver goblet.

Several agonizing seconds of silence pass. The ghoul expects a surprise attack at any moment. He turns to Mr. Haemo, thinking he may strike, but the mosquito only palms the ghoul's face and turns his head, like a parent would a child's, back to face the scene.

Out of the middle house, a seventh person appears. She is swaddled not in white, but red. From her neck to her toes, she is covered in a writhing dress of tightly packed and fitted vermillion veins. The woman is ancient, an unearthed relic too dusty and worn for even the most skilled archaeologist's brush. She has no hair, and no eyebrows, and her mouth sinks in because it has no teeth in it. Seeing this, and then seeing how she moves so effortlessly, so gracefully, down to the front yard, the ghoul realizes this: the vermillion veins aren't a dress, but her actual body.

The seventh woman breaks the circle and places herself at the center. Her face and her eyes are vacant. She is lost in a twilight beyond Dementia, beyond Alzheimer's, but her body, or rather, God's body, is oriented and aware, and filled with dark intentions. She holds her arms out to the side. Vermillion veins snake down her fingertips and stab into the earth.

And then the earth begins to rumble.

"Girl's got game," Mr. Haemo whispers, snickering.

The ghoul presses his hand against the wall. The whole house is shaking. "Who is that?"

"Lillian."

The ghoul swallows hard and chokes on the air. "L-Lillian? The Lillian?"

A body flings across the window with a vermillion vein, like a fishing line, attached to it. The vein slams the dead body into the ground outside the circle of seven. Nobody notices, or seems to care.

Lillian flexes her arms.

A second body, followed by a third, followed by a fourth, drops outside the circle from the vermillion veins lifting out of the ground.

"She's out in the open," the ghoul says. "Someone's going to attack her."

Mr. Haemo shakes head. "I think they already tried. Obviously."

Lillian opens her toothless mouth and mumbles.

A great tremor rocks Six Pillars and then stops as soon as it started. Long shadows slither over the circle. Light gives way to darkness.

Hearing a loud crash on this house's roof, the ghoul jumps. There is a tumbling, and the scratchy sound of shingles sliding over one another.

A body falls in front of the window. And then another. And then another.

The ghoul presses his face to the glass and looks to the sky.

Except there is no sky.

There are only veins. Vermillion veins knitted together for as far as he can see. And hanging from their weeping ends are bodies. Hundreds of bodies.

All at once, the bodies fall from their bloodied boughs and break around the circle. Never stacking, the corpses carpet the neighborhood with a grotesque geometry. The bodies do not explode when they hit the ground. They keep, as if petrified, as if preserved. As if something had been saving them for this moment.

Once the last body hits the ground, the vermillion shield retreats back into the earth, like a forest growing in reverse. The shadows disappear, and the light returns, and Lillian is smiling.

The ghoul says, "What is she—"

But doesn't finish his sentence.

The circle closes around Lillian, their chalices outstretched. She raises her arms. Two of her followers take out daggers. She nods to them. They jam the daggers into her armpits and rip them out. Thick streams of blood pour down her body.

"The Blood of Before!" Lillian shouts at the top of her feeble lungs.

The followers crowd around Lillian, filling their goblets with her blood. She bleeds more blood than she could possibly have, for on her hands, she has the blood of billions.

Once the last cup glows crimson at its brim, the followers back away. They raise their chalices to Lillian.

Lillian reaches into her chest, pushing her arm through the vermillion veins of which it is comprised. She pulls out a piece of jewelry, a silver, white-gemmed necklace, and dangles it before her followers.

"The Agony of After has been too great," she shouts. "May our prayers be enough. May our souls be the soil the Worm finds favorable."

Lillian puts the necklace around her neck.

Her followers guzzle their chalices, spilling blood down the front of their white robes.

Lillian takes the necklace's gem in her hand and kisses it. She screams, "I offer myself to thee!"

The followers go stiff. The chalices drop from their hands and bounce along the ground, drained.

Lillian releases the necklace as it begins to glow. She tips her head back, and the vermillion veins that are her body crawl up her neck and cover her skull.

A flash of white light bursts across Six Pillars. The ghoul covers his eyes, but Mr. Haemo's thousands drink it in.

The ghoul stumbles to the window, rubbing vision back into his eyes.

The followers are shaking. Their mouths open wide and split at the corners, giving them a horrifying grin. Their heads tip back, their jaws unhinge. Jellyfish-like chandeliers of white light heave their way out of the followers' mouths and stretch upwards to the sky, like seaweed.

From the hundreds of bodies scattered across the neighborhood, the same glowing growths sprout from the dead, until Six Pillars is covered in them.

Terrified, amazed, the ghoul stares in wonder at the malignant blades of light swaying before him. At this moment, he feels such a strong want for God's love that he cannot help but weep.

Sensing this, Mr. Haemo puts his arm around the ghoul and, patting him, says, "There, there. There, there."

"It's beautiful," the ghoul says, touching the glass; wanting nothing more than to be enveloped in the light.

"Beautiful only on the outside," Mr. Haemo says.

Another tremor shakes Six Pillars. The chandeliers of light bend forwards, towards the center where Lillian still stands. The tips of the white stalks seem to be pointing towards the silver necklace, as if drawn to its pulsating light.

The jellyfish-like chandeliers rip free of the corpses and the followers. On an otherworldly current, they slash violently through the neighborhood towards Lillian. Once they reach her, they shrink and tighten. Each chandelier wraps around the other, forming an intricate weave over Lillian that almost looks like fabric.

When the final strand of light wraps itself around Lillian, she looks like nothing more than a mummy. But then the light from the necklace, which is underneath hundreds of layers of this ethereal, organic material, breaks across the fabric.

Where it goes, features follow. Arms and legs are given definition and flesh tones; feet and hands are next, and then fingers and toes, flexing. A torso is shaped, and breasts are chiseled into it. A long, slender neck is formed like a funnel.

But where there should be a head, there is nothing. The light cannot form it. Instead, the wraps of light tear from their places on Lillian's body and rush to that stump. The worming appendages take on millions of shapes as they build a brain and bones, fat and flesh, until what remains is the head and face of a young, somewhat sad woman.

The remaining wraps, which the ghoul now identifies as white worms, pour off her neck and face like rain, and cover her naked body in white pants and a white tunic.

She stares at the dead around her, sighs, and sets off into the world.

The ghoul and Mr. Haemo watch the White Worm for as long as

they can.

And when they no longer can, the ghoul says, "What the fuck just happened?"

"Something special," Mr. Haemo says.

"Are you going to kill her?"

"No. She's going to make this land so rich with blood, I'm going to need a dentist when she's through."

The ghoul hesitates: "She's going to take over the Lillians."

"Yep."

"I could kill her and impersonate her."

"I don't think so. I don't think your stomach would find her kind all that agreeable. Besides, I brought you here to kill something else."

The ghoul furrows his brow. "Who?"

"Them."

Mr. Haemo points out the window, to the five Night Terrors working their way through the neighborhood to the summoning spot.

"She killed her enemies."

Mr. Haemo curls his proboscis inwards. "You think all those dead people are her enemies? Those are martyrs, baby."

"Why didn't they attack her?"

"They're Night Terrors," Mr. Haemo says. "When you're the one running the scales, you get to say what's balanced or not."

"You want their blood."

"Can't get it myself," Mr. Haemo says with anger. "Something wrong with it. I do want their blood, but I want something else's blood even more. You're going to help me get it."

The ghoul's stomach turned. "Who's blood?"

"A homunculi's."

7

The Night Terrors move like the beasts they embody. The Boar hurries along Lillian's house in short bursts, constantly scanning his surroundings for prey and predators. The Monkey leaps over the porch's railing, holding his spear limply, and slips inside the house. The Lion goes wide, forming a perimeter around the corpses before he settles in the grass, knives at the ready. The Vulture coasts the scene sluggishly, picking at the bodies with her sword, and then perches herself atop a severed telephone pole.

But it's the last Night Terror to arrive that truly moves the ghoul from fearful fascination to abject horror. The Ram, with her bleached skull and massive, twisted horns, sprints towards the ghoul and Mr. Haemo's hiding place with vacant determination. Her furs, bleached black with years of dried blood, cling to her body as if they'd grown into it. She wields a single halberd under whose blade four children's skulls have been fixed. There are still bits of muscle and flesh on their bones.

The ghoul stumbles away from the window. Tripping over his legs, he slams into the ground, busting his knee.

Mr. Haemo mumbles, "Shit," and backpedals. He steps over the ghoul, grabs his arm, and drags him out of the living room, down the hall, and into the kitchen.

The front door is kicked open. The Ram's feet are like hooves against the hardwood floor. There is a musicality to their demonic claps.

The ghoul, bracing himself against Mr. Haemo, stands in the kitchen. His breaths are heavy, so he stops breathing altogether. His hands are shaking, so he makes them fists and presses them to his mouth. He raids the closet in his mind and puts on every suit he sees, rapidly changing between the men, women, and children he's eaten over the years.

More sound from the front of the house. The Ram starts for the living room, stops. The ghoul hears her hit the halberd hard into the ground. The tiny skulls on it clatter like a baby's rattle.

Mr. Haemo nudges the ghoul. He points to the door that lets out to the backyard. Ducking down, the seven foot mosquito makes for the exit when—

The Ram hoofs it through living room, down the hall, and comes to a dead stop in the kitchen, inches away from the ghoul.

He sinks his teeth into the tops of his fists. His eyes meet the Ram's. Hers are massive inside the skull, and tattooed around her already dark irises are the halves of black rectangles.

Mr. Haemo straightens up like a thief caught in the act and steps behind the ghoul. "Well," he says, "it's now or never."

Mr. Haemo shoves the ghoul at the Ram.

Shocked, the Ram slams the halberd, handle first, into the ghoul.

But the ghoul keeps going. It takes the blow, takes the handle in both hands, and kicks both legs forward, sinking his feet into the Ram's stomach. She gasps, lets go of the halberd, and flies backwards.

The ghoul hits the ground, hip first. A sharp, solid pain, like a block of ice, runs through his body. He tips his head back, cries at Mr. Haemo, "Help, goddamn it!"

But Mr. Haemo only nods forward.

The Ram, wheezing, rises to her feet. She runs headfirst, horns out.

The ghoul gets to his knees. She barrels into him, driving the horns through both shoulders. They slide, her on top of him, back into the kitchen, bashing against the rusted oven.

"Fuck!" the ghoul screams.

Mr. Haemo, now sitting at the table, drooling blood into a dirty coffee mug, says, "Quiet, you're going to wake the neighborhood."

The Ram rears back, ripping the horns out of the ghoul's shoulders. Chunks of his terse flesh fling through the air and smack against the walls. She punches him in the face, each hit sending his head into the oven.

The ghoul's vision blurs. The kitchen fades. His face feels like clay in this unmaker's hands. He grabs her wrists, but she swats him away, and keeps pummeling. He'll be dead soon, he knows, and so he goes to his mind to find a suit befitting his funeral.

No pressure. No pain. A cool wind kisses his cheeks, dousing the bloody fires raging across them. He opens one eye; the other is swollen shut.

The Ram is staring at him. Her eyes, once so alien with their horizontal slits, are wet and worried. Blood and skin slip off her fingers as her fists unravel

The ghoul glances at his flesh. He's become someone else. Mind like mush, he can't remember who he has chosen. Is the Night Terror surprised by his ability? Or does she recognize him? A ghoul's body is a graveyard. What spirit has he unearthed, and what does it say to her now?

The ghoul hears voices outside the house. Her companions have come to investigate.

The Ram's eyes tighten. The spell is broken.

But before she can act, the ghoul lunges forward, knocking the skull from her head. A face underneath, just as human as any so-called Corrupted's greets him. He pins her to the ground. He clamps his jaws around her throat and rips out a dripping strip of skin and muscle and quickly gulps it down.

The Ram tries to apply pressure to the wound, but her hands can't get around his face, which is now buried deep in her esophagus. He chews on her cartilage like jerky, and tongues her larynx. With his fingers, he widens the wound and then goes to work on the bones, prying them open like stubborn oysters.

The backdoor slams open. The ghoul, with a mouthful of Night Terror, whips around and finds the Monkey standing there, gasping.

The front door cracks back. The Boar and the Lion stumble into the hall outside the kitchen, while the Vulture drifts back towards the second hallway on the kitchen's opposite end.

Mr. Haemo takes one last, loud, obnoxious sip from the coffee cup and shifts in his seat, seeing each Night Terror that surrounds them.

The ghoul slurps up the Ram's blood. Hunger and hate subside to the gnawing reminder of his own mortality.

Seeing the panicked look on his face, Mr. Haemo waves his hand. "Finish eating, ghoul," he says, coming to his feet. "There are starving kids in Africa who would love to have a meal like that."

The Monkey jabs his spear forward.

Mr. Haemo flings the coffee cup at his mask. It shatters on the skull. The Monkey recoils, the shards protruding from his eyes.

The Lion and the Boar bear down on the ghoul. Reaching the end of the hallway, ready to impale him where he lies feasting upon their friend, Mr. Haemo conjures a cloud of mosquitoes and floods their masks with the winged demons.

They scream, go sideways. They paw at the wall, but their hands slip on the ghoul's shoulder meat pasted there.

The Vulture hurries down the opposite hall, sword at her side, her forearms bulging. She runs into the kitchen, slashes diagonally. Mr. Haemo turns sideways, swings around, one wing out. The wing cuts through the skull as if it were paper, severing the beak… and the Night Terror's jaw.

The Vulture drops her sword. Her tongue lolls over the gushing cavity. Screaming, she turns to run, but Mr. Haemo is faster. He grabs her by the tongue, rips it out of her mouth, and smashes what's left of her head against the side of the table, killing her instantly.

The ghoul scoots away from the Lion and the Boar. Mr. Haemo shakes his head, tells him to stay, and steps over him. He grabs the two Night Terrors swarmed by his children and hurls them down the hall, one after the other.

The Boar bashes against the wall, while the Lion goes headfirst into a linen closet.

Mr. Haemo snaps his fingers and the mosquitoes disappear. He crouches down beside the disorientated Boar, dusts off his chest piece.

"Please," the Boar says.

Mr. Haemo tips back his head and laughs. "A flesh fiend begging for mercy? If you ask me—" he lowers his head and faces the Boar, "—evolution did you no favors." And stabs his proboscis through the Night Terror's chest, straight into his heart.

Mr. Haemo takes a long sip of the Boar's blood, and then retches. "Trash," he says, vomiting. "Trash blood."

Out of the linen closet, the Lion stumbles.

Mr. Haemo, still crouched, still vomiting, raises his claw at the Lion and makes a fist.

The Lion screams a scream unlike any the ghoul has ever heard before. A scream of such immense, unfathomable pain that it makes him cry and cover his ears.

The Lion flies forward, as if pulled by some invisible force. Halfway to Mr. Haemo, the Night Terror's vein and arterial systems rip through his flesh, complete and still functioning. The Lion stops, collapses to the ground.

The veins and arteries fold into a ball and glide into Mr. Haemo's hand. He crushes them and then comes to his feet. With the remnants in his palms, he dips his other fingers into the blood and begins to paint the walls.

"If you had any doubts that this was going to end well for you," Mr. Haemo says, creating in blood the crude image of a mosquito, "well, sorry, I'm not sorry."

He stops, smears what's left of the Lion's veins and arteries all over the Boar's face.

"That doesn't mean I'm going to kill you, though," Mr. Haemo says, cheerfully.

The ghoul stares down at the Ram. There's still so much to go. He sinks his fingers into the wet folds of her neck and starts to undress her, flesh first.

"Get the homunculus' blood, and I'll teach you to hear the blood, make pacts with the flesh."

The ghoul stares at him. "If I possess a life, I'll still be what I am."

"Will you?" Mr. Haemo cleans off his proboscis. "Is that what you want?"

The ghoul thinks back to the suits in his mind and says, "Apparently not."

"Didn't think so."

"What's a homunculus?"

Mr. Haemo shakes his head, picks up the ram skull, and says, "Don't talk with your mouth full. Make sure you clean your plate. We need to be in Brooksville by nightfall. I've got a date with a Maggot."

6

On a stomach filled with one drifter, one wife, two daughters, and a Night Terror, the ghoul is grateful for Mr. Haemo's silence. In his gluttony, he's become much like the mosquito. Covered in blood and swollen, his stomach sloshes when he walks. He moves like a drunkard, and drips with the sweat of his sins. Yet, he is confident in a way he hasn't been since his awakening. In a comfort food coma, he drifts, untouchable. He has never killed a thing unless it was necessary, and now that he's seen that he can, he feels like the father he was, and the father he should have been: The quiet protector his children could look up to, and whose wife couldn't take her eyes off of. But no matter how much he does for them, no matter how much he changes for them, they'll still be dead.

He forgets this, sometimes. He's been through this before. When one of his best friends had died, he found himself picking up his phone to text them months, even years after the funeral, wanting to check-in. He knew his friend was dead, but in that brief moment of forgetfulness, his friend was not. That moment, it was neither good, nor bad. He's imagined this must be the closest one can get to going back in time. If you lie yourself into a life that once was, forever can it be.

Six Pillars bleeds into Bitter Springs, but there isn't much differentiation between the two. It is hard going across the raped earth. The bruised ground sinks beneath their feet, while the scabby stretches of parasite-infested stones stick in their toes. Stretched chasms gasp words of warning, and they heed and steer clear. Stinking puddles of stagnated water reek of rot, and they go the long way around them, careful to avoid the gelatinous bottom-feeders feeding within. Tumbledown buildings moan within their vermillion constrictions—towers of rubble, they threaten to topple; and distant tents, white and Lillian branded, show their emptiness to the wind, the bitterness of ritual all around them, like static before a storm.

They reach the debris-dammed riverbed of what once was the Tri-County River. Without water, it's hardly recognizable. It betrays the ghoul's memories in the way these ravaged vistas do not. He has no personal attachment to the river, but it was the binding between the cities; their lifeblood, their contaminant. That's how he knew he was still human: he got stupid with sentiments, sometimes. But if water ran these banks again, would the river be the same? Like a word forgotten for an object later rediscovered, would there be a difference?

Wild dogs and stray cats roam the riverbank, but to the giant mosquito they are no equals. They scatter.

Overhead, a Lord beast clears the river in one leap. The ghoul can't make sense of the creature or its kind. A moon cat, likely, given its dark fur and celestial markings. Five-to-six-hundred pounds of muscle and claws like knives. And it's running. From Night Terrors most likely. The ghoul's wife was the bleeding heart when came it to animals, but to him, this doesn't seem fair. In this life, certain things, no matter what, can't catch a break.

And hearing the soupy gore in his gut, the ghoul wants a break. He won't get one the way he is. Today, he is a monster, and according to the Corrupted, responsible for the Trauma. Tomorrow, it will be no different. He'll still be a monster, and a blight. He will bear humanity's burdens like a pack mule, so that they won't have to. And when he no longer can, they'll butcher him and look for something else to blame. He could live among them, in disguise, but not truly. He would know the truth, and in turn, in time, they would, too.

He turns to Mr. Haemo. The bug pays him no mind. He still holds the ram skull closely. He already knows what's going to be said. He's known all along. The ghoul wants history. He wants to possess. He wants to forget, and he wants to remember. This chameleon gift of his is a weapon he'll come to loathe. Surely, he thinks to himself, there is, was, or will be someone else out there in a similar situation as himself. A ruined man, maybe, wanting to get back to a family forlorn. He hopes never to meet them, though. They can never meet, men like that, like himself. They will see their paths diverged, and spend their lives reaching out to the other to justify the choices they've made.

Hours pass. The river narrows. Around the bend, two commercial airplanes are smashed into one another. Seats and buckles and oxygen masks spill out of the cabins like grubby guts. The bellies of the rusted fuselages have been split open. Fresh, frothing liquid rolls languidly over the tears. Inside, the ghoul hears pattering feet and the frantic search for weaponry. Shining eyes meet his from the ruin's dark. It is difficult to tell whether they are human or not, but these days, it doesn't matter. Trying to make the distinction is more dangerous than it's worth.

For once, the sky is clear. Seasons are strange during the Trauma. Summer and winter are two hateful lovers wrestling over the specifics of an endless divorce. Mornings can be cold and distant, and afternoons, suffocating and hot. It isn't until the evenings when all energies are spent and all battles lost that the temperature steadies out. But today is different. It has to be past noon, and the weather is decent. Only some parts of the land will catch fire.

Does the blood speak? Does the flesh make promises? Can it? Will it? The ghoul glances at Mr. Haemo. Even with his thousands of eyes, the bug won't make eye contact. He feared him because you were supposed to fear him, and he still does, but not in the way the mosquito expects him to. He killed four Night Terrors without breaking sweat, and he can spellweave without any effort. But he had chosen the ghoul for a reason. He said it was to infiltrate the remains of Brooksville Manor, to find the Night Terror encampment and the homunculus stationed there, but the ghoul knows there is more to it than that. The ghoul is needed. He can harbor blood and flesh of the Night Terrors in a way the mosquito cannot. But if Mr. Haemo can turn him into a blood slave to control, why the cordiality?

So, after hours of silence, the ghoul breaks it: "How long have you been watching me?"

"A long time."

"I didn't know."

"That's the point."

"Why?"

Mr. Haemo shrugs. He's not going to give him straight answers from here on out.

"You could've shown yourself sooner."

"It wasn't time."

"For what? What were you waiting for?"

"Things to be in their proper places." Mr. Haemo cracks his knuckles. "I'm old. I was here before the Trauma, and I'll be here buzzing along well after it. Waiting is nothing."

The ghoul mumbles, "Can you see into the future?"

Mr. Haemo looks at him. "Only if it's already happened."

"The hell does that mean?"

"Bloodlines are timelines. They grease the Dread Clock's dark hands. I know them well."

"What the fuck are you talking about?"

Mr. Haemo pokes the ghoul's nose with his sharp finger. "I'm the abortion that survived."

The ghoul shakes his head, says, "Don't cut yourself on all that edge."

"I grew too slow," Mr. Haemo says with a sigh. "I could have shown the Old World such a good time." He spits out a wad of blood. It forms a name: Herbert North.

They begin to make their way up out of the river. The bank is dusty and crumbles beneath their weight. When the ghoul stumbles, Mr. Haemo takes his hand like a child in a crowded mall and helps him along.

The ghoul feels sick constantly equating the bug to a parent.

At the top, they stop. The sun sits low over what once was Brooksville. The ghoul hasn't been here in untold years. It is unrecognizable to him. There are no buildings. Every building, of which there had to have been thousands, is gone. It is a field of craters and vermillion veins filled with ramshackle huts and the ramshackle shufflers who might call them home. The ghoul counts thirty people in total, but there may be more farther on. In the field is a field of their own; crops—corn, potatoes, and wheat—and plants—Null, Respite, Antagonist, Numb, and Warmth.

This is a community, and everywhere where he's gone, he's seen nothing but an intense need for community. Humanity has been traumatized. God left, and those that didn't chase It, chased one another down, and chastened. Seeing the crops and the people here, the ghoul thinks there may be a chance at reconciliation. There may be a chance God will come back.

The ghoul snaps out of it and says, "What is it? A homunculus?"

"Manmade," Mr. Haemo says. "They are the original flesh fiends. The original Night Terrors. Their progenitors. They were supposed to be a perfection of humanity, a mold to teach more conscious, free-thinking creatures—"

"Night Terrors."

"Yeah. They were supposed to guide and educate the Night Terrors into working with humanity. But you've seen how that's worked out for everyone."

The ghoul nods.

Mr. Haemo stretches his wings. "The thing is the homunculi are completely capable of spellweaving."

"That's what you do."

"That's right. And something bio-organic such as themselves shouldn't be able to do that."

"Can Night Terrors spellweave?"

"Only a rare few."

"Why do you care what homunculi can do? They don't seem to be any threat to you."

Mr. Haemo snorts. "They're not. But I want what's inside them. I want to know how they do it. I want to know what Ødegaard did. I want what's in them. I want to hear its secrets and promises."

Several Corrupted in the field turn and take notice of the ghoul and the mosquito. Quickly, they hurry away from the riverbank and settle in behind a few large trees that lead into the woods farther on. Maidenwood, that was what they used to call it. Now they don't call it anything at all.

"I can track Corrupted. I can't track Night Terrors. That doesn't sit well with me. They're up to some fucked up shit. I want to keep tabs. I want to be there when the blood spills."

The ghoul doesn't buy Mr. Haemo's last line, but keeps that to himself.

Mr. Haemo presses his claw against one of the trees, says, "This'll do," and then, with both hands, grabs the bark and rips outwards. The tree opens to him like a womb, and inside, waiting all along, as if it'd been there all along, is the red, shadowy light of Exuvia.

"Have to wait until nightfall. Have to teach you a thing or two about a thing or two until then."

Mr. Haemo steps into the tree.

The ghoul follows after, never even considering the fact he could run.

Unlike Earth, Exuvia is unchanged. The ghoul emerges from the red, shadowy light onto the hill where they'd sat around the cold camp-fire. The fire is still there, too, frosting the air with its flames. Across the golden way, the convent's bells peal, and the ghoul has a suspicion they might even be for him and the bug.

Mr. Haemo takes a seat beside the fire.

The ghoul does the same.

"Put on the Night Terror."

The ghoul's attention drifts back to the convent. Small shapes in habits are climbing across the roof, leaving behind what appears to be patches of hair in their wake.

"Put it on," Mr. Haemo demands.

The ghoul closes his eyes and opens his mind. He goes to his flesh closet and finds the Night Terror there. He slips into her skin. It's no different than anyone else's. Without the violent entitlement, the Night Terror is no different than any other Corrupted—Corruption with-standing. He will not be convincing as her. He doesn't even know her name.

"Yep, that's her," Mr. Haemo says.

The ghoul opens his eyes and looks down. His figure is bulkier than his natural frame. He has breasts, but he's long since gotten over that shock. What throws him off more than anything else when he's a woman is the looks he gets, the way conversations change; how what's between his legs is simultaneously celebrated and debased. Monsters had better manners than most Trauma-born men and women.

"Her party was sent out from Brooksville Manor to observe the transubstantiation of Lillian into Mother Abbess Priscilla or whatever those bible thumpers have decided to call her. She was a captain."

He tosses the ghoul the ram skull. "Put it on."

The ghoul catches it, does as he's told. The skull is bulky and digs into his head. It's not comfortable, but no one ever said the life of a flesh fiend was.

"You saw what happened with your own eyes, thanks to me, so you don't have to BS that part of it. We'll have to cover you in blood to explain why you're the only survivor." Mr. Haemo snaps his fingers. "I'll cover you good."

The ghoul shifts the mask. It smells of rot.

"But Night Terrors are freaky little fuckers. You're going to have to play the part to a T, or you're going to get pinched. I'd say put on your

SCOTT HALE

best Nazi impersonation, but knowing you, you'll start speaking German and heiling away. So…" Mr. Haemo's proboscis extends to its full length. "Here's what we're going to do."

Mr. Haemo stands. At seven feet tall, wings expanded and proboscis erect, the mosquito is gargantuan to the sitting ghoul. He steps around the fire, goes up to the ghoul, and says, "Open your mouth, baby."

The ghoul doesn't.

"I'm not jerking you around about what I can teach you. I'm going to show you right now. I'm going to give you a taste. You're going to possess this Night Terror. It'll be temporary, and you'll still be you in there, but you'll also be her. All the way."

The ghoul opens his mouth enough to speak. He is muffled as he says, "What you're going to teach me… can it be undone? The real thing?"

"If someone knows you well enough and gets inside your head enough, like moi, yeah. But other than that, you'll be awash in ignorant bliss. Lucky you."

"You're not going to turn me into a blood slave, are you?"

Mr. Haemo laughs so hard he starts to cough. "You're already doing everything I want. You're the best blood slave I could ever hope for. Open your mouth. You're going to like the way she tastes."

The ghoul doesn't budge.

Mr. Haemo reaches out, takes him by the throat, and digs all five claws into his neck, penetrating the skin and muscle.

"Open up," the mosquito says. "You've come too far for a change of heart."

The ghoul, gasping, opens his mouth.

Mr. Haemo rips his claws out of his throat, and the wounds heal instantly.

"Don't forget to swallow," Mr. Haemo says, touching the tip of his proboscis to the ghoul's mouth. "Spitters are quitters."

The ghoul closes his eyes. He sees his family in the dark there. Ava, Zoey, and Faye. He wants to tell them he's doing this for them—a family man's favorite phrase and justification. But the truth of the matter, he's not doing it for anyone or anything, but to drown and die in the undertow of ignorant bliss.

He opens his eyes in time to see what appears to be a magnified germ drop from Mr. Haemo's proboscis onto his tongue. The green,

268

spiked orb, surrounded by tens of floating globs, stabs its way toward his mouth. Panicking, the ghoul clamps his teeth down on his tongue to stop it. But the germ scales his teeth like walls and melts into his gums.

Everything does not go black. Everything becomes everything. Innumerable images flood his mind at an incomprehensible rate. Memories he cannot possibly have coalesce and co-exist alongside his own. He feels his mind splitting apart. New cavities are created. His body shakes. Or rather, her body shakes. Their eyes roll back in their head. Auditory hallucinations, or maybe just remembrances, wrack his skull. He, she... they are foaming at the mouth. A seizure in the wake of this schism.

Mr. Haemo grabs the ghoul, or the Night Terror, and starts to chant frantically.

This was not how it was supposed to go.

5

The ghoul's brain itches. He imagines it splitting, like cells dividing. Trying to reconcile his thoughts with the Night Terror's is getting him nowhere. His mind aches in the way puzzles make it ache during that one insurmountable step before being solved. He knows he can do it, but he doesn't know how to do it, so he lets the process take him where it wills.

He returns to the moment of her death. She is staring him down, except in his eyes, she sees a moth staring back. It reaches out to her with bladed fingers.

Memories mount one another, each one trying to secure their place at the top of an infinitely growing pile of experiences.

He goes farther back. He's smaller now—a child—because the world is larger than it should be. He's in a swamp. White tupelos sit swollen on the shore, getting their fill of the placid waters beyond. Thick, brightly colored tussocks decorate the ground, like fallen pompoms from a clown's suit. He turns, because the memory turns, and finds a village behind him—Traesk, likely. There are huts as far as he can see, which isn't very far, given the Night Terror's height and being nearsighted.

He hears something. She moves forward. Night Terrors cross paths with her, but pay her no mind. She rounds corners. Her fear becomes his fear. They are panting together. Someone screams out.

The screaming melds with moaning. Traesk gives way to the texture of blushing flesh. They rear back from a sweating neck to a sweating body. The naked woman beneath them is on her belly and bound, and Corrupted. They tug on the rope to tease her. The woman is begging for them to stop, but instead, they go all the way in every-which-way they can.

The woman cries out in pain. They laugh, and grind themselves against her backside, going purple with power. Someone whimpers. They look up. More Corrupted lay on their sides bound to one another in the corner. They are covered in blood. Their faces have been turned into a pink mash. They are upset that one of them is still alive. It is embarrassing.

The memories shift. They sit beside a fire, their hand in the hand of the female Night Terror beside them. They are teenagers, and they are in love; a deep, stupid kind of love; the kind that could rival electricity if such a force could be put to use for things other than fawning and fucking. The ghoul doesn't think this. The Night Terror thinks this. She thinks this as she remembers this moment for him from another moment later in her life. She is dead, but inside him, she is alive.

The swamp puts on a show. Fireflies take to the black stage and fill it with bioluminescent bravado. They drift across the air, making shapes that only these two young lovers can find meaning in. They squeeze the girl's hand. Her name is Callie. She is a vulture.

They lean into one another and, going in for a kiss, miss each other's mouths. They close their eyes and try again. Callie's lips are wet and slightly chapped; kissing her turns their insides in the best way possible.

When they pull away, they are back in Six Pillars, in the house of Filipa. They are on the ground in the kitchen, a ghoul on top of them, tearing at their throat. Callie is coming down the hall to save her.

They die. They live.

Traesk screams. It has been this way all day and all night. Fifty Corrupted lie in a chain, their heads hacked from their bodies. The public execution has every Night Terror in attendance. The elders insist for them to remain calm, but the hot blood has made them hot, and soon they are down on all fours, reveling.

They step up to the Corrupted on the chopping block. They grab him by the back of his hair and scream into his ear, "Where is it? What's its name?"

The Corrupted tries to wriggle. Another Night Terror, the Dog, steps up to him. The Dog takes two fingers and plunges them into the blood collected around the block. Then, the Dog shoves them into the Corrupted's mouth, enough to make him vomit. He does this, over and over, until the Corrupted is the color of a stillborn baby and there is nothing left in his stomach.

"Lacuna," he says, bawling. "Off the c-coast from Nachtla." He heaves. "God f-forgive m-me."

They laugh and step on his neck.

"I love you."

They are in the Night Terror's room. They are tucked into bed. A candle burns on the windowsill, its flame moved by the heavy air coming off the swamp. Their mom and dad are in the room. She is sitting on the edge of the bed, holding their big toe from over the blanket. He is standing near the door, smiling in the shadows; his arms crossed, covered in a thick mat of hair they always like to pull on to make him mad.

"We love you, too, Emvola," Mom says.

Brooksville of years after and hours before bursts through the floor. It is the morning of their death. They are underground. The Monkey (Caine), the Lion (Rusaf), the Boar (Domuz), and Callie, the Vulture, stand at their side.

In front of them there is a massive hole, like an abscessed wound. It is covered in a wreath of millions of feasting maggots. In front of that stands a strange creature. A sexless, genderless humanoid without any armor or weapons. Its eyes are like two cracked marbles still covered in the grit of the games they'd played. Its hands are clenched. Liquefied maggots drip from the creases. There is already a large puddle of the creatures around the humanoid's feet.

It is a homunculus. They know this. Very few do.

"Do not intervene," the homunculus says. "Without the Lillians, there is no telling what the next dominant religion will be. We need not taunt Exuvia."

They nod.

"Kill no one. Rape no one."

They and their companions grumble ridiculously, like sitcom actors.

"We must be better if we are going to make the world better. Go, now, and see history."

"What about the Maggot?" they say.

"The Maggot knows me well, Emvola. If it is here, I will find it. Go, and be more than what you are. I trust you."

I trust you. The statement makes them feel that deep, stupid kind of love again. *I trust you.* They can't remember anyone ever saying that to them in their entire life. Most had never been given cause to. *I trust you.* They throw their arm around Callie's shoulder and squeeze her into them.

They walk out of Brooksville in a series of choppy vignettes. When they reach Six Pillars, they are sixteen again. They are sitting on the chest of their first Corrupted kill. The heart has already been removed and placed in the proper bag. They will be a full member of the tribe soon. She picks at his skin and slips a piece into her mouth. The elders have recently forbidden cannibalism, stating that it could lead to genetic defects in future births. But the Corrupted and Night Terrors are not of the same species, and how does that saying go?

Oh, yeah. That's right.

Old habits die hard.

4

The ghoul goes it alone. He came out of the mental stitching by himself. He'll carry this conjoined consciousness on his own. He's had enough of his mosquito chaperone.

One hour; Mr. Haemo had warned he had one hour. As he follows the river to the final resting place of Brooksville Manor, he counts the seconds in his head, her head—their head. Emvola, the Night Terror whose life he now possesses, is quiet at the moment. Her last thought was that she was dying. Now, she cannot understand why she isn't. He wonders what will become of this ghostly mind inside his own. Can it form new memories? And when this hour is up, what will stay behind, disguising itself as his own recollections?

"You have one hour to eat the homunculus," Mr. Haemo had told him. "If you can't eat it, then swallow as much blood as you can. One hour, and you're back to being you. After that, it'll be up to your charming personality and your... ghoulish... good looks."

There had been people outside when they first arrived in Brooksville, but not anymore. Impersonating Emvola gave him the kind of wide berth from others you couldn't get short of being a cruise liner or a comet. He knew why, too. Those memories were fresh. They still had a temperature and smell to them. They were hot, and they smelled of sweat and rust. Emvola and the others, while the homunculus had been asleep, had snuck out of Brooksville Manor to terrorize the Corrupted living here. Not to send a warning or "balance the scales," but because traveling with the homunculus had forced them to be civil. Six women, eight men, and five children were slaughtered, raped, and impregnated by the time they were able to scratch that "itch."

"If the Maggot is down there, don't go near it," Mr. Haemo had told him. "Don't go into the hole you saw in her memories. You won't come out. And I won't come save you."

The ghoul didn't want this. He didn't want Emvola's memories, or the ones he'd fashioned when he took on the fashion of others from his flesh projects. And what about his own memories? What good were they to him anymore when the ones he kept them for were an afterlife away? His wife was Ava; his daughters were Zoey and Faye. And he was... He couldn't remember his name, anymore. He remembered being a banker, or a manager of a bank. He remembered Zoey was a C-section, and Faye came out so tangled up in her umbilical cord she might as well have been playing cat's cradle with it. He remembered meeting Ava. They met their freshman year of college in the library. She'd ended up getting pregnant six months later. She had cussed him and his "no good, deadeye dick" out for two hours before laughing herself to tears. They were married for ten years before a Lillian put a bullet in her head.

"But if you can do this," Mr. Haemo had said, "then I'll teach you the secret histories of the body. It's the best fresh start you're going to get in this rancid world."

But if he found the perfect life and possessed it, would he forget everything else? Just having Emvola's corpse of consciousness lying beside his was spiritually and mentally nauseating. It made him want to vomit out both and be done with the experience. Yet, if he allowed everything to be scratched and scoured from his synapses, would it be worth it? What had he been doing this whole time? A family man convinces himself everything he does or will do will be for the sake of his family. But he has no family; just people he's orphaned and invaded.

"You'll have to hibernate, eventually," Mr. Haemo had said, waving him off. "But you might just get to live just shy of forever. A new life and young wife every hundred years or so? You scallywag."

The ghoul doesn't want to live forever, but he doesn't want to die.

He is a ghoul, not a human—not even a Corrupted—but he knows he's foolish to think he's all that different from them. He just wants meaning. God was his meaning once. And maybe God still can be. But until then, his curse can be a gift. He could carry on a life nearing its end; bring happiness to those who aren't ready for their loved ones to go. No one has to see him die. He could be the stalwart protector standing on the precipice of time; rotted, ragged, ravaged; a skin cloak like Mr. Haemo's fastened around his neck; waiting for that preternatural pat on the back. And then, yes, then, and only then, can he let go and see Ava, Zoey, and Faye again. Finally, he'll be able to look them in their beautiful eyes and tell them why he had been spared when they had not been.

Brooksville Manor creeps on him in the way most repulsive things do. He doesn't see it until he can't help but see it everywhere he looks. That is the boon of repulsive things. They do not belong, but the world compensates around them, so that they do. It is the only way to explain why they should exist at all.

The three-story, low-income housing complex used to tower over the Tri-County river, but ten years before God awoke, it collapsed upon itself. Whether the collapse was the result of an accident or malicious intentions, it was never substantiated; but Brooksville Manor was never rebuilt, and its debris had never been fished out of the river. They were simply left to drift into the distant sea.

Brooksville Manor was nothing. The only reason the ghoul knew to call it that was because he remembered it had been here once. Brooksville Manor was a blown-out piece of hill, like a bombed bunker, that had been walled off by row after row of barbed wire, broken glass, metal shards, and stacks of cars that burned infinitely with the same cold, black flames from Exuvia. There were bodies, too; hundreds of them, strung up in the air by silken threads connected to nothing but the wrinkles in the sky. Each of them had their eyes gouged and their bodies split, from their asses to their mouths.

Fifty feet out, the ghoul stops. He straightens the ram mask and slips into Emvola's thoughts. He doesn't know how important this homunculus is, but clearly it didn't need much of a guard while Emvola and the other Night Terrors had been away. Brooksville Manor looks how a cataclysm might when preparing for the apocalypse. But there had to be a way in. And if there was, he already knew it.

Emvola's memories drift like motes of dust across his mind. He reaches out to them. Lenticular imagery flash before his eyes. He sees a stack of cars braced by a vertical white van. Black flames immolate the mechanical pyre. Everything burns. Nothing melts. Emvola steps through the cold fire unscathed, and goes through the van, out onto the cars, to the second layer of this transplanted hell.

The ghoul goes around the outskirts of the Manor. He spies the vertical white van. Squeezing the handle of the halberd, he adjusts the ram mask and gets as close as he dares to the black flames. Here, unlike elsewhere, they're not cold. They're not anything.

He takes a deep breath and reaches out. The black tongues caress his hand. Expecting pain, he feels pain; and then, realizing it's nothing, he feels nothing. This part of the fire is an illusion.

Climbing into the van, the ghoul snatches another memory from Emvola's molting life. After the cars come the metal shards and the broken glass. Protruding from the earth and tightly packed, it's impossible to step off the cars without impaling your foot or scrambling them into boney confetti. Yet, Emvola does just that. She drops from the cars and into the second layer. She steps from shard to shard, and each time, they disappear beneath her feet, as if they weren't there at all.

The ghoul replays the memory over and over. When he's comfortable enough to do anything but call it quits, he lowers himself from the wall of burning cars and plants one foot in the exact location Emvola had yesterday. The shards give to his weight. He can't even feel them beneath him.

Reaching the end of Emvola's memory loop and the beginning of the barbed wired third layer, the ghoul stops. The barbed wire walls are just that—walls of barbed wire—and stand at least ten feet tall. They are memorials to massacre. Their brutal, sharp points are bloodied knots upon which flesh, feathers, scales, and tissues are fixed.

Sensing movement across the wall, the ghoul looks to his left. There, he spies a lamb caught between the dense, cutting layers. Its fur drips pink with pigheaded pride. It does not whine as it works itself to the bone to get to the center. It is indifferent.

More movement. Spastic vibrations. The ghoul glances to his right. Farther down, an elderly Corrupted couple are caught in the barbed wire. Their emaciated bodies, soaked with blood, glow radiantly against the cool, uncaring steel. At first, the ghoul thinks they are trying to escape the wall's clutches, but then sees they are merely trying to get farther in. They sound like they are praying. Epiphanies in evisceration.

Emvola's memory glides over his consciousness, teasing him to take it. He does, and recoils as what he finds there. She doesn't pass through the barbed wire as if it were an illusion or secret passage like he thought she might. Instead, she holds out her hands; and from one of the suspended corpses above, a silk rope drops from between its mutilated pelvis. She grips the rope, and the corpse reels her up, over the wall, where she drops and descends into the hollow of Brooksville Manor.

The ghoul goes back to the lamb. One little leg, sheered to steel, sticks out of the wall, dripping blood from its toes like a paintbrush.

The ghoul wonders about the elderly. They didn't get much farther from when he last saw them. They're dead in each other's arms, except one appears to be holding the other back, as if they meant to be the first one through.

Sighing, shaking, the ghoul glances over his shoulder. He's come this far. He can't even say how far he's come. But he'd like to know where he was going for once. So, he holds out his hands.

He counts ten corpses closest to him. One turns slowly towards him, its silken noose glittering around its mushy, bruised neck. A faint, green mist oozes out of its empty sockets and slacked jaw. It considers him intensely in a way only the blind could. Then, from its dry, yawning perineum, a silk rope unravels.

The ghoul steps back. The rope hits the top of the barbed wire wall and slides down it. He fixes the halberd underneath his arm, presses it against his body.

The hanging corpse gives the rope a tug.

The ghoul grabs the rope, holds it above his head.

The corpse begins to reel him in slowly, effortlessly.

The ghoul tucks in his legs to avoid having them catch on the wall, but the corpse is pulling him at an impossible angle, adjusting his trajectory, despite not moving from where he hangs.

Ten feet up, the ghoul clears the wall. The corpse lowers the rope. When he's close enough to drop from it, he does. The ghoul falls four feet and hits the ground. The halberd slips out from underneath his arm. He scrambles to his feet, but the weapon is out of reach. It bounces along before falling into the Manor's hollow.

The rope rises past the ghoul's face. He looks up to see the corpse stuffing it back into the hole between its legs. The green mist rolls in reverse back into his eye sockets and mouth, and for now, it is dead again.

The ghoul approaches the hollow. He doesn't know what to expect, because Emvola's reconstructed mind has gone dormant. The stitching between his and hers is fraying. He can only remember what she remembered for him—fragments of fossils from a shape he doesn't have the imagination to imagine.

"I'm almost out of time," he says to himself, going to the lip of the hollow.

The last of Brooksville Manor is subterranean. Inside the hollow of the blown-out hill is a partially destroyed cement staircase. It plunges narrowly into the glistening dark beyond.

The ghoul puts one foot on the top of the stairs and stops. His stomach turns. He turns. He wants to run away, but he can't remember the way. Beyond the corpse's rope, the rest is a blur of nervous hesitations and anxious second guesses.

No different than anywhere else, at any other time, he thinks to himself.

And thinking that, he descends.

3

In the hazy depths of Brooksville Manor, the ghoul and the homunculus he's come to consume are not alone.

As he moves down the crumbling stairs, he hears two voices below. One from the homunculus of Emvola's memories. The other belongs to a woman with a strong speech impediment.

"Ou… y'ave et?" the woman struggles to say.

The ghoul leaps over four weak steps and catches himself against the wall. The cement and old pipe dig into his bones. He takes off the ram skull and holds it at his side, to see more clearly.

"Yes," the homunculus says.

Their voices echo around the ghoul. It's too dark to see where the homunculus and this woman are, but he's certain they are near. He smells fire—real fire—and sees the glow of it just beyond where the stairs appear to stop.

"When will you use it?" the homunculus asks.

The ghoul creeps to the bottom of the stairs. He sees the halberd a few feet away, sidesteps towards it, and scoops it up. Donning the ram's skull, he drifts in the dark towards the fiery glow—and the two

277

figures huddled around it.

"N'yver. They w-will."

"You have the Blood. What else do you need for your Communion?"

"The Body."

The ghoul is dripping in sweat. The dark is sweltering. The shapes become more defined by the fire with every step he takes. He probes Emvola's mind, but there is no reaction, no response.

"How will you find the child?"

"They w-will 'ring him t' me. They w-would give me all their c'ildren if they could. I will find him."

He has seconds at best before this phantom mind becomes a phantom limb. What does he need to know? What will the homunculus ask him? Was there a passphrase? Was he, she, them even supposed to come back—

"Someone's there," the woman says. Her speech impediment is gone. "Someone's in the dark."

The homunculus clears his throat. The ball of fire they and the woman are beside lifts into the air, touches the earthen ceiling, and then explodes into hundreds of tinier, yet equally bright orbs. They rush across the ceiling in every direction, until the entire hollow is no longer completely dark, but instead, dimly lit with cloudy bulbs, like a Podunk bar on Christmas Eve.

The homunculus and the woman, once Lillian, now the White Worm, stand before him. Behind them, the massive, abscessed, maggot-wreathed hole from Emvola's memory gapes. Between them, an old, dirty, metal hospital bed sits lopsided; butcher's knives lay across it.

The White Worm looks no different than she did before. Her tunic and pants bear no stains or rips from the barrier above, as if she passed through it perfectly, or somehow avoided it entirely. The only thing different about her is the box in her hands. It's constructed from a deep red wood; and the locks and hinges fixed to it are milky white. She holds this box so tightly that the flesh in her fingers and hands bunches up from the tension.

The homunculus cocks its head, concerned. Sexless, genderless, and without armor or weapons, the creature shouldn't scare the ghoul as much as it does, but it does. It's not the cracked marble eyes, or the bird-like features of its mouth. It's not its slightly elongated arms, or its fingers that come to a point. It's the complete and total control of itself and the environment around it. The surety in the way it carries itself. It is the way in which it resembles a flesh fiend in its purest, most undiluted form. It is the embodiment of violence and depravity, without any of the telltale signs. It is unpredictable.

"Emvola," the homunculus says, sounding slightly relieved. "You're alive."

The White Worm disagrees. She unlocks the wooden box and opens it. Inside, sitting upon a cushion, is a silver, red-gemmed necklace covered in what appear to be worm-like adornments. She mumbles, "Guess you were good for something, Ruth," and closes it.

The ghoul shuts his eyes. He invades Emvola's mind with his own, but finds himself creating memories for her. Some slip through before he realizes, and now he can't tell what's real and what's not.

"She's not alive," the White Worm says. "She and the others rushed off to Filipa's house to kill some voyeurs. That's not Emvola."

The homunculus nods. It turns to the White Worm, bows, and says, "What will you call yourself?"

The White Worm taps her lips in contemplation and then: "Mother Abbess Priscilla."

"And after that?"

Mother Abbess Priscilla laughs, gives the homunculus a weak shove, and walks into the hole. The maggots close around her, and when they disperse, she is gone.

The ghoul's heart is beating so hard he's certain the homunculus can hear it. He finds himself drifting towards his flesh closet, desperate to put on another suit. He stays his hand. He can do this. He's so close. He's seen enough of Emvola. He doesn't need her to be her. The details differ, but most courses are always the same.

"What the hell was the point of watching her if she was going to come back here, anyway?" the ghoul shouts, ramming the halberd's end into the ground. That sounded like Emvola.

"She was supposed to come back with you," the homunculus says. "Callie had orders to escort her back. Where is Callie?"

The ghoul stiffens. Tears fall from his eyes. Callie. The love he never loved and yet the love for which he would now kill himself.

The homunculus approaches. "I am sorry." It holds out its hands for him to take. "I am sorry for all of your deaths. You should not have come back."

The ghoul says through his teeth, "She died… because of you."

"She died because of you. I asked you not to kill, and you were killed because of it."

"Are you fucking kidding me? I'm standing right here before…"

The homunculus reaches the ghoul and takes the ram mask by its sides and lifts it off his head.

By the time the mask is gone, so is this grotesque glamour. Emvola's flesh melts into his own and finds its place upon a rack in his mind.

"That is better," the homunculus says. "It is nice to see the truth in a world of lies."

The ghoul imagines stabbing the homunculus with the halberd. But he can't bring himself to do it. Not yet.

"You are a ghoul." The homunculus lays the ram skull at his feet. "You impersonated Emvola to reach this place. That is very clever. Was it to meet the White Worm?"

The ghoul shakes his head.

"Was it to see heaven?"

The ghoul is confused.

"Heaven." The homunculus points to the maggot hole behind him. "Well, it was a way into heaven. The Vermillion God is gone, and so the way to It is shut for now. Yet, people and things are drawn to this place. I am sure you have seen them caught in the barricades outside. What is a place that once was heaven and is no more if not hell? It is important they do not reach this place until the maggots have finished cleaning the wound."

The homunculus pauses, as if it has realized it is speaking too much and says, "You came for me."

"I did," the ghoul says.

"Not the Maggot?"

"I don't know what that is."

"We all hold our undoing within ourselves," the homunculus says. "Even God, I believe. I hope." It touches the ghoul's rough cheek with its soft finger. "What do you want from me?"

"Your blood."

The homunculus smiles.

"Not me. It's not for me." The ghoul hangs his head. "It's for the mosquito, Mr. Haemo."

"Ah."

"You know him?"

"Unfortunately."

"What has he promised you?"

"A life. A way to have a life."

"What is wrong with the life you have now?"

"They're not mine. Mine's gone. I'm a parasite. I'm a cuckoo bird."

"Is that not your nature?"

The ghoul doesn't respond.

"You can be yourself, and you can be more." The homunculus takes a step back. "We have been telling the Night Terrors this for years. Some are listening. Emvola did not."

The ghoul sneers. "Maybe you shouldn't have given them horrible principles to base their life around."

The balls of fire on the ceiling begin to glow brighter.

The homunculus makes fists and then, slowing its breath, says, "That is what you do when you do not believe in the subjects you are trying to mold. You appeal to what they are, in the hopes that, one day, they will become what you have.

"I am sorry, ghoul, but I do not have blood to give you."

The ghoul stammers, "W-What?"

"I am bloodless. I only have the oil from the Mokita machine. It is yours to have. That is what the mosquito wants."

"Why are you helping me?"

"I have just committed a terrible sin by giving Mother Abbess Priscilla that box. I appealed to her nature with the hopes it will make more fruitful our own. I wish to atone."

The ghoul nods. The hollow is going dark. The homunculus' weavings are beginning to wear thin.

"You're manmade," the ghoul says.

The homunculus nods.

"But you can spellweave."

Again, it nods.

"How?"

"The Mokita machine. Its oil."

The homunculus presses its hand to its chest and tears a piece of it away. The porous material in place of flesh comes free in one, dry hunk. Behind the material lies the creature's chest cavity. Inside it, artificial organs with a plastic sheen throb with calculated movements.

The homunculus reaches deeper into itself and wraps its hand around its heart. The container is rich with a dark, swirling liquid inside it.

"The liquid is the oils of Exuvia," the homunculus says. "When man could not be God, he tried to be Its opposite, instead. They lie to themselves about the nature of angels and demons. They only see the wings."

The homunculus rips out the heart container and hands it to the ghoul.

As soon as the ghoul takes it, the homunculus collapses upon itself into a pile of dust.

Overhead, on a cue, he hears buzzing and the flapping of wings, and Mr. Haemo's grating voice.

"Just one more thing you have to do for me," he says, landing behind him, resting his claw upon the ghoul's shoulder. "Just one more thing."

2

Bowie cracks his back at the crack of dawn and wakes his wife, Starla, with the dramatic gyration.

"What're you doing?" she rumbles, one half of her still in last night's cups. "What time is it?" She opens an eye. There is no light coming in from the casement window. "Go back to bed. You need to sleep!"

Bowie lets her go on like this for another five seconds or so before sleep, having realized she's slipped its grips, comes to get her. She's gone by the time he gets out of the bed.

He's seventy-two. Older than anyone he's ever met, Bowie expects some insomnia in his twilight years. Starla hates it, though. Being his wife makes her, by default, his most trusted physician, and according to her, it isn't right or natural to have him awake at all hours. Then she usually tells him he didn't use to be like this. Then he tells her she didn't use to nag him so much. And so on and so on.

Bowie stumbles in the dark out of the bedroom. In the hall, he smells the candle they pinched out an hour ago and wishes they hadn't. He kicks at the wall until his feet hit something hollow.

Reaching down, his bones crack like branches underfoot. He shudders in delight and grabs the pot beside the wall. Holding it in one hand, he takes his dick out and pisses into it. His bladder thanks him as it shrinks. When the stream is nothing more than a drizzle, he gives himself a few healthy shakes. It's ceremonial at this point, though. He could stand here and slap himself around through breakfast, lunch, and dinner, and still he'd dribble as soon as he put this useless thing away. "Good enough," he mumbles with final jerk.

He puts his dick away. A single, sadistic drop of piss hits his linen not a second later.

Bowie takes the pot and shambles down the hall. He and his family have been in this house for twenty years. He knows it well. If he were to spin around in this Black Hour blackness, he would still find his way to whatever room he needed and not run into anything on the way. No, he wishes the candle was still burning because the world got worse when the lights went out. If you're sleeping, you can't see it, but he doesn't sleep, so he sees it all.

Bowie, dodging chairs and a table, gets to the backdoor. The cold comes in under it and chills his toes. When you're only skin and bones and your two ten-year-old daughters combined weigh more than you, a gust of cold air is all it takes to get your teeth chattering.

He reaches into the dark and comes back with a heavy coat from off the wall. He steps into the boots beside the door, and sinks. Holding the pot of piss, he cringes and then opens the backdoor.

It's snowing again.

Only at night, blanketed and glittering, can their town of Nyxis gain some sense of comfort. At any other time on any other day, Nyxis is a restless child—all gnawing gums and growing pains. It used to be a barren field covered in scorch marks and satellites, and small hovels that were homes to the witch covens that roamed here. But then the witches' children wanted more than to sow suffering, so they sowed seeds and reaped fields, and those from the smolders of Vold (now Elin) saw and left their city lives for the country.

The town is ten miles wide at this point, but it continues to expand. That's where the gnawing gums come in, and the growing pains. Nyxis creeps across the land, be it by shack or field, taking more and more of the Trauma-enriched soil of the Heartland for itself. But with this potential for prosperity comes those desperate to prosper. Rich and poor and those getting by; good and bad and those myopic menaces— they all come Nyxis to claim their stake. It's led to a town structured around being unstructured; a cultural wave crashing against a socio-economic typhoon. It's led to some of the town's greatest achievements (socialized medicine) and most terrible transgressions (prostitution, and weaponized sexually transmitted diseases).

But in the snow, you can't tell. The moonlit white and the frosted dark hide these things without prejudice, bias, or lies. Gone are the buildings–those built up at the center, those falling apart at the ends; gone are the midnight marauders and the late night life takers; gone are the howling voices from those who have too much and those who don't have enough at all; gone is the blood, but when it's not, when it's there, eating through the snow, reflecting off the ice, at least it's beautiful.

Bowie doesn't share these thoughts with his family. He and his wife have been around long enough to remember a time when the world was closer to ending than beginning. When he does sleep, the memories haunt him. It's gotten better, but mostly, the world has gotten better at hiding its inhumanity. It's no longer so raw, so primal. Violence goes not naked into the street, but clad in the clothes of priests and politicians.

At times, he misses when he could trust no one but those he loved, and days were spent in solitude. It was a crueler world, but in some ways, an easier world. But these are words of a victimizer, not a victim. He knows this, and knows if the tables had been turned, he would not think so fondly on the follies of the past.

Bowie hurls the piss from the pot into the snow. The stream steams in the air and lashes the top layer. With the piss, he sends these negative thoughts, too. He doesn't need them, anymore. If he really misses seeing a world undone, he knows he need only wait for his hour with Death. She'll show him.

He wipes his runny nose, turns to go back in the house, and stops. Something catches on the corner of his eye and reels him around. There it is. A tree. Moonlight running like streamers through its outstretched branches. It sits on the edge of his property, snow packed around its roots, old as the land it's grown from.

And it shouldn't be here.

Bowie sets the piss pot down and wades through the five inches of snow on the ground to get at the tree. He and his family have been in the house for twenty years. And this tree here? It wasn't here a few hours ago. He should know. He was just out here at midnight, pissing, staring at the same spot he was staring at now, except it was empty.

"Where the hell did you come from?"

Because he's old and incurably stubborn, he touches the tree. There's a rough, scabby scar that runs vertically along its base. From it, a warm, viscous fluid oozes. Hard seeds cling to the liquid. He considers picking one out and tasting it, but common-sense kicks in and he considers otherwise. It's then that he realizes the tree isn't made of wood, nor is it lined in bark. The whole thing is comprised of this dense, dark, viscous material.

He's never seen anything like it.

And he doesn't like it.

Bowie hears Starla's voice in his head. "Get back inside," she tells him, "or you're going to catch your Death."

Wiping the fluid on his fingers on his pantleg, Bowie backs up and goes back inside. He shuts the door and stands there at it for a moment, thawing. The strange tree has taken root in his mind. Even if he could sleep, he couldn't anymore. Not with that thing that shouldn't be there being there.

Something bites his neck. He slaps the spot. The pain stops. He pulls his hand away, holds it to the crack in the door where some moonlight comes through. A smashed mosquito lies bloody in his palm.

Bowie goes to check on the girls. On his way, he grabs the candle from the hall and lights it with the tinderbox and wooden split. Their house is one large room that doubles as a living room and a kitchen; the single hall is short; one side leads to his and Starla's room, the other to their daughters'. It's not big enough for a family as big as theirs, but on nights like these, when it's dark and cold and strange trees are growing from the ground, and strange insects are riding on the air, the house is just the right size. He wants to be able to see everything all at once.

He goes to the girls' room and pushes open the door. He holds the candle high, lets the light crawl over their sleeping bodies. Duška and Sethe are out. They've pushed their beds together, and are wrapped up in each other's blankets. Their eyes move behind their lids, dreaming, most likely, of warmer days.

Bowie backs out, slips into his room—Starla is snoring up a storm—grabs a blanket off their bed, and brings it back to the girls. He lays it over them in equal parts. But like the hairs of a flytrap, as soon as it lands on Sethe's arm, she quickly snatches it away. And like the younger she is, even if it's only by weeks, Duška fusses about this from her slumber.

Bowie leaves, and leaves their door open on his way out.

He goes into the family room and sits in his chair. He sets the candle on the table beside it. A surge of wind rushes up against the house, shaking it before receding. It does this over and over, and the temperature in the house dips with every attack. Bowie grabs the quilt from off the back of his chair and wraps it around himself. The wind stops after that.

Thinking about the tree makes his stomach hurt. In a post-Trauma world, in a town built by the children of witches, day-to-day oddities were absolute certainties. Night Terrors still visited them, though not as often as before, and Lord animals were known to pass through on occasion. A few even claimed to have seen the Black Hour. Revenants attacked the outer parts of Nyxis in the spring and lamias preyed on the orphanage and foster homes in the fall. Some said they'd seen a ghoul down by the river earlier this week.

Even this winter was said to be unnatural. Archivists in Elin, Geharra, and Six Pillars had all agreed it might last for years.

But never in Bowie's days had he seen a tree like the one in his backyard. And why was it in his backyard and not the old crone's next door a half mile down the way?

Bowie rubs his thumbs against his fingers. He clears his throat with his whole body. He convinces himself he has to piss again, so that he can see the tree again.

The candle's getting low. And if this winter is going to last half as long as they promised—weathermen never get it right—they're going to need all the candles they can get. He snuffs the flame. The cold closes in on him. He pulls the quilt tighter against his body. Pushing out of the chair, he comes to his feet after fifteen seconds and then waits there, until his body gives him the go ahead to go ahead.

When he was young, he didn't have to be so deliberate. Now, everything has to be accounted for.

Bowie turns to face the backdoor and hears something hit the one at the front. He spins, gets dizzy; waits until it passes. Again, something hits the front door. There's a short sword beside it against the wall. He gets that first, and then, mustering his courage and strength, he opens the door.

Snow blasts across the threshold. It gets in his many wrinkles and forms tiny icicles there. He squints, because squinting makes him see better, and tries to make sense of the storm swirling before him. Nyxis is nearing a whiteout. He leans into the outside air. His ears prick up at another sound. Footsteps through snow. And as soon as he hears them, they stop.

Bowie panics. He steps inside, shuts the door, locks it, and then tosses some firewood behind it, as if that'll make a difference. He and Starla have lived in Nyxis a very long time. They've gotten to know just about everyone who lives here through their trades—she as a seamstress, he as a "Renaissance Man," whatever that means. He's sold Old World relics, repaired stables, tended fields, copied manuscripts, fished, mined, dabbled in dentistry, and of late, made the same candles he now uses to light his house. Never in that time had he ever made any enemies. But now it felt like he had some. Now, it felt like he had been marked.

Bowie turns around and cries out.

Duška and Sethe are standing behind him, blankets wrapped around the both of them. They look like two twins conjoined by comfort.

"Be quiet," Sethe tells him.

Bowie glances at the door. He must've woken them. The girls were light sleepers. When he and Starla found them eight years ago by the abandoned mill, they were covered in markings of the occult. They quickly took them to the local Lillian priest and had them blessed. Since then, they, like him, never slept for long, and never all that soundly.

"Sorry, girls."

"Why were you outside our room?" Duška asks with a whine.

"I was in the backyard."

The wind kicks up and rattles all the doors in the house.

Sethe's eyes droop. "Don't try to scare us."

Duška crosses her arms and nods her head.

"What... what did I do?"

"Ugh," the girls say simultaneously.

"Your daddy's old." Bowie scratches his head like a monkey. "I forget things."

The trees outside creak. A branch snaps off and hits the side of the house.

The girls jump. Their eyelids snap up so hard they're stunned.

Bowie grabs his heart, thinking, *Don't you dare fail me now,* and laughs uncomfortably. "It's okay... Just the storm."

"I don't like it when you do that," Duška says.

Bowie furrows his brow.

"When you talk to us through the walls. It's mean."

Sethe tugs on the blanket, taking some away from Duška.

Duška pouts and tugs it right back to where it was between them.

A chill shoots up Bowie's spine that has nothing to do with the winter raging around them. "T-talk to you? Through t-the walls?"

"Yeah, we heard you," Sethe says. "Why did you keep saying 'blood' over and over and over? That's weird, Dad."

Bowie realizes he's still holding the short sword. He smiles at his daughters, gives them an unemphatic, "I don't know," and goes around them, to their room. They don't have any windows in here, so he doubles-back, his head swimming with dark paranoias; lights the candle again.

He hurries into their room and goes to the farthest wall—the only one where he could have supposedly spoken to them through.

Duška and Sethe waddle up to the doorway, refusing to drop the blankets they share.

"Wake your mother," Bowie croaks, pressing his ear to the freezing wall.

He hears nothing, but inside his head, it's all warning bells.

His girls go pattering down the hall, their warm feet sweating on the cold floor.

Bowie smashes his face against the wall and moves along it. Is this place haunted? Wouldn't be the first in Nyxis. Maybe that tree in the back is an ill omen. He thinks as far back as he can manage, trying to recollect any wrongdoings. But he can conjure no such thoughts. He's seventy-two. He doesn't do much of anything anymore except annoy Starla.

Sethe screams.

Bowie straightens up. His back snaps and a sharp pain lances him.

Duška screams.

Bowie cries, "What is it? Come to me. Come to me!"

By the time he gets to the door, the girls are running past it into the family room.

"What's wrong?" He goes to chase after them, but he's drawn farther down the hall.

"M-Mom," Duška cries.

"She's…" Sethe can't get the words out.

A blast of cold air winds down the hall. It shouldn't be there. It shouldn't be this cold inside the house. The candle goes out. He turns into his room.

The casement window is wide open, and Starla is hanging out of it, her face upside down and staring directly at him. She has a hole in her head. Blood falls languidly from it, freezing before it hits the ground.

Someone laughs outside the window.

The rest of Starla is wrenched through it, into the white dark.

And then Duška screams.

1

Bowie's body forgets it's seventy-two. A surge of adrenaline takes over and unlocks muscles that gave up so long ago. He hurries down the hall. More snow blows through it from the family room.

"Girls! Girls! Don't touch them whoever…"

The front door is open. A cloaked figure stands in the doorway, holding Duška against him. Snow blows over them, builds up around them. She doesn't have her blanket. She's scared. She's shivering so badly.

The back door is open. A cloaked figure stands in the doorway, holding Sethe against him. Wind and shards of ice trickle down around them, tinkling when they hit the ground in a magical kind of way that makes the scene sicker. Sethe has her fingers dug into the figure's arm, her teeth into his hand. The hate is all the warmth she has right now.

Moonlight pours in through the two doors, but the living room between remains pitch black. That is, until a red light flickers into existence. It stands freely in a grotesque, clawed palm.

Bowie looks back and forth between the two figures holding his daughters hostage. They're both too far away from him to do anything. And if he does anything, then one of the girls isn't going to…

"Look familiar?"

The voice comes from the center of the room. From the thing holding the red light.

"Not exact, I know, but that's on you," it continues. "Time to wake up."

Bowie buckles over. He takes heavy gulps of air. What little adrenaline he had is gone. His body is on fire. His mind is twisted up inside his skull, trying to work out solutions. He thinks of Starla, and before he knows it, his face is soaked with tears.

"Gunshot wounds to their faces, right?"

Bowie looks up. "What are you…?"

The cloaked figure at the front door takes out a pistol and blows Duška's face off.

Bowie's voice breaks as he screams, "No!"

The cloaked figure at the back door takes out a pistol.

"Daddy…" Sethe says.

Bowie runs towards her, pleading, "Don't, don't!"

And then the cloaked figure pulls the trigger.

Bowie gets to her by the time she hits the ground. He can't recognize her anymore.

"Why?!" he screams until his voice gives out.

He glances up at the cloaked figure. Its face is mangled and covered in dried blood. The ghoul… the ghoul the townspeople saw…

Bowie takes Sethe in his arms and goes to Duška. The cloaked figure steps aside. He looks like a ghoul, also. Bowie scoops her up, too, and with each of them slung over his shoulders, he goes, bawling, back towards his room.

"And the Oscar goes to…" the voice in the dark whispers.

Bowie stops. The girls are too heavy to carry. He shakes as he cries and sets them back down. He lays them out and then falls onto his haunches. He can't get up. He'll never get up again.

The voice in the dark speaks again. "Not the life I would have chosen, but I can see the appeal. Cozy, for sure."

Bowie ignores him. He takes his girls' hands in his and says, "Just fucking kill me."

"No, no. That's not why I'm here at all."

The red light increases in intensity. Holding it is a giant, seven foot mosquito bundled up in a skin cloak. On a different day, Bowie might say it was the worst thing he's ever seen. But today, his daughters lie dead beside him.

"I missed you, ghoul."

Bowie's breath catches in his throat. His mind goes elsewhere. Quickly, he refocuses onto the mosquito.

"I gave you decades upon decades. You did good, you did. But now, it's time."

The mosquito steps up to him. His cloaked cronies fall in at his sides.

Snow builds in the doorways. The house is pale with moonlight. It looks like a tomb.

"Go on, ghoul. Put on your killing suit."

Bowie's vision goes dark. He slips inside himself and finds a closet within. Many faces stare back at him. Many lives he's never known and yet has the greatest affection for. He reaches out to one.

And one reaches back.

The ghoul jumps to his feet in the Night Terror, Emvola's, flesh and lunges for Mr. Haemo.

Mr. Haemo laughs and catches the ghoul by the wrists and drives his proboscis straight through his neck.

The ghoul gasps. Dark blood seeps out of the wound. He can't speak. He can't breathe.

"My little cauldron," Mr. Haemo says, tipping the proboscis so that it goes down the ghoul's throat, rather than out the back of it. "You've stewed and simmered, and after this time, you're finally ready. One part starved ghoul, one part flesh fiend; hundreds of dead bodies; exposure to a Worm; the acids of depriving yourself a much needed sleep; and of course, a homunculus' oil.

"You see, we all have the same Skeleton in our future. I'm glad it's you, though, that he'll be reborn from. If the Dread Clock is right, you two will get along very nicely."

Mr. Haemo pushes the proboscis directly into the ghoul's stomach.

"Now, we have a long journey ahead of us. And years of winter. You're going need your rest. I'd hate for you to remember any of this."

0

The ghoul wakes to a mouthful of a dirt and an earthworm on his eyeball. Instincts kicking in, he starts digging upwards, raking at the earth. Augmented by hunger, he rips through his shallow grave, from the coldness of his rest, to the heat above.

One hand explodes out of the ground. He grips the grass and sends his other hand through. The ghoul lifts himself out of the earth and into a hot summer evening. The humidity is thick. He's swimming in it.

"Goddamn," the ghoul says, heaving himself out of the ground and collapsing upon the grass. "Goddamn."

He rolls over, sits up; gets his bearings. An abandoned, ripped apart chapel looms over him. And behind him, a haphazard graveyard stretches into the dirty night.

"Alright, that's what I'm talking about."

The ghoul gets up. His senses are making his mouth pucker. There are so many bodies here to feast on. But where to start? Where to start?

His nose picks up something sweet, something fresh. He wheels around in search of it until he's back at the chapel. Realizing it's coming from in there, he goes in.

Past the pews and chipped altar is a piece of the floor that's sunken in to recently disturbed earth. There are flowers there, and a tiny, unmarked headstone. It's a new grave. A new grave for a new soul.

The ghoul grumbles. He's so hungry, but he can't bring himself to eat a baby. He'll have to settle for less.

The ghoul turns—

And a man slams into him, bringing them both to the ground.

The ghoul kicks the man in the stomach. A cloud of alcohol explodes from his lips. The man crashes into a pew.

The ghoul scoots backwards. He's shaky with hunger. It's been a long while since he's killed someone, but if he's got to, then he's got to.

The man staggers to his feet. He's lean, black, and somewhere in his early thirties. Veins bulge from his frame. He's killed before, the ghoul knows, and right now, has no qualms about doing it again.

"Get the hell away from there," the man says, slurring his words.

The ghoul glances at the tiny grave.

The man moves towards him.

"I'm not." He holds out his hands, stopping him. "I'm not. I wouldn't do that."

The man straightens up. He rumbles out a slow belch. It slides over his lips like vomit would. "What're you doing here?"

The ghoul shakes his head. "I just woke up. Don't know how I got here."

"Well, get."

The ghoul stays put.

The man licks his lips, pushes sweat from his forehead into his hair. He rubs tears out of his eyes.

"You okay?"

The man stares at him with daggers in his eyes.

"Is that your little girl in that grave?"

The man's mouth quivers. "How'd you know she was a girl?"

The ghoul taps his nose. "I'm sorry, man."

"Vale." The man sniffs his nose. "Her name, for a moment, was Vale."

The ghoul nods, whispers, "What's your name?"

The man looks at his surroundings, as if he can't believe he's having a conversation with this creature. "Atticus," he finally says, sobering up. "Most just call me Gravedigger."

The ghoul can't remember much, but he remembers cordiality going a long way with the so-called "Corrupted." So he extends his hand to the Gravedigger and says, "It's nice to meet you."

The Gravedigger is hesitant. But after some deliberation, he wipes his hand on his pantleg and takes the ghoul by the wrist. "What do they call you, ghoul?"

The ghoul opens his mouth to speak, but no words come out, because he doesn't know what to say.

He remembers he had a family once. They're dead now. He remembers he had been awake before this. There were strange creatures. And the world wasn't right. He remembers mosquitoes. And blood. And the smell of old people. And snow. And there's this dark place inside his head, and he sees a lot of flesh he used to possess, but now its stretched and wrinkled and discolored from disuse. He couldn't wear them, not even if he wanted to.

And oddly enough, with this Gravedigger guy, he doesn't want to. He doesn't want to be anything but his decrepit self. He sees a man hurting, and in the corner, the object of his hurt, and thinks maybe, just maybe, something could be done about this.

The ghoul smiles. He can't remember his name, but being a smartass, or at least having once worn the skin of a smartass, he gets clever and tells Atticus: "It's Gary. Gary the ghoul."

The Gravedigger's scowl turns upward slightly into the hint of a smile. "You hungry, Gary?"

Gary nods. "Starving."

The Gravedigger exhales loudly, blinks the tears out of his eyes. He shakes, fighting back another meltdown, and staring at Vale's grave, says, "Well, let's see what we've got to eat around here. Keep your head low. Clementine'll take it off if she sees you kicking around in the dark."

"Okay," Gary says, laughing. "She your wife?"

"Yeah."

"Pretty?"

"Prettiest."

"Lucky man."

"Yeah."

Gary clenches his jaw. "Got another child?"

The Gravedigger shakes his head. "No. Not sure we ever will. But there is this kid that keeps coming around these parts. James. He's a timid thing.

"Listen, you got me in a bad way. I'll cut you a deal, Gary. I'll let you have your run of the corpses if you keep an eye on my baby Vale's grave here. Don't let nothing get to it. I haven't had a friend…"

Gary grabs the Gravedigger's hand and shakes it. "Deal."

"Alright, then. Now, since I always do everything all ass-backwards and complicated-like," the Gravedigger says, "let's go walking in the moonlight so I can get to know you some. I'm sure you a got story to tell."

Gary didn't.

But he would.

YOU HAVE BEEN READING

"THE AGONY OF AFTER."

ABOUT THE AUTHOR

SCOTT HALE is the author of *The Bones of the Earth* series and screenwriter of *Entropy, Free to a Bad Home, and Effigies.* He is the co-owner of Halehouse Productions. He is a graduate from Northern Kentucky University with a Bachelors in Psychology and Masters in Social Work. He has completed *The Bones of the Earth* series and his standalone horror novel, *In Sheep's Skin.* Scott Hale currently resides in Norwood, Ohio with his wife and frequent collaborator, Hannah Graff, and their three cats, Oona, Bashik, and Bellatrix.

Printed in Great Britain
by Amazon

68416798R00203